By Any Name

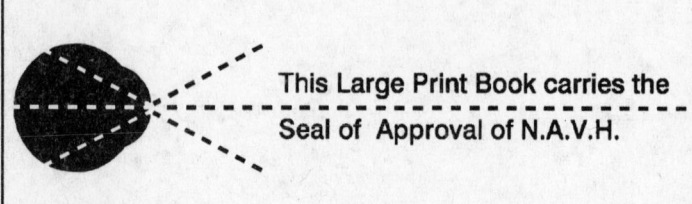

This Large Print Book carries the
Seal of Approval of N.A.V.H.

BY ANY NAME

CYNTHIA VOIGT

THORNDIKE PRESS
A part of Gale, a Cengage Company

Farmington Hills, Mich • San Francisco • New York • Waterville, Maine
Meriden, Conn • Mason, Ohio • Chicago

Copyright © 2017 by Cynthia Voigt.
Thorndike Press, a part of Gale, a Cengage Company.

ALL RIGHTS RESERVED
This is a work of fiction. Names, characters, places, and incidents either are the product of the author's imagination or are used fictitiously. Any resemblance to actual persons, living or dead, events, or locales is entirely coincidental.
Thorndike Press® Large Print Clean Reads.
The text of this Large Print edition is unabridged.
Other aspects of the book may vary from the original edition.
Set in 16 pt. Plantin.

LIBRARY OF CONGRESS CATALOGING-IN-PUBLICATION DATA

Names: Voigt, Cynthia, author.
Title: By any name / by Cynthia Voigt.
Description: Large Print edition. | Waterville, Maine : Thorndike Press, a part of Gale, a Cengage Company, 2017. | Series: Thorndike Press Large Print Clean Reads
Identifiers: LCCN 2017029037| ISBN 9781432843762 (hardback) | ISBN 1432843761 (hardcover)
Subjects: LCSH: Large type books. | BISAC: FICTION / Historical.
Classification: LCC PS3572.O33 B9 2017 | DDC 813/.54—dc23
LC record available at https://lccn.loc.gov/2017029037

Published in 2017 by arrangement with Diversion Publishing Corp.

Printed in the United States of America
1 2 3 4 5 6 7 21 20 19 18 17

To Woody, Molly, Andy, and Fritz
— even if it isn't a portrait.

■ ■ ■ ■

PART ONE:
RIDA, LIKE
HAYWORTH

■ ■ ■ ■

Prologue:
Mumma's Childhood

My three older sisters did the work of finding out as much as they could about our mother's childhood, sparing me the aggravation. They asked the questions, first out of the desperate affection of little children and then, when they were older and more independent, out of an analytical curiosity. As teenagers they asked — so they claimed — just so they could figure out what planet she was from.

I am the one who collected together the various answers they were given, who gathered their memories up into a single album and then scrutinized the information, noting contradictions and unlikelihoods. The facts are few and they are these.

FACT: *She was born in the fall of 1924.*

The precise date is not known. Mumma celebrated the fall equinox as her birthday, enjoying its inconvenient variability. When she was left at Saint Catherine's Home for

Abandoned Females in Eureka, California, the sisters estimated her age to be between five and eight weeks. Neither well dressed nor well nourished, the infant was nevertheless — by her own subsequent report — robust and possessed of an indomitable spirit.

FACT: *She was never adopted.*

My sisters and I tried our hardest to pity our mother, poor little thing, first abandoned, then rejected. We asked her to receive our sympathy and Mumma's response was typical: "They didn't know what they were missing."

FACT: *For the first eight years of her education, she attended the convent elementary school.*

Mumma claimed to have been an excellent student, inherently more intelligent than the other girls, her relentlessly high grades achieved without effort. She was popular, she reported that, too.

"Who was your best friend?" my sisters asked. "Were you a Brownie?"

"You know how I feel about best friends," Mumma told them. "But what you don't know is that in those days there were no Brownies. You're lucky you were born at the time you were, and that you have the mother you have, or you wouldn't be in the Brownies either."

"But if you didn't have a best friend and you were popular, who *did* you have?"

"I had myself, and everybody else."

FACT: *The high school Mumma attended was a Catholic girls' school from which she graduated (probably the truth) and at the top of her class (debatable). She was seventeen and a half, that June of 1942.*

"So you were the class valedictorian."

"Saint Catherine's wasn't that kind of a school."

"Did you have any boyfriends?"

"What do you think?"

"But if it was a girls' school, how did you get a boyfriend?"

"There were youth clubs. There were dances, and you know what a good dancer I am. Everybody always wants to dance with me."

"What did you wear? Who bought you dresses?"

"We wore uniforms. It saves a lot of trouble, wearing uniforms."

"Did you like school?"

"I was happy to graduate, I can tell you that. I was ready to go to work."

"But what work could you do?"

"We had to take typing, all four years, and stenography."

Mumma claimed to have excelled at both of those skills, and it might well have been true.

FACT: *Immediately after graduation, she went to work in a law office.*

"The sisters placed me at Alcott and Hastings and they found me a room in a respectable boardinghouse, too. They didn't just put their girls out on the street. After four weeks, Mr. Alcott already wanted to send me to law school." But it was 1942 and there was the war. Mumma left the law to join the USO — where if a girl told them she was eighteen, and told them she could dance, they asked no further questions. "I had a career in show business, did you girls know that?"

FACT: *Her troupe was sent to the Pacific, charged with the task of boosting the morale of soldiers and sailors and airmen.*

"Then your father fell in love with me and the rest you know."

In the way of children, we often envied Mumma's motherlessness, and that our mother was without family of any kind also piqued our curiosity. But she never admitted to the traditional doubts and miseries of an orphan — food, clothing, lack of privacy, lack of diversions — and there was nothing to be discovered from Saint Catherine's.

The building had been taken over as a military hospital in 1943 and the orphanage records transferred to a warehouse that burned down under suspicious circumstances late in the 1940s. We lamented the lost chance to discover if there had been any kind of clue to our mother, anything to lead us to who she was.

"You know perfectly well who I am."

"How do we find out what's in our gene pool?"

"You already know as much as you need to about your gene pool, which — except for your father — isn't anything to write home about."

Only once in her life was Mumma willing to talk about her childhood, and then it wasn't to her daughters. "It's not like in books," was all she would tell us. "It's never like in books," and whether she was speaking of life in an orphanage or life itself she left us to decide.

However, once she met Pops, Mumma's history became knowable — insofar as anyone's life is knowable to another person. Especially, I could say, as any parent's life is knowable to her own children, and especially again, a parent like Mumma.

Don't get me wrong. I loved my mother. But I loved her as she was, not as she wanted to be seen, and when I think of her stories, fitting them into the narration of her long life, only the earliest, the ones she told herself, make an orderly construct. In Mumma's life, things were infrequently logical and often inconsistent, although, I am interested to note, the stories do tend to lack the common unnecessary unhappinesses most people endure. Quite possibly my mother is too much a part of my own life for me to be a reliable witness to hers. I'm not confident that I can give it form or recognize its significances. The story of my mother's life, as I imagine it, is like nothing else — unless perhaps the story of my own life, when my own daughters will tell it.

1.
MUMMA'S WARTIME ROMANCE

They met in 1943. He was a lieutenant (j.g.) in the Navy, the communications officer on a destroyer based in Honolulu; she danced in the chorus line of a USO show that traveled around the military bases on the islands. "If it hadn't been for the war, we never would have met," Mumma told us. "And who knows *what* would have become of your father."

The encounter was brought about by Katy and Louella, women in their late twenties, professional dancers — unlike Mumma, who was only a natural, unschooled in dance as in all else. They dragged her along with them to a Saturday dance at the Officers' Club. Most of the men, they knew, would be married, but Katy and Louella, themselves a couple, preferred to deal with the hearts of married men, and since Mumma was engaged, all she could do was flirt. This, theoretically, was what the USO-

15

sponsored showgirls were there to do: dance with the men — enlisted or officers — flirt with them a little but not too much, give a temporary normalcy to their lives, and be fun. They were for morale, the USO girls. The sponsoring organizations — the Salvation Army, YMCA, National Jewish Welfare Board, National Catholic Community Service, Travelers Aid Society — were probably aware of a certain ingenuousness in this view of their girls, and their service clubs, and their camp shows. But they were aware also of the nature of war, its propensity for ironic as well as ordinary everyday cruelties, compared to which ingenuousness and even sex might well have seemed much the lesser evils.

This particular dance, because it was at an Officers' Club, not a USO Servicemen's Club, promised good food and a real band, as well as alcohol. Katy and Louella were high livers and enthusiastic partygoers. They were not about to decline even the offhand invitation to "Come on along and bring your prettiest friends."

(My sister Meg doubted this version. "Personally? I think they probably crashed it and the guys were too drunk to notice — that's if they'd have cared if they had *noticed. You know what Pops says about those shore*

leaves and how much he had to drink to forget what was going on." As the oldest, Meg was the authority on the topic of our parents' romance, and she never missed a chance to remind us that she remembered things that younger, later arrivals — me, for example — could not hope to know.)

That evening, Pops was wearing his dress whites and Mumma wore an orange dress with big red poppies all over it, her good-luck outfit, with cap sleeves, fitted bodice, and wide skirt. On her feet were gold pumps with the high heels that showed off her ankles. She and Pops didn't meet immediately. They didn't glimpse each other across the crowded room and fall into love at first sight. The stories might have varied, but that version was never on offer.

The dining room of the Officers' Club was dimly lit and filled beyond capacity, men crowding around the bar, dancers crowded together on a small dance floor, each table crowded with several officers and two or three women — nurses, staff, even a few of the local girls, and most of the USO troupe. There was a heavy odor of whiskey and cigarettes in the air; there was the sound of the band, rhythmic and melodic; also, people insisted on trying to talk. Mumma entered with her two friends. Pops was

17

among the men settled in near the bar. They probably didn't even notice each other for a long time, that was our guess, although Mumma maintained that from the moment she stepped out on the floor — with a boy from Ohio, an ensign — from that instant, Pops never took his eyes off her.

(Amy maintained it was the dress. "He must have been astounded by her bad taste. Not to mention those shoes." Amy inherited Mumma's concreteness: "Picture it," she advised us. "Orange? Big red poppies? Gold high-heeled pumps?")

Mumma sat down beside her Ohio ensign when he rejoined his friends, and they all wanted to dance with her. "They were all — you know — attracted," as she told the story. But she wanted to drink her drink and look around. This was the first Officers' Club she'd ever been in, and she was trying to decide what she thought. She begged off the requests to return to the dance floor, fended off her admirers. Then she noticed Pops, standing by an open window, staring at her.

In the formal commissioning photograph Pops sent to his mother, it's clear what Mumma saw: a big, blond officer, not so young as her ensign and undeniably handsome. All of his life Pops struggled with his

18

good looks. He was square of jaw and blue of eye, broad of shoulder and over six feet tall; his round glasses gave him a trust-worthy, intelligent expression. He looked as if he had gone to some fancy famous college, Yale or Harvard (which he had), and he looked rich, like a young man with a trust fund, or maybe two (also true). Added to this, he had an easy smile, like a man who enjoyed his own charm, and the loose walk of a natural athlete. Both of these belied his true nature, which was in fact anxiously thoughtful, even pedantically philosophical, and unathletic often to a comic degree, except Pops was no comedian. He could, however, laugh at himself, which he frequently had cause to do, and his upbringing had, perversely, produced in him the generous, grateful nature of a man who had neither looks nor money to make life easy for him.

For a long time Mumma stared back at him. Then she rose from her seat and made her way across the room. She claimed to have had no particular reason to do that, except he wasn't making the slightest move toward her, and patience was never one of her strongest characteristics. He piqued her curiosity, challenged her vanity; also, he was easy on the eyes. She pushed through the crowd of people to plant herself in front of him. "You want to dance with me," she told him, and held out her hand.

"No. No, I don't. Thank you," Pops said. Back in Boston, everybody knew he couldn't dance, any more than he could sing. His sisters had teased him about it and tried to teach him, his brothers had gloated and mocked and showed off their own easy movement, his mother had sent him to dance classes and sat resolutely watching while he failed to learn. In his circle, Pops was a famous non-dancer. You didn't want him for a dance partner, or to escort you to a cotillion, a debutante party, a hunt ball, or any occasion when you might possibly have to dance with him. "Thank you, no," he said again, when Mumma neither retracted her hand nor went away. Pops was a man who understood his limitations.

In the dim light and with the difference in height, they had to peer up and down to see each other's faces. With the noise of voices and music, they had to lean toward each other and speak loudly to be heard.

"But you do," Mumma corrected him.

"No, really, I don't," he maintained. Then exactitude struck, and he added, "That is to say, I don't dance."

Mumma thought about this briefly. "Like

20

the song," she concluded, typically getting it wrong in the precise wording but right in its essential meaning.

"What song?"

She sang the first bars, unintelligible with all the noise in the room, "I won't dance, don't ask me . . ." He pretended he could hear until it had been enough time to say, "Never heard it."

"Yes you have," Mumma insisted. "You must have," she explained.

"Well, but I never did," he said.

(We know as much as we do about this first conversation thanks to the perseverance of Amy, who collects details. And if Meg was the one who insisted on hearing the story, over and over, while Amy elicited the facts, it's Jo — the most romantic of the four of us, the dreamiest, or laziest and least practical, but without a doubt the most empathic — who understood what Pops didn't want to talk about. "Pops must have been a fish out of water in the Navy, in a war. He wouldn't know the first thing. Everything would go against his nature.")

"You must have heard it," Mumma insisted. "Don't you listen to the radio?"

"I listen all the time." This was, however, one of Pops' private jokes, because monitoring radio transmissions to and from his ship

21

was part of his job. Another of his jokes at that time was: What else would the Navy do with a philologist?

Mumma didn't get it, so she pressed on with the conversation. She almost never got Pops' jokes and almost always pressed on. "What's your name? Mine's Rida."

"Spencer Howland," he said.

"Like Rita Hayworth, only with a *d*."

Pops studied the girl in front of him. "You've got red hair like her, but you're not nearly as tall, and you have a different build. You're plumper."

"Maybe, but you have to admit it's in at least two of the right places," Mumma said.

Which made Pops laugh. And for a minute, laughing, he forgot where he was, and why. He also forgot the bright orange and red splotches of her dress, and the heavy application of lipstick and mascara and perfume — that is to say, her dubious taste. *That* he forgot forever.

"If you won't dance with me," Mumma said, "then what would you like to do? Within reason," she warned him, because soldiers, sailors, airmen, all boys at war, sometimes they got their hopes up.

"I'm always within reason," Pops told her, truthfully.

Her initial response was flirtatious. "I bet

you are." Then she looked into his mild eyes and figured him out. *("I always understood your father, from the first. That's one of the things I liked about him, right away.")* She suggested a walk. "Or don't you walk, either?" After all, he could be wounded, or even crippled. All she'd seen him do was stand still.

"That's an odd question," he said, then told her, "It happens that walking is my favorite form of exercise. I don't enjoy sports," he added, as if she would want to know about that.

They exited the room through French doors that opened out onto a stone patio that, in daylight, would overlook the golf course. Pops, protecting Mumma from discovering to what uses the soft, grassy greens might even at that moment be being put, kept close to the well-lit clubhouse as he led her around to the front, through the rows of parked cars, and eventually down to the broad Pacific beach.

Stars burned in the black night sky and a three-quarters moon floated in front of them. Its light flowed silver over the surface of the dark water. The scent of flowers blended into the salt air smell on a velvety black breeze that brushed gently against their cheeks. Mumma carried her shoes by their high golden heels, one in each hand; Pops slung his white jacket, with its single gold stripe, over one shoulder. Noticing how the breeze pestered her hair into her face, he offered her his tie. "To keep it out of your eyes," he said, and held her shoes while she wrapped the tie around her head, never losing a beat in her insistence that he had to have heard "I Won't Dance," ignoring his disclaimers, and, either ignoring or ignorant of the fact that these lyrics were by Oscar Hammerstein, explaining to him that it was the cleverness of Cole Porter's songs that made them less American than Tommy Dorsey's dance band because not everybody liked cleverness but everybody liked to dance. "Maybe so, but America's a country that idolizes individuals," he said. "Which is, by the way, why communism will never present a real danger to our country."

Mumma had an argument to win. "Everybody dances," she said. "Dancing is basic to human nature."

"Although, Americans do like team sports," Pops pointed out to himself, then cited his proof. "Baseball. Football."

"In the Middle Ages, too, and even before then," she argued.

"Perhaps I'm making a false distinction," he said.

"Although I don't know much about the Egyptians, but I bet they did, too. Dance," Mumma added, when she saw his expression in the bright tropical moonlight.

Pops took a breath and shifted conversational course, to follow her. "Nobody actually knows much about the Egyptians," he said. "You see, most of our information is necrophilic — that is to say, it comes from temples and tombs. Even our knowledge of the language, which has as its text the *Book of the Dead.* What we know of the society and daily life, architecture too, is derived from tomb paintings."

They walked on in silence until Mumma thought to remark, "You sound educated."

"I should. I am."

"I've met some pretty stupid educated people," Mumma observed.

For some reason — perhaps all the gin and tonics — this made Pops laugh. Again. "So have I. In point of fact, I could well be one of them. Do you mind?"

"If you're stupid?"

"If I'm educated."

"How educated are you?"

He spread his jacket on the sand for her to sit on, and they talked, taking drinks from the silver flask his Howland uncles had presented to him as a commissioning gift, with the observation that Dutch courage was better than none. Pops told Mumma this, looking out over the uneasy black Pacific, wondering in the back of his mind if he would — his body, that is — end up rolling around in its lightless depths. Dead. Once he was dead, he reminded himself, his body wouldn't matter to him, and he took the usual comfort from the familiar thought against the familiar fear.

Terror, really. He swallowed brandy and watched a shadowy wave creep up the sand to reach him where he sat telling this girl the story of his silver flask.

"How many uncles do you have?" she asked.

"On my father's side, two. And there are three more on my mother's."

"Real uncles or are they married to real aunts?"

"You mean by blood," he told her. "They're almost all by blood. Why?"

"Do you have lots of aunts, too?"

A pause to count. "Seven. Including by marriage. One of my mother's brothers isn't married. I've got twenty-one first cousins."

"That's a big family."

"I guess it is," he said.

"Why is it Dutch courage when you're drunk? Are Dutch people drunk all the time?" Mumma asked. "Or do you mean they're cowards? I don't get it."

"Not drunk. I'm not drunk."

"No, you've just had too much." She turned her face to him. "Probably you'll forget all about tonight." She didn't sound worried about that eventuality. "But I won't forget you."

"That would be a kindness, because it seems to worry me that I'm not likely to be remembered by anyone for very long."

"Just for starters, I've never met anyone from such a big family before."

"I've accepted it, though. I'll be gone. Erased. As if I never existed."

Mumma never had any trouble conversation hopping. "How could that happen with all those people who know you to remember you?"

"If I'm the only one of us who dies, maybe they'll remember me."

"Why should you die?" Mumma demanded.

And Pops laughed again, making it at least three times that night, maybe five, which was at least three and maybe five more times that he'd laughed than . . . Thinking back, he thought he'd had one good laugh in San Diego, but he'd been drunk at the time and the memory was not clear.

He reminded her, "I'm a soldier."

"A sailor," she corrected him. "And an officer."

"Metaphorically, I'm a soldier. Soldiers die."

"I suppose if your ship goes down," she granted him. "But until then your odds are much better than if you're in the Air Force. And much, much better than the trenches in the last war. Everybody says," she concluded her point. "But in that case, why waste drinking for Dutch courage now, when you're on land? You should save it up, for when you need it."

Pops decided he could let himself confide in her. "All I really want — what I'm really afraid of? I mean, other than some horrible wound — although . . ."

She offered comfort. "If it's *really* horrible you'll probably die."

He laughed yet again and admitted, "I just want to die well. Bravely. You know? Honorably."

"If I were you, I'd want to live. You can live those same ways. Why waste them on dying?"

"It's not up to me," he reminded her.

"I know that. I may not be educated, but I'm not stupid."

"I never said —"

"I'm an orphan," she told him. "A foundling, too. Somebody dropped me off at the hospital. At the door. The emergency room door, because it was night, but it was summer so they knew I wouldn't freeze or anything. I don't know how you feel about orphans," she said. "I mean, foundlings. Because of your big family. Nobody ever adopted me," she said. "Not even when I was little. I had bright red hair, and lots of people don't care for red hair. And then there's my name, which they gave to me because of course I didn't have one when I was found."

"It's a fine name. Rita Hayworth uses it."

"Not Rita, Rida. It's not Hayworth either, it's Smith."

"Were all of the orphans named Smith?" Pops wondered.

"Or Davis. Or Jones. Or Thomas." Then Mumma made her own great confession. "It's not Rida, really. It's Elfrieda, which I hate."

"In alphabetical order, one after the other," Pops guessed, not distracted by her odd name, and maybe that's when she began to love him. "So if you'd arrived one baby later, you'd have been Rida Thomas. But Rida? Think about it this way: When you're a foundling, you could have been

29

anybody. You can *be* anybody. There's no restriction on who you might be. My family has been around for centuries — since the *Mayflower* —"

"Only three," Mumma pointed out. "That's not exactly centur-*ies.*"

"I think I might like to be a foundling."

"I don't mind," Mumma told him. "It makes me different, so I stand out."

"You'd stand out anywhere," he told her sincerely.

"Thank you," she said.

It was a fact Pops was stating, not a compliment he was paying, but Mumma didn't make any distinction between the two. She was satisfied by his admiration and he was satisfied by her practicality. When he walked her back to her quarters, he said, "I'll see you again."

"When? Tomorrow?"

"Tomorrow we go out on ops. Just training, although even in training ops, accidents happen."

Mumma wasn't concerned about the theoretical. "For how long?"

"Four days. Sometimes, even when they're just out doing exercises, boats go down. Things can always go wrong." He looked at his watch. He had only four more hours on land.

"That doesn't usually happen," she pointed out before returning to her main point. "So you'll call me Friday?"

"You'll have forgotten me by then."

"No I won't. I told you I wouldn't, and one thing about me is I mean what I say. You'll like that about me. And you'll remember me. Because you said I stand out," she reminded him, and added her own embellishment, "in any crowd." He laughed again and forgot for another minute where he was, and why.

The ship docked early on a bright, hot Friday morning, but it was midday before Pops was allowed ashore. He had quarters on board the ship, but the showers at the Officers' Club had an abundant supply of water that was not only hot but also fresh, and thick towels, too, hotel-quality terry cloth, so the first thing he did was head off to the club for a cleanup and maybe lunch, a couple of beers. *("He said he'd forgotten all about calling me," Mumma told us. "But I knew better. He was crazy about me. And if he wasn't going to call, why did he go right by the phones?")* Since midmorning, she had been standing beside the pay phones at the gates to the dock, waiting, wearing a yellow, green, and blue flowered dress, her bright

31

hair tangled by the wind. You couldn't miss her, standing there, so Pops didn't, especially when she called out to him, and waved wildly.

"What's this, Spence?" commented one of his fellow junior officers. "You never said you had a date." There were three of them, counting Pops, and they approached her together.

"I thought I'd save you the trouble of making the call," Mumma said. "Besides, I have to return this." She reached down into a bright red carryall to pull out his tie. Pops took it and thanked her, and the four of them then stood in an awkward silence. Mumma had settled in her own mind what was happening next, so she didn't say anything. The two companions were waiting for Pops to speak, so one of them could strike up an acquaintance with her if Pops was going to drop the ball, Spence being an odd duck and known ball-dropper, but an okay guy and tireless out at sea, a good man to stand watch with.

Finally Mumma asked, "Are you going to introduce me to your friends?" and Pops obliged, finding that he *did* remember her, that he did know her name, and that he was glad to see her.

"Rob, Marty, this is Rida." After the

pleased-to-meetchas, another awkward silence rose up among them. *("They were curious, and they wanted to know me better. They were* attracted, *you know. But your father had found me first and they had to play fair.")* She said to the three of them, "Every one of you needs a bath and a shave, don't you? We can all go together to your Officers' Club, but Spencer plans to take me out afterward. You'll want me to wait at the bar for you," she told Pops.

The truth was, Pops was exhausted. When at sea, he barely slept, from anxiety about where he was, and why, and the fear — of a torpedo, an air attack, something unpredictable and unpredicted, even a great white whale with the skeleton of a man still strapped to its side. At sea something terrible could easily happen, with him unconscious on his bunk, his quarters not much bigger than a coffin, a shared coffin at that. Fear and dread and the necessity of sobriety kept him awake. But his exhaustion was as much nervous as physical; he knew from experience that he wouldn't sleep until he had relaxed — which meant a couple of hours of drinking to stupefy himself, followed by reading a couple of chapters of Aristotle to give his brain something else to chew on. The truth was, the last thing Pops wanted to do was go on a date. But exhaustion made him too slow to elude this unexpected girl. By the time he realized that his usual manner of coming ashore was at risk, it was too late. The four of them were walking along together toward the Officers' Club, and Rida was attached to his arm.

It wasn't all bad. For once, he was the one with the girl, and this was not the kind of girl anyone would miss seeing on your arm. Just her hair, to start with. That unruly, untidy, unorganized red mass grabbed attention, and her high-heeled shoes were bright yellow, and nobody could deny that she had a fine figure. She was utterly different from all the girls and women he had ever met. If he was going to die — and he was sure that he was, although probably not for a couple of weeks now that he was safely returned from maneuvers and the ship was in harbor being stocked and fitted for its next tour, a process that would take at least two weeks and maybe three . . . If he was not going to die immediately, Pops thought that he might enjoy the novelty of this girl, and be diverted by it. This Rida wasn't educated; she'd said as much. But she had to have some ideas, didn't she? It was human nature to have ideas. Just as Socrates believed that each one of us desires the good, Pops believed that everyone wanted to have a life of the mind, and as it turned out — granted that her idea of an intellectual life differed in content and approach from his wider, more disciplined one — he was absolutely right about Mumma.

On that day, she held a large carryall, something she'd picked up cheap at the market, the kind of colorful woven straw bag the local women were seen with, from which they would extract food, clothing, changes of diaper for an infant, towels, flowers, newspapers, kerchiefs — just about anything a woman needed to get through a day. This was not the kind of bag to hang off a lady's gloved wrist as she shopped for a hat, or to set down beside neatly crossed ankles when she took a chair. This bag hung shapeless from the shoulder, and when Pops — showered and shaved and in fresh civilian trousers and shirt — walked out on the beach beside Mumma, she pulled out of it Spam-and-Velveeta sandwiches wrapped in waxed paper, a thermos, a blanket to sit on, and a bottle of beer for him. She never drank, she told him, and went to the water's edge to bury the bottle up to its neck in the wet sand. "To cool it," she told him. "You don't want warm beer."

"Didn't you have a drink the other night?"

he questioned her. The day was warm and only gentle breezes blew, here on this empty beach, only a mild offshore breeze of "under two knots," he would be able to tell her if she asked his professional opinion. He looked off across the ocean, to the horizon. He preferred the Pacific seen from a blanket on the beach in daylight, no question about that. From a blanket on the beach, he might actually *like* the old bastard.

"That was an exception." Mumma poured a thermos cap of pineapple juice for herself, offering to share it with him.

"*Never* doesn't admit of exceptions." He stretched out on his back on the cotton blanket. The afternoon sun — hot even in early spring on that exotic island — poured down over him; the sand was warm under his back and legs. He closed his eyes and heard, instead of the thrum of engines, the equally regular rush of waves on the sand. He closed his eyes and felt the deep earth steady beneath him.

"What's the best book you ever read?" her voice asked him.

He opened his eyes and sat up in surprise. "Why?"

"You tell me what and I'll tell you why."

"You don't strike me as a bookish girl."

"I bet you know a lot of those," she said.

"Are they terrible bores?"

He considered this alternative to everything he'd ever thought or been told to think. "Only sometimes. Like me."

"You mean people in glass houses shouldn't throw stones."

Unable to follow the leap and parry of her mental processes, *"War and Peace,"* he told her.

"Is that a book?"

He had her full attention, and he registered for the first time the mahogany color of her eyes and felt the intensity of her gaze, as if the answer to this question mattered deeply to her. Her mouth was not pulled up at the ends by the little flirtatious smile with which the girls he knew, including his cousins and especially his sisters, his sisters being the girls he knew best, masked their intensities. He noticed also how unfashionably dark and definite her eyebrows were, and he'd already, at some unacknowledged level, registered the soft roundnesses of her body, arms and breasts, hips. He gave her his full attention right back.

"A novel by a Russian —"

"Not an American?"

"Most Russians aren't," he said, then wished he hadn't given in to intellectual snideness, then — when she laughed, a sound as round as her thighs — forgave himself. "If you'd asked me my senior year, I'd have said *Moby Dick,* which *is* by an American."

"Anybody can guess the story of *War and Peace,*" Mumma said. "But what's *Moby Dick*?"

"A whale. Everybody hunts him, and dies — well, except for one man, Ishmael, but everybody else . . . Moby Dick attacks the ship and sinks it. In the Pacific," he pointed out.

She failed to sympathize. "Can a whale do that?"

"One did, in the last century; it sank the *Essex.* The story was in the newspapers when Melville was a young man."

"Who's Melville?"

"He wrote it."

"Is it good?"

"It's — it's *great.*" He thought of how to express it to her, so she could grasp the importance of the valuation. "It's about good versus evil, or maybe good *and* evil. It's about man, nature, God, fate, life, everything important. It's a terrific story and the writing is . . . Melville uses traditional narrative, and theater, irony, science, descriptive essay, comedy —"

She was no longer interested in *Moby Dick.*

"But now you like the Russian better. Are you a Communist?"

"It's so human," Pops said. He was thinking that he could introduce her to literature, be her teacher, educate her. She clearly had curiosity, and curiosity was a sure sign of intelligence. He could be a Socrates in his own *Meno* for what could well be the last two or three weeks of his life. "*War and Peace* takes place during the Napoleonic Wars in Russia." He lay back down, considering this new idea, thinking that then she *would* always remember him, the doomed young sailor who changed her life. "So it's early nineteenth century. It has an incredible cast of characters, all levels of society, all kinds of people, a wonderful hero — two heroes, actually — and one of the most interesting heroines —"

"Don't tell me," her voice interrupted him. He thought she must be bored, and probably wasn't ready for a project the size of *War and Peace,* which logged in at about 1,400 pages in his Modern Library edition at home. He wondered where to begin with her — Thucydides? *Pride and Prejudice? The Scarlet Letter?* He didn't think he himself ever wanted to read *Gone with the Wind,* but for her that might make a good first step. But did he have time to waste on such a first step? Not Shakespeare. *Huckleberry Finn?* Not Aeschylus. *Little Women?* He heard his own voice saying, "*Little Women,* have you read that? It's a bible for all the girls I know." His voice sounded to him as if it were from a distance, babbling. "My sisters loved it, my female cousins, all their friends."

When Pops awoke, the sand was cool under the blanket, and the eastern rim of the world, off at the ocean's distant edge, was fading from pearly gray to pink. He had no memory of the night, as if he had slept the unbroken sleep he only remembered these days: the kind of sleep he hadn't enjoyed since his last summer on the Cape, the summer of 1941; the kind of sleep the anxiety of senior year and then the anxiety of his time in history had made impossible. Rolling over, seeing the girl silhouetted at the water's edge, looking out, he didn't *think* it was sex that had granted him such a sleep. Sex like that, he would have to remember it, wouldn't he? Because he hadn't had anything to drink, had he?

Rida, that was her name. She seemed to sense his awakened state and turned from the horizon to approach him. The rising sun backlit her windblown hair, and he stood up. "What are you doing here?" he asked her.

"You fell asleep," she told him.

"I know that."

"Do you know any place you could get me a breakfast? Because I ate my picnic for lunch yesterday and by now I'm really hungry," Mumma said. "The bus leaves at noon and I haven't packed, so I have to get back. Now that you're awake," she reproached him.

He walked her to her quarters, carrying the red bag, apologizing for his ignorance of all-night eateries, promising that he would find her some breakfast, somehow, and he'd be back ASAP with food. She told him that the USO troupe was leaving that day on a ten-day tour of the islands. He discovered that hunger made Mumma snappish, so he gave up trying to talk to her. He left her at the steps to the women's barracks, and by the time he got back she had packed, changed into khaki coveralls for the journey, and was in a fine bad temper.

"Is that beer still buried in the sand?" he asked, offering first a banana, then a milk bottle, being sure to wait until she had bitten into her second doughnut before he took anything for himself.

"I never drink," she said, and glared at

him, daring him to contradict. "You can go back for it, if you want it so badly. But you drink too much."

Pops didn't argue and he didn't make excuses. Having nothing better to do, he walked her over to the camouflaged bus, into which girls carrying duffel bags climbed. They waited for the driver, also female but older than the USO girls, and the WAC officer in charge of getting the show to the airport.

"Where will you be performing?" he asked.

"The walls have ears," she answered, "but I'll be back."

He knew — although he didn't say it — that in two days' time she would have forgotten him. After ten days, he would have become one of a mass of uniformed young men, all faceless.

Mumma seemed to read his mind. "You can take me to dinner my first night back. Six o'clock, a week from Thursday."

"If we're still in port."

"You will be," she told him.

They stood face-to-face by the bus, waiting for the final call. "You can kiss me goodbye," she told him. So he did, bending over because she was so short, and as they kissed she placed a warm palm softly against his cheek. He drew up at the end, feeling bemused and oddly satisfied. Also, distinctly eager to kiss her again. She looked up at him, her mahogany eyes sparkling. "You love me."

"No I don't. I can't, really, you know. There's a girl, back home." He realized that for the last fourteen hours he had forgotten Abigail as thoroughly as he had forgotten his own imminent death, although when you propose to a girl because you're confident that you won't live to marry her, it's the kind of engagement a man might easily forget. "I'm engaged."

"That's all right," Mumma said. "I am too. With the ring to prove it. In fact" — she laughed softly, reaching up to touch his cheek again in a gesture he found more intimate and seductive even than the willing softness of her mouth — "I've got four of them. Rings, I mean. I mean, I have the fiancés too." And then it was time to get on the bus, and she left him with a careless backward wave of her hand.

Immediately, Pops started to accept the fact that he'd never see her again, which was actually — now that he thought clearheadedly about it — something of a relief. She disturbed his equanimity. She undermined the stoicism he had worked so hard to achieve. And she thought he drank too much. Also, she had — by her own admission — four fiancés, four men she had encouraged enough to propose marriage, each of whom she had accepted. And she had never — also by her own admission — even *heard* of *Moby Dick*. He could almost hear his mother asking, "Is she really your kind of girl, Spencer? This — what did you say her name was? Something melodramatic, rather affected, don't you think? Rida? Not your type at all, I'd think. Oh, but," the voice growing indulgent, "I should remember that you're at war." His mother's was the voice of reason, the voice of his better self, and that voice gently inquired, "You haven't forgotten the promises you made to Abigail, have you? But I know you'll do the right thing, Spencer. You've been brought up to do the right thing."

Pops spent the next ten days alone — or, perhaps more accurately, apart from Mumma, because one of the most discouraging things for a man like Pops about being in the service was the lack of solitude, so he was not ever alone, as he remembered it, as he told the stories. Low-ranking young officers shared living quarters with other low-ranking young officers, and unlike the prospects in the two other branches of the military, a battlefield promotion to a rank offering more private quarters wasn't likely, since his particular field of battle tended to go down with all hands.

Pops filled those ten days with drink and dread in the relentless company of his fellows, checking in supplies and stores, making sure the radio room was outfitted for the ship's upcoming tour of duty. He forgot about Mumma, her return and their dinner date, until another lieutenant j.g. announced at morning mess that the USO girls were giving a show on Saturday and that he for one intended to be at whatever they were using for a stage door, with whatever he could find by way of flowers with which to attract to himself the companionship of whoever was available to him. Pops was nursing a relatively minor hangover, so it wasn't until the words "USO girls" penetrated his consciousness that he remembered his date, and the girl Rida. But it all happened in time for him to bow out of the poker game and be waiting at the foot of the stairs when she emerged from the wooden barracks, wearing a sky-blue dress splotched with yellow flowers, her bright red hair in its usual disorder.

"Hi there," she said, holding out her hand

to shake his as if they had never kissed and she had never touched his cheek in that way, which was in fact the same seductive way she later sometimes touched the faces of her daughters, saying "What a little face," as she cupped it within her palms, delighted that it was just that particular little face she was looking into.

"Good tour?" he asked, shaking the offered hand.

"I read the whole thing." She tucked her left hand under his right arm to walk off with him.

"The whole what thing?" He couldn't help noticing that she wore a ring on every visible finger of the hand that had wrapped itself around his arm.

"Where are you taking me?" she asked. "Because I'm real hungry. I hope it's got good food."

"War and Peace?" he guessed.

"What did you think? And it was a good thing that the prince died, wasn't it? Because otherwise Natasha wouldn't have been able to marry the count, who makes a much better husband. Did you think, when you read it, that there are some men — like you — who are destined not to die in whatever war is going on? Like that count, even though he was pretty stupid about risking his own life."

"You read all of *War and Peace*?"

"You didn't tell me how long it is. You could have warned me. But it's okay, I'm a fast reader."

He took her to the Officers' Club, where she seemed pleased to talk — and dance — with anybody who came by. His shipmate Rob pulled a chair up to the table for two that Pops had booked and invited himself to join them for dinner.

"Spence is a pretty limited conversationalist," Rob told Rida, who listened with interest. Pops could tell she thought Rob was amusing, which he was, a born comedian. "He's a Gloomy Gus, which can't be much fun for a girl like you."

"Like me meaning what?" Mumma asked.

"Meaning a real live wire. Now, *I'm* a talker. I'm good at talking, and Marty" — a second chair was pulled up and they were joined by the second young officer, who greeted Rida like an old friend even though he'd met her only once, and briefly — "Marty dances like a dream. Like Fred Astaire."

"And you've got that Ginger Rogers look about you," Marty added, a comparison particularly appreciated by someone like

Mumma, someone with short and not shapely legs, however delicate her ankles. "I'm right, aren't I? You do like dancing?"

"Who doesn't?" Mumma riposted. She sipped at her ginger ale, then asked, "What about him? What's special about Spencer, unless you can only talk about yourselves? What's he got to offer a girl?"

"You've got me there," Marty said, and grinned at Pops, while Rob suggested, "Looks?" and Marty realized, "He's nice, you know, a nice guy."

"Between the three of us, we make one perfect man," Rob announced. "If you don't mind there being three."

Mumma laughed, delighted.

"Like Cerberus," Pops suggested.

"Who's Cerberus when he's at home?" Mumma made a joke of it.

"That's what I mean by gloomy," Marty remarked, and Rob agreed.

"But I can *learn* things from him," Mumma told them. "I get smarter every time I talk to him." *("They were falling in love with me and I didn't want them to get their hopes up," she told us.)* "Spencer's ed-ucated."

"We're all educated," Marty protested.

"But he's really interested in it, he really likes it, and you two think — You think education is like some suit of clothing, if you pay for it you have it, and the more expensive it is the more you can be sure it's better than anybody else's. But education's not like that, it's like a meal, you have to eat it to have it. Except, really, education is like a smile. I mean, a good smile. A good smile makes people smile back at you, and if you're educated, when you talk to people, you make them smarter. But you don't care about education, it's just something somebody bought for you," Mumma told Marty. "I bet you've never read . . . oh, *War and Peace.* No, I didn't think so. Or *Moby Dick* either I bet. I don't think any the less of you, I promise. And I surely do love to dance." She covered the back of Marty's hand with one of hers, the one bearing all the rings, adding, "and I *am* a big talker," as she covered the back of Rob's hand with the other. She raised her face to smile at Pops. "So who is this Cerberus?"

Much later in the evening, Mumma and Pops went to a bar so small it didn't even have room for tables. They set two chairs side by side on an open patio, facing across the sand to black water that surged onto the shore like some great blind animal in the throes of death, or of birth, struggling for breath just beyond their sight. Over the water, stars crowded the sky, in the dark of the moon.

"You're a flirt," Pops said to Mumma. The statement was in part the result of observing her all evening with Rob and Marty, but even more it concerned her several engagements. All evening, these had been worrying him. He had decided that she didn't know what moral peril she had put herself in. As the evening went on, he had determined to help her toward a clearer position vis-à-vis men, and herself, and also her life. "You're a terrible flirt."

"No I'm not." Mumma had ordered a stinger, arguing — when Pops reminded her that she said she never drank — that something so sweet was dessert, not drinking. And who was he to complain at her about drinking anyway? She'd been counting; he'd had too many. "In fact, I'm pretty good at flirting. It's not as easy as it looks, you know. I bet you think it's easy, but I notice you don't even try."

"Who are these fiancés?" he asked. "How can you have four of them?"

She held out her left hand, for both of them to admire. "I never wear just one of the rings. I always wear all four if I wear any. I don't like to play favorites."

He didn't know how to respond. Was she

joking? Should he laugh? Or if he laughed, would she just get insulted, and if she were to feel he'd insulted her, what would she do? What would a girl like this do, if she thought you were laughing at her? This unpredictable girl, this Rida. He almost wanted to try to insult her to find out. A sudden curiosity on this subject burned in him, but he couldn't think of how to go about it, so he stuck to his point. "Who are they?"

She told him, name, age, service, rank.

"And every one of them said he wanted to marry you? And loved you?"

"Of course."

"And you in turn told every one of them you'd marry him? I mean," he paused to give more weight to the point, "you said yes to each one when he proposed?"

"Of course."

"You promised that you'd be faithful to him, in your heart, and," Pops struggled to express his sense of the weightiness of betrothal, "not flirt, for one thing, with anyone else. Not kiss anyone else. Not fall in love with anyone else."

"Of course not. Why would I promise any of those things? I never *promised* anything like that. I only said yes I'd marry them. I write to them, at least once a week, or every ten days sometimes, and each one gets his own different letter, not just the same letter sent to four different places."

"Do they know about one another?"

"Of course." She could see that he was confused, so she explained. "Each one does think he's the real one, that's only human nature. But they're just *boys,* and they're going to *war.*" She looked at him measuringly. "You aren't going to think badly of me, are you?" Then she smiled. "No, you won't. Because you love me, so you don't want to, so you won't. Probably you're jealous."

"That's ridiculous," Pops said.

In the shadowy light from the low candles, she peered into his face for a long time. "No, you never would be jealous, would you."

"What makes you say that?"

"Is *your* fiancée the jealous type?" Mumma asked. "Because I know some girls aren't. I'm not. What's her name? You should tell me her name. I feel sorry for her, you know?"

"Why would you feel sorry for Abigail?"

"Because I'm guessing she's like that Hélène. Remember her? With the shoulders?"

Pops remembered. "Abigail's not . . . sexy." He hesitated, wondering if that was an acceptable word to use with this girl, but she seemed unoffended by it. Then he started to wonder why she wasn't offended, but he got distracted by what she'd just implied about *him.* "That would make me Pierre."

"Hélène isn't sexy either, she just looks like it and besides, it's not just sexy women men fall in love with. You know that. Anybody knows that. Men aren't so dumb as everybody says."

"I don't think I'm as muddle-minded as Pierre," Pops said, although he would have to admit that he might be as clumsy. "Tell me more about your fiancés."

Happy to talk, Mumma started with Tony because, "We've been engaged the longest, almost a year."

The next evening Pops took her out again, and then they spent the weekend in each other's company, from morning until late at night. During the days Pops spent with Mumma, he had no time to think about his forthcoming death and his implacable fears. He had, for one thing, these men, these fiancés, to get her to do right by. If she wanted to insist to him that he was in love with her, he would deal with that misapprehension later, after he'd helped her clear up this *mess* she had made.

They talked about other things, too. Of course. She asked him about the schools he went to and no sooner had he recited their prestigious names than she informed him that she wasn't sure she liked the sound of a family that sent its children away at such a young age.

He thought that perhaps her orphaned state was the root cause of her inability to turn down suitors. "If I asked, you'd probably get engaged to me, too."

They were on the beach, in bathing suits. No Rita Hayworth, Rida did not appear to advantage in her one-piece suit. She looked round, and soft, like an overripe pear, but she seemed unaware of this. And in fact to Spencer Howland she was plump and delicious, a succulent pear. She was also easy to be with, and fun, and lively. She kept surprising him and making him laugh, and letting him forget where he was, and why. She supported Roosevelt and admired Eleanor, although she "didn't blame him a bit for the other women because what man wants to always be talking about everything that's going wrong in the world? He loves her, though. Anyone can tell. I'm not so sure about her, though. What do you think — do you think she really loves him? You know this kind of people, don't you? I don't —

how could I? Although, I tend to think people are pretty much the same, no matter how much money they have. But don't go thinking I'm a Communist. I expect to take care of myself."

"By getting married," he pointed out.

"Of course."

"To one of these fiancés."

"What's the point of getting engaged if you don't ever get married?"

He laughed, and she laughed too, and she leaned over to kiss him in that way she had, her palm against his cheek.

"How can I convince you not to get engaged to everyone who asks you?"

"You'd have to marry me," she said. "Because then it would be illegal. To get engaged to anyone else," she explained, since she seemed yet again to have confused him.

"Marry you?"

"Since you love me," she told him, for the hundredth or so time, and this time he realized that she was right. He did love her. He heard himself ask, "Will you? Marry me?"

"Of course. But you have to give me a ring to make it real."

"No, Rida, I mean marry-marry. Not engaged-marry."

"I know that."

"And you have to break it off with those other fiancés."

"I will. But we can't get married right away, you know. It takes time, and you have to give me a ring to show you really mean it."

He knew better. "My captain can marry us. I'm not kidding about this, Rida."

"I know you aren't. In the first place, you're not a kidder. And besides, you're crazy about me. Of course you want to marry me."

"I am!" he laughed. "I do!" He hoped the captain, a paternalistic type, would go along with this project. Because suddenly he found himself able to hope.

When he made his request, first thing on Monday, the captain observed, "I'll say this, Howland, she's good for your nerves. We sail Tuesday."

"That's tomorrow!"

"It's already been delayed three days. So get the girl right over here, Lieutenant. You've got a ring? The girl has to have a ring. You take care of that, I'll do the paperwork, and you be back here by 1600 hours. She's eighteen, isn't she?"

Pops had no idea getting married could be so simple. Mumma, on the other hand, would have been both surprised and displeased had things not gone along quickly and smoothly. Not because she trusted Pops, nor because she trusted the Navy — neither of these being in her opinion particularly efficient entities — but because it was what she wanted. So she and Pops stood up in front of the captain to make their vows. They used a ring from Mumma's collection, a silver band with a turquoise stone set in it, which she'd been given by an Air Force fiancé who trained in Arizona where there were Navaho silversmiths. They had a wedding dinner at the Officers' Club with their friends — Katy and Louella, who had been instrumental in their meeting, and Rob and Marty. *("Those men got pretty drunk but you couldn't expect them to be too happy when it was my wedding dinner to someone else.")* After the dinner, and a final drink at the little bar on the beach, they went to a hotel.

The next morning, Pops left port and Mumma stood on the dock watching until the ship could no longer be seen in the oceanic distances. *("I was a wife now. I had to stay and wave as long as the other wives. So I did. And I didn't lay eyes on him again for years. Talk about being deprived of a honeymoon. You girls have no idea.")*

2.
A MARRIAGE IS ANNOUNCED

The telegram arrived on a spring morning in 1943. Grandmother was alone in the Boston house — alone, that is, except for the servants, including the housekeeper, Mrs. Cook, to whom the maid passed the yellow Western Union envelope, holding it out in front of her between two fingers like something particularly nasty, which — it being wartime — a telegram was likely to be. Mrs. Cook put the thing on a small silver tray and carried it in to Grandmother, who sat at her desk in the front parlor, tidying up some corner of her many-cornered, much-tidied life. Always preferring not to show emotions *devant les servants,* or *devant* anyone else, for that matter, Grandmother excused the hovering housekeeper before opening the telegram to learn that her second son — Spencer, always something of a disappointment — had gotten married, in Hawaii of all places.

Because lunch in the big house on Louisburg Square was at twelve thirty, precisely, Grandmother had the time to respond immediately to Spencer's telegram, and she had the stationery, too. Her name appeared engraved at the top of the sheet of thick, cream-colored paper, each black letter slightly raised: DOROTHY SPENCER HOWLAND. Under that name, in equally elevated letters, were printed both the in-town address and the summer address on the Cape. Upon her marriage to Brundage Howland, the Howland mansion on Louisburg Square had become her home, but it was she who brought into his family the property on Cape Cod. More than any of the trusts or inheritances, investments or acquisitions, these two houses exemplified the fiscal self-definition of each of my grandparents. Grandmother took pride in the ever-escalating value of shorefront acres on the Cape, while Grandfather boasted of a family home with the kind of history no amount of money could purchase. For three months every year, the family rusticated out on the Cape; the remainder of the year they spent on Louisburg Square, in the heart of Boston, where, on that spring morning, Grandmother sat at her desk to write to her second son, on her second-best stationery.

From under her engraved aegis, Grandmother let Pops have it.

Honestly, Spencer, I cannot for the life
of me imagine what you were thinking
of. Your thoughtlessness leaves me
speechless. Your selfishness — I can only
remind myself you're still a boy, you
don't understand. But isn't it time you
grew up? Intellectual as you are, you still
cannot be so absentminded as to have
forgotten about your poor brother. I
mean Brundy, of course; Ethan, as you
have probably also forgotten, still has
another year at Groton, and by then
either the powers that be will have
recognized that the country has need of
an educated class, although I do find this
an unlikely prospect, or this particular
world crisis may have passed. Because
surely, at some point, all of this must be
finished. Although since it has already
gone on as long as the last time and
shows no signs of abatement, Brundy
will simply have to languish in his captiv-
ity and make the best of it. It has been
five months now, but Barth is a seafront
city, which will give him some consolation. I realize that you cannot write to
him, but I do hope you spare him a

thought. Perhaps you will be more considerate of your brother than you were of your mother. I can at least hope for that.

But where was your brain? And you credited with such a high IQ. (Well, I have always been dubious about those IQ tests.) Be that as it may, even you must have known the effect a telegram would have, arriving here, with two sons in the service, and I always alone in the mornings. Suffice it to say, I am disappointed in you. I don't know how I could have failed to teach you basic consideration for others. When Mrs. Cook carried in that dreadful yellow envelope, I almost had a heart attack on the spot, with only Mrs. Cook and little Louisa in the house should I need help, seeing as although Martina can cook wonderfully she is too excitable to be of any use in an emergency. As soon as I saw the telegram, I knew something terrible had happened.

I trust I have made clear to you just what you have done. I can only hope that understanding it will lead you to mend your ways. In the meantime, I will pass on your news to the rest of the family. They will communicate to you directly, if they wish, although they are all quite busy, Anne with her nursing courses, Juliet at school, and your sister Phyllis expecting her second child, and I tell you frankly, I don't know about that. This doesn't seem like a world into which one wants to bring a child, however privileged its position will be.

That is the news from home, Spencer. We are all as well as can be expected. I hope I have made clear to you how very strongly I feel about your tendency to communicate by telegram. If you ever do something like this to me again, I will not be able to forgive you.

With love,
Mother

In Louisburg Square, the entire household assembled for luncheon — its three courses too stately to be a mere *lunch* although not elaborate enough for *dinner.* Our tall, handsome, hawk-nosed grandfather always left his office at twelve twenty, precisely, to arrive in time to take his place at the head of the table. In those years, Lally, whom Brundy had married in 1938, was living with her in-laws, her life in limbo until her husband's fate was fulfilled. Also in residence and required to attend the meal were the two younger daughters: Anne, for whom it was often an inconvenience, and Juliet, for whom Grandmother had only to procure the necessary permission from a day school, which presented no difficulty. It was to this gathered assemblage — including Little Louisa, who was serving from the tureen of soup, and through her to Mrs. Cook and Martina, when they had their own lunch later, in the kitchen, and through them to Dennis the chauffeur/groundsman, too old for the draft, and his gardening assistant, too young for it — that Grandmother announced Spencer's marriage.

I picture Grandmother's table, set with plain linen mats as befitting the midday meal, and the dimly lit dining room around it, all dark wooden wainscoting and dark silvery chinoiserie paper with scenes of Chinese gentlemen standing beside Chinese rivers or beneath improbably conical Chinese mountains. I picture the slow procession of courses, soup and then whatever light hot dish Mrs. Cook had arranged and Martina had prepared, to give Grandfather the strength to get through his important afternoon. For dessert, at lunchtime, there would be only a plate of cookies or bars and a selection of fruit. I see Grandfather as he appears in photographs, a distinguished figure in the charcoal-gray three-piece suit he always wore, and I picture Grandmother at the opposite end of the long table in a cashmere sweater set, her pearl necklaces draped over her narrow bosom. Little Louisa, who was no longer at all little when I knew her, ladles tomato bisque into bowls, and when everyone has been served, Grandmother lifts her spoon and says, before Little Louisa is out of earshot, "Your brother has gotten himself married." The scene became one of Aunt Anne's favorite family stories, to which all of us children were an eager audience; it is lodged in my memory, narrated in my aunt's laughter-drenched voice.

At Grandmother's news, everyone, except for Grandfather, sputtered satisfyingly. She waited for them to swallow, and to respond.

"But Brundy's already married," Juliet said, glancing at the young woman seated next to her, reminding them, "to Lally."

"Isn't Ethan too young?" Anne asked. "Don't boys have to be twenty-one? Girls it's only eighteen, I know, without parental consent, but Ethan's barely seventeen."

"I speak of Spencer."

Grandfather reminded her, "The boy's engaged."

"I think we may safely assume that the

engagement is off," Grandmother said. "And I imagine also that it will be up to me to inform Abigail. Spencer would never have the courage, even if he had the wits to think of it. At least," she consoled herself, "I can count on Abigail to behave well."

"The boy's a fool," Grandfather said.

Anne always enjoyed shocking her father, who took pride in never being shocked, so she said it out loud: "Maybe she's pregnant."

"Anne," her mother breathed correctively.

Grandfather told her, "Abigail is in Boston while your brother is in Hawaii. Surely those nursing courses you insist on taking have taught you enough basic biology to realize that under those conditions pregnancy is an impossibility."

"I didn't mean Abigail. I meant — maybe he *had* to marry her. This other girl, maybe it's a shotgun wedding."

"What's a shotgun wedding?" Juliet asked.

"For God's sake," Grandfather expostulated.

"Nothing you need to know about," Grandmother responded. Juliet, who in fact already knew, grinned at Anne.

"Moreover, given the number of things you young people know at much too early an age, I suspect that the question was ingenuous," Grandmother said, surprising them. "Don't you try to play me for a fool, young lady."

But Anne had just realized the most serious consequence of Spencer's act. "Now we won't have Abigail in the family. How could Spencer do that to us? Not to mention that of all the girls we know, she's the only one who's perfect for him, not to mention that she's the only girl he's ever met who knows as much as he does, not to mention she's the only one I've ever seen who likes talking to him. What's the matter with Spencer?"

"Who is the bride?" Lally asked. "Have I met her?"

They were too surprised by her asking a question to answer immediately. Lally was grieving for Brundy as if he had died, whereas in fact he had only been taken prisoner and as far as the family knew was still alive. But Lally not only dressed entirely in black, she also went veiled when she left the house. This she did only to take twice-daily walks, always the same route, down across the Commons, across the Gardens, then back up to Louisburg Square. The family sympathized with the poor girl and felt she should be allowed to carry on as she saw fit, but it did make her a detriment at the table. She'd been a sunny child when

Brundy married her, a pretty girl from a good family, with a sweet, cheerful disposition. The prolonged absence of her husband and his undecided fate transformed her into what Grandmother called — only when Lally was out of the room, however — a wet blanket. They felt sorry for her, of course, but it *was* wartime and they wished she would snap out of it. So when Lally showed curiosity about this wife of Spencer's, everyone turned to Grandmother for the answer. "What's her name?" Lally asked.

"I have no idea," Grandmother said. "Smith, nobody we know. Rida, he said her name was, I think. He must have found her in Hawaii. Perhaps she's a nurse?"

"What if she's a native girl, an islander?" Anne suggested. "Or Oriental, I mean Chinese. Or mixed, native and Oriental?"

Grandmother dismissed the possibility. "Where would Spencer meet a native girl? Rida with a *d,* of all the odd things."

"Or there are a lot of Europeans living in Hawaii," Anne added. "Artists go to the South Seas, like Gauguin did, Mother. Is she an artist? Or maybe she's a refugee, from somewhere in Europe. Do you think — Could she be Jewish?"

"Anne," Grandmother admonished again

while Grandfather repeated, "For God's sake."

"Probably not, with a name like Smith," Anne decided.

"Even Spencer would know better," Grandfather decided.

"In any case, he should never have sent a telegram," Grandmother maintained. "*And* he should never have left the job of telling Abigail to me."

"She'll be new blood," Juliet said. "The family could use some new blood. Not that you aren't, Lally, but you aren't, you know, new, are you?"

"Should he be lost in action the whole issue will prove moot," Grandfather said. "Unless there *is* a child. I must say, I'm sorry now that I instructed the will I did for him. But in my own defense, I did think — we all thought — that when he married it would be to Abigail. That girl would have been the making of him. She'd have done the right thing with Spencer's estate should he die, and now — Now, anything could happen."

"Exactly," Grandmother said. "That's exactly what I've been saying."

"You know how Spencer is," Anne reminded them. "He never listens to anyone."

When Little Louisa came to remove the

soup plates and set down the platter of chicken salad for Grandfather to serve onto the pile of Limoges plates she also set in front of him, they spoke of the weather and the war until she had returned to the kitchen.

Then: "I cannot imagine," Grandmother admitted with unwitting correctness, "what kind of a girl Spencer would pick out, on his own."

"She'll have married him for his money," Grandfather predicted retroactively. "Not his brains."

"Nobody ever married anyone for his brains. Or for hers, either," Grandmother announced, not the last time her preconceptions would mislead her about Mumma. "I dread meeting her."

"Maybe we'll like her," Juliet said. "I wonder what made Spencer fall in love with her?"

"I don't think you have much to worry about," Anne decided. "Spencer's such a stick-in-the-mud, he won't have done anything too shocking. I think I'll write and congratulate him."

"I have already written to him," Grandmother said. "And put it into the mail. He won't be sending any more telegrams," she announced with satisfaction.

■ ■ ■ ■

In this, Grandmother was absolutely correct. In fact, it was one of her lifelong complaints about Pops that he did what he was told, especially in regard to what Mumma told him to do, just as it became her lifelong complaint about Mumma that she was simply perverse. According to Grandmother, "You tell her one thing and she will do the opposite, your mother. You can count on her — which I suppose is something." Grandmother was not as right about things as she thought, but in the matter of the telegram, she predicted Pops accurately. When he was radioed the news, in August 1946, that his wife had given birth to a baby girl in the naval hospital at San Diego, he immediately passed the good news on to his mother, but not by telegram. He wrote a letter that same day which, while brief, was saturated with his happiness. He assured Grandmother of the child and mother's well-being, revealed the details of weight and length and name, and then signed off, to spread the good news among his shipmates and to telegraph Mumma.

But he was part of the force occupying Japan when he wrote his letter home, and it was weeks before the letter arrived in San Francisco; even on dry land it made slow progress across the country to arrive in Boston just when Grandmother was busy organizing her household for its annual remove to Cape Cod. This was an irritatingly inconvenient time, as well as being news that was weeks overdue.

Honestly, Spencer, she wrote to him, sitting down to that task immediately.

What were you thinking of? Have you never heard of telegrams? Certainly, the birth of the first direct-male-line Howland grandchild, even if it is a female, is important enough to merit a telegram, never mind the cost.

I'll pass on your news to the family, and I am sure everyone will be pleased for you and your bride. But whyever did you select the name Meg? There has never been a Margaret in the family, and your aunt Esther would have been so honored, and even you must remember that she is childless. Not after the young princess, I hope. There are entirely too many of those kinds of Margarets and Elizabeths around already.

We expect Brundy any one of these weeks, once he regains the strength his ordeal took from him. We are all looking forward to having him home with us again, so that life can get back to normal. Anne may not have written to tell you that she is in England now, nursing the wounded outside of Bristol, and Phyllis has had yet another child, although not the girl they both want. Ethan is living at home while he attends his Harvard classes. They rush them through in two and a half years these days. I don't like to think of the long-term cost of that policy, the kinds of doctors and lawyers who will have the running of the country in two decades. Or three. I find that thought frightening.

With love, Mother

(It was Amy who first raised the question. "But Mumma always said she didn't see him for four years after the wedding, so what about Meg?" she asked. There could be no doubt whose child Meg was, with her feminine equivalent of Pops' lanky height and firm jaw, and she had his same long-fingered hands as well. "Mumma never told me about any leave" — Meg did the math — "that December. She only told me about being removed to San Diego, as an officer's wife, and pregnant." I could explain this, with the clarity of mind *characteristic of twelve-year-olds: "For Mumma, truth isn't an exact science"; but Jo, as usual, had a view contrary to mine, and nicer, too. "Mumma sees things differently from other people."*

"We have to ask them," Meg decided, and, "You do it," the rest of us agreed. When Meg did, one dinnertime, Pops answered inattentively, "Of course I had leave. Of course I was sometimes in port. What did you think?" and Mumma snapped, "Don't you girls have anything better to think about than my love life?")

When Juliet was told about her new niece, she asked Grandmother, "Are you going to write to Spencer's wife? And introduce yourself, and welcome her to the family?"

"I don't know where the woman is living," Grandmother answered. "She hasn't written to introduce herself to me," she pointed out. "Which I must say doesn't speak well of her upbringing. I don't see her fitting into the family, not like Lally," she said, and Lally thanked her. "Not like Abigail would have. I have to tell you, I am not looking forward to meeting this woman Spencer chose to marry."

"Maybe he'll settle on the West Coast," Juliet suggested, "and you'll never have to meet her."

"Our family has lived in Boston for more than two hundred years," Grandmother reminded her. "I cannot imagine Spencer living anywhere else."

Pops didn't bring Mumma east — by which he and his family meant to Boston or the Cape — until the summer of 1947. His ship had been part of MacArthur's occupation forces in Japan at the end of the war, and it wasn't until fall of 1946 that Pops was discharged from the service and set ashore in San Francisco. At that time, Mumma and Meg awaited him in San Diego. Other wives made the train trip north, to be at the docks or at the airfield when their husbands came home from war, but not Mumma. She couldn't see the point of the long, crowded train ride, with a nursing infant, and she didn't have the time. In San Diego, she had formed an ad hoc committee of the Navy wives — both officers' wives and the wives of ordinary seamen — to offer cooperative babysitting services. Some of these women Mumma had found jobs for *("Unless they had the gumption to go out and get one for themselves, which most of them didn't")*. Others she had enrolled in the nursing courses or teaching courses offered by the local college, for postwar employment. Mumma was especially concerned about the widows, particularly those widows who didn't want to return to the Midwest or South or even New England, not as widows, not to lives that would offer them only years of single-parent- and social-pariah-hood. ("*A woman without a husband, I don't have to tell you girls this, she has a hard time making friends, especially among married couples. You know how possessive women can be about their men. And any woman knows what men are like. Men look around. Especially if the odds are in their favor, and the odds were in their favor those days, the way the odds always are after a war. Except for the men who'd been crippled, of course.*")

In San Diego, Mumma had the lives of her various wives to look after, and she had Meg to look after; she wrote daily letters to Pops and read the books he recommended, if the base library had them; and she had the wounded men in the base hospital to visit, and do what she could for. Her life in San Diego was both useful and busy. She couldn't drop everything to go meet Pops, when it was just as easy — in fact, easier — for him to find a car and come join her.

Not that she wasn't looking forward to seeing him, she could promise him that, promise him the kind of warm welcome waiting for him that any man would want coming home from war. It was just that not everyone had come back unwounded, not everyone had come *back,* for that matter, and there were people depending on her and she couldn't let them down. It was just that he was the one with the trust fund, which meant the ready cash to buy a car and drive it down the California coast. They had the rest of their lives, so what was the big hurry?

Besides, she concluded with canny insight, or maybe wisdom learned from encountering too many men deprived of the solitude and quietude necessary for them to shed their military pasts and reposition themselves for a civilian future, Pops had never seen the California coast, had he? He'd been living in crowds, didn't he want some time to himself? He could take as long as he liked on the way south. He should see the sights of San Francisco and talk to the University at Berkeley, because didn't he say he was planning on going back to take his doctorate? He could see the mountains, and the little city of Monterey, with its canning factories. That would be almost like home, wouldn't it? Mumma guessed so, anyway, from what he'd told her about Cape Cod. Not Boston, she knew better than that.

There was no fishing out of Boston, she knew, and no industry, either; she'd looked it all up in the encyclopedia at the base library. Pops could stop in Hollywood, maybe meet a starlet. All in all, he should buy that car and have a holiday. Otherwise, what was the point of having so much money? What was the point of living through a war? She would see him when she would see him, although she would certainly enjoy a few phone calls. She had almost forgotten the sound of his voice, she wrote him.

The little family didn't leave San Diego until March, and even then, since Mumma had never in her whole life been east of the Sierra Nevada, and since a crawling infant, as Meg then was, shouldn't travel for long hours, they took their time crossing the country. Pops showed Mumma the Grand Canyon and the Grand Tetons; he took her to Yellowstone National Park. He also had never seen these sights. They wandered across the Arizona desert and the mesa country of New Mexico, then through the oil fields and cattle ranches of Texas, to see the Louisiana bayous. They made a huge loop north along the Mississippi River from New Orleans to Saint Louis and Chicago. Mumma drove while Pops held Meg on his lap and read aloud to them both — Zane

Grey, Mark Twain, Willa Cather, Theodore Dreiser. He was reading *Ethan Frome* when they came to New England, via the battlefields of the Civil and Revolutionary Wars. Mumma had enjoyed the long drive, the geography she'd seen and the history she'd heard. She suspected that once Pops got back to the East Coast, the only places he'd be willing to travel to were in Europe, and she had her doubts about Europe.

They were due to arrive at the Cape on a Friday in mid-July of 1947. There, Pops would be reunited with his family, Brundy having returned to his father's law practice almost a year earlier, and there Mumma could finally meet her in-laws, not to mention the rest of his family. Pops had told her about the various connections, the first and second cousins, the aunts and uncles, the relations by marriage. He drew family trees for her to study. He described the Spencer compound, seven large original summer cottages and several more recently built smaller homes, which occupied the broad point of land stretching out into Buzzards Bay. He related the history of summers spent there, a great gathering of all ages, from the most elderly and rickety to the least self-reliant newborns, and everything in between, a mass of children running around together. Mumma had been memorizing names and relationships. Pops had called his mother before they left San Diego, and again from Saint Louis, and finally from Gettysburg, first to estimate, then to establish the day they would arrive, next to verify, and finally to confirm it. They were, Mumma knew, expected.

("I wasn't nervous. I was curious. I wasn't expecting anything in particular. Except, of course, Jo, I was expecting Jo. And then, once we got there, it took me about five and a half minutes to take their measure.")

They had spent four days in New York City and then driven up the Connecticut coastline, along the Boston Post Road. Rhode Island — a state Mumma always scorned for both its size and the extravagances of Newport — went by in a minute, half a minute, on their way to the Massachusetts state line, and then came the high Bourne Bridge over the Cape Cod Canal, which had originally been built by private investors, but after more than ten years was purchased by the federal government, as Pops informed Mumma. *("Your father knows everything, and don't you girls ever forget that. How else do you think I've learned so much?")*

They crossed that bridge and they were on Cape Cod. They turned off Route 6 onto a narrow paved road that snaked through the geographical shoulder of the Cape's long arm, through summer towns where Boston's wealthier families escaped from the hot city to a quieter, simpler life, broken only occasionally by such events as weddings and funerals, large parties assembled to celebrate major birthdays and anniversaries, the Fourth of July, and the opening and closing of the summer season on the Cape, Memorial and Labor Days. Mothers and children and servants spent whole summers in the saltwater environment; fathers came out for long weekends, and — now that they could take them again — vacation weeks. Children spent days in bathing suits, by the water, in the water, on the water. Mothers sat on beach chairs keeping an eye on things. Seaweed floated up onto the little curved beaches, and horseshoe crabs plowed their blind way along the sand at the edges of the tides. Low, marshy islands could be explored when the tide was out, or visited by rowboat in high water. Clams could be dug, fish caught. On rainy days, of which there were many, especially in July, wooden jigsaw puzzles came out, and fires were lit, and children swarmed from one kitchen to another while cooks produced tarts and cookies and slabs of frosted cake, vying to be the most visited.

During the long years of war, these summers were a sanctuary for the children, and in part for the parents, too. As much as was possible, summers had gone on as before, the only real difference being that there were almost no young men and there were only a few young women. But now the war was over, rationing had ended, the men had returned, and normalcy been reassumed.

Wampanoag was a little crossroads town, one gas pump in front of the general store/post office/lunch counter, on a back road between Bourne and Falmouth. The town lay two miles inland from the irregular coastline where summer houses at the ends of long driveways overlooked the protected water of Buzzards Bay. Pops drove through the town center and along Beach Road, where a small public beach was bright with bathing suits and umbrellas. A few miles beyond the beach, he turned in to an unsignposted dirt road that led them into Spencer territory, where a loose tribal society had been established among the homes of Spencers and Spencers-by-marriage (like the Howlands). For Pops it was home and he knew he had no choice but to return.

And so they finally met, Mumma and

Grandmother. Grandmother had girded her loins for a great enemy, against whom she would need all of her many weapons for the inevitable victory. Mumma never girded, she just prevailed. (*"Do you think he ever understood what was wrong about her?"* Amy *always wondered, and Jo agreed,* "It never crossed his mind they wouldn't love her, too," *but,* "I was their ticket in," *Meg claimed.* "The family line, the family name, even with Mumma for my mother, I was still her granddaughter.")

Having at last arrived, the young couple climbed out of the car, Meg asleep on her father's shoulder. But they did not enter to the relaxed seaside life Pops had been describing. A pair of men passed by them carrying panniers that clinked of glassware and china, to load them into the back of a small van; a sedan, its rear seat piled with linens, drove out past them; men and women took trays covered with kitchen cloths out to a second van while an open-topped convertible came up and parked behind, waiting for its next load.

The house remained impervious to the activity swirling at its hems. The Howland-Spencer house sat on a wooded ridge of hill that would have looked down to the harbor if dense summer foliage hadn't almost entirely concealed what lay beyond. This setting was about house, not ocean. It was a typical summer cottage, with a large two-story central section and wings that spread out on either side. The shingled exterior had weathered to a silvery gray and the many windows had small glass panes. At the end of an ascending walkway, a single slate step led up to the front door, which opened wide for Pops and Mumma and Meg.

In the door stood a scrawny girl whose hands were clasped in front of her. She had pale brown hair pulled back into a knot; she wore a shapeless, pale blue cotton dress buttoned down the front; she was a nice-looking girl, although you wouldn't have noticed it to look at her. *("If you girls ever have maids, you make sure to dress them well, you hear me? Life is too short to make the people who work for you miserable.")* "Mr. and Mrs. Spencer?" she asked, and when they said they were, she said, "Come in, please. Mrs. Howland is expecting you in the library." She preceded them with self-conscious adolescent steps across a broad sunny hallway to a paneled wooden door, which was closed.

The house hummed with invisible busyness, distant voices calling out to one another, the muffled sounds of feet. Every table in the hallway bore a large display of cut flowers. "Who died?" Mumma asked Pops, and, "It's the party," he told her, but before she could demand, "What party?" the little maid had knocked on and thrown open the door.

As impervious as her house, Grandmother was standing in front of a fireplace flanked by long windows. *("Like a portrait of that tsarina of Russia, you know the one, the kind of portrait that makes you see why there was that revolution, poor woman, even being the daughter of the Queen of England couldn't save her.")* Once they had had a moment to view her, Grandmother stepped forward, arms outstretched. "Give me that beautiful child."

Pops passed over the sleeping Meg, and in the brief time it took Meg to wake up and take center stage, the three adults considered one another. "You look quite well rested, Spencer," his mother greeted him, offering a cheek should he care to bend and kiss it, which he obediently did. Before he could say anything, she turned her attention to Mumma. "You must be Rida, but nobody names a child Rida. What is your real name?"

"Rida," Mumma answered mendaciously. She turned to ask Pops again, "What party?"

Once again Grandmother forestalled

Pops' answer. "And you were raised in California? Are your parents there?"

Mumma went straight to the point of what Grandmother wanted to talk about. "I'm a foundling, so I can't tell you anything about my parents. I don't have any background."

"Oh. My. Then —"

With characteristic good timing, Meg saved the moment — there never was a chance for the day — by opening her eyes and lifting a pudgy hand toward this new stranger, making almost-word noises to express her curiosity as well as her readiness to accept whatever attentions this person would offer her. Meg was accustomed to the kindness of strangers.

"She has taken a shine to me," Grandmother announced.

"She likes everybody," Mumma answered truthfully. "Strangers don't frighten her. What do you want me to call you?"

"Call me?" Grandmother played for time. "What do you mean, call me?" She wasn't accustomed to playing for time with someone who had so many reasons to be currying her favor.

"You're not the Mom type," Mumma explained, and Pops laughed, further confusing Grandmother, who was also unaccustomed to Spencer laughing. "Should I call you Mrs. Howland? Because Mother Howland sounds like a woman whose sons go out and rob banks. You'll call me Rida, of course. Unless you'd rather call me Mrs. Howland, too?"

"I hadn't given a thought to that question," Grandmother said — her turn for mendacity, since immediately after the relevant wedding ceremonies she had instructed her previously acquired daughter- and son-in-law to call her Mother H. "I'm not sure —"

"Mrs. Howland would be a little formal," Pops said, to help things along, although to whom he was saying this was not clear. "Even pompous."

"What's your given name, then?" Mumma asked Grandmother.

Luckily, at that moment Meg reached up her other adorably pudgy hand to pull on Grandmother's triple strand of pearls, so that she could respond "Dorothy" to the harmless grandchild, almost still a baby, not this young woman with her alarming mahogany eyes and abrupt — Did she mean to be rude? — way of speaking. "This little girl will have to go out to meet Mrs. Cook. Mrs. Cook is going to take care of you this evening," Grandmother informed Meg while Pops told Mumma, "Mrs. Cook is the housekeeper. She knows all about babies."

Mumma was not distracted from what she perceived to be the hidden, if not the main, point. "What about a party?" she demanded of Grandmother, but before Grandmother could answer, she turned on Pops. "What party?"

"The party to announce Spencer's marriage, of course. Just a few family and friends, people who have known Spencer, and the family, for years. They have to meet you."

"You knew about this," Mumma accused Pops.

Grandmother intervened. "I instructed him not to tell you. I made him promise. Don't blame Spencer. It's my fault."

Sensing unease, Meg reached out to her mother, so Mumma took her back and stood with the child against her breast, facing her husband and his mother. She stood on an Oriental carpet worn pale by years of afternoon sunlight and dozens of pairs of bare feet, but Mumma was not quelled by her environment. "I certainly will blame Spencer for making a promise to keep something secret from his wife. He knows better. Although he probably doesn't realize how difficult it is for me to meet everybody all at once, so I don't blame him about that.

I don't blame you for that either, although I think you do know perfectly well. What I blame you for is putting secrets between a husband and wife."

"We wanted to spare you the worry," Grandmother suggested.

Mumma gave her the gimlet eye. She didn't believe it for one minute. "I wouldn't have worried."

"You're going to have to meet these people sooner or later," Grandmother pointed out. "You might as well get it over with."

"Are you trying to undermine my marriage?" Mumma asked. "Because I should tell you, Spencer is very happy with me. Although," she turned to Pops, "I warn you, another trick like this — ever in our life, I mean — and that's the last you'll see of me."

"It's not his fault," Grandmother repeated.

"Oh, I know whose fault it is. But Spencer and I have a marriage here."

Grandmother, tall and straight in a light flowered chiffon garden party dress with one of the large lace collars she favored at the time, made an effort to resume control of the situation. "I've put you in the Capstan house," she told Pops, referring to the small building nestled at the bottom of the hill below the big house. "You can live there for as long as you need — we'll settle all of that later — but right now you have only an hour to get bathed and changed. You'll want to get started getting yourself ready. Spencer will show you where everything is," she said to Mumma, "and baby will be here with me and Mrs. Cook. I've had some dresses hung in your closet since I can imagine what condition your wardrobe is in, after having been on the road for so long. Just so you know you don't have to worry."

"I'm not worried," Mumma said. She wasn't. She was furious. At both of them.

Then Grandmother surprised her by saying, in a considering tone of voice, looking down at Mumma from her extra four inches, "You're not at all what I expected."

"Spencer sent you a photograph," Mumma reminded her.

"Yes," Grandmother said.

"Or do you mean . . . ? I get it, you mean I'm not what you expected of Spencer. For Spencer. I'm looking forward to meeting Abigail."

That was the first time Mumma saw Grandmother's real smile, which occurred no more than once a week, and sometimes not for weeks at a time. This smile was not only rare, it was also brief. It lit up her stern face like a flash of lightning, gone as soon as seen; it didn't change her appearance or attitude, it merely revealed — and only for that flash — her sense of irony. *Isn't this just the kind of trick life gets up to.*

Pops escorted Mumma down the dirt-and-log stairs to the Capstan house and opened the door to her new home. Without even looking around at the furnishings in the living room or out the window at the view, Mumma told him, "Don't bother unpacking."

She didn't try to explain anything to him, but she didn't have to because his family often made him feel the same way, like an unwelcome stranger. Either Mumma would settle in or not, and whether or not he unpacked would make no difference. Besides, the blue-and-white-striped seersucker suit he'd be expected to wear was waiting for him in the closet, so he didn't need to unpack much of anything. Moreover, he didn't feel like fighting with anyone, ever again, not even a squabble, in his whole life. So he said to Mumma, "Just what I'd take out in a hotel," and set about the process of getting dressed for his mother's party to introduce his bride. He knew who he was, and where, and what to wear.

So did Mumma, whatever anybody might think to the contrary, although when she looked into the closet and saw the dresses Grandmother had hanging there, she had a moment's doubt — not about what to wear, and not about who she was, but about where she was.

(This was the point in the story where Mumma began her refrain of, "Don't remind me. I don't want to talk about it," which prefaced her answers to any of our questions about this first meeting with Pops' family. "What were the dresses like? Did they have those awful lace collars?" "Don't remind me about those dresses." "Where was Grandfather? Why wasn't he there to meet you?" "I don't want to talk about your grandfather. I'd already heard all I needed to know about him by the time I saw his face.")

Mumma was out of the bath when the same little maid who had opened the door to them arrived at the door of the Capstan house to deliver Meg, with the message that Mrs. Cook thought the baby needed a feeding. Once Meg was attached to a breast, and quieted, Mumma had a visit with the girl, who had been instructed to wait and then return the baby to the big house. Pops was having a postwar bath, a long, leisurely soak, so Mumma had the time and privacy to get to the bottom of whatever it was that was keeping this girl so scrawny and uneasy.

Her name was Polly Grangery and she was fifteen, just summer help, but she wished she could quit. Not that she minded the work, she never minded work, hard work wouldn't hurt you, long hours wouldn't hurt you. It was the people. Not that she minded Mrs. Howland, for all her carry-on, and she didn't mind Mrs. Brundy either, and she didn't mind the daughters. Juliet was often quite friendly, not at all stuck up, not like Phyllis, and Anne was in Bourne for her nursing job, so how could she mind someone who wasn't even there? Although Mrs. Howland said it was probably some man there and not a job at all.

Polly didn't mind the housework either; the rest of the staff was very patient, explaining things to her, helping her, so she had nothing to complain about, did she. Mumma rocked in her chair, and nursed Meg, and listened, then asked, "What is it you *would* complain about? That you're not mentioning although it's obvious to me there's something."

"That's Mr. Howland," Polly answered, the first but not at all the last occasion on which she and Mumma followed perfectly one another's mental leapings and torturous grammars.

"Men," Mumma said.

"I know he's just being friendly," Polly said. "Everyone says." She smiled brightly and then burst into tears, a child's helpless tears born of fear and rage. Then, "I'm sorry, Mrs. Spencer. But you wouldn't be willing to ask to have me work down here for you, would you?" she asked. "I'll be all right," she said, wiping her eyes and nose on the back of her hand, wiping the back of her hand on her starched uniform apron. "After all, a girl has to learn how to take care of herself, doesn't she?"

"Who have you talked to about it?" asked Mumma. "Besides me, I mean."

"I'd never," Polly said. "They'd fire me and I need the money. I'm saving."

"Saving for what?"

"To go to school. To be a secretary, maybe for a doctor, maybe for a lawyer. You meet men in offices," Polly said, and blushed. Polly Grangery was a terrific blusher; her face turned brick red with excitement or anxiety or embarrassment, with anger or impatience, and also — most frequently — with laughter. "I'd like to get married someday, like you, and have a baby, like this one, like you."

"We will not be staying on here," Mumma told her.

"You aren't? But Mrs. Howland said —"

"I haven't told her yet."

"I was hoping you'd stay," Polly said, bright red. "I was hoping I could work for you."

"You are a planner, aren't you?" Mumma observed.

"If a girl doesn't have her own plans, she could end up with a baby and maybe not even married, and then where would I be? I don't mean you. You're married. If I could marry someone like Mr. Spencer, I'd think I'd done well for myself. He's going to be a professor, or anyway that's what they're saying. I could be a secretary in a university college. They have secretaries in those places, don't they?"

Mumma shifted Meg to the other breast and told the girl sternly, "There's more to life than a husband."

"For children you need a husband. You can't tell me you don't agree with me because you're pregnant again, aren't you?"

It was seldom that anyone surprised Mumma. "I guess you *are* observant."

"How am I going to get ahead if I'm not? With this baby, and being pregnant again, you're going to want help in the house, and I could work for the whole rest of the summer. And weekends and holidays, after."

"Maybe. But I don't want anyone having

an influence on my daughter who puts up with the kind of behavior from men you were talking about."

Polly considered that. "I can't tell Mrs. Howland."

"I never thought you would, and she probably knows anyway. It's him you tell. Tell him to stop. Tell him if he doesn't, you'll tell your father."

"My dad has worked for the Howlands for years, and my mother too, and everybody says that's the kind of thing you have to put up with when you work for summer people. They pay much higher wages."

"Well then, tell him you'll tell the authorities."

"You mean the police? The minister? They're all afraid of him, and anyway, he's a lawyer, from the city, from Boston." Polly tried to make Grandfather's status clear to Mumma. "They'd never listen."

"Then quit. And say why."

"But I need —"

"Once you get the gumption to quit, and say why, come talk to me about a job."

("I don't know where Mumma got off being so authoritarian with Polly that day," I say to Amy but "Mumma taught Polly to stand up for herself," Amy tells me. I correct her. "Mumma taught Polly how to be her servant.")

"Polly had three children, and a good hus-band — even if he wasn't a lawyer or a doc-tor, or a WASP either, if that matters, if you've turned into as much of a snob as Grand-father," Amy answers. Having temporarily silenced me, she finishes the job. "Although I admit she never got to be some man's secre-tary and work long, tedious hours for low pay, getting home late and too tired to enjoy her family, that's if she found a man other than her boss to fall in love with. Gee whillikers, Beth, maybe you're right. Maybe meeting up with Mumma did ruin Polly's life.")

On the Cape, Grandmother held parties at the long crescent of private beach below the house, but only the footwear — or, rather, the lack of footwear — nodded at sum-mertime informality. Everything else met higher standards. A marquee was put up, with tables and chairs set out under its cover, as well as the long serving tables for food and drinks, and a special wooden floor for dancing. Grandmother didn't give cook-outs or lobster roasts or clambakes; hers were garden parties, to which the women wore light summer dresses, and some even sported broad-brimmed organza hats, their crowns circled with wreaths of silk wildflow-ers. The men wore seersucker suits and striped ties, and the gayer blades sometimes a panama hat. This was a Boston crowd, so the jewelry — with the exception of engagement rings — tended toward pearls, strings of which, in those days, women wore to the beach, believing that the warmth of the sun and the oil of their bare skins promoted luster, just as the washing and buffing of their silver by the servants promoted luster — luster being acceptable, glitter not. Because the party was at the beach, however, the women didn't wear stockings, and nobody wore shoes. Guests set their shoes neatly side by side on an old swimming float the family kept at the foot of the steep road to the beach for just such use, twenty, fifty, eighty, a hundred and twenty pairs of shoes, wingtips and sandals, arranged in neat rows.

It was hard for Mumma to understand that although she was wearing the swirly red satin skirt edged with black lace, and the off-the-shoulder white blouse edged with ruffles, both of which she had purchased in New Orleans, with big gold hoop earrings for her pierced ears, she couldn't complete the outfit with high black Cuban heels. Giving up her footwear was bad enough, but when Pops told her that they were expected to stand with his parents to greet guests, she sat down in the living room for the third time, announcing for the third time that she wasn't going to this party. The first time was when he suggested that it might be politic to wear one of the dresses Grandmother had hung out for her, without earrings, since nobody else would have pierced ears, not in that crowd. Mumma sat right down, declaring, "I'm not going out to meet people looking like a sack of potatoes — and a sack of peeled potatoes at that." The second time concerned shoelessness. "What kind of people are they? Whoever heard of a formal picnic? Are they trying to have the worst of both worlds?" At mention of a receiving line, Mumma plumped herself down on the sofa and once again announced her refusals, but she knew she had to go along, however much going along went against her grain.

The receiving line *("Don't remind me about that receiving line folderol of your grand-mother's — I've never felt so unnecessary in my life")* formed up just beyond the shoe float, where the stones and pebbles washed down by rains gathered, which encouraged the now barefoot guests to move swiftly along onto the warm, soft sand toward the well-stocked bar and the abundant platters of food. The line itself was not long, a traditional wedding receiving line, the only real difference being that there were no parents of the bride to add two more hands to be shaken, two more polite congratulations to be offered. "Or," Grandfather announced to Grandmother as the four of them set themselves up in a line, "to foot the bill." He knew Mumma heard him, so he smiled and added, "Nothing personal . . . Rida? I can see" — here he leered — "why Spencer chose you."

Mumma refused to stand next to Grandfather in line *("He had the look of a pincher")*, so the guests were greeted by — and offered their appropriate pleasantries to — first Grandfather, then Grandmother, then Mumma, and finally Pops. Grandmother would welcome them and mention a name, saying "Mary," or "Mrs. Gillespie," or "Cousin James, I want you to meet Spencer's bride Rida, she's only just arrived." All that Mumma needed to do was say Hello and Hello and Hello. Nobody cared what else she might have to say, they just wanted to clap eyes on her. "I've heard so much about you," the guests said, over and over. *("You can bet your boots they had, and they'd probably said a lot, too. I don't want to talk about it.")* The first people through the line were members of the immediate family, sisters and brothers, sisters-in-law and brothers-in-law, then more distant relations, and Grandmother would mumble some introductory phrase like, "One of the North Shore Campbells," or, "Her father is a Villier," and Mumma would say Hello. She met Brundy, and Phyllis, then Phyllis's husband, Rich, then Ethan and Juliet and Anne, and all except for Brundy said, "I'm so glad to meet you at last," and "I can't wait to get to know you." Brundy, a lean, handsome man like his father, said nothing, but he did really look at her, for one lingering glance. *("Different from your uncle Ethan's kind of lingering, and if you don't know what I mean, ask me. A girl needs to know these things.")* Cousins went by, Spencers and Norths, as well as more Howlands. After them came family friends, Gillespies and Maddons, Dawsons, Sawyers, and younger people, Pops' age, Tommys and Billys and Bettys and Susies, postwar young people who, like Pops, had survived, and at the last a slender, tall, pale woman, introduced only as Abigail. "This is Abigail, of course."

Abigail Smith was quite lovely, wearing a sleeveless linen dress of pale silvery blue, the broad white collar of which set off her slender neck. She wore her long, pale hair up in a chignon. Mumma tried to catch her eye as they were introduced, then while she was shaking the hand of her ex-fiancé, but Abigail Smith would not look up from those clasped hands, until she moved quickly on to join a group of young people standing, talking, with their feet in the shallow water.

("I knew it right then and there — he'd never written to her. I don't know why I didn't do what Huckleberry Finn says and light out for the territories. It was your father who stopped me, because I couldn't abandon him in that nest of vipers. Even if they were his own blood vipers.")

From where she stood, Mumma could see a long curve of beach, more crowded with each passing minute by arriving guests, and beyond that the water of the cove, protected from the bay by narrow barrier islands of marsh grass. The cove required only this minimal protection because the bay was itself protected on the east by the projection of land out from Woods Hole and on the west by the coast of Rhode Island. *("Just the kind of overprotected place the Howlands liked, and I don't know how your father turned out as well as he did." "But Mumma," I pointed out, "Wampanoag's where we grew up." "You had me," she explained.)*

On the day of Grandmother's party, the water rippled gently in the sunlight, fluffy white clouds floated across a glowing sky, and a breeze cooled the air with no more troubling effect on shore than a seductive stirring of skirts. It was a perfect day. Guests in summer dress and bare feet held tall champagne flutes, and barefoot waitresses wearing crisp white aprons moved among them, offering delicacies on silver trays. Uncle Ethan, who had learned photography in case the war kept going on — photographers as a rule seeing less combat than other servicemen — took photographs. The high Spencer forehead appears on many of the guests, and the square Howland jaw, as well as a tendency toward youthful balding. In the wedding portrait taken that day, Mumma has her hand on Pops' arm, and his hand covers it; her hair is wild around her head and bare shoulders; her mouth is set, her face grimly expressionless. She's rather frightening to look at, not at all the glowing bride, or even — as her outfit promises — the fiery gypsy. Pops looks merely handsome; his bare ankles belie the formality of his dress and expression.

Mumma had to work hard for the few moments of pleasure she got from this party of Grandmother's, where nobody wanted to know her. The sisters of the groom, deprived of the opportunity to be bridesmaids on display — and in one case bridesmatron as

well as the envied mother of the flower girl
— gathered Spencer's bride under their col-
lective wing. They wouldn't leave her alone.
They took charge of her in shifts, escorting
her from group to group. "This is Mrs.
Gillespie, she went to school with Mother,"
"You haven't had a chance to talk to Cousin
John Spencer, Father's brother's second
wife's daughter's husband," and "Oh, and
here's Jonquil. Jonquil Cartenbury, Rida.
Jonquil, this is Rida, Spencer's bride from
California. You two will have a lot in com-
mon, Rida, Jonquil's from the South —
Georgia, isn't it?"

"Virginia," a pretty young blonde woman
of about Mumma's age answered with a
sweetly indulgent smile for Phyllis's geographic limitations. She turned her smiling
face to Mumma to add, "Charlottesville.
That's in the foothills of the mountains, but
I'm not a mountain girl, oh my no. My daddy's family removed there during the war.
For safety."

"From Nazi attack?" Mumma wondered.

"I mean the War of Northern Aggression."

"What war of northern aggression?"
Mumma demanded.

Jonquil looked sympathetically at Pops,
then lowered her eyes to her own clasped
hands to murmur delicately, "Sherman."

"Sherman who?" asked Mumma. *("I could see what she was up to, but life is too short to fly off the handle at every little thing and I already had your grandmother to take care of.")*

"The Civil War, Rida dear," said Phyllis.

Mumma glared at both of them. "The names wars get . . . sometimes . . . It wasn't very civil, that war, from what I've read."

"Did you enjoy *Gone with the Wind*?" asked Jonquil, all wide blue eyes.

"Of course, the book and the movie. And how did you like Sandburg's biography of Lincoln?" Mumma shot back before concluding her point. "Like calling that other one the War to End All Wars. You'd think people would learn."

Jonquil Cartenbury nodded, smiling, waiting, but Mumma was finished. Finally, Phyllis said, "You two will have to get to know each other." Jonquil Cartenbury fingered her pearls, then tucked her blonde pageboy behind a delicate ear to display the pearl earrings, leaving it to Mumma to disagree grimly, "No, we don't."

It became clear to Mumma that Pops' sisters were among the enemy. Juliet, who had at last figured out that her favorite brother was no longer going to stand at the edges of a party joking with her the way he used to, blamed Mumma for her loss and glared from a distance, or glared from Mumma's side as she inserted her new sister-in-law into yet another small, happily chattering group. Since Mumma had never had sisters, she took this dislike at face value. The older two disliked her with more finesse. When someone quite politely inquired about something as harmless as Where had the young couple met? How was Rida enjoying Cape Cod? or, What did Spencer plan to do now? Before Mumma could even start to answer, her attendant sister took over. "During the war, Spencer was in Hawaii, I don't know if you knew that. But was that you I saw on the golf course this afternoon? How's your putting?" "They just got in this afternoon, you know how Spencer leaves things to the last minute. I don't think the poor girl's had time to bathe, much less see the dunes and beaches. But what do you think of this idea of building a breakwater off the Point? Will it really control the silting?" "Spencer's returning to Harvard, to do a doctorate, and he'll probably decide to work there, or MIT. What's Timmy going to do, now that he's settling down, has he told you? Timmy's not here today, Rida, so you haven't met him. He always wanted to go into business, didn't he?"

Mumma put up with this until a sister interrupted the sixth or seventh group of strangers to introduce Spencer's bride and bring their easy conversation to a grinding, unwilling halt before setting it off on leaden feet in a new direction: "Are you sailing in the Wednesday twilight series this year?" At that, Mumma simply extricated her arm and walked away. She made no explanation, made no excuse; she just broke loose. Phyllis stared after her, and when Anne came over immediately to ask her where Rida was going, just shook her head in palpable amazement at her brother's wife's odd behavior. The two sisters stood shoulder to shoulder, stupefied by Mumma's unmannerliness. Then they set off together to report to their mother.

On her own, Mumma gravitated toward the musicians, who had been playing unobtrusively, as instructed, as usual. At Grandmother's beach parties there was always music. It was a point of pride with her, and there was always dancing. Mumma planned to ask the bandleader to play a tango. Any dancer knows the special pleasure of a tango, which she hadn't danced in a long time. To get to the bandstand, Mumma had to pass by Grandfather, who was standing with Brundy to watch the festivities. Both of them were drinking purposefully, the handsome, hawk-nosed, white-haired man in his seersucker suit, his tie loosened and his face beaded with sweat, and the tall, tanned younger man, who was one of a few wearing white linen. Brundy even had a white linen vest, and he had removed his jacket and rolled up his shirt sleeves, as handsome as his father and much more attractive.

As Mumma passed near, Grandfather's arm snaked out and wrapped around her waist; he spread the fingers of his hand up over her ribs toward her breasts; he pulled her toward him and she smelled the aroma of whiskey, like a cloud of perfume all around him, as he suggested, "How about a kiss from my new daughter-in-law? A kiss for the new man in her life," with the smile of a man who knows no woman will say no to him.

Mumma didn't even bother putting her hands up flat against his chest, in the time-honored way girls can fend off undesirable attentions while pretending not to, so as not to offend, hoping — however much they might be offended — to be themselves inoffensive. Mumma wasn't that kind of girl.

She looked right at him, and when his eyes rose to her face, that look wiped the smile off his and loosened his grip. Before he could pull back, she said, without changing her expression, "I've known a lot of men just like you."

Unaccustomed as he was to rebellions, Grandfather was momentarily wordless. Then, "I don't know what Spencer is doing, trying to bring you into my family," he said, and turned to Brundy. "Your brother always was a fool. A brain, none of us can equal his brains I'm often told, but the boy has no sense."

"Dad," Brundy protested, but he was protesting to his father's back. Grandfather had walked off. Brundy started to apologize to Mumma. "Dad just —" but she cut him off.

"I've met worse. Not much worse, and not many, and I don't know why you all don't either make him stop or get rid of him. Frankly."

At that, Brundy laughed out loud, and she smelled on his laughter more of the same whiskey perfume. Brundy was drinking, but he was not drunk. She looked into his face, looking up, since like all of the Howland men he was over six feet. Looking up, she could see that however much he had drunk, he was stone-cold sober.

"I was going to ask them to play a tango," she told him. "Do you tango?"

"I did, in my day. I haven't for a while," he said, a sad statement, saturated with unspoken losses.

"Good," Mumma said. "Let's do it."

Tango music cleared the dance floor of couples moving in sedate small squares, leaving it entirely in the possession of Mumma and Brundy. "Spencer won't mind?" Brundy asked, putting out his hand for her to lay her palm flat against.

"Spencer doesn't enjoy dancing, but I was a dancer when we met. Only USO, only the chorus, but still, I was."

They stepped, wheeled around the turn, and leaned their cheeks together for the next passes. Brundy was a good dancer, relaxed, fluid — no surprise, since Spencer had boasted about his brother's coordination. Brundy was the athlete in the family; he had a dramatic flair, too, and when he threw his head back to look down into her eyes, she realized how little expression his own dark blue eyes had held up until that dance. With the music pulsing around them and nobody able to overhear what they were saying, she remarked, "You had a bad time, didn't you." When he didn't respond, she looked carefully at him, concluding, "And this is worse."

That was when the music's rhythms halted and the two dancers looked around to see that the rest of the guests were gazing out over the tranquil harbor with averted eyes, while Grandmother was stepping away from the musicians and Lally was approaching them.

"In the camp," Brundy said to Mumma with the first genuinely welcoming smile she had seen since she arrived at the Point, "they called me B-24."

"The Liberator?" Mumma was a war bride, she knew her planes.

Brundy grinned, a boy again briefly, and devilishly good-looking.

"B-24 it is," Mumma told him, and at that moment Lally arrived to say, "You haven't danced with me yet, Brundy."

"First," Brundy told his wife, "I want to find Spencer and congratulate him. He's my brother, Lally, and I've barely seen him to say hello to. You can find someone else to partner you, although I don't think Mother's ready for the dancing to begin."

As he left the two women, Mumma said only, "Your husband is a good dancer."

"You should know," Lally answered, sorrowfully. "If you'll excuse me . . ." But she warned Mumma before she turned away, "He hasn't been himself since the war. Since the camp. Since he got back."

"What did you expect?" Mumma asked, but Lally didn't want to discuss it and drifted off, leaving Mumma once again alone. Mumma was ready to leave by then, and for good, but Pops had been sent to join a group of men and women his own age and she couldn't catch his eye. She could understand that he wanted to visit with cousins and summer friends. She didn't expect him to stick close to her side; she'd always exercised autonomy, even before she knew what the word meant. So, figuring she had been there for everyone to see for at least an hour — and those people had taken full advantage of the time she'd given them — she exited up the sandy road.

("But Mumma, what about talking to Abigail Smith?" We couldn't get used to Abigail Smith actually having once been engaged to our father, even if Mumma was the one he married. The idea that Abigail Smith might have been our mother took our breath away. "That," Mumma said. "Don't remind me about that. You know I don't like to boast.")

Abigail was the only guest Mumma had wanted to talk with, but Abigail had been standing among the Howlands, keeping someone between herself and Grandfather with practiced skill. When Mumma saw Abigail finally going off to join another group, she intercepted her, hand outstretched to reintroduce herself. She was not warmly received. *("And I didn't blame her for that, not one bit. As far as she was concerned, I was the home wrecker.")*

"I was wondering which one of these houses belongs to your family," Mumma said. She was trying to be friendly, since after all, Abigail was someone who had agreed to marry Pops, so she must have loved him, so maybe she was someone Mumma would like.

"I've always been a guest of the family. In the big house." Abigail's cool smile was sent in Mumma's general direction.

Of course Mumma understood that the woman's pride had been injured. She had no doubt, however, that her heart was intact. "You're so cool and also so pretty," Mumma said, which was true. "No wonder they wanted you for his fiancée, I don't blame them a bit."

"That's very good of you."

"But *you* know, even if they don't, because they don't appreciate him at all. *You* know you're not his type."

"I beg your pardon?" Abigail protested. "I

have to differ. I am exactly his type. I am exactly the type of person Spencer prefers. I've known him all my life. We're cousins, distant cousins, but still, we're the same kind of people from the same kind of background and education. We have the same goals in life. We live by the same standards. If I may be brutally frank, you're the one who doesn't belong here."

"Oh I know *that,*" Mumma agreed. "You don't have to tell me that. But that has nothing to do with being his type, does it? Anybody can see Spencer needs someone to look up to him. Not someone to admire, and he'd have to admire you, wouldn't he? But I'm thinking about you, really, because, you know, you remind me of Sonia."

"Sonja Henie?" Abigail was practically laughing out loud at Mumma.

"I thought you were so educated," Mumma said. "But I guess not, unless you've just never read *War and Peace.* Sonia Rostov — the cousin, I mean. Or unless the one you really remind me of is Amy, Amy March, and I know you've read *Little Women.* The sister who marries the rich boy who really loves Jo."

"I don't know what you're talking about." As many Hollywood moguls discovered, Abigail Smith's angers were icy and elegant.

"But I do," Mumma assured her. "If I were you — Did you know my maiden name was Smith too?"

Abigail pinpointed the important difference. "You aren't descended from the family of the Abigail Smith who married John Adams."

"I *could* be," Mumma maintained. "Nobody knows who a foundling is related to. But that's not what I meant to say. I meant to say that if I were you, I'd go somewhere entirely different from here. I'd go to California. Here, you're nothing special, you're like everybody else, only poorer. Except prettier than most, but it's not as if you're beautiful, is it? Out there, they'd think you were extraordinary."

"Even though," Abigail said through clenched teeth, "I'm clearly not."

"I don't know about that," Mumma said. "But if I were you I wouldn't stick around for the little life that was waiting for me here. I'd go — You ought to go to Hollywood," she decided.

"Oh, really? Really? And become — what? An actress, I suppose. Where *did* Spencer come across you?"

"At the Officers' Club," Mumma told her, "and no, not an actress, you'll have to figure out for yourself what to do, but you can do

114

that easily, if you really are so smart. Which I think you probably are."

"Thank you for your good opinion. I can't tell you how honored I am," Abigail responded, with an ever-increasing weight of sarcasm, but Mumma proved unsquashable. "Of course, I could be wrong. It could be that this is the best you can do."

(*"Abigail Smith wasn't one of those women who get pretty with anger," Mumma told us. "I am. When I'm angry, my eyes sparkle, my color heightens, but not her. She had that fair, fine skin, and those cool gray eyes, they had no flash at all in them, and her neck mottled red, the way fair people's necks do. So I knew she was angry, even before she huffed off. I was the making of her," Mumma concluded, taking credit for Abigail Smith's legendary career as a Hollywood casting director and eventually film producer. "If it wasn't for me, she would never have thought of it."*)

After leaving Grandmother's party, Mumma picked up Meg from the big house for feeding and Polly for company, taking them both down the hill with her. She and Polly played gin rummy until it was time for Polly to ride her bike home. Eventually, Pops returned.

"Everybody missed you," he said, the nearest thing to criticism he felt up to. His mother's parties went on for hours, and seeing that introducing Rida had been the putative reason for the event, the guests got to be shocked, appalled, and offended by her early exit. He'd come in for a lot of unmerited (as he felt) sympathy. Especially his own family had had much to say, and then say again, on the subject. His mother's "Honestly, Spencer" about summed up their collective thoughts. Except for Brundy, who seemed to have enjoyed his new sister-in-law. "My brother likes you," Pops reported.

"Your brother wants to sleep with me," Mumma corrected.

"Brundy?"

"Ethan. That boy's got too much of your father in him. I hope you warn people. Your father's a terrible snob, do you all know that? And your sisters are jealous — they have no personality, and they know it. And no style either."

"Ethan wants to sleep with you? What did he say? Did Father do something? Did Brundy?" Pops didn't talk about it, but he knew what his family was like.

"Brundy liked me. I like him, too. His name in the camp was B-24, Spencer. That should tell you something. It's a name he likes being called and that should tell you something too."

"My sisters always go nutty at Mother's parties. If anyone, it's her they're jealous of."

"Because your mother respects me," Mumma explained, against all the evidence, and correctly.

By the next afternoon, Mumma and Pops were gone from Wampanoag, leaving a Scylla and Charybdis of gossip behind them, past which only Grandmother, like Odysseus, sailed with a clear head — Grandmother and Uncle Brundy, that is, although Brundy was a useless ally, since he moved out shortly after, moved out on his wife and on his family, too, returning to Europe and never coming back to this country. "How could he do that?" Grandmother demanded. "He wasn't a cruel boy — competitive, of course, but that was athletics. He was always a gentleman; how could he be so cruel to us? And Lally, too. What happened to him?"

Pops tried to explain. "He wasn't in the Navy." But Mumma thought Grandmother needed more. "When you send boys to war, what do you expect? That they'll come back the same?"

Grandmother objected, "Most of the time, he was only a prisoner of war."

3.

MUMMA IN BOSTON

The next morning they made their farewells and left Wampanoag. Mumma had decided to find a place to live across the river from Boston, in Cambridge, within walking distance of the university. But of course the three of them would stay at the Louisburg Square house, Grandmother announced. In fact, they could settle permanently there, which would be in many ways convenient. *("I didn't ask her what ways. She'd already told me twice in one morning that I needed to learn how to fit in.")* Once Grandmother had stopped protesting about their brief stay on and hasty exit from the Cape, Louisburg Square became the very place she wanted them to be, the best thing, really, despite Rida's objections. "You'll be perfectly adequately looked after," Grandmother told Pops, as he and Mumma stood by the car's open doors. "As you know, there is more than enough room — Take the girls' rooms, they're cooler. Also, Rida will be just around the corner from Dr. Irving." She turned to Mumma; she knew Mumma couldn't have yet found her own obstetrician. "Everybody goes to him for their babies, and Boston Lying-In is a wonderful hospital. We won't be able to join you at home until after Labor Day," she told them, probably disingenuously, although with Grandmother it was sometimes hard to differentiate between disingenuity and mendacity, "but there's Martina. She has nothing to do all summer long. And she's been with us since the Crash, so you can trust her with little Meg. As well as the two dailies. You'll be well looked after and so will the new baby when he arrives."

"By that time we'll have our own home," Mumma said.

"You have a home with us," Grandmother repeated. "But," she added, in response to a glance from Mumma's mahogany eyes, "if you insist on paying rent to someone, we have plenty of friends."

When Mumma's expression only intensified, Grandmother predicted, "You'll change your mind once you see what's available. You haven't forgotten that there's a housing shortage, have you?"

Pops said, "We'll see how things work out," with which neither of the women could argue. The car waited by the entrance. It was a sunny day, and hot, there being no breeze that morning to cool the air. Grandmother was holding Meg close, her fingers spread protectively wide across the baby's delicate back. "You have the list of names and numbers I gave Spencer?" she asked.

She didn't, but, "I do," Mumma said. *("I always tried to keep the peace with your grandmother, which wasn't easy, it never is with a woman who's so used to getting her own way — And just what is it you girls think is so funny?")* Then Mumma took Meg into her own arms and went to sit in the car, waiting until Pops joined her and they drove away.

They reached Boston in the midafternoon. Pops parked in front of a tall brick building, one of a ring of four-story homes that kept careful watch over the long oval garden they surrounded. Each home had its three layers of bay windows, each was topped by a pair of dormer windows. Looking at the Howlands' house, identical to all the other tall houses, Mumma warned him, "I'll unpack, but I'm not planning on staying one day longer than we have to. And that won't be long, if I have anything to say about it."

"Of course you have something to say about it," he told her.

Mumma turned her attention to the central garden, a strip of green planted with well-spaced trees and flowers, kept safe from prying eyes by thick rhododendron bushes, entirely enclosed by its high, spear-tipped, black, wrought-iron fence. There were no pathways crossing the garden, no sandboxes and no swings hung from low branches. In fact, she couldn't even see a gate through which one might enter. She knew there must be an entry, however, because the grass was mown as smooth and level as a golf course. She had seen plenty of golf courses out in California, and she knew the kind of care they took. She explained it to Pops: "Because I don't want Meg living where she can't go into a garden and play, and where even if she could, most of the rest of the world wouldn't be allowed in. Or Junior either," she said, laying a protective palm on her belly, which was just beginning to puff out.

Where they might live presented real difficulties, in the housing shortages of that postwar era, but it wasn't an immediate problem. Grandmother had told them that they would want to take the girls' rooms on the second floor, but Mumma decided to claim the attic, despite the steep back staircase that was its only access, despite the small windows and low ceilings, despite those having been the boys' rooms and therefore furnished in blue and brown, stripes and plaids, and despite only two of the rooms being available, since Ethan had locked his door and the one remaining room was used for storage.

When she stood at the center of Pops' boyhood sanctuary, considering the brown-striped wallpaper and the shelves of old schoolbooks, the framed photographs of statues of Greek gods — Zeus with his arm held high, about to throw a thunderbolt, and what Pops identified for her as the Winged Victory — the twin beds jammed in under the eaves, covered with brown-and-blue plaid spreads, Mumma just nodded. Brundy's room, joined by a connecting door, had shelves lined with trophies and corners crowded with sports paraphernalia, lacrosse and ice hockey sticks, bats, gloves, balls of all shapes and sizes and colors. "Meg can sleep here. She doesn't know she's female, so what does she need a pink fluffy room for? She's not sleeping downstairs and neither am I. I don't know why anyone bothers getting married if they're going to keep half a house apart," she said to Pops. Pops didn't answer. He had no desire to argue with Mumma, since he shared her marital bed and bedroom preferences; also, he had no desire to think about his parents' sex life, whatever it might be, in their separate bedrooms, one at the front, one at the rear of the second floor, both with twin beds, and the distance of the three girls' rooms between them.

"Your sisters are fenced in by their parents down there," Mumma observed.

"Given the way Anne runs around, that makes sense," he answered.

"As if your parents are the guardian watchdogs," she continued.

"Girls these days need protection, even if they resent it," he pointed out to her. "Don't you plan to protect our daughter?"

"Yes. But not from life, and not from sex either. That's the double standard and you know how I feel about that. We're going to push these two beds together, aren't we? It's not as roomy up here as down there, or as pretty, I know, speaking of the double standard, but it *is* private," she pointed out.

What precisely the double standard had to do with the bedroom arrangements at Louisburg Square we had to work out for ourselves, later in our lives. While Mumma spoke easily of sex, she didn't talk specifically about it. We deduced that the three boys, up in the former servants' rooms, didn't get the same close supervision as their sisters. They could come and go as they pleased, which they did. Or, as Pops told it — disclaiming for himself any wild youth and Ethan having been one of those children able to seem not to be disobedient no matter what they get up to — Brundy could come and go as he pleased. Grandmother never seemed to notice when Brundy hadn't slept at home. If he appeared at the breakfast table still wearing his tux, she didn't notice. If his shirt and trousers had obviously been slept in or vomited on, she kept silent about that, too. All three boys could be in or out for all three meals without informing Grandmother or Martina or Mrs. Cook. The daughters, however, were closely monitored, their escorts required to meet visual, oral, and social-placement standards, their curfews strictly enforced, their clothing purchased under Grandmother's surveillance, their plans subject to overrule, and their friendships proscribed: the double standard. As it happened, only one son took open advantage of his freedom, and only one daughter rebelled against her confinement, and I've never figured out just what that says about human nature.

About Brundy in his youth, the double

standard meant that he was a real boy, sneaking down the back stairs to join packs of friends to go prowling around the Square, or Charles Street, or even across the Commons, looking for trouble. Later, it meant he was a real man, unlike Pops, who spent hours studying and reading, and enjoyed playing Monopoly with Juliet, when she could persuade him to a game, or jacks with Anne. About Anne, at that time, the double standard meant she was fast. What fast meant, in the '40s and early '50s, we could never be certain. What did they actually *do,* those fast girls? There were, of course, no fast boys.

Even safely removed to the top floor, tucked away into former servants' quarters with no neighbors, Mumma held firm. "I want to be out of this house by Labor Day, Spencer. And so do you," she told him. What Mumma exactly wanted was: first, not to live among Howlands, and second, her own home, decorated by her in the bright fabrics and colors she liked, with meals cooked by her and served on her own plates, eaten with her own utensils, its rooms cleaned, its windows washed, its laundry folded and ironed by her. *(What did I know? Once I had all the work of keeping house on my plate, every day, every week, it took about two months and then I saw the light, I can promise you that. I was always grateful that your father had money so we could afford to hire Polly. I'd have murdered him in his bed, if he didn't. Or one of you. Or all of you. Nobody has an easy time of it, not even housewives, not that I've ever seen, whatever things look like. I can see what you're thinking, and you're right. I have an easy time of it. Who knows why? Maybe somebody up there likes me.")*

Back in Boston, Pops settled down to studying, classics this time, the professors he'd talked to having assured him that there was no future in linguistics. "There'll always be a need for classicists," they promised him at the Harvard Graduate School of Arts and Sciences, and Pops didn't argue. He had his doubts, but he enjoyed the field, so he took down from his bookshelves the Cassell's dictionaries, the Chase and Phillips Greek textbook, Liddell and Scott *Greek-English Lexicon*, the Scudder *Second Year Latin*, all the worn books of his prewar studies. He submerged himself in the languages and histories of the ancient world. *("Besides," he told us, "it was no small consolation to realize that humankind has always been if not equally efficient at war, at least equally vicious.")*

Mumma, meanwhile, despite being at the end of Jo's second trimester, moved energetically around Boston, Meg thrust in a pram out before her, shopping for a home of her own. She was confident that this second child would be a boy, which meant they needed not only three bedrooms but also a yard. Any son of hers would, she knew, be a lively child, so a yard was essential. She read the classified ads and talked to rental agents. She didn't need Grandmother's help, thank you. She had always looked out for herself. Mumma liked having possibilities spread out in front of her, looking them over, comparing them, and finally selecting the best. (*During the season of her life when she read Emily Dickinson, Mumma relentlessly quoted, " 'I dwell in possibility,' " continuing on with a raised voice over our outbursts of laughter at any claim of her similarity to the reclusive, self-effacing spinster of Amherst, " 'a fairer house than prose' I don't know what's so funny.*")

That August, the pre-air-conditioned city of Boston sweltered in such heat and humidity that its citizens spent as many hours as they could outside, preferably in rain. They crowded the garden spaces, waiting for the sun to make its nightly retreat behind the horizon, dragging the temperature down with it, and as they waited they complained to one another in companionable misery.

Mumma, however, never complained about the weather, or minded it. Maybe she didn't notice it. Certainly it couldn't affect her mood, or her plans. She had set herself the goal of finding them a home. Across the river in Cambridge would be most convenient, but given the housing situation, anywhere in the city would do. Anywhere, that is, except Louisburg Square.

"I can't walk on these streets," she explained to Pops, as if the cobbled streets of Beacon Hill were his personal responsibility, or at least his family's direct doing. "I could break an ankle, and then where would you be?"

Pops would never point out to her that the high heels Mumma wore to make her legs look longer and to exhibit the delicate bones of those same vulnerable ankles should never be worn on the steep and cobbled streets surrounding Louisburg Square. Nor did he warn her that the streets of Cambridge, although not at all steep and entirely uncobbled, were surfaced with bricks that surged up and sank down with the winter freezes and the spring thaws, making them a pavement to which high heels were equally unsuited. On matters of her dress, Pops left Mumma strictly alone. Also on matters of politics, home décor, religion, friendships, food, and finances. He quarreled only, and that rarely, about education and about family, that is, his own family, their own children. *("Your father and I saw eye to eye on everything. Everything important, anyway, except he had a real stubborn streak about you girls.")* Pops was occupied by his studies and that left Mumma free to drive across the river to Cambridge, where she parked on one of the broader streets, Brattle or Mount Auburn, and walked around the residential areas, Meg in the pram. Mumma looked for signs in the windows of houses, of which there were none, this being New England, and even more, being Boston, the self-appointed heart of New England. She sat on a bench on the green that faced the old Unitarian church, reading the classified pages as well as the newspaper that preceded them, and striking up useful conversations with the strangers who stopped to coo over Meg. She inquired among shopkeepers. She left no stone unturned, as she often told us. She even overcame her inherent distrust of bureaucracies and inquired at the Office of Student Housing at Harvard, but they were entirely unsympathetic to someone who already had living quarters, even if Pops was a war veteran and entitled to preferential treatment.

The little family hadn't been long at Louisburg Square when Anne arrived. "Only for a night or two," she said. Anne was working at the hospital in Bourne, but she hoped to be able to move back into the city, to which end she had a job interview, maybe, in the morning, at Boston Lying-In, and wouldn't it be fun, she asked by way of distracting Mumma, if she were the nurse on duty when this baby arrived?

"No," Mumma said, undistracted.

"Anyway, I have a date tonight, I won't need dinner. And don't wait up," Anne said. "There's no need for you to go waiting up for me."

"A date with who?" Mumma asked.

"You wouldn't know him. Spencer might, but he's just someone. We have dinner every now and then. It's not serious," Anne told Mumma.

"He's married," Mumma guessed.

"His wife doesn't understand him," Anne told Mumma.

Mumma warned Anne, "You don't understand him either."

"What do you know about it?"

"Nothing, and that's how I plan to keep it," Mumma told her. "Don't ask me to meet him."

"Don't tell Spencer," Anne asked.

"What is it about your family?" Mumma demanded. "What is it with all these secrets? Why would I marry a man so I could keep secrets from him? Or sleep in single beds or not have my own house, don't you people know anything about anything?"

Anne backed away, going up to bathe and dress and get away from Mumma, which was the usual result of Mumma's exasperated response to the Howland modus vivendi and also, not incidentally, exactly the response she wanted. Anne went out to dinner with her married man and did not return until the next midday, at which time she left to return to the Cape. Whether or not there had been a job interview, Mumma didn't know. But she overcame her own reluctance and accepted the help of Grandmother's connections to solve the housing difficulty. She did not, however *("Not that I didn't think of it. Not that I wasn't tempted")* say anything to Grandmother about Anne's dinner escort, an older man, as she deduced from the graying hair and silver-dollar-size bald spot viewed from her bedroom window, an older man in a lawyer's dark three-piece suit, his fedora held in the same hand as the bouquet of flowers he presented, his other hand free to hold on to Anne's shoulder as he leaned forward for a prolonged kiss, while a taxi waited. Anne was over twenty-one, had a profession, and had been assigned by her family a reputation that this particular date would merit. Grandmother already knew Anne's reputation and Mumma was already reluctant to ask for the help she was about to have to ask of Grandmother. Any further conversation would have been excessive.

As it turned out, her reluctance was well-founded, if ill-informed, being a prejudice or intuition rather than a reasoned conclusion. If the space on offer ("We're only making it available to our kind of people") wasn't a tiny garage apartment, unoccupied and uncleaned since an unreplaced chauffeur went off to die in North Africa, it was a carriage house whose owners set restrictions, on animals ("No animals, not any kind, not even a goldfish, you know how people take advantage, my dear") and children ("No more than one. Oh? You are? Did Dorothy know about this when she telephoned me? Well, then, no more than two, and they will of course be in bed by seven.")

Distant cousins were willing to rent out bedrooms in their own now inconveniently and expensively large homes, or to offer apartments in buildings acquired during the Depression, when there had been so many bankruptcies and so many buildings had come onto the market at such good prices. There was a single floor of one of the tiny houses originally built to house Civil War widows (two widows per house, four small rooms per widow) in the back streets between Brattle and the Charles; the house had been in the family forever, originally constructed as a patriotic gesture and, really, more trouble than it was worth to maintain and keep occupied. Mumma looked at all of these but saw nothing that suited her needs, nothing desirable either, and certainly nothing at a fair price, not in this seller's market.

"You're related to a lot of slum landlords, did you know that?" Mumma asked Pops, who hadn't known and was sorry to hear it. "Your parents' friends treat their servants like dirt," she told him. When thwarted, as in this matter of a home of her own, Mumma's critical faculties grew sharper, especially when she was predisposed against a person, or a situation or, as in the case of the Howland-Spencers, most of an entire large family. "I'm glad I don't have to be one of their fancy friends," she said. "I'd have to worry about what a creepy Crawford

I was, if I was one of those friends. Or maybe I wouldn't," she decided, "because they do think well of themselves, don't they?"

"It's human nature," Pops told her.

"What? Human nature which? To think well of yourself? Or to be greedy and self-serving, and act as if yours was the only important life in town?"

Pops took the question as unloaded. "Both, I'd say. All."

"That's not what I mean," Mumma said. "You know what I mean."

"I don't think I do."

"I don't want to live like that, to live here. Are your friends like that?"

"Well," Pops said, and thought about it. "Not yet. Not all of them. I don't have many friends."

"I don't much care for that kind of person," Mumma warned him.

The only one of these connections of Grandmother's whom she found sympathetic was an older woman, a widow, who over the years of war had lost not only a husband but also her two bachelor sons. This woman would have welcomed a young and growing family into her big empty house. But the square stucco building, overgrown with ivy, its garden unweeded

134

and grass rarely mown, was so dark and dismal and steeped in sorrow and death Mumma was sure it would permanently distort her children's characters. "You can't expect a child not to be affected," Mumma told Pops. "Think of all those children in Europe."

"And Japan," he said. "And the rest of the Far East, and now India, too, and the Mid-East."

"Life is hard enough without growing up in a mausoleum," Mumma agreed.

"Children would brighten it up, though, wouldn't they? I remember playing with Allen and Rich in Mrs. Ralster's garden. It was — We played hide-and-seek there, we all —" but that was not a line of thought he wanted to dwell on. "She was an avid gardener. I think she grew vegetables, too; she let us pick peas. She showed us how to shell them."

"I'm not risking my children," Mumma announced. "Meg and I will visit her, and I'll think of something for her to do, maybe library work. Yes, libraries are quiet, it's work a lady would be comfortable doing, librarians are kind people. She'll be comfortable in a library. Where is the public library in Cambridge?"

Pops didn't know. He didn't know if

Cambridge had a public library. Mumma thought that was just like him, just like his family. He agreed that it was, and did she want him to find out where it was? What did he think? she demanded, from which he deduced her answer. So he set about getting her that information, and finding out which family friends were on the board. The rest became history, once Mumma got started. *("Who do you think built up the children's collection there? And funded the Ralster Children's Reading Room?" "I thought it was Mrs. Ralster who did all that," Jo would respond, or I would. "Yes, but who do you think put the idea into her head? Which made her last years so much happier than they were being before.")*

Their second week at Louisburg Square stretched into a third and entered a fourth and Labor Day grew close. Anne returned, twice, ostensibly for job interviews. She must have really had them, because by the end of the summer she had turned down a position at Mass General and decided to continue working in Bourne. This made no sense to Grandmother, who tried unsuccessfully to persuade her middle daughter to return to Boston, but Mumma had her theories. The end of summer meant a man's wife would be returning, from the Cape or the Vineyard, Watch Hill or Blue Hill. The end of summer meant the end of the affair.

Meanwhile, Mumma had opened her mind to the possibility of purchasing a home rather than renting one, but she discovered that there were almost as few opportunities in that market. There were, however, two apartment buildings, side by side, unfortunately situated in North Cambridge, and also unfortunately in need of a great deal of repair, renovation, and redecoration. "I can't believe those cousins of yours with all their money don't fix the apartments up for the tenants," Mumma said.

"They'd lose the income," Pops said.

"They don't need the income," Mumma argued.

"I know, but they like it," Pops said.

"Fixed up, the buildings will rent for more and sell for more. They'd be a good investment."

"Real estate isn't an investment. It's property."

"I'm not going to turn into one of those slum landlords," Mumma warned him.

He agreed entirely. "I never thought you would." They both understood without speaking of it whose vision and ambition was being served in this.

"Does that mean you don't think I should make an offer on the buildings?" Mumma asked.

Pops said, "No. The opposite, in fact. But I'd be hopeless at the renovation and no good at overseeing the work any contractors were doing. You know how I am, I don't —"

Mumma cut him off. "I was thinking of me, because I *can* do all of those things, and with one hand tied behind my back."

"Then I'll talk to Mr. Talziewicz and he'll get you the money."

"Mr. Talziewicz? I thought it was *your* money."

"He's the trustee."

"The trustee?"

"Well, actually there are three, but Mr. Talziewicz is the only one who does anything. He's the one we talk to about the trust funds while the other two — it's a sinecure really, they're cousins, much older and for one reason and another, they don't have much. They do whatever Mr. Talziewicz says. He's the one who actually manages the investments, the distributions, the taxes."

"You have to ask him for your own money?" Mumma asked.

"Do you want me to?"

Then Mumma wasn't so sure. Possibility, when it turns into prose, loses some of its allure. It gains substance, but that substance might well be not what one hoped for, or planned on, or could keep control over. Prose, like children, might grow into something ungovernable. "I have to think about it," Mumma said.

However, the more she thought about it, the more confident Mumma was that she could make it work. "We could live there if we have to, if we want to," she told Pops. "It's not that bad."

"You'll find a house."

"An apartment would be all right for a temporary home, once the wiring and plumbing, furnace, a new roof — once they're in place, with the bathrooms tiled, fresh paint on the walls, the kitchen . . ." *("And that was the start of me, the start of my business," was the way Mumma liked to conclude her telling of this story. "I hope you girls know how important it is to marry the right man.")*

Brundy showed up at Louisburg Square the day after Pops got the check from Mr. Talziewicz and deposited it into Mumma's bank account so that she could — after the ten business days required for the funds to travel the several city blocks from Temple Street to Brattle — conclude her purchase of the building. Mumma had arranged it so that the renovation work began immediately on signing of the contract; three-quarters of the tenants would be staying on, having decided that enduring renovations was their best option in this particular housing market, with this particular landlady. They must have been pleased to note that she arrived every morning to oversee the work, despite the toddler she pushed before her in a perambulator and the unborn child she was carrying. Mumma and Meg had returned to Louisburg Square after the morning's labors, for a nap (Meg) and further study of building codes (Mumma) on the day Brundy came to the Louisburg Square house for the last time, and asked to see Mumma.

Martina made the trek up three flights of stairs, the last flight only dimly lit and entirely uncarpeted, to knock on the door of Mumma's room and tell her that Mr. Brundy was downstairs and he was wondering if he could have a few minutes. Mumma didn't want to leave Meg so far from anyone who might hear her cry out, but she was equally unwilling to wake her up, since whenever Meg was short of sleep her character suffered. So Martina agreed to wait upstairs for Mumma's return and maybe she would just take a load off and lie down with the baby, because that way she could be sure nothing would happen to the dear little thing.

Mumma went down to where Brundy stood in the front hall. He had a large leather suitcase beside his long legs. He was jacketless and tieless. There was nothing odd about his casual attire; the temperature that day had risen to over ninety-three degrees and heavy, humid air choked the city, so she wasn't surprised that he had decided not to put on the usual suit and tie, even for a day of business. In fact, he probably could have worn a bathing suit and Mumma wouldn't have paid much attention. Her mind was occupied with radiators and venetian blinds, and now with the question of whether she should offer Brundy a sisterly kiss or whether to a Howland that would seem an untoward show of emotion. She didn't even think to wonder what he was doing in the high-ceilinged foyer of his parents' house, on a weekday, in the early afternoon, with a suitcase.

"I know you weren't expecting me," he said. "I'm sorry."

"I don't mind," Mumma said, and she

meant it. She enjoyed a handsome man, and Brundy was a very handsome man, especially now, with his fair skin tanned, his golden hair streaked blond by exposure to salt water and sun, his blue eyes as dark as an early evening sky. "It's your house," said Mumma, who never shied away from stating the obvious. *("People — Half the time they don't see their noses in front of their faces, their forests for their trees.")* She told Brundy, "Martina is upstairs with Meg, but can I get you something cold? Iced tea or lemonade? You don't want a drink at this hour, do you?"

"Not anymore," he said, which caused her to look at him more carefully, however handsome he might be. *("You girls think it's so easy if you're pretty, but just because everybody's looking at you doesn't mean anybody's seeing you. So count your blessings.")*

Handsome, fortunate Brundage North Howland III, who liked being called B-24, straight-backed, broad-shouldered, tall, and smiling, looked like a man who had already taken a snootful, although he didn't smell like one. Mumma was puzzled, and curious. "Let's go to the kitchen. I'll make you coffee," she announced.

Leaving his suitcase in the hallway, he followed her down the back staircase into the big cellar kitchen, its small windows too high up in the walls to see out of, although, since they faced the Square, they did let some daylight in. He sat down at the long table where Martina and the help took their meals. Brundy was accustomed to having his coffee made for him and brought to him. He never thought of offering to help, and that was probably part of why he got along so comfortably with Mumma, since she never thought of herself as helpless. Seated, he set his hands together on the table, fingers interlaced, and pronounced his good tidings: "I've left."

"Left what?" Mumma was filling the percolator with water and measuring tablespoons of coffee from the can into the basket.

Brundy stood up then, as if unable to sit still for excitement, or maybe to give his announcement a proper formality. He stood up and said, "Everything," then sat down again to specify, "Home, the firm, the family. Lally."

"Unless you'd rather have hot tea? Coffee will be better for you."

"Left my car, too," he told her, confirming her opinion of his sobriety. She set the percolator on a burner and lit the gas, dropping the match into a little stoveside dish Martina kept handy for that use. Brundy reasoned, "Lally should have a car, don't you think?"

Mumma got down cups and saucers and asked, "What do you like in your coffee?" At that, Brundy started to laugh. *("He laughed like a maniac. I had a bad minute there alone with a drunken maniac in that kitchen down in the cellar, while he was having a postwar nervous breakdown.")* Brundy laughed and laughed, while Mumma fixed him with her best gimlet eye to sober him up, or calm him down, she didn't care which.

Eventually he said, rather quietly, considering, "I should be opening a bottle of champagne. We should be having a toast. I could kiss you."

"You've already had enough to drink. Champagne isn't necessary," Mumma told him.

"Believe me, I know that. But I could kiss you anyway. I'm going to Paris. I'm getting a divorce. I'll get another car, over there."

"Over there Paris?"

"Where else?"

"Mexico?" Mumma suggested. "Rio de Janeiro, Morocco, or California?"

Then the coffee started to percolate and

she fell into thought, as she waited for it to brew. She poured two cups and sat down next to him, still thinking. They drank in silence. "Paris is probably your best choice," Mumma conceded.

"I know some French already. I'm good at languages."

"Not me," Mumma said. She raised her cup to her lips again and took a swallow. "Well, B-24, I hope you find someone to love you there."

This conversation about Brundy's homosexuality had both more content and more sympathy than any of the other Howland conversations on the subject. After his abrupt departure from Wampanoag and the country, all of the Howlands, except for Mumma and Pops, referred to him as Poor Brundy, weaving the myth around him of a young man so disturbed by his wartime experiences that he was able to live only in a country where nobody spoke his language, so that nobody could understand the extent of his mental lapses. That was the Howland family line on the eldest son, the sum total of what they said when they spoke of him at all, which was almost never. "Poor Brundy, he was never the same. One of the walking wounded, Poor Brundy."

Mumma and Pops, in this as in much else,

differed from the family. The two brothers in fact, somehow, by virtue of living so far apart from each other perhaps, grew closer. They maintained a regular correspondence, and later, when Pops took Mumma to Europe, they spent a lot of time in Paris with Brundy. The three of them — sometimes four, if Brundy took a friend — traveled together in Italy and Greece, Yugoslavia, Scotland, Portugal. Uncle Brundy always sent us chocolates for Christmas, boxes and boxes of Belgian and French and Swiss and Italian chocolates. "I can't choose between them, and I don't want to. Have them all," was his message. He remembered our birthdays, with a card and a check. He was our favorite uncle. Uncle Brundy's sexual orientation was not one of Mumma's bugbears, as Brundy probably sensed from the first. They drank coffee together in the cellar kitchen of the Louisburg Square house. "I came to get my passport," he announced jubilantly.

"Meg's asleep," she told him, then saw the need for further explanation. "In your room."

"And I have to talk to Old Tally, before I can leave. I better get to him before Dad does."

"Old Tally?"

146

"Talziewicz. The trustee."

"You call him Old Tally?"

"Spencer's told you about him, hasn't he? Of course, Old Tally is a Jew, but a lot's going to be different about Jews now. After Hitler, and all."

"I never minded Jews," Mumma told him. "Even before. But then, I could be Jewish. I could be anything, which is part of what your family thinks is wrong with me."

Brundy laughed again and offered, "You could come to Paris with me."

"It would never work, believe me," Mumma told him.

"Dad would rather I was running off with Spencer's wife."

"So you *did* tell him."

"I didn't tell anyone."

Mumma stared at him. "What about Lally?"

"She'll be relieved. I've been making her nervous."

"She's your wife and she hasn't guessed?"

"Lally's a *nice* girl. She doesn't know about things like me."

Mumma got up to refill their cups, and didn't sit down again. "You have to tell your wife. You could ruin her life going off without telling her."

147

"She was ruining mine," Brundy maintained.

Mumma lost patience with him. "That was *you* ruining it. And I don't mean because of *that.*" However enlightened her attitudes, Mumma couldn't actually say any of the words out loud, at least not to his face. "Because of pretending it wasn't true, that's what was ruining your life."

"What do you know about it?"

"Not much," Mumma admitted. Then she claimed, "I have to know something, don't I? If I'm a human being and you are too, how much difference can there be? Besides, what do you have to lose by telling her? I mean, you personally, since you're leaving anyway."

"You can explain it to her. You have my permission."

"Yellowbelly."

"Of course," he said. "What do you expect? You're impossible, Rida. Let me ask you, since you're Miss American Honesty, does Spencer know what he's gotten himself into with you?"

"Of course he does. I'm good for him and he knows it. You don't know anything about your brother, none of you do."

"Well, he doesn't know anything about me, and neither do they, so we're all even.

Except you," he added, more wary now. "I'm going upstairs; I'll take Phyllis's room. In three days I sail from New York, so —"

"You can't stay here," Mumma told him.

"This is my home."

"You just said you left home."

"Oh, for Christ's sake. So I guess you're not so open-minded after all."

Mumma, who knew perfectly well that she was practical rather than open-minded, pointed out to him, "They'll call here to ask for you. This is the first place they'll call and I'm not much of a liar, so you'd better find a hotel. But we should go to a restaurant for dinner. Spencer will want to have dinner with you."

"You won't let me stay in the same house but you'll go out for dinner with me?"

"I want to talk to you about investing in real estate," Mumma explained. "So tell me what restaurant and what time, and go get a hotel room so you can telephone for your appointment with Mr. Talziewicz. They might just show up here, instead of calling."

"They won't even figure out until tonight that I'm gone. They'll give it until morning before they do anything."

"I'm glad I'm not your wife," Mumma said, then gave him fair warning. "If they don't call here, I'm calling Lally."

Brundy shrugged. It was no longer his problem.

As things turned out, Mumma didn't have to telephone the Cape house. Instead, the mountain came to Mohammad, as she used to say, after Grandmother telephoned Louisburg Square and Mumma couldn't give her the name of the hotel where Brundy was staying. The day after Brundy's boat had left New York, which was two days after his meeting with Mr. Talziewicz, Mumma and Meg returned from a walk around the Public Gardens to find Grandmother in residence and the whole house in an uproar, rooms being aired, furniture uncovered and dusted, suitcases unpacked, and Lally settled in the library, behind a closed door, weeping.

Grandmother emerged from her bedroom to corral Mumma, who was on her way upstairs. "Brundy was here. He was here and you didn't telephone. We would have stopped him. We could have, if you had telephoned."

This being entirely true, Mumma could see no reason to comment on it. "Moreover, my husband tells me that Spencer is purchasing some tenement building, in a slum."

"*I'm* buying it," Mumma said. "Not a

slum, it's in North Cambridge. Off Massachusetts Avenue."

"You aren't going to live there, are you?" Grandmother asked.

"I haven't decided," Mumma said.

"Well," Grandmother said. "Give me the baby. You need to explain your actions — by which I mean your inaction, of course — to Lally. The child is upset. Very upset. You should have telephoned."

"Brundy should have telephoned," Mumma maintained.

"Everybody knows that Poor Brundy hasn't been himself since his dreadful experiences," Grandmother announced. "We can't blame him. I'm sure you can explain it to her better than I can. You're both young, you understand her better because of that. What could I say to her? He's my son," Grandmother reminded Mumma. "It's up to you, Rida."

("So what did you tell Lally?" we asked. "I explained about her financial settlement, I explained about divorces, about what desertion is, I tried to get her to move to Texas."

"Texas! Why Texas?"

"Or New Mexico, or Montana. Lally would have remarried in a minute out West, she'd have been irresistible. But she wouldn't leave Boston. But you girls already know that sad

151

story, I don't plan to go into it again. And she never wanted for anything. Your uncle Brundy saw to that. And yes, I told her about him. She didn't believe me.")*

It took only three days for Lally to pack up her married life and move back to her parents' big house on Brattle Street, the house she lived in for the rest of her life, waiting for them to die, then waiting to die herself. None of them ever forgave the Howlands, and by association the Spencers, for her husband's desertion. *("Oh, they could all go to the same parties and symphonies, but they never spoke to anyone in your father's family, not even me. It wasn't a feud. Bostonians don't have feuds, but they are good haters.")* During the days of Lally's departure, however, Mumma was most often out of the Louisburg Square house, and Meg with her, so she missed the excitement, if there was any. Mumma had plumbers to talk to, electricians, roofers, housepainters. She was lighting fires under her contractors, to keep the work moving along.

Grandmother returned alone to the Cape and then Anne returned to Louisburg Square. "They don't like my friends," Anne told Mumma and Pops, having joined them at the dinner table. "I told Mother she should send me to Paris to take care of Poor

152

Brundy, since after all I am a nurse, but you know them. They worry about foreigners. They don't trust me."

Mumma held her tongue.

"I'm going to really try to get a job in the city," Anne told them, "but there are so many nurses around, because of the war work, and the ones who served in combat areas get preference. I never got to a combat area," she told Mumma. "I was like you. Not the entertainment part, but I was always kept back in the safe zones. Personally, I suspect that my parents used connections. No wonder Phyllis married so young, just to get out from under. Juliet will do the same, just watch. Whatever she says now about marriage. You can't believe what girls say. When I was her age all I wanted was to get married. Imagine!" She laughed. "I'm going out later," she told them with her brightest smile.

"Not with that married man, I hope," Mumma said.

There was a long silence before Anne said, "No, Rida. That's over. That was just — He was just lonely, it wasn't serious. I can warn you, don't ever leave Spencer alone for summers like that, that's my advice. I'd never be serious about a married man myself, but not all girls have my standards. Whatever

Mother may think of me. Our parents are hard to have for parents, aren't they, Spencer?"

"Don't pay any attention to them," Pops advised his sister.

"They won't *let* me not pay attention to them," Anne said. "I'm not the family intellectual absent-minded professor, I can't get away with things. But I'm not letting them pick my friends. They can't tell me who to like."

Less than an hour after that declaration of independence, Pops answered the front door of the tall brick house to set eyes for the first time on Giancarlo Ruscelli. Giancarlo was obviously foreign, and just as obviously of Mediterranean extraction, with his olive skin and wavy dark hair, more hair than any true Bostonian would even think of possessing, and his velvety brown eyes. Also, he had an accent, vaguely Italian but also oddly British, and the cautious speech habits of a foreigner — a foreigner, moreover, who has learned his English not in America. Also, it was clear that Giancarlo worked in the open air, and with his hands, but Anne whisked him away after the briefest of introductions, deaf to Pops' tentative inquiries. She deflected Mumma, too. "I would have thought you'd believe in taking people for who they are. Not who their parents are. Not what work they do or where they live. I would have thought you of all people wouldn't be like my parents. Giancarlo's fun, which is more than I can say about a lot of other people."

("I don't know what bee she was having in her bonnet. I was talking business with Giancarlo and he liked me.")

Giancarlo was an attractive man, with a muscular body and a fine head, strong cheekbones and a Roman nose, full lips made for kissing. Giancarlo had Mumma for an ally, at least to the extent *("I would never lie. You girls know that about me")* of not telling Grandmother about this foreigner who drove from Bourne to Boston three or four nights a week to see their daughter.

Grandmother didn't ask, so Mumma didn't have to tell.

Grandmother couldn't imagine that an Italian, working as a gardener, might have met her daughter in England while he was a POW assigned to the grounds of a British hospital, might have then come to Cape Cod because she had made that a familiar part of America for him, might have followed up the flirtation begun during the war. Although born into an entirely bourgeois family of Paduan landowners and merchants, Giancarlo didn't want to return to his native country, where Mussolini had been so admired and the Fascists had permitted so many injustices. He thought he had a good chance to win Anne's hand. He had been an officer, after all, and he was a university graduate. Granted, he'd been the enemy, but he wasn't a German. Women liked him, he liked women, life would be good to him, and he would enjoy all the good things life offered.

The next Howlands to arrive at Louisburg Square were Grandfather and Uncle Ethan. A week after Brundy sailed, they came for a couple of days to meet with Mr. Talziewicz and put whatever spikes they could in Brundy's fiscal wheels. Anne retreated to the Cape. "Mother's a pain, but Father's a ferret," she said, climbing into her car. "I feel like I'm deserting you," she told Mumma.

"You are," Mumma answered. "But I'm not worried. I know how to handle lounge lizards."

"My father is not a lounge lizard," Anne protested. "He's just a drunk, and Ethan's a womanizer, that's all."

"Lounge lizards," Mumma repeated. "I know."

"Oh, for God's sake, Rida. Sometimes I

156

wonder about you. I mean," said Anne, who enjoyed a battle, "what do you think people are saying about *you*?"

"I don't," Mumma said. "Think about it. I know what people are like. But I can tell you this, nobody would ever call me a lounge lizard. And if I had a father like yours, I wouldn't run away from him. I'd stand and fight."

"I'm glad I'm not you," Anne said.

Mumma got the last word. "Me too."

Mumma almost always got the last word in any argument. You knew that no argument with Mumma was finished until that last word was uttered. You could always recognize it when it came to say The End, with absolute finality. The only exceptions to this pattern were Mumma's arguments with Grandmother, who sometimes won her point. It was nothing Grandmother could count on, persuading Mumma to alter an opinion. Grandfather, on the other hand, never did, not even when he had Ethan beside him to back him up, not even when he was apoplectic with confidence that his version of things was the correct one.

At the Louisburg Square dinner table, after Anne had fled and Ethan and Grandfather had spent an afternoon with Mr. Talziewicz, an anxious Little Louisa served the meal while Grandfather finished his scotch and started on the merlot, which he took with the meat course. He drained his first glass and remarked to Pops, "What kind of tomfool idea is this that Tally's been telling me? Do you think you can explain yourself?"

Pops had the most elegant table manners of anyone I've ever known. He managed forks and knives, spoons, any utensil, however specialized, with skill; he ate slowly, savoring each individual bite. Pops also believed that the purpose of a dinner was conversation. He admired Mumma's ability to keep conversations interesting, and he helped her as much as he could. When Grandfather made that conversation-killing demand, Pops continued chewing, and then he swallowed, set his fork down quietly on his plate, and brushed his mouth with his napkin before responding. "What is it you don't understand?"

"Nothing, there's nothing I don't understand, except for one simple thing, which is: What the hell you think you're doing liquidating your New York, New Haven, and Hartford stock. Unless you've been gambling, in which case you'll just have to bite the bullet, and I can only hope you've learned your lesson."

"Do you mean the principal I've withdrawn?" Pops asked, to clarify what his father might be talking about.

"You know perfectly well what I mean, boy. I don't remember authorizing any such sum."

("As if that man could remember anything that got talked about after ten in the morning. I don't know who he thought he was fooling but he wasn't fooling me.")

"After I turned twenty-five," Pops reminded Grandfather, since his father seemed to have forgotten the terms of the Howland Trust, "I no longer required your authorization. Mr. Talziewicz notified me, when I turned twenty-five, that I was the sole signatory."

"Tally will do anything to undermine my authority with my own family, the stupider the better, like putting an armload of cash into your woolly-headed hands. I always heard Jews were so smart with money, but he's starting to smell like an exception," at which witticism Ethan snickered and Grandfather raised his glass in acknowledgment.

"It's less than two percent of the total capital," Pops pointed out and cut himself another bite of roast beef. (Grandfather would only eat roasts, and those had to be what he called real meat, beef or lamb;

anything else, he maintained was not a dinner, except lobster, and the unavoidable holiday turkeys.) Pops lifted his fork to his mouth and gracefully set it back down empty on his plate, and chewed.

"We're wondering," Ethan said, then turned to his father for corroboration and permission to speak. "What we wonder is: What do you want the money for?"

Mumma ate away at her meal, ignoring the men insofar as she could, filling her mind with ideas for renovations, books to read, and good thoughts about Pops. Mumma believed that a baby's surroundings during gestation affected his disposition and spirits. If she ignored Grandfather, she thought, he would have no effect on her son's character. She concentrated on the mashed potatoes with their brown pool of gravy, on the sweet tiny onions nestled among bright green peas. She concentrated on happy thoughts about good food and bright white linen, heavy silver and pure crystal, her child asleep upstairs and her husband seated beside her.

"For an apartment building," Pops said.

"You've bought an apartment building? What is wrong with you, Spencer? I thought you were going for your doctorate. In — I can't be expected to remember, something nobody else is interested in. What do you want with an apartment building?"

Mumma had no desire to say anything. His father was Pops' problem, and she wasn't about to take the man on as one of hers.

"Actually, it's Rida's building. It's in her name. She found it."

"You gave her that money? All that money? Get it back, boy. That's no way to use your trust fund, buying run-down apartment buildings in North Cambridge where nobody with any sense wants to live. You don't want to start giving large sums of money to your wife. Bad enough you married her."

Mumma rose from the table.

"Can't take a joke?" Grandfather glared at Mumma and grimaced at her in a show of merriment. "Make her sit down, Spencer, she's your wife." When Pops didn't obey him, Grandfather demanded, "What are you, afraid of her? Are you a man or a mouse?"

"Yes," Mumma echoed the question, looking down at Pops. "Which one are you?" *("I thought he would be standing right at my side already, like a knight. Like Lancelot and Guinevere, but he stayed sitting, as if he was thinking over what that old drunk was saying. It was a bad moment in my marriage, I can tell*

161

you girls that. A very bad moment.")

"I'm not afraid of Rida," Pops said to his father. "I'm not afraid of you, either. And as to the man-or-mouse question, in the way that you are using the words, I'd say I'm a mouse." Then he looked up at Mumma. "It would seem that I can be a mouse for you or a mouse for them."

"You'll do better with me," Mumma advised him.

"I'm not going to ask you to sit down," Pops said to her, "but if you would do that, I'd be grateful."

Mumma sat. "I'll pay you back the money for the building," she told Pops, ignoring Grandfather and Ethan, who snorted in a duet of disbelief. "With interest," she said, ending the discussion.

But she knew even then that they couldn't live in an apartment in the midst of renovations, so that was the first of the few arguments with Mumma that Grandmother won. In the matter of a house, Grandmother insisted on a compromise that Mumma could go along with. The apartment building was obviously uninhabitable when Grandmother returned to Louisburg Square, the day after Labor Day, explaining, "Mr. Howland will follow in a day or so. He's closing up the house."

"We'll have moved out by then," Mumma told her.

"You're not going to live in that tenement, are you? It's not safe for Meg, or a baby, all that dirt and noise. You can't live there."

"I thought we would live in the Capstan house. Spencer can drive in for classes and sleep here if he's too late to drive home," Mumma said. "I'll have Polly Grangery there, to help with the house and children."

"But I've told Anne she can live there, because she's going to stay with the job in Bourne after all."

"Then it will have to be the big house."

"Oh, no, Rida, I can't let you do that. It's not winterized. There's no heat. What about the baby? You haven't forgotten that you're going to have a new baby, have you? What does Dr. Irving think of this?"

"I can have the baby in Hyannis."

"And bring it home to that big drafty place? You're asking for colds, and croup, and probably only bronchitis, if you're lucky, not pneumonia."

"By then I'll have found somewhere else. We'll have our own home by then."

"You'll come in from the Cape a few weeks before the baby is due," Grandmother instructed. This was her compromise. "You can live out there until winter if you like, but my grandchild is going to be born at Boston Lying-In."

On this point, Mumma gave way. After all, she was as concerned about the health of her children as any normal mother; she wanted the best for her son, and she trusted Grandmother's sense of what was the best. So Jo — not a boy after all — was born in Boston, and after two postnatal weeks in the house on Louisburg Square, Mumma moved her family into one of the renovated apartments in her building.

In June she moved the family again, into the house she had finally found for them, not in Cambridge but out on Cape Cod. They were still in the town of Wampanoag but right on the border of West Falmouth, miles from the Spencer houses and without even a water view. From Wampanoag, the commute to Cambridge was long and hard, especially in the winter months, so at the end of his second year in graduate school, Pops transferred to Brown, on the basis of Mumma's convincing arguments about wanting him not to be killed in a car wreck on some winter evening.

Of course Pops did what she told him he'd prefer, and in fact he was much happier at Brown than he'd been at Harvard, finding like-minded, like-spirited friends among professors and fellow students. Mumma was entirely satisfied with her home and her husband. Pops, too, was satisfied, and Grandmother, who had won the battle, accepted her undeniable loss of the war.

4.
MUMMA AND THE
SOCIAL ORDERS

THE ENGAGEMENT

"Fast girls get pregnant, look what happened with your aunt Anne."

This constituted Mumma's contraceptive counsel as we grew up, and it made a convincing argument until Amy pointed out to us that it was *girls* who got pregnant, pregnancy having to do with the *girl* part of the sentence, not the *fast*. Aunt Anne, she pointed out, could have gotten pregnant without being *fast*. For example, Aunt Anne could have gotten pregnant the first time she slept with anybody, whenever that was, and whoever, rather than getting pregnant eventually, which, as Amy pointed out, wasn't the same as inevitably.

In those postwar days, if you got pregnant, you got married. In those days, if you got a girl pregnant you married her — that is, if you didn't disappear, leaving no forwarding address. So Anne and Giancarlo Ruscelli were getting married.

Grandmother undertook the task of breaking the news to Spencer and Rida. She telephoned the apartment building in North Cambridge, as required, but she was too rattled to give the usual three-hour notice, time for a daughter-in-law to tidy up and ready the children and perhaps bake a little tea cake, as if those were things Mumma would have done, even *with* notice.

"I'm coming over," Grandmother said. "It's a very important matter and you know I don't use that word lightly. Be sure Spencer is there."

"He's working."

"It's only studying and he can set it aside for an hour. I've been to college, I know about this."

"I never interrupt Spencer's work," Mumma said.

"Just tell him I say it's important," Grandmother instructed, and hung up before Mumma could repeat her refusal.

Of course Mumma didn't fetch Pops down from the room she had set aside for him, two floors above the noisy confusion of their crowded family quarters and as much a light-filled aerie as an apartment. She didn't put away the children, either, although Jo happened to be asleep; she didn't tidy up and she didn't get a cake into the oven. She went ahead with whatever she was doing, and not until Grandmother had actually arrived did she put on a kettle. "It's too early for a drink," she told Grandmother.

"I could use one," Grandmother said.

"All we have is beer. You'll prefer a cup of tea."

"Where's Spencer?"

"Sit here in the dining room. The kitchen is a mess. You could read a story to Meg," Mumma suggested, "while I'm busy."

She parked Grandmother at the dining room table and returned to the kitchen. With Meg on her lap, Grandmother entered the world of the little engine that could, with its primary colors and sturdy heroine. (*"One thing about your grandmother — you girls should know this about her — she was a person who read things. Where do you think your father got all his brains from? They had to come from somewhere, so whenever your grandmother had gotten herself all het up, I'd have her read to one of you to calm her down, at least enough so she could be talked to."*) After Mumma had poured cups of tea, and offered Grandmother sugar and milk to put into hers, and given Meg her own chair with a coloring book and crayons, Grandmother broke the news. "Anne has gone and done it. She's getting married. It's that Giancarlo man, of course, and Brundage is . . . Well, not to put too fine a point on it, Brundage is furious."

"I know," Mumma said.

"I mean — and I'm trusting you not to say a word to anyone, Rida — she *has* to marry him."

"I know," Mumma said again, because Anne had come to her for advice. (*"I told her to tell her mother, and she got angry at me. I don't know what she expected me to say. She's a lot like her father, now I think of it. Except, she doesn't drink the way he did."*)

"So the wedding will be almost immediate. We've got four and a half weeks," Grandmother said, "and I'm going to need your help. Can I count on you?"

"I don't know," Mumma explained "My days are pretty full. What did you have in mind for me to do?"

"Anne has her heart set on a wedding like the one Phyllis had but with a guest list of only two hundred. You won't be aware of this, but in our circles girls usually give their family at least a year, at least that much time, to plan a wedding. A big wedding doesn't seem so hole-in-the-corner, which could be reason enough to indulge Anne, but four and a half weeks . . . Well," with the sigh of a mother much martyred by her children, "needs must. There will be a shower, of course. A girl has to have at least one bridal shower after we announce the engagement, and we'll also be responsible for the rehearsal dinner. The man has no family here. Fortunately, he's not insisting on a Catholic ceremony. I don't think I could get Brundage to set foot in a Catholic church, so at least I'm being spared that. What people will say . . ." Grandmother squared her shoulders and then gave Mumma her instructions: "I know just what everybody will be saying, and I personally do not plan to dignify them with any response at all. I'm going to ask you to hostess a bridal shower, as well as see to it that Spencer does everything that's expected of him."

Mumma considered her own plans and necessities, then thought about how she might fit this new activity into her crowded days. She could do it. "When is it?" she asked. "I have some houses to look at next week, on the Cape."

"You don't want to live out there, not year-round," Grandmother said, accepting another cup of tea. "There are the schools, for one thing, and you can't ask Spencer to commute, for another. Where do you plan for Margaret to go to school?"

"Her name is Meg."

"Yes, I know, but her baptismal name is going to be Margaret," Grandmother told Mumma.

"No, it isn't. Why would I name her something nobody will ever call her?"

"Is that true of Josephine also?"

"Of course."

"Well, dear, since they haven't actually been baptized yet, it's not too late to rectify that."

"Yes they have. We had both girls done at the same time."

"Did you? But Rida, we weren't there."

"When do you want me to give the bridal shower?" Mumma asked.

"The week after next, I'm afraid. The announcement will be in the paper tomorrow."

"I can do that."

"And you'll help with the wedding, too, the invitations, and ordering the flowers for the groom and groomsmen, and probably with the groom's gifts for the bride, as well, *and* for the groomsmen. I particularly need you to help me with the groom, because I'm practically positive the young man knows nothing of how we do weddings over here. We don't know anything about him. Not

171

one thing about his background, which is probably a blessing, because Italians . . . We know only what he tells us about himself. I don't know, I just don't know. Brundage is very upset, you can imagine. I can admit it to you, Rida, that Brundage is not the most broad-minded of men. Especially when it comes to who his children marry." *("No, I didn't take offense. Why should I? Your father was lucky to have me and he knew it.")* "Also, Brundage doesn't care for the Italian people, I'm sorry to say. After Mussolini, and the war."

"Maybe he'll change his mind when he has a half-Italian grandchild," Mumma said.

"Rida! It's just that the young people don't want to wait, and why should they?" Having made her admission and filed her complaint, Grandmother reassumed her impregnable cloak of denial.

"Actually, they *can't* wait," Mumma said. "That's the actual truth."

"You need to keep your opinions to yourself sometimes, Rida," Grandmother counseled. "You can get a little strident about truth, and after all, the truth is a pretty flexible commodity. You know how people will talk."

"I know people can count to nine," Mumma said.

"Whatever that means," Grandmother riposted. "Never mind that, because the shower has to be a week from Saturday, so I've talked to Jonquil Cartenbury and she'll be your co-hostess. Because if you think about it" — Grandmother waved a hand in the general direction of the other rooms of Mumma's apartment — "the Cartenbury house is a much more appropriate setting. You could barely squeeze eight people around this table, and besides, it's half covered with papers."

Mumma was happy to explain. "They're important records: contracts with electricians and plumbers, carpenters, painters, and daily logs, projected completion dates, progress charts, receipts for payments, inspection certificates, rent receipts —"

"That's not what I meant. No matter."

"If a person doesn't keep records, keep track, a person can't say she's doing a good job of managing. Managing anything, I mean, not just a business."

"You have to admit —"

"No I don't."

"— that you might be overdoing it," Grandmother finished. "You *are* something of an over-doer, my dear. I don't know why you need to worry about money anyway."

"I'm not worrying, I'm managing. Making a profit."

"You met Jonquil at my welcome-home party last summer. She's from Virginia and knows how to do these things. I'm so pleased she's here to help you out — that is, to help us all. You will be able to work with her, won't you? For Anne's sake." She looked at Mumma. "For the sake of the family," she amended. "Spencer's family, and where *is* the boy, by the way?"

"He's a man," Mumma said. "I don't disturb him when he's working."

"You spoil him," Grandmother told her. "But it's obvious how devoted to him you are. I *do* notice how happy you make my son." Then Grandmother, having complimented Mumma on that area in which she felt Mumma had earned her good opinion, returned to her primary purpose. "So you will do it? Be the co-hostess, with Jonquil."

"I'll telephone her tonight."

"I'd rather you went to see her today. I can drop you off. You can take the children and bring the pram so you'll have a nice walk home. Isn't her boy not much older than your Jo? The nanny can easily see to the children while you two girls make plans. Jonquil knows everything that needs to be done. Really, whatever you might want to say about Southerners, they know how to raise a lady. Please don't start your quarreling with me about that, Rida, I know what you think and I've had too much to deal with today to be having one of your quarrels about what is important in the world." *("She really thought I had ever quarreled with her, which I never did. Your grandmother didn't know what people were really like. She only knew how they were supposed to act.")*

Grandmother had one final request. "I need Spencer to be one of the ushers, since Giancarlo's family won't be there — which is a blessing — and I have no idea who he'll have for a best man. I'm a little concerned, I have to tell you that."

"You could have a small wedding," Mumma suggested.

"Don't think I wouldn't prefer it. But you know what Anne is like when she makes up her mind she wants something."

For once Mumma chose not to say what she was thinking and chose instead to offer comfort. "I'm sure it will be a very successful occasion, Dorothy." *("When I called your grandmother by her first name, well, I can tell you, I felt like I was throwing myself off that high cliff in Acapulco into deep rocky water. I had to make myself do it. I wasn't even in my mid-twenties, remember, still just a girl, young. Or maybe it was like making myself swallow something really strange, like the first time I tasted caviar — and never again, I can tell you girls that. But really, it was like making myself go to the doctor for a shot, saying her name like that, Dorothy, to her face. And she didn't like it any better than I did, I promise you. It was almost fun, watching your grandmother's face when I called her by name.")*

In my opinion, that bridal shower was the actual starting point for the rivalry between Mumma and Jonquil Cartenbury, or maybe it would be more accurately called a feud, or even a duel, or perhaps simply a general and inclusive mutual dislike that went on for over forty years, almost — although not entirely — without interruption. The antipathy on which it was based had been planted at their first meeting on the Cape, which also transpired at Grandmother's hand; a seed of mutual ill-will germinated over the months when both Mumma and Mrs. Cartenbury were wives of students at Harvard graduate schools and reached full flower at Aunt Anne's shower. It was the most natural thing in the world, a contest between those two women.

Jonquil Cartenbury was everything Mumma wasn't: the mother of a son, the wife of a decorated hero, the darling of her

176

in-laws, descendant of an old, if regrettably Southern, family; she was a pretty girl with pretty manners, who dressed well, not to mention being a college graduate. Moreover, she was a person who disclaimed credit for achievements: "I didn't do anything really, it was not one little *bit* of trouble." She disclaimed even compliments: "This old thing?" She kept her eyes modestly cast down and her voice openly admiring of others and was regularly to be found at stage center, in a leading role.

That Mumma was ambitious to outshine Jonquil goes without saying. During the first winter of graduate school, while Mumma was having Jo and moving her family into its temporary apartment, and overseeing a complicated schedule of renovations, Jonquil Cartenbury established herself at the social center of the Harvard graduate schools, settling around herself like the skirts of her wedding gown (visible in the photograph so proudly displayed on top of the grand piano in the double living room of the Cartenburys' Cambridge home) a circle of young women to admire and envy her. Mumma, having no natural talent for admiration or for envy, was not a member of that inner circle. Jonquil Cartenbury took Mumma's absence for criticism; she understood Mumma's single-minded self-satisfaction as dislike. Mumma was always pleased to boast, "I was a thorn in her side, from the first."

Mumma accepted Grandmother's offer of a ride to the discreetly magnificent edifice on one of those small shady streets between Brattle and Huron, but she declined to be escorted in. "I'll be happy to stay and ease any awkwardness, Rida," Grandmother offered, as Mumma extracted the pram from the trunk of the Lincoln. "That won't be necessary," Mumma responded. "You should go now." In the large, flower-filled entry, Mumma's two girls were taken into the care of the nanny, a person brought over from England for the important purpose of caring for Jonquil's son and, as Jonquil confided prettily when she greeted Mumma with a significant glance at the nanny, "his little brother, in not very many months. It's certainly in the air, isn't it?"

"What's in the air?" demanded Mumma, who met any challenge head-on.

"Oh, nothing. Nothing at all. It's just my silly way of talking. You don't have to worry about a thing, because Nanny is very good with children. Your girls will love her," Jonquil said with a bright and welcoming smile.

Mumma had her doubts but held her tongue. *("Making it twice in one day," as she told the story. "Something of a record," we remarked.)* Without comment, she watched her two children being led and carried away up a broad staircase. *("Was Mrs. Cartenbury doused in that perfume she always wore?" Amy asked. "What was it, was it Chanel or Guerlain? I really remember that perfume.")*

Mumma gave her hat and coat to a hovering maid and put her gloves in her purse, which she kept with her. She did not look around the entry hall with interest and admiration; she was not curious about the portraits and landscapes on the living room walls nor the photographs set out in silver frames on the piano. While the two young mothers talked, seated in armchairs facing each other in front of a bay window that looked out over flowerbeds where gardeners were at work, tea was served from a Sèvres set. Jonquil poured, offering little crustless cucumber sandwiches and tiny pastel squares of petits fours.

Mumma declined refreshment. Or, rather, she attempted to decline. "No, no tea, thank you," she said, and her hostess smiled benignly, "Of course you do, will you have milk or lemon?"

"I'm not hungry," Mumma said, and her

hostess did not insist, agreeing, "I know, isn't it lucky these are so little and light?"

It wasn't really any kind of a conference at all, as Mumma soon realized. Grandmother had drawn up a guest list, Jonquil had decided on a menu, Aunt Anne's pregnancy determined the date and time, and for everything else Jonquil had the answer. "I know just who will do perfect flowers," she said, and, "I know just the right place for invitations and since it's all happening so fast," she said, and paused, waiting. "I picked some out I know you'll just love, because we don't have time to really decide things together, do we?" Pause. "To *really* work on a shower would take, why, *months.*" And Jonquil smiled, waiting.

Mumma said nothing, and continued to say nothing until she finally ended the silence with the suggestion that they could use the time that afternoon for addressing envelopes, and she would be happy to drop them off at the post office, on her way home.

"I don't know, Rida." Jonquil became diplomatic. "In our schools, I mean at home, in Virginia, I mean, you know, they didn't always teach us the same things you Northerners think are important. I do understand that. I have realized that. Although, now I recollect myself, you aren't a

180

Bostonian either. We are the both of us outsiders, aren't we?"

"What is it?" Mumma asked. "Do you think I won't be able to copy names and addresses correctly?"

"Goodness, no. I have certainly noticed how smart you are. Why, everybody notices that, my goodness. But — I doubt — did they teach you the Palmer method? I mean, calligraphy."

"Not if it's the one with all the loops, they didn't. But I write a clear hand and I think we should get something done, since I'm here. I've had enough tea for one afternoon." *("Maybe it was my own fault, too. If people don't get along with you like that, it's partly your own fault. I know that and I accept my share of the responsibility for all of the bad feeling between me and Jonquil Cartenbury. I won't deny it: The woman has always been my Achilles' heel.")*

"It's only that I don't want you troubling yourself. That's all it is," Jonquil said to Mumma. "I know how busy you must be, with that whole apartment house you've bitten off, and the two baby girls besides, because you don't have any help at home, do you? So you can just leave everything to me. Why, I have nothing better to do with my time," she said. "Really, there's no need

181

for you to be bothered."

"Then why am I here?"

"Oh. That's because Mrs. Howland — don't you just adore her? She needs a family member to give the shower for Anne. I don't know if you know, but it's traditionally a cousin, or an aunt, or a sister who gives the shower, but on such short notice Phyllis can't come up from Washington and of course Juliet is too young, so there was only you. And Mrs. H thought I was a person who would know how these things are done, which, for my sins, I surely do. She is absolutely right about me — Why, there was nothing but engagements and marriages in my whole huge family, all through the war, and every single last one of them done right, done up proud."

(" 'Proud' would be the operative word for Jonquil Cartenbury," Mumma told us. "But never for you," I wisecracked. Mumma ignored me. Jo said, "Maybe Mrs. Cartenbury was trying to be friends. Maybe she envied you, your independence, the way you bought that building and envied your business ability. Or maybe? She probably felt just as out of place as you did." "I never felt out of place anywhere in my life," Mumma maintained, "no matter how hard they tried."

"Mrs. Cartenbury is a real traditionalist," Meg

182

reminded us. "Remember how we hated her boys?" I asked. Mumma agreed, "She was always farming them out to some nanny or some camp or some boarding school. Those boys didn't have a normal mother.")

With everything now made clear about the shower, Mumma set down her Sèvres cup on a spindly side table and stood up. "I'd better be getting along. Jo's liable to get hungry."

"You're not feeding her on demand, are you?" Worry clouded Jonquil Cartenbury's violet eyes, so Mumma put her out of her misery. "I am," she said, and then she added in the hope of shocking the woman into movement, "I'm nursing her, so it's easy." *("I should have known that instead of stiffening her backbone, it would just turn her legs to jelly to hear that. I should have known better. She stayed planted in that chair like some statue, or maybe like some azalea. But really she was like a creeper, a Virginia creeper, as if she needed that chair under her or she'd just flop onto the ground. It was all an act, of course. She didn't fool me.")*

"But what," Jonquil almost gasped it, "what does Dr. Irving say about that?"

"I didn't ask him. He couldn't nurse a baby if he wanted to, so why would I listen to him? You know, women have fed their children that way for centuries, so anybody who did anything famous that you've heard of at college — Tolstoy, or Leonardo, Napoleon, Queen Elizabeth? They were all breast-fed." Ignoring the palpitations taking place in front of her very eyes, Mumma asked, "Where are the children?"

"The children, yes. They'll be in the day nursery, with Nanny. Shall we fetch them?"

Mumma took up her purse and gloves, while Jonquil Cartenbury rang a little silver bell to let the maid know that the tea things could be cleared and that Mrs. Spencer Howland's coat and hat should be fetched, after which she had regained her strength and could rise to her feet. The two young matrons ascended the broad staircase side by side, their footsteps muffled by thick Oriental carpeting. From down the long second-floor hallway came the sound of Meg, crying. Howling, actually, with that ragged, persistent unhappiness small children can achieve. Despite her high heels, Mumma broke into a run.

Jonquil followed at a more stately pace, but the sound of Meg in misery gave Mumma sure direction and she flung open a door that knocked Meg — who had been clinging to the other side of it, trying to open it, trying to escape — flat on her back.

Mumma scooped her child into her arms, sat down on the floor, and —

("A day nursery?" wondered Amy. "What kind of stuff did the Cartenburys have in a day nursery?" "How would I notice and why would I want to? I had your sister to tend to, after that witch woman from England had been doing who knows what to my children.")

Once Meg had entered hysteria, Jo had of course joined her, sibling sympathetic vibrations at work. The nanny remained unmoved, seated at a low nursery table where Jonquil's son was quietly drawing. Jonquil arrived at the doorway and asked, "Nanny? Whatever is all the commotion up here?"

"That child refuses to settle," the nanny reported, and turned to Meg. "Now you've got your way, missy, and I hope you're satisfied."

"Who's a little face?" Mumma crooned, crouched in front of Meg, cupping the wet, red cheeks with her palms. Meg clutched at Mumma and sobbed, but with diminishing urgency. Jo was already at the hiccupping stage.

"And she got her sister going, too," the nanny reported.

"Neddy's not giving any trouble, is he?" Jonquil asked from the doorway.

"Mumma's here now," Mumma soothed

Meg. "Everything's all right now."

"He's a good boy," the nanny said. "He'd never cry like that. Would you, my little manny."

"Shall we go home?" Mumma asked Meg, rising and setting her on her own feet.

"Home! Home!"

Little Francis Edward Cartenbury IV colored on, his fat fingers wrapped around the thick crayon.

"*And* she's not in training panties," the nanny reported to Jonquil.

"Nanny! I've asked you before not to make comparisons between Neddy and his little guests," Jonquil reprimanded her, before turning to Mumma to say, "My goodness, those girls are just miserable, aren't they? I thought you'd like to color with my Neddy," she said to Meg.

Meg wrapped her face in Mumma's skirt, sniveling and drooling.

"Only her mother would satisfy this little missy," the nanny said.

"Oh," Jonquil said, in that tone of voice that implies all of the many thoughts that are going to go unspoken. "Well. My goodness, Nanny, you know that not every child can be as independent as Neddy. Why" — she smiled at Mumma — "I do believe I could be gone all day and he'd barely notice."

The nanny denied it. "I hope you don't think that, Mrs. Cartenbury."

"Well, of course I don't really. Neddy is devoted to his nanny, I realize that, but he does love his lessons with Mommy. Don't you, sugarpie?" She told Mumma, "We do letters and numbers and Neddy can count to five — can't you, sugarpie? Do you want to count to five for Mrs. Howland, Neddy?"

"No," the child said.

"Another time," the nanny said.

"And I'm sure Margaret already knows all of those things, anyway, with two such smart parents. Have you started her on letters, Rida?"

"No," Mumma said. "And her name is Meg. I don't use nicknames."

"My goodness. Aren't you original."

"Not particularly." Mumma gathered Jo up into her arms, hung her purse off her free wrist so that Meg could take her hand, and instructed, "Say thank you, Meg."

"Thank you," Meg mumbled, her eyes downcast and her fingers wrapped tight around Mumma's.

"You should have called me," Mumma said to the nanny.

The nanny stared at Mumma out of unresponsive eyes, and said nothing.

Mumma outwaited her.

"I don't believe in spoiling children," the nanny finally said.

"I don't believe in nannies," Mumma answered.

"Let me walk you downstairs," Jonquil said. "And have you decided what you'll wear to the shower?" Jonquil asked her. "Because I surely would enjoy a girls' expedition over to Peck and Peck, if you're planning on a new outfit. Oh, and there's the wedding too, isn't there? I know you'll want to do Mrs. H proud at the wedding. We could make a day of it, shopping. Wouldn't that be fun? And we could end up with a tea at the Ritz and I'd feel — oh, a hundred years younger, a girl again."

("As if I couldn't read her mind. As if I didn't know what those two were up to with me.")

"I'm already fixed for dresses," Mumma said. She was already at the front door, which the maid held open for her.

Jonquil called down from the top of the stairs, "Just give me a tinkle when you change your mind. And you'll plan to be here an hour early on the Saturday, won't you? Because you should be, I don't know if you knew that. Will your girls be all right with Nanny, do you think? Because we don't want them ruining Anne's party."

THE BRIDAL SHOWER

On the day of Aunt Anne's bridal shower, Mumma arrived an hour in advance, as instructed. Jonquil herself opened the front door, aproned and distracted. "Just take the babies up to Nanny and then I need you to come right back, Rida. I need your help down here." She turned away to attend to some other crisis and never even noticed that Mumma hadn't brought her children.

Mumma entered the hall and waited to be told: where to put her hat and coat, purse and gloves; where to be useful; what to do to be useful. The hall was festooned with urns of flowers and empty of people. She didn't have to wait long; in a few minutes Jonquil hurried into view again. "Girls all settled upstairs?"

"No," Mumma said. "They're at home with Spencer."

"With Spencer?" At last Mumma had Jonquil's full attention. "Does he know anything about children?"

"If he doesn't he'll find out."

"I guess you know best. Let me show you where we're putting the coats." She led Mumma to a guest room at the top of the stairs, its bathroom door invitingly open,

"For anyone who needs to wash her hands, or spend a penny," Jonquil said. "Although, I expect most will use the downstairs washroom, don't you?" Before Mumma could construct an opinion on this question, Jonquil was leading her out of the room and back down the stairs.

Mumma wore a bright banana-yellow dress, with thin vertical black stripes edged with even thinner stripes of claret red; the skirt was full, the waist fitted, the neckline scooped, the short sleeves puffy; her high-heeled shoes were in two shades of leather, black and red. In contrast, Jonquil wore a pale blue dress with lace at the neck and wrists, the fitted bodice adorned with a double strand of pearls; her dyed-to-match pumps had heels of a tasteful two inches. "I hope you can manage the stairs in those shoes," she remarked as they descended. "I am amazed you don't totter more than you do. You are amazing to me, Rida, I swear you are."

Twenty-nine guests were expected. Originally Jonquil had predicted thirty-four, guessing that of the thirty-eight invitations she sent out no more than four of the women were likely to decline on principle. This, however, appeared to be an occasion when Southern principles differed from

Northern. Jonquil had either underestimated the moral intransigence of the ladies of Boston, or she had overestimated their goodwill. To be precise, she mis-estimated by five, one of those an older Spencer cousin, to whom Grandmother never again said more than "Hello, so nice to see you" and "Goodbye, we must get together more often." So there were twenty-nine guests, at roughly three age levels — the girls, the mothers, and the Greats. Girls constituted those between their early twenties and early thirties, several of whom were in fact matrons, their children delivered up to the nanny in the day nursery. Their husbands, it seemed, either could not be bothered or could not be trusted with children. The girls wore full-skirted dresses, pastel pink and pastel green, one lavender, with matched belts cinched tight around their trim waists and low-heeled pumps dyed to match. The mothers, like Grandmother and the senior Mrs. Cartenbury, wore rose and silvery gray, while the Greats wore black and navy blue. Everybody had pearls to one degree or another, single or double strands, and Mrs. Cartenbury had a triple.

Anne also had been instructed to arrive early, which she did, accompanied by Grandmother, at which point Jonquil's mother-in-law descended to join the party. Anne, as guest of honor, took her seat on the living room sofa, while Grandmother, as mother of the bride, remained in the entry hall with Mrs. Cartenbury, the mother-in-law of the co-hostess. Mumma was detailed by Jonquil to show the guests where to put their coats and hats and then, while new arrivals were being formally welcomed in the hallway, to add their wrapped gifts to the display mounded on the polished top of the grand piano in the living room. Jonquil, as co-hostess, remained in the hall with Grandmother and Mrs. Cartenbury, to welcome the guests. Mumma's duties, as Jonquil assigned them to her, left her no time to welcome or to be introduced or to make introductions. Which is to say, Mumma had been demoted to helper; which is to say, she had been entirely upstaged; which, on this occasion, seemed fair enough to her, since she had done none of the work of preparation.

The party gathered in the long double living room, where windows let in the bright spring sunlight and vases of aromatic flowers sweetened the air. The guests grouped themselves, girls with girls, mothers with mothers, and the Greats, of whom there were four, seated side by side on a long sofa, their eight feet resting side by side in four pairs of sturdy laced shoes. At one end of the room, nearest to the dining room and farthest from the piano, a round table had been set for five because, as Jonquil whispered to Mumma, the dining room table could stretch to only twenty-four. The separation was unavoidable.

Pre-luncheon conversation centered on Anne. Her sisters and cousins and friends exclaimed, "Isn't it exciting?" and asked one another teasingly, "Do you remember when you were so wildly in love with your husband that you didn't want to wait a single week to marry him?" Anne turned prettily pink and promised them that when her fiancé came to pick her up, they'd all see right away why she wasn't about to let him run loose any longer than she had to. "And you all know how I've always felt about long engagements," she said, with little rippling laughs. "Especially now, women our age, isn't that right, Rida? If you've been at all close to the war like we have, the old conventions don't have the same importance. Isn't that what you think, Rida? We don't see the point of doing things the old way." After which Anne added tactfully, "Unless it's what a person wants. You agree, don't you, Rida?"

Mumma said, "I don't know what the old conventions were, so I couldn't say."

Into the silence that followed this unexpected response to a traditional pleasantry, Jonquil spoke. "I've heard it said that in California — I mean, out West, everywhere out West, we just *call* it California — things are very different. I often think, myself, that the way the settlers lived, the first settlers of a place, I mean, determines the character of a place. So that when you think of out West, with all those ranchers and gamblers, the Gold Rush, and silver mines too, and oil too, all those overnight fortunes, the way they had to live. They were governed by what they called the law of the gun, I've read that in a lot of books. You can't expect them to have much interest in conventions. Why, they had other things to think about — Indians, I mean, and blizzards, and rustlers. It wouldn't be reasonable to think they'd care about how things ought to be done. I just think America is the most interesting country," Jonquil concluded.

Mumma stuck to her point. "I know of some long engagements in California."

"And those movie people set such a bad example. Everybody thinks they can get divorced and remarried like there's no tomorrow," somebody offered.

"For a lot of people there wasn't," Mumma reminded everybody.

"I for one am a big fan of the movies," somebody said. "Clark Gable, just to mention a really handsome man."

This did divert Mumma. "Gregory Peck," she seconded.

"The movies are quite the social equalizer," one of the Greats remarked, after which no one could think of anything to say, except perhaps Mumma *("I'd never thought of that before. Have you girls ever thought of that?")*, but before she could open her mouth, Jonquil whispered into her ear, asking her to go out to tell the cook that it was time to serve. Jonquil turned back to the group to say brightly, "Aren't you lucky to be marrying a European, Anne. Tell us, he isn't a prince, is he? Don't they have just scads of princes over there? Especially in Italy. Did you rope us in an Italian prince?"

For the luncheon, Mumma had been seated at the table in the living room with the four Greats. In hurried whispers, Jonquil told Mumma that it was important for those older women to have a hostess at their table; it showed proper respect. However, it couldn't be her, since she had to be at the table with her mother-in-law, since after all it was Mrs. Cartenbury's house; and Mrs.

Cartenbury had to be on Anne's right, as the honored guest; while Mrs. Howland had to be on Jonquil's right, as the honored guest; and besides, Rida hadn't yet paid her calls on the older ladies of Boston, had she? Or Cambridge, either, two of them actually lived in Cambridge, and they were all dying to get to know her. Jonquil knew that for a fact.

Another fact was that to seat Mumma with the Greats in a separate area was as direct an insult as to have seated her at the children's table at a Thanksgiving dinner. Everybody knew it, even Mumma. Everybody, especially the four Greats, pretended not to know it. Everybody except Mumma, that is.

The Greats managed the introductions: Mrs. Howland ("Young Spencer's wife, isn't that correct? What is the boy up to these days?"), let me introduce Mrs. Allworthy, Mrs. Worthington, Mrs. Penworth, Mrs. Worth *("Or some names like that, people who'd known one another since they were babies, and their parents before them, the Worthies")*, four blue-haired ladies with permanents, in black with pearls, or navy blue with pearls, three of them plump as pillows and one as thin as a rail, and at least one a former beauty, with those facial bones that last forever.

It was determined again from which part of the country Mumma derived, one about which no one had anything to say or any curiosity about, and what part of Cambridge she was living in, about which also no one could think of anything to say. The Greats asked one another about various relatives and common acquaintances, always including Mumma. "Have you ever met . . . ? You must have run into . . ." These conversational gambits took them as far as halfway through the first course, which was vichyssoise, at that time exotic to Boston. Filtering in from behind them, crossing the hall from the dining room, came the sounds of a successful party. Voices spoke rapidly, two or three lively conversations conducted simultaneously, occasional bursts of laughter, every now and then a single voice remarking, "Oh, that is just so romantic," or "Oh, this is just so flavorful." Jonquil Cartenbury's silken drawl moved through the sharper voices and the metallic clinking of silver on porcelain like the wind weaving through the leaves outside the open windows.

By way of contrast, talk at the table backed into a corner of the living room was faltering. Mumma didn't want to know about where the Greats had come from, which she already knew, or where they lived, which she could guess. Everybody took slow spoonfuls of the creamy soup, and swallowed slowly, and an awkwardness as heavy as the linen it was swathed in settled over their table. The Greats began to talk about the weather, this spring, last winter, last fall, last summer, and Mumma couldn't turn them to any other subject, not the chicken salad, not books, not radio shows, and she knew better than to try politics. They didn't seem to want to talk to her about themselves, either, and the meal limped on. Finally, as they waited for their plates to be cleared, one of the Worthies asked Mumma, "Can you give us any idea how young Brundage is taking the marriage?"

"He's living in Paris."

"No, no, my dear, we know that, we know all about the son," another said. "We mean the father. Young Brundage was never what a person would call generous of spirit." She waited; they all waited.

"He wants Giancarlo to change his name," Mumma reported.

What Grandfather said, which Mumma didn't quote precisely although perhaps to this quartet she didn't have to, was that he didn't want any daughter of his named like some Eye-talian greaser, or any grandchild either. If Anne wanted to throw her own life away, she wasn't throwing his good name away too, he could promise her that. If Anne expected him to do anything for the two of them — just for starters, to pay for this misbegotten wedding her mother had her heart set on — then what did Giancarlo have to say about changing his name he'd like to know.

The Worthies had not yet heard about this, and were surprised into real interest. "Oh my."

"Oh my."

"I have to say that is just what I'd expect from young Brundage. It's drink, of course."

"But will the boy do it?" they asked Mumma, leaning back to give the servant access. "The fiancé."

"I think so."

"You could be wrong."

"Probably not," Mumma said. "I'm usually right about things," she explained.

They hmphed, then asked, "What are you giving Anne today?"

"I didn't bring it," Mumma told them.

They were concerned. "But you know, Rida, it's customary, for a shower, to bring the gift with you. The unwrapping of the gifts is a high point of the party, when you see her with all the fine things for her new home."

"Mine isn't for home décor. It's practical, for both of them. Giancarlo is practical."

"Oh," they told her, "the groom isn't to be thought of in the bridal shower."

"In my book he is," Mumma said.

"Well, yes, of course, dear," they soothed her. "But this is our book."

"I'm sorry to say, it isn't," Mumma said. "I'm sure it used to be," she soothed them.

"I'm sure it still is," they warned her, not without curiosity about just who this young woman was and how she was going to enliven their lives. "Tell us, how did you and young Spencer meet?" they asked, and since this was one of Mumma's favorite stories, especially with such an interested audience, she smiled and leaned forward, to begin it.

Then dessert plates were set down in front of them and before they could eat, or drink the tea and coffee put down for them, the group from the dining room, hastier eaters, moved past them into the living room to begin the next stage of the party. The five women agreed, without a word spoken, to forgo dessert and end their lunch together. They rose from their table.

"A lovely luncheon," one of the Worthies

praised Jonquil.

"How clever of you to start with a cold soup. It quite reminded us that summer will soon be upon us," another added, the kind of compliment that could be worried over for weeks.

"And you are entirely correct, dessert really is too much for people as old as we are," said a third.

"Oh, really," the fourth said, shaking her head at her old friends. She turned to Jonquil. "It was very kind of you to seat young Rida with us."

The others echoed her. "A lovely shower, a lovely luncheon, Anne is looking so well."

Mumma held her tongue.

The occasion dragged on well into the afternoon, gifts being exclaimed over and their ribbons twined into a remembrance bouquet for Anne to take home and treasure, four identical sets of guest towels from the Greats (all purchased at the same well-known purveyor of quality linens), causing both Anne and Grandmother to laugh merrily and Jonquil Cartenbury to speak with disappointment about Makanna's clerks, who she felt should have caught the duplications, while the Worthies twittered, "So silly of us, we should have consulted one another, so sorry, such silly-billies," and, "Do exchange them, please, for something you find that you need, Anne." *("They were no fools, those old ladies," was Mumma's opinion.)*

It was Jonquil Cartenbury who voiced the question, "But Rida, where is your gift?" This was just before the audience had disbanded to talk among themselves for a last few minutes as they waited for the groom-to-be to arrive to pick up his fiancée, which would be their signal of release.

"I didn't bring it," Mumma told her, and didn't add that a perambulator was too large to be put on top of the grand piano. Eyebrows were raised, and eyes were rolled, but that was, luckily, when the doorbell rang, causing a silence, the whole long double living room silent with its damask drapes and chintz-covered furniture, its landscapes and still lives, its grand piano and the display of unwrapped gifts, and all the women too, all in readiness for the grand finale, the arrival of the groom.

Giancarlo entered, confident of his good looks if not of his lines, but aware of which was more important to the occasion. "I am not too prompt?" he asked. "I don't interrupt?"

Anne rose to take his hand and kiss his cheek, then, placed at Giancarlo's side, she turned to face the group. "You're right on time. Everyone? Here he is. Those of you who don't yet know him, this is my fiancé, John Brooks. Johnny, let me introduce you around. I want everyone to meet you."

Mumma, of course, refused to call him Johnny, or even John, and all of her life continued to call him Giancarlo; and so we did, too, unless we were talking about him to one of the other Spencer-Howlands. To us he was Uncle Giancarlo, and a great favorite of ours, and not just for his good looks. Uncle Giancarlo let us dig in his gardens and later, when we reached our teens, was willing to give us summer employment that wasn't babysitting. He assumed we were in the know about various Howland-Spencer carryings-on, thus becoming a major source of information about many things Mumma considered none of our business. He wasn't tall and slim, like the stereotypically handsome Italian, but he had an exotic quality despite a square, muscular body; perhaps it was his nose. Uncle Giancarlo's nose didn't slope gently out from below his eyes like the rest of the noses we knew. It fell down from high in his forehead, like the beak on some raptor bird. He looked stronger, perhaps more dangerous, than the usual kind of men we saw. He worked in the outdoors as much as possible, even when the business acquired a corporate identity with its own multistory office building just off Route 128, so he was always as tan as a fisherman. He was a romantic vision, in fact, our uncle Giancarlo Ruscelli. I understood why Mumma declined to let him be toned down to John C. Brooks.

All of the ladies at the shower fluttered with pleasure in his presence. "Now I've seen you up close," Jonquil Cartenbury said, "I can understand why Anne is so ready to forgo a long engagement. If you were mine, I'd want to have you signed, sealed, and delivered as soon as possible, too."

Mumma stood back, as did Grandmother, while the others fussed. Giancarlo came to greet them without Anne, who had remained behind at the center of an excited group.

"Johnny," Grandmother said, holding out her hand to him. "You do Anne proud."

"I hope, yes," he said. "They like such things, girls do. This I remember from my sisters."

Giancarlo didn't greet Mumma as he had Grandmother and the others, with a formal bow over their outstretched hands. Instead, he put a hand on her shoulder and kissed her first on the left cheek, then on the right, in the Italian way. Mumma loved that, as he knew. Mumma always believed that had she not been so obviously devoted to Spencer, Giancarlo might have given over his attachment to Anne and tried to win Mumma. *("But you know she thought every man she met was in love with her."*

"Except Grandfather," Jo reminds us.)

At the end of the afternoon, Grandmother and Mumma were the last to make their farewells to the Cartenburys and leave that spacious house. Grandmother had a car waiting and she would drop Mumma off before crossing back into the city. As soon as they had settled themselves into the back seat, Grandmother made her move. "I expect we can ask you to give the rehearsal dinner, Rida. That is, I hope," she corrected, because she was getting to know Mumma's nature, "that if asked you will say yes. The young man has no family," she added cannily.

"I thought he had a big family."

"Yes, of course, but they're in Italy. They're Italian. They can't be here for the wedding — which *entre nous* I admit is something of a relief. However, of more immediate importance is the fact that they can't be here to undertake the traditional responsibilities of the groom's family. We'll have the rehearsal dinner out on the Cape," she added. "You can't get Trinity Church with less than twelve months' notice, so the Cape it is, Saint Stephen's it is. I am resigned to that. It won't be a large dinner, no more than forty, I'd think, there are only fourteen in the wedding party, and then immediate family, and then Frances and Jonquil Cartenbury."

"Is Jonquil one of the bridesmaids?" asked Mumma, who was not.

"No, of course not. But if a person is a close enough friend to co-host the bridal shower, it would look odd if she weren't included in the rehearsal dinner. And I have my hands full with next weekend's party to introduce John to our friends, as well as to the entire family, so since you two did such a lovely job with this shower . . ."

Mumma didn't respond. She was thinking about the exams Pops had to take, and those he had to grade, and their upcoming move out to their new house on Cape Cod.

"Besides, I've asked Jonquil if she could lend you a hand with the rehearsal dinner and she has quite sweetly agreed. I don't know what I would have done without her at this time. Do you? What, I mean, *we* would have done without her support, and help, and generosity."

"I'll do it," Mumma decided. "But I'll do it alone."

Grandmother turned her face to study Mumma's expression. "You aren't jealous of her, are you? What good does that do, Rida?"

"I'm not," Mumma assured her, but Grandmother was unconvinced.

"She could be a useful friend to you. She has such a graceful way about her, and lovely taste, and she seems to instinctively understand how to make things go smoothly. You could do a lot worse than watch how Jonquil does things."

Mumma could agree to watch. "But if you want me to give the rehearsal dinner, Dorothy, you have to let me do it by myself."

Grandmother considered this, then stated her compromise position. "You'll let me advise you?"

"If you want. Also, I can read about rehearsal dinners in Emily Post. What were you thinking of advising?"

Grandmother commenced. "In the first place, that we give it in the big house. They're opening it for me this weekend. Aired, cleaned, and polished, it will be an appropriate setting. A formal dinner, seated, with place cards, we have all of the linen and silver, place settings, that's all taken care of." Then Grandmother returned to her primary interest. "The wedding reception is at the Club, a more modest affair than Phyllis's, but Anne will just have to make do, and I have to say that in the circumstances, a little modesty seems appropriate. I need all of the help you can give me, Rida."

The car stopped outside of Mumma's building in North Cambridge.

"I'll give you all the help I can," Mumma assured her.

Grandmother was puzzled by this qualified promise. "You aren't pregnant, are you?"

"Not that I know of," Mumma assured her. "I could be," she added, because in those days, unless she was actually menstruating, a woman couldn't be sure.

"Perhaps this is a good time to think about getting rid of this distraction," Grandmother suggested with a slight wave of her hand, barely able to look at the three-story clapboard building. "Since we'll be needing so much of your time, and energy, for Anne's wedding, and your children make many demands."

"There's Spencer, too, at the end of his school year," Mumma said. "Also, the building next door is still for sale and it would be smart to buy it."

"My goodness. Can Spencer afford that? With his school costs and all."

"You don't have to worry about Spencer. I'm already paying him back. I can take care of everything."

"Yes. I'm sure you can. That I *am* sure of."

Mumma had been away from her daughters for hours, and was eager to return, but she took the time to ask, "When will you have the guest list?"

"I have it right here" — Grandmother took a sheet of folded paper out of her purse — "with all the phone numbers. Because I was so hoping you *would* agree to do it. And I do want to help you in whatever way I can. I'm grateful to you, Rida, as is Anne, as well. That goes without saying."

"Actually," Mumma told her, "I'm doing this for Giancarlo. He's the one without any friends around here."

INTERLUDE: GRADUATION EVENTS

Mumma wanted to be a good wife to Pops, and this was the end of the academic year, when a rush of social events presented opportunities to win the assistant teaching assignments and research positions awarded by professors to their most deserving, or demanding, or maybe even just most beloved, students. His wife made a big difference to a student and Mumma knew that. What she didn't know, what she never knew, was how to flatter some man whom she privately considered not half as bright as Pops, or a windbag, or even — this was the worst in her private lexicon of academic vices — a phony. Mumma didn't know how to make useful friends and then make use of them. She didn't know how not to say what she thought and she never figured out that many people, maybe even most people, disguise, conceal, and even deny their true thoughts and opinions and emotions. She never paid any attention to, or had any curiosity about, what others might be privately thinking; it was the words they actually uttered that she attended to. If people didn't mean what they said, they shouldn't have said it: that was her opinion; they were phonies and cheats so she didn't want anything to do with them anyway. This was not an attitude likely to win her friends at the graduate school, not among students and not among professors. Also, Mumma was not good at being an underling, or the wife of an underling, and students, even graduate students at prestigious universities, are paradigmatic underlings.

As a wife, Mumma was often a liability. Not that Pops ever thought that.

That May marked the end of Pops' first year. The final graduate school gathering, held on the Commons outside the Widener Library, took place between Anne's bridal shower and her wedding. Rhododendron and azalea and dogwoods were in flower and even the myrtle offered up bright little blue blossoms. All the young men came dressed in lightweight gray suits, their ties striped blue and red and silver, their shoes polished. None of the young men wore uniforms, not even those who were more prepossessing and dashing in them, or who had earned the right to wear medals, thus declaring their deservedness of special notice. Likewise, none of the gray-haired or white-haired men wore academic robes or, in those few cases where they could have, their own military uniforms. Their suits also were gray, but often inexpertly pressed, and their shoes were often scuffed, which reminded everyone that their minds were on higher things. The women present, all of them student wives, most of them young mothers, wore light, flowery cotton dresses in pastel colors; except Mumma, of course, who had chosen something electric blue splotched with white flowers, with high-heeled white sandals.

Undercurrents of ambition and envy eddied around the ankles of the chattering guests. Pops sequestered himself off to one side of the party, on higher ground. He waited out the time next to a rhododendron in the company of a couple of equally awkward and earnest fish-out-of-water friends; they stood with their gin and tonics in one hand and, should one of the Alumni House waitresses seconded to the occasion happen to have recently passed, some small edible in the other, while they discussed perhaps some fine point about the nature of monads or the question of property left to female beneficiaries under the Code Napoleon. Mumma mingled, seeking out interesting conversations in which she might take an interesting part and thereby bring notice to Pops, the man who had such a wife. She had no idea what Pops' particular ambitions were, since he hadn't confided any to her, but she identified the important men present: Jonas Jackman, who held the Carnegie Chair of Economics, the mathematician Tex Pauley, and Hampton Court, who had the distinction of having had for his Harvard roommate a man who now sat on the state supreme court, so that every year one of Professor Court's law students was assured a clerkship in that judge's office.

Mumma avoided the mathematician *("I knew my limits. It's always good to know your limits and I knew I had nothing to say about numbers. Or pi.")* and joined the group gathered around Professor Court. They were still discussing the March suicide of Czechoslovakia's foreign minister, Jan Masaryk, which everyone knew had been murder, an example of Soviet methods of securing power, representing the threat of Soviet communism to a world that had so recently sacrificed so much to stay free. Professor Court supported the establishment of the House Un-American Activities Committee in response to this threat, with dire warnings to the encircling young people about Communist ambitions for world domination. "It's a stated objective of Stalin's foreign policy," Professor Court said, to murmurs of agreement and self-important noddings of heads. "Anyone who watched the partitioning of Europe not so long ago has to be aware of how they work. Not to mention Berlin. It's lucky we're the only ones with the bomb," he said.

"According to Bernard Baruch, we aren't," Mumma reminded him from her position at the outer edge, adding, "And I personally think that's maybe lucky for everyone else in the world."

"Oh?" Professor Court looked around him with a conspiratorial smile before turning to put her in her place. "You'd better be careful where you offer opinions like that, my dear," he advised her. "You know what people will think."

"Think," said Mumma. "Ha!" She always enjoyed a conversation with substance. "People *don't* think. That's why we have laws."

"I'd say, rather, that that's why we have a representative government," Professor Court riposted. He was a tall, broad-shouldered man, with a mane of white hair and bright blue eyes, a type everyone would recognize as the noble judge or professor, wise and kindly, a part written for Spencer Tracy.

"Congress," said Mumma. "Ha! They're about to pass this Mundt-Nixon legislation, do you know that?"

"I rather hope they will and I certainly think they should," the professor said. "The Communists are taking advantage of America's constitutionally guaranteed freedoms to infiltrate our institutions so that they can set about destroying this country from within. Correct me if I'm wrong, but I thought it's to protect the citizens that the

Committee on Un-American Activities has been created."

"I'll tell you what *I* think is un-American," Mumma said. "Telling people what they can't believe in. I always thought that was a founding principle of this country."

"Religion isn't the same as political belief," Professor Court asserted. When Mumma opened her mouth to expostulate "Ha!" for the third time, he forestalled her. "You *have* heard of the principle of separation of church and state, haven't you?"

At this, his listeners permitted themselves a little ripple of laughter, but Mumma, being in pursuit of an idea, was undismayable. Or maybe she simply didn't notice. "All right. So. If they pass this bill, and you're a Communist, I mean a real one, not one of these theoretical people, these fair-minded liberals who don't rule out anything, like a lot of people around here are, so careful to think things through that they can defend any position. Like what they said about Socrates in Athens, do you remember that?"

"Your point is?" he inquired.

In case he had forgotten, or never known, the precise charge, Mumma reminded him. " 'He makes the worse appear the better cause,' that's what they said about him. Because if I was a real Communist about

215

the last thing I'd do is register myself as one. If you see what I mean. I wouldn't even consider obeying that law. So the law will only catch the people who respect it, and live by it, and all the people the law wanted to catch will evade it. Maybe that's American, but it doesn't seem too smart to me. So why do *you* want them to pass the bill?" she asked, and waited with interest to hear his argument.

Into this conversational mayhem stepped Jonquil Cartenbury, who saw that none of the law students felt ready to do so, although every one of them was aware that the redheaded young woman was well beyond the pale. This aggressive young woman — whose wife was she, exactly? — didn't seem to understand how to speak with professors, that is, the art of asking a question in the response to which a professor would appear both well informed and witty, sometimes even benign as well. Jonquil Cartenbury took Mumma by the arm *("and she almost blinded me with that hat of hers, the rim almost sliced my eyeball in half")* in a fondly repressive gesture that also managed a wordless apology to the great man for whatever discomfiture this awkward person might have caused him, at the same time assuring him that of course everybody was aware that someone like this person could never really trouble someone like him.

"I'm perfectly sure," Jonquil Cartenbury said in her velvety voice, "why, I'm practically positive not a one of us would ever be a Communist. So what is there to worry about? Here? In this place, where — Why, it's been here since 1636, and that's three hundred and twelve years if my subtraction is correct, although I was always terrible at carrying," she admitted prettily. "I know Rida didn't mean half of what she said," Jonquil confided to Professor Court. "She just loves to argue. Argue, argue, she'll argue all day long with you if you give her a chance. I sometimes think *she* should be a lawyer," Jonquil suggested with a light laugh. "But I think Spencer was looking for you," she told Mumma.

For a while after that, Mumma dragged Pops around the party, visiting with some of the other couples from the classics department who were, in part, friends, although Mumma never felt they gave Pops the respect he deserved. As far as she was concerned, this gathering was a waste of a sweet spring afternoon, when she could have taken her family for a picnic by the Charles. Mumma was just waiting until they could leave, and Pops at a party was always

217

killing time until he could go home. Then Jonquil Cartenbury came up to join them. She ignored Mumma but took Pops confidingly by the arm. "I am always so glad to see you, Spencer. You are just a breath of fresh air," she said. "And I am so looking forward to seeing you in full regalia at Anne's wedding, because what girl doesn't like looking at a handsome man in his tuxedo? And speaking of the wedding, Rida? I've invited Professor Court and his wife to our little rehearsal dinner. He was telling me that he's never been out to Cape Cod, and how he's heard so much about it from some of his students, about their summers on the Cape. He just sounded so wistful, like a little boy, I couldn't stop myself from asking him, and he is so excited, it's quite flattering to you all. I'm sure Mrs. H will be pleased to meet him. She'll have heard of him, I'm sure. He's a distinguished jurist, very well known."

"You did what?" Mumma asked. "You can't do that. It's a rehearsal dinner, immediate family, members of the wedding party."

"But I'm not immediate family. I'm not a member of the wedding party, either, and we're invited, so it can't be all that strictly private. Is it, Spencer?" She smiled up at Pops.

"I don't know anything about these things," Pops said.

"I don't either," Mumma acknowledged, "but I do know he wasn't on the guest list Dorothy gave me. You'll have to dis-invite him."

"My goodness, Rida, I can't do that. You can't invite someone and then uninvite them. My goodness. Anyway, it's too late, it's a fait accompli."

"A what?"

"That's French," Jonquil Cartenbury informed Mumma with pretty patronage. "It's French for something that's already been done, so it's too late to stop it. Like," she added, as if she thought Mumma could be blackmailed, "if instead of this big old fancy wedding they're having, Anne and her handsome Johnny had decided to elope and present Mrs. H with a done deed, they'd call it a fait accompli."

"*I* wouldn't."

"Yes, but I don't think — Correct me if I'm wrong, and I know you will — I don't think you ever studied the French language?"

"*I* have to disinvite him. That's what you mean."

"You can't. No, really, Rida — it would be — everyone would think — and it means so much to Francis, to be able to do this little favor for Professor Court. I know he's probably going to get the clerkship anyway —"

"Then that's not a problem," Mumma told her.

(*"You don't think she really did that, did she?"*

"According to Mrs. Cartenbury she did."

"You asked Jonquil?"

"You call her Jonquil?"

"Good for Mumma," I said. "And what about the clerkship — did Mr. Cartenbury still get it? That's what I want to know."

"Maybe he didn't and that's why Jonquil kept thwarting Mumma's ambitions. Do you think?"

"When did you start calling her Jonquil?")

Mumma didn't just abandon Pops to Jonquil Cartenbury, who always made him a little nervous, which he concealed behind an impenetrably elegant formality. Before setting off to tell Professor Court that he was no longer invited to dinner, she gave Pops a subject to talk about. "Spencer had a brilliant idea about the ablative case. Explain it to Jonquil, Spencer, she'll be so interested, she's quite the linguist, you know. She studied French at college, she'll understand it much better than I can."

"I'm sure Jonquil doesn't —"

"I'd surely love to hear all about it, Spencer, but right now Francis needs me. Well, it's just a look he gave me, but a wife knows when her place is at her husband's side. You'll tell me about it some other time, won't you? You promise, now."

"I promise," Pops said, and then to her back, "although it's not nearly as long and tedious as Rida would have you think, and not difficult at all to grasp. It's just an insight," he called, as she got farther away. Then he turned to Mumma. "You shouldn't pick on her, Rida. She's a lost soul up here among all you bluestockings. And you know she's not very bright. It might do her a kindness if you could befriend her," Pops suggested.

"She's not my kind of person," Mumma told him.

"Oh," he said. "Well, then. But I thought — I thought Mother told me — and you gave that shower together."

"She's more your mother's kind of person," Mumma explained, and then she went to tell Professor Court that he wasn't welcome after all. She was usually willing to explain things to Pops, which is more than she did for the rest of us.

Mumma offered no explanations to Grandmother about the rehearsal dinner. She
listened to Grandmother's suggestions, she
read Emily Post, and she went her own way.
She also talked with Giancarlo about what
his mother would have served on such an
occasion, and she was probably instrumental
in arranging to have the senior Ruscelli
present for his son's marriage, which he was
proud, happy and able to be, much to the
chagrin of Grandmother and the distaste of
Grandfather. But Giancarlo rejoiced.

Massimo Francesco Ruscelli took a train
from Padua to Bologna, Bologna to Milan,
Milan to Paris, and from there a boat train
to London, where he boarded an airplane
for New York. Giancarlo and Anne met him
there and drove him north to Cape Cod for
his first introduction to the Spencer-
Howlands. This took place at Mumma's
rehearsal dinner.

Introductions between people who do not
speak one another's language tend to consist
of handshakes and smiles, followed up by
regular smiles and nods, to indicate goodwill. When the children of the two parties
are about to get married, a little extra effort
seems appropriate. Signor Ruscelli had
made that effort and could greet these

American in-laws-to-be in a clumsy and limited English — *'ello, 'ello* — and say *tanks you* and express his happiness about the occasion and the forthcoming child, "Is to me very please." If he wanted to say more than that, Giancarlo translated for him, probably accurately, although how accurately he translated to his father what the Americans were saying Mumma didn't know. She was pretty sure he omitted the more offensive (that source primarily Grandfather) and insensitive (most of the rest of them, at one time or another during Signor Ruscelli's brief stay) things the family had to say.

Of course Mumma and Giancarlo's father got along famously, despite having no common language. They communicated without words. *("He was half in love with me. A ladies' man for sure, like all those Italians. Jonquil wanted to horn in but she made the mistake of trying to teach him English words. Poor Jonquil, she never did understand men.")* Mumma called him Capo Max, convincing him that Americans had a way of giving pet names to people, as they had to his son, as acts of welcome. In return, he called her Contessa Rida. "Contessa?" he offered her a glass of champagne, and "Capo," she accepted it, then patted the place beside her on the sofa. He sat there, content to talk and not be understood. When Giancarlo joined them they could speak of one thing and another, but they were quite happy to be silent side by side, two shoe people, his pointed leather toes polished to a black brightness, her heels high, and red.

At the dinner, she kept Capo Max on her right and Giancarlo on her left. "But you can't," Jonquil Cartenbury told her, explaining that Mr. Brooks should be on Grandmother's right and Grandfather on Mumma's, that Giancarlo and Anne had to be seated together, the bridal couple, at the center of the long table. "That's the way it's done," she said, offering herself in place of the absent Mrs. Brooks for Mumma's left and Mrs. Cartenbury for Grandmother's left, since "She's the oldest. The best man sits on the groom's right, the maid of honor on the bride's left, and where do you want to put Spencer? Let's seat Francis with Ethan, don't you think? Because Francis flew over Italy, you know, and bombed them."

Mumma overruled. Not only did she seat people as she thought best — notably both Ruscelli men next to her and Grandfather at the most distant end of the table, with Anne next to him and the best man on Anne's other side — but she also served a dinner menu that had been advised by the grocers of the North End. "A person should feel at home when he eats," was Mumma's theory of foods. "What would an Italian family serve if the son was getting married?" she had asked, and then, "Is there a cook I can hire for an evening?" Mumma's meal had many courses, presented one after the other: two pasta dishes, grilled chicken with rosemary, grilled lamb chops, broiled fish, sautéed chard, eggplant with tomato sauce, roasted potatoes, roasted leeks, followed by fruits, cheeses, nuts, with two *dolci* to conclude, one a traditional *torta della nonna* with pine nuts, the other a dense chocolate *budino,* and after that a chilled Vin Santo served in small glasses, for which course little plates of warm *cantucci,* for dipping, were scattered around the table, and small bowls of chocolates and nuts. The two Ruscellis were delighted, and some of the other guests were dubious only about one course or another, while a few people disliked the whole unfamiliar thing. Jonquil Cartenbury remarked to everybody near her that this was typical Italian food, she was sure of it, and wasn't it clever of Rida to serve it? She herself would never have had the courage, but wasn't Rida original?

"Eye-talian food," Grandfather announced, putting down his fork, ignoring the glass of wine in favor of his glass of gin. "What's the point of whipping them if we have to turn around and eat their food?"

"Oh, Mr. Howland, you are just the most terrible man," Jonquil Cartenbury laughed, and removed his hand from her arm, or thigh, wherever it had landed. "You like spaghetti, don't you?"

"It would be just like a wop to serve spaghetti when he's marrying my daughter," Grandfather said, and his voice carried into one of those unpredictable silences that can fall over a large dinner table, the ones that people explain by the position of the hands of the clock, twenty before or twenty after the hour. His voice fell into a silence and squatted there, and it took the table an endless long minute to displace it. ("That did it for me, I can tell you. That man almost ruined my rehearsal dinner, and he wouldn't have minded if he had. Mine and Giancarlo's, and I wasn't sure at that time that Giancarlo could look out for himself. Which he can.")

After they had risen from dinner and removed to the living room for a final burst of conviviality before dispersing, Mumma bearded Grandfather. Grandmother stood beside her husband, and Jonquil Cartenbury was chattering away at them, but that didn't stop Mumma from laying down the law. "Those things you say, the names you're calling them," she began. "I mean the Ruscellis."

Grandfather smiled unpleasantly and looked to the two tamer women for support. "Now what's the matter with her?"

"You know what I mean," Mumma said.

"Such a lovely dinner, Rida," Jonquil Cartenbury was saying, and, "Surely this is neither the place nor time," Grandmother was saying. Mumma ignored them both. "You know exactly what I mean. You're not *that* drunk, not any drunker than usual."

"You have no sense of humor," Grandfather told her. "That's the trouble with the girl, she has no sense of humor," he repeated to Grandmother, and snaked an arm around Jonquil Cartenbury's waist. "I don't know what's getting you so hot and bothered," he told Mumma. "It may have escaped your notice, but the man doesn't speak one word of English," which struck him as a very funny remark.

Mumma ignored him, too. She had something to say and she had a plan. "If you don't stop, I'm warning you. I'll be putting ipecac into your drinks. Whenever I feel like it, I'll put drops in. I have plenty of ipecac, for the girls, a mother does. If you don't know what effect ipecac has you can ask Dorothy. And that goes forever. I don't mean stop just today, or just this wedding, or just this particular name-calling. I've had enough of it and don't pretend you don't know what I mean. You should know by now I mean what I say."

"Rida, I think that waiter is trying to get your attention to ask you something, maybe out in the kitchen," Jonquil Cartenbury said. "She doesn't mean it, Mr. Howland. I'm sure she doesn't."

Grandmother knew better. "I'm sure she does mean it, and I can't approve." She hesitated, then added, "Of talking to your father-in-law that way, Rida."

"Somebody needs to," Mumma maintained.

"That is your opinion," Grandmother said.

"I don't know what my son was thinking of, marrying you," Grandfather said. "I know what *you* were thinking of. Anybody with an ounce of sense could tell us that."

"Just remember, I warned you," Mumma repeated, before heading off for the kitchen where, as she knew as well as Jonquil Cartenbury, there was nobody needing her to offer an opinion.

THE WEDDING

Perhaps it would be true to say that as long as he lived, it was Grandfather who was Mumma's great enemy, and it was only after his death that Jonquil Cartenbury came to occupy that position, although it could also be truly said that it was only Jonquil Cartenbury with whom Mumma maintained a lifelong competition. Toward Grandfather she felt only distaste, disaffection, and a deep dislike, all of which he reciprocated. In the black-and-white photographs of the family at Aunt Anne's wedding, however, the visible emotion Grandfather displays is his unassailable pride. Grandfather was photogenic, tall, trim, and elegantly white-haired, his features strong, his morning coat perfectly fitted, his expression one of implacable dignity. Grandmother had equally strong bones, although hers were cast in a finer mold; also, she had carriage, a straight back and shoulders, her chin high, her hats modest. Grandmother was queenly. Beside them, Massimo Ruscelli is clearly from another world, although clearly he is an equal.

Clearly, at least, to any onlooker. It was never clear to Grandfather, and Grandmother was only dimly aware of how well their daughter had done, marrying Giancarlo, not only because of his cultural background and his own business successes but also because of his ability to endure and ignore, as if they did not matter, Howland assumptions of his inferiority. This for a man whose ancestors had been minor princes, and warriors too, long before either the Howlands or the Spencers had established their status by being among the first to set rough-shod feet on a wild new land. There were distinguished bastards in Giancarlo's family tree, and in the photographs Signor Ruscelli has the look of a man with that kind of ancestry — alert, confident, and a little dangerous. Standing beside him, Giancarlo looks like his father.

No wonder Mumma took to Giancarlo, and to his father as well. Between their good looks and goodwill and the combined rudenesses of the Howlands, there could be no contest for Mumma's partisanship. She didn't blame Pops. (*"Your father is a wonderful man,"* she used to tell us, *"but his head is in the clouds. It's not that he lacks the courage, he just doesn't notice. Once I tell him, he's always ready to do the right thing."*) At the ceremony itself, being an usher, Pops couldn't do the right thing alongside his wife, although he undoubtedly would have been told to and probably would have agreed. When Mumma arrived in the church, one daughter in her arms and the other at her side, she took the usher's crooked elbow and answered his traditional question with the word "Groom." Being a Spencer cousin, or a Howland cousin, the usher was surprised, but he was also a gentleman, and he did what the lady asked. Mumma and Meg and Jo were taken to join the scattering of people sitting in the left-hand pews of Saint Stephen's Episcopal Church in Wampanoag, employees and employers of Giancarlo's, a few friends, some of them with wives. She declined Capo Max's hopeful invitation to sit beside him *("The front row at a wedding is for the immediate family of the bridal couple, you girls remember that")* and had herself seated directly behind him *("So he would know he wasn't alone")*.

Jonquil Cartenbury was sent over to correct the error in urgent whispers. "I know," Mumma said. "So come back over with me," Jonquil Cartenbury concluded.

"I don't think so," Mumma said.

"But everybody —"

"You can explain. Explain however you like."

"But, Rida, you're supposed to —"

"I don't know that I *want* to sit down with

231

the family of the bride," Mumma said.

Jonquil Cartenbury hovered, the organ playing behind her, more guests arriving and being seated; eventually she retreated to the crowded right-hand side of the church. Nobody commented on Mumma's solipsism except Grandmother, who came up to her at the reception, gathered Jo into her own arms, and remarked, "I am not taking that personally."

"You're not one who should," Mumma assured her.

"Yes, well. A woman doesn't apologize for her husband," Grandmother told her, and hesitated a second before adding, "Or for her daughter-in-law."

("Your grandmother thought — no, she believed, it was like a faith for her, she believed it the way some people believe in God or science. She believed that it was the rules that made her life so easy. She thought life was about the rules people make for it, as if life was some kind of a board game and if you had a little luck, and you kept to the rules, you'd end up winning. Or maybe she thought it was like a game of solitaire and once the cards had been shuffled and laid out, if you had a good draw you were safe, as if it was arranged for you to win. Or to lose, although Grandmother considered herself someone

who had won, since all she had to do once she was born was follow the rules. But really, life's like a game of bridge: You're dealt a hand and it can be a winning hand or a losing one, but that doesn't necessarily mean that you'll win or lose because there are other people at the table, your partner for one, and the other team for another, that's three people —" "I can count, Mumma." "— playing too, and people make mistakes, multiply that times three and even with a bad hand you can win. Or you can fool people, multiply that times three too, or you can just be smarter than they are. And luckier too, because anybody who sits down to play bridge or life without figuring out how much luck is involved is making a Big Mistake. I don't want you girls doing that.")

MARRIED LIFE

The wedding behind them, the bridal couple sailed to Italy in the company of Signor Ruscelli and remained there for an extended honeymoon, returning early the following fall to a landscaping business in arrears, with a son of inexact age.

Grandfather was pleased with the boy; at least, he was pleased with his gender. At one of the long family dinners surrounding the holidays, he tackled Pops. "Even that greaser" — with a glance to see where

233

Mumma was — "husband of your sister's can get a son. When are you going to give me one to carry on our name? A Howland grandson: Is it too much to ask of you?"

"You've got Ethan, too," Pops answered, but Grandfather said, "The boy's not going to settle down for years, and why should he? It's up to Rida, but she seems determined to produce only girls."

"Actually," Pops told him, "it's the man who determines the gender of the child. That is to say, it's the sperm. Scientific fact, Father."

"I don't believe it," Grandfather said, and then having thought about this point, "What's wrong with you, then?"

Amy was born a year later, and then there was me, and at every birth Mumma had to listen to Grandfather comparing his son's masculinity to that of his sons-in-law. By then, however, Mumma had settled her family out on the Cape, and Pops had settled in contentedly at Brown, because, as Mumma pointed out, at Brown they knew his worth, they were pleased to have him as a doctoral candidate in their classics department, and they made it easy for him to work there. Living on the Cape, they went into Boston only for Mumma's weekly business meetings, for the inevitable family occasions, or if Mumma's real estate investments needed some direct interventions, since by the time I was three she owned and had renovated and rented out under separate managers six apartment buildings in North Cambridge. During those years, Mumma's business interests had to share her entrepreneurial attentions with the enterprise of her children, first the three, then the four girls, whom it was her job to raise and mold and advise and ultimately present to the world.

When Grandfather died — relatively young, in his early sixties, of cirrhosis — Mumma didn't want to go to the funeral, but Grandmother said she needed her there. The death somehow took Grandmother by surprise and, moreover, she felt the loss deeply. During the weeks that followed the funeral, Mumma often sat for hours in the living room of the Louisburg Square house while I slept on her lap, or on Grandmother's. It was not until a year and a half later that Grandmother finally emerged to reenter society. She had loved her husband. *("Of course she did, she had to, he was her husband. A woman can't despise her husband until they're divorced. Unless of course she's European; they do things differently over there.")*

■ ■ ■ ■

PART TWO:
LUCKY TO HAVE ME

■ ■ ■ ■

Prologue:
A Life

There followed the whole rest of my mother's life, years crammed with activities and commitments, weeks busy with conversations (some) and monologues (many), day after day balancing her maternal, business, and civic duties, being always herself. She was always herself, Rida Howland. Because all four of us bore witness to those years, we possess a plethora of facts, most of them presented through four separate and perhaps equal points of view. Thus, there is an overabundance of information, and that is the first of the three great obstacles to understanding our mother.

The second is the woman herself. What was she thinking? What guided her in the things she chose to tell us and what she required of us, what advice she gave and which opinions she aired? Did she even have a plan? We seem unable to determine this, although I see to it that we keep on trying.

And that is the third obstacle: Me. My obstinacy. I insist on continuing to try to understand our mother, apparently convinced, first, that this can be done and second, that I can do it. I am after all a scholar, as well as a long-time observer of the woman. I possess both direct information — she said that, she did this — and inferred — that is, all the material I have gleaned by observing the women my sisters have become, guided and shaped as they were by the experience of our mother. I listen to what they say. That each of them has reached a different conclusion doesn't surprise me.

"She was a realist," Amy announces.

"And a perfectionist," is Meg's opinion. "About everything, and all of us, too."

"Can a person be both a perfectionist and a realist?" I ask.

"A genuine humanist, too. I mean, as she got older," Jo remarks. "Didn't you think?"

"A humanist-realist-perfectionist? Is that possible?" I wonder at them.

"How about laying off the Socratic method for five minutes?" one of them will request, and another will comment, "What else can you expect from a *college professor*," pronouncing the last two words if not with an actual sneer then certainly stripped of the respect usually accorded us.

"Pops was never like that," the third will say.

"He had Mumma," I point out.

"She wouldn't have stood for it," we agree.

We mimic her voice: *"I was ahead of my times,"* and laugh.

If the early part of Mumma's life seems to have a narrative structure (one hurdle after another, o'erleapt), I suspect that this is only because they are the stories Mumma told about herself. She presented herself as she intended to be seen, perhaps made simple for our more simple minds, although it is equally possible that this is the person she believed she was. If she were telling the story of these subsequent years herself, would they also have clear dramatic shape and didactic purpose, as well as the same redoubtable heroine? Probably, but the only way I can present them is as a thematic narrative, involving swerves, not vaultings, growth, not change. Although, as far as I can see from observation of any woman's adult years, from the four women's lives I've observed most closely, this is entirely common.

Except, of course, that I'm talking about Mumma. Thus, while the topics are common, because it is Mumma who lived them

241

they assume capital letters: Motherhood, Wifehood, Friendship, Age, and then, inevitably, sadly . . . But not Death, really, so much as Absence. (Although in the case of my mother, this last is proving to be something of a *vale atque ave,* she having left behind what I can only think of as Aftermath, in the person of her youngest grandchild, Sarah, who is also and not incidentally — there being nothing incidental about Sarah — my own daughter.)

If we tend to mother the way we enjoyed being mothered, as I believe we do, and also the way we would have liked to have been mothered, that is to say by reflection and reaction, then I persist in the hope that by examining Mumma from all of the angles available to me I will learn. Not learn how to be a good mother to Sarah, who abandoned me on the sidewalk in front of the school building on the first day of kindergarten *("I don't need a mother anymore"),* but rather, to understand her, to know when to stand at her shoulder, when to sit in the stands and cheer her on, when to place myself squarely behind her, and when to throw myself in front of her onrushing train. Or even, maybe, when to come after her balloon with a hatpin. How to help her see that

she is loved and to know, about herself, that
her love is welcomed.

5.
MUMMA AND HER DAUGHTERS

HER DAUGHTERS AND MUMMA

It wasn't easy being Mumma's daughters; that was one thing we could all agree on when I was finally old enough for my sisters to treat me like a fully enfranchised human being. That age was ten, if I remember correctly, although it should be noted that among us four sisters, remembering correctly has always been a sore point and a hotly debated issue.

Since I was four years younger than Amy, then if I were ten Amy would have been fourteen, and she was two years younger than sixteen-year-old Jo, who was two years younger than Meg. Meg would have been starting college in the fall, so it must have been during the summer that I achieved my new, and proper, status.

It would have to have been summer also because we sat at the breakfast table, just the four of us, and we were eating bowls of cornflakes. During the school year such a thing could never have happened, the four of us alone at the breakfast table eating cold cereal. During the school year, Mumma's family always had a hot breakfast — eggs and toast, or pancakes with real maple syrup, oatmeal with raisins and brown sugar — always together, five days a week at 7 a.m., weekend mornings at 8, no matter what time you got to bed the night before. Dinner was another meal at which attendance was mandatory, but that was true year-round. There was no summer vacation from Mumma's dinner table and only rarely a day off. Friends, if any lingered until dinnertime, were asked to sit down with us, boyfriends, girlfriends, anybody to whom Mumma could show off her cooking. All of her life, once she got started, Mumma cooked eagerly and ambitiously, and also well. When Julia Child introduced American TV audiences to the arts of classic French cooking, Mumma took it as a personal vindication. *("You girls can laugh, but I was one of the first to eat from other countries. I was always ahead of my times.")*

That Cape Cod summer morning when we sat alone together at the breakfast table, I had just finished reading *Little Women* and announced my stunning discovery: "We're named the same as them. Do you think she did it on purpose?"

"What do you think, stupid?" Amy answered.

"Because if she did, I should be the one named Amy," I continued.

"Maybe she hoped we'd turn out like them," Jo said. "She probably wanted to be a mother like Marmee. She never had her own family, remember."

Amy decided, "They were Boston names. You know? Probably that's why she named you Meg, Meg, being the first, and then, you know how she is, once she makes up her mind she doesn't change it, she just keeps going."

"So I should be Amy," I repeated.

My sisters all looked at me with the same expression of impatient tolerance. They all had Mumma's thick curly hair and Pops' fine facial bones, as well as his blue eyes, although in Amy's case the blue was more gray, sometimes green, her eyes more of a light hazel than real blue, and in Jo's it was watery and pale. Meg and Jo were short, like Mumma, but Amy was tall, like me the tallest in her class, girl or boy. I had the misfortune to have gotten Pops' lank, colorless hair plus Mumma's thick eyebrows and determined chin. I'd also inherited my father's poor vision and so, like him, had to wear glasses for everything except close work. I was pretty much a disaster, genetically speaking; everyone agreed about that. They also — except for Pops — agreed that I was a disaster in all other respects as well. Stubborn, too. According to Mumma, stubbornness was my greatest fault.

But at ten I knew I was smarter than my sisters, and not just because Mumma told me I'd inherited my father's brains *("And don't let that go to your head, young lady")*, so I made it simple for them. "Amy should be Beth, the second youngest, and I should be the youngest, Amy, if we're named after the book. Which is what you all just agreed we are."

"Mumma gets things wrong," Amy said. "Haven't you figured that out yet? She gets a lot of things wrong. Like you, you're one of her mistakes."

I asked, "What did she say when you asked her about our names?"

"Why would we ask her?" they wondered.

"The woman has no idea why she does most of what she does," Amy said. "I'd have thought Bethy would have figured that out, if she's supposed to be such a girl genius."

"Don't call me Bethy!"

"I wouldn't go asking Mumma about our

names," Meg advised. "I know you're thinking of it."

Jo told me why. "Mumma likes to think we don't figure things out."

"And we like her to think she's right," Amy added. She always joined up with the other two, three against one. So of course I asked Mumma.

Actually, I didn't ask her so much as shriek it at her, in the midst of one of our heated quarrels. "You named me Beth because you want me to be the one to die!"

"I don't want anyone to die!" Mumma shrieked back at me. "What's the matter with you!"

"I should be Amy!" Then I was struck by a disquieting and yet exhilarating thought and I stopped shrieking. "You *did* get it wrong. You can be wrong, you'll just never admit it."

"You can change your name legally if that's what you want, when you're eighteen," Mumma answered.

I reported this back to my sisters. "I can change my name, legally. When I turn eighteen, Mumma said."

Jo groaned. "You didn't *tell* her."

"I think actually it's fourteen," Amy said.

"How could you do that to us?" Meg asked me.

"Do what? It's the truth, after all. I *should* be Amy. Anyway, it doesn't matter," I assured them, and I remember thinking that my sisters often lacked proper perspective.

Disparate and divided as we were, we still thought of ourselves as the four Howland girls, although my sisters subdivided us into three of a kind, with bright brown hair and regular fine features, and me, the unfortunate final fourth. We were unquestionably a band of four under the same relentless guiding hand, or, as Mumma might have said, we were the four tires of the family car of which Pops was the driver while she was the chassis. (We would have said *she* was the driver.) Pops sometimes called us the Four Horsemen of the Apocalypse, and at other times the four leaves of his lucky clover, but Mumma's metaphors emphasized our differences, making us the four seasons, the four points of her compass. "You were all pulling in different directions, all the time," she said. "No wonder I didn't have a life of my own until I was almost forty, what with a husband, and you girls, and the house, plus my business."

"What about Polly?" I asked. "Polly kept your house for you all those years and you've forgotten her? Most of your life when you had young children, Polly was there."

"After Polly left," Mumma specified, "it wasn't easy. One child is a full-time job. Especially if it's a girl," she said, with her baleful eye fixed on me.

"It's not like you were trapped at home. What about all those meetings you hauled me to?" I asked, but, "You were too young to remember them," Mumma said.

Whereas my own childhood was spent sitting in one corner or another of Mumma's purposeful life, my sisters had Mumma sharing every corner of theirs. Before I learned to be grateful for that, I was jealous. When I was fourteen, just starting high school, I tried to let my sisters know I hadn't had the same amount and quality of attention as the three of them and to complain about how Mumma treated me differently, no matter *what* she said *("I treated all of you exactly the same, always," she maintained)* — and I had my evidence at the ready: "She was always worrying about *your* problems, *your* grades, *your* boyfriends. She always talked about you three and how she could help you out."

"Don't you get it? You didn't have any problems. She didn't need to go barging around into your life, straightening it out. You're the one she left alone. No wonder we hated you."

"*That* I did notice," I told them.

"Not really," Jo said. "We didn't really hate *you*. Just as a sister."

"And I *did* have problems. In case you remember, it was Meg who was the perfect daughter."

"I had to be, didn't I? I'm the oldest, the firstborn, she was all over me. She never let up, she never left me alone. No wonder I married so young."

"Actually," I said to my oldest sister, "the wonder is that you stayed married for more than six months. Mumma was pretty relentless about getting you away from Jack Cartenbury."

But Meg was on a rant and didn't pay any attention. "I didn't have the *choice* to do badly in school. Don't you remember the first B I ever got? It was the end of the world."

"I remember that it wasn't until you were a junior in high school," Jo said. "And I remember that for me, a B was over-the-top excellent."

"Mumma went ballistic over that B I got," Meg remembered.

"No," Jo said. "Ballistic was Mr. Smithers."

Amy covered her face, and we were all silenced by the memory of that spring of

1959, and Mumma. "It was all so . . ." Amy spoke from behind her hands. Then she lowered them, and her cheeks shone pink. "I've never been so embarrassed. And furious too, for all the good that ever did me with Mumma. I'll never forgive her," she promised.

MUMMA AND AMY

Mr. Smithers taught Amy's sixth-grade class, and he was one of those unusually charismatic practitioners of the teaching trade who sometimes come along. I've seen a few of them in action and I never know whether to think of them as saints just back from the desert, with their visionary eyes and compelling certainties, or as pied pipers, who lure the young away into mountain fastnesses. They are always the popular teachers. They are usually young men, young women with these qualities tending to find other arenas more satisfying and more rewarding, just as most such young men are found in politics or on a stage. They are rare in education, such young men, and even rarer at the elementary school level. Mr. Smithers was one of them.

He was young, he rode a motorcycle, he wore a jacket and tie to school, he was funny, he worked hard, long hours at full attention, and every Thursday his wife baked cookies for him to give his class at Friday lunch. Mr. Smithers was loved by his students and thus their parents, and naturally also the school principal. He was envied by other teachers. His sixth-graders presented no discipline problems. They did not cheat on tests or assignments. They did their homework carefully and went to school gladly. Amy was in his class and I, a second-grader, could bask in some of the glory of that accomplishment. "My sister's got Mr. Smithers, and he says . . ." I could report to my classmates. He had been at Wampanoag Elementary only since September, but already by Halloween Mr. Smithers was a legend.

So that when Amy for the second February morning in a row complained of an undefined sickness, maybe in her stomach, she thought she might throw up, Mumma was suspicious. Her early-warning system was always up and running, her vigilance perpetual, her red alert formidable.

Also, Mumma had read Freud, who in her opinion didn't know as much as he and everybody else gave him credit for, as well as Jung and Winnicott, plus Melanie Klein for a woman's point of view. She took pride in her knowledge and understanding of human psychology, and in her ability to ferret out the hidden pistons that drive and define character. She was ready for Amy that second morning.

"You're trying to get out of going to school."

"No I'm not. I'm sick."

"You don't have a temperature."

"I feel nauseous."

"You don't look nauseous. You ate all of your breakfast."

"You made me."

"If you were really sick I wouldn't be able to make you eat. So what's the matter at school?"

"Nothing," spoken in the sullen, secretive way that really means *I'm not going to tell you.*

"The rest of you go brush your teeth, I want to talk to Amy in private," Mumma told us. Pops had already left on his commute to Providence. It was midwinter, raw and cold on the Cape. Once she had Amy alone, Mumma asked, "Tell me. It won't go any farther, you know you can trust me."

About that she was right. We did know it. Even so, Amy insisted, "I'm just sick."

"Is there a test you haven't studied for?" A shake of the head. "Are you in trouble?" Another shake. "Have you had a fight with

255

Jeannine and Helen?" Not that, either. "I don't have all day, Amy. You'd better just tell me."

A shake of the head.

This began to seriously puzzle Mumma, since Amy was not the stubborn, pigheaded one, that being my role. Amy had the part of the reasonable daughter. Meg could be asked for cooperation, as a favor, and Jo tricked into it through her empathetic nature, but Amy could be persuaded.

"If something's wrong —"

"Nothing's wrong!" Amy cried, so impulsively that Mumma was immediately confident that she had her finger on it.

"How can I fix it if you won't tell me what it is?"

"Why can't I just not go to school? Why won't you leave me alone when I'm sick?"

"Because you're not sick, as you very well know. Are the boys saying or doing things?"

Mumma asked this because in sixth grade many of the girls were "developing," as the euphemism of the time went. The suggestion that there was anything any boy in her class could get up to that she couldn't handle pricked Amy's pride. "They wouldn't dare."

"But you're ashamed."

"I'm not."

"All right, embarrassed."

"Never mind. I'm going to school, and if you have to come get me in an hour don't blame me."

"I never blame any of you for being sick. You know that perfectly well, Amy Howland, just as perfectly well as I know that something is going on. You can go ahead to school, but don't think I'm not going to look into it, when something is going on with one of my daughters."

"Mumma?" Amy was all anxiety now, pleading. "Don't, please? I'm really sorry. I won't do it again."

As she plowed through the busynesses of her day, Mumma decided that the difficulty was that Amy had a crush on her teacher and wanted to stay home so that she could arouse his interest by getting him to worry about her health. Moreover, in Mumma's opinion, Amy was not the kind of girl to be shallow about this. Overly emotional Jo *was* that kind of girl, but Amy was serious and realistic, the sort of girl to feel her first crush deeply. Satisfied with her insight and this analysis, Mumma decided to ignore it. The path of wisdom, for a mature woman and a good mother, was silence.

But silence was never a path Mumma traveled for any distance. Only one or two days later, going into Amy's bedroom to say good night, she turned the conversation to school and thence to Mr. Smithers, to sing his praises and gauge Amy's reaction, which was, "He's not so great." Amy turned her face into her pillow so that her words came out muffled, unclear. "Everybody thinks he's so great."

"You said the same. In September, I remember you saying that."

"Did not. I never." Amy turned around to face Mumma, her cheeks flushed. "That was you, you said it. I just didn't argue back. I don't like to argue with you because why bother because you never let anyone else win."

"You're tired and cross," Mumma answered. "Get a good night's sleep. You'll feel better in the morning."

At Amy's door, struck by a bolt of insight, Mumma wheeled around. That she spoke without thinking goes without saying. "What is it about Mr. Smithers, if it's not a crush?"

"A crush?" Amy sat up in bed. "That's just — That's *sick*. You think I have a *crush* on him?"

"So it's the antithesis." This was Mumma's reading in psychology coming in useful again. "And that means you're afraid. What is it, Amy, does he . . . ?"

Here, words failed her. The 1950s were not years when anyone spoke openly about being groped by boys in the cloakrooms, or other perils of adolescence for girls, and never the dubious responses of many older men to those ripening bodies. This was an era when menstruation was called The Curse and sexual education consisted of presenting ten- or eleven-year-old girls with copies of *Growing Up* and *Being Born,* two slender books with an absence of mechanical details, not even the accepted Latin terms that doctors used. *Down there* and *It* constituted the sexual vocabulary of well-brought-up girls at that time. So Mumma didn't know how to ask her daughter if the teacher was copping a feel, or worse.

"Does he try to kiss . . . ?"

"You're disgusting!" Amy cried, and covered her head with the bedclothes. "Can't you leave me alone? Please!" From under the bedclothes came muffled sounds of unsuccessfully stifled weeping.

This convinced Mumma. "A mother knows," was all she planned to tell us and, moreover, being Mumma, that mother knew just what she wanted to do about this . . . this *teacher,* if her suspicions were correct, not to mention that mother being as well the secretary of the PTA, over whose collective eyes he had so successfully been pulling so much wool. But if the '50s was an era without a vocabulary, especially among nice people, it was also an era that idealized its professionals.

In the '50s, professionals were an Olympian breed, above questions, beyond reproach and, perhaps not incidentally, almost uniformly male. Doctors were all skilled and sober, lawyers hungry only for justice, bankers wise conservators, priests saintly, and teachers, of course, reliable arbiters of intelligence and behavior. Children might lie and cheat, but teachers were morally upright. Parents did not doubt teachers, any more than citizens doubted their president or the nation its warriors. It was, in short, an innocent and unsuspicious era. The '50s often failed to protect its children, its patients, its clients, and its citizens from a variety of evils, many of which more modern times have named and numbered and guard zealously against. Mumma was not, however, one to jump to conclusions. She prided herself on objectivity and thoroughness. If it happened that most of the conclusions she reached after objective and thorough inquiry were the same as those she would have jumped to, had she jumped, that did not surprise her.

In the case of Mr. Smithers, she inquired first among other PTA parents. Those with children in lower grades were figuring out ways to maneuver their sons and daughters into his sixth-grade class. Those with sons in the sixth grade spoke with relief about his easy management of their unruly offspring. Some parents of girls were not so enthusiastic, although neither were they concerned; any changes they put down to "developing." All of the parents Mumma talked to were mothers, although they spoke for two: "We're hoping she'll get this moody phase over with quickly; she's always been such a sunny child"; "I guess we were hoping she'd never grow up"; "He even cares about getting his homework done, we can't believe it."

Mumma then took her suspicions to the principal and the principal resisted, probably put off by both Mumma's directness and the idea itself. Mumma cited her proofs, pointing out the physical maturity of those girls whose attitudes to school had changed and the physical immaturity or the gender of those children who were apparently untroubled, even glad to be in the class. "I think he's taking advantage of some of the girls," Mumma said, employing another euphemism of the time.

The principal leaned back in her chair for judicious thought before she announced, "Girls. Well. You know what they're like, Mrs. Howland, you have . . . four of them, isn't it? And two in the upper grades, so you know what adolescent girls can be like."

"I'm not talking about the girls. I'm talking about the teacher," Mumma said.

"Dealing with adolescent girls can be tricky," the principal said.

"So you're not going to do anything about it," Mumma said.

"I didn't say that."

"Then what are you going to do?"

"I'll look into it, of course. But I have to ask you to remember, Mrs. Howland, that he is a young man with a family to support. I'm sure you don't want to destroy his reputation. I *will* tell you that there was no hint of anything amiss in his recommendations from his last school, which was in Troy, New York. Everyone knows how excellent the New York school system is. Possibly the best in the country. Everyone knows how irrationally adolescent girls can behave. Think of the Salem witch trials."

"I'm not saying he's a witch," Mumma answered. "Or a warlock," she specified.

The principal ended the meeting. "The matter is in my hands now. You can leave it to me, Mrs. Howland."

Of course, Mumma didn't do that. Giving Polly charge of her family, Mumma drove off to Troy, New York, to be thorough, which for Mumma meant: Not giving up until you proved that you were right.

She met with the principal of Mr. Smithers's former school, and then talked to two or three parents, and the evasions with which she was presented convinced her. *("When people start trying on half-truths, and dodging subjects, they might as well just go ahead and tell the truth and I don't know why they don't because who do they think they're fooling?")* By the time she returned to the Cape, where spring was just beginning to soften the blues of the sky and the crocuses had only that week come up, hesitant and untrusting, she had devised a plan of action. That plan was typical Mumma, unnervingly direct and disquietingly subtle. Mumma announced to the principal that she was thinking of going into teaching, so she needed to observe a successful teacher in the classroom, and who better for that purpose than Mr. Smithers? How could the principal refuse?

All spring, Mumma went to school with Amy, every day, and remained there from homeroom to dismissal, stuffed into a desk at the rear of the classroom. At first, Amy was furious and embarrassed. Then she was miserable and ashamed. Every morning there was a scene at the breakfast table, Mumma implacably maintaining her career goals and Amy reduced more and more quickly to hysterical tears. There were classroom repercussions for Amy, as well, and recess repercussions. Even I suffered the shock waves, former friends now shunning me as the daughter of the mother who was going to sixth grade.

Every morning of that unending spring, Mumma entered Mr. Smithers's sixth-grade classroom. She wore a bright flowered dress and high heels, stockings, lipstick; she carried a purse and a briefcase; she sat at her desk, sometimes writing, sometimes reading, never changing her story. "I'm learning how to teach. I'm observing." She even went outside to enjoy the fresh air at recesses. I could pretend not to see her and run away when she called me, but Amy was not so fortunate.

"I'm really getting to know your sister, and that's an added benefit," Mumma said, giving the rest of us cold chills as she assured us, "Don't ever think I wouldn't do the same for any one of you."

All that spring, Amy's refrain was "I hate

you! I hate you!"

"No you don't," Mumma assured her.

"You've ruined my life," Amy insisted. "You're ruining my life!"

"I'm not," Mumma promised.

Mumma never directly accused Mr. Smithers. She just sat in his classroom, curtailing his activity. As she told the story in later years, after a couple of weeks he did ask, "Mrs. Howland, just what are you doing here?" and she answered, "You know." Apparently he did, because although he was offered a contract for the next school year, Mr. Smithers decided to decline it, and — on Mumma's good advice, she claimed, and Mumma never lied — left teaching. "You work well with people," she told him, more of her unsolicited opinions. "You don't drink, and you've got a good sense of humor."

"Why are you telling me this?" he asked her.

"He was falling in love with me," Mumma assured us, "and when someone loves you they believe what you say, which makes it a lot easier to help them out. I told him he'd be good in a liquor store, or a bar, and I happened to know where there were some opportunities in that field in Boston, for his fresh start." Thus Mr. Smithers moved out of our school system and out of our lives.

"Nobody is speaking to me!" Amy cried, all that summer. She had always been the popular sister and solitude preyed on her spirits, undermining her characteristic practicality, so that her every remark was desperate. "It's all your fault! You ruined his life! I've ruined his life and they all blame me! I never said anything about him and you just decided you knew everything! They all hate me!"

Mumma predicted, "You'll end up thanking me."

"You don't understand!"

Mumma knew better. Hadn't she seen the effects on her sisters-in-law of growing up with a drunken bully? "People may be the ruin of their own lives, but it's other people that get them started," was Mumma's analysis.

"I don't care about Mr. Smithers!" Amy shrieked from behind the hands that covered her face whenever his name was mentioned.

"It's not Mr. Smithers I'm worried about. It's men," Mumma told her.

Amy regained her practicality, muttering, "It's not men who are so bad, it's mothers."

"What's that, young lady? After everything I did for you this spring?"

"You mean ruining my life?"

"Didn't you hear what I said? Only *you* can ruin your life. But I'm not going to let that happen."

ENTER OLYMPIA

Mumma asked our family doctor and he recommended Olympia Frieling, the silver lining to the dark cloud Mr. Smithers had spread over our family. Olympia, as she insisted everyone call her, became Mumma's personal parental aid, and she helped us, too. She was our personal child aid. Except for me, that is.

Twice weekly, all that summer and on into the fall, Amy was dropped off at Olympia's office in Hyannis, to be picked up an hour later. At first, Mumma grilled her on the drive home ("What did you talk about? What did she say? What did you ask her?"), then Olympia asked Mumma to come into the office. Amy delivered the message to Mumma, at dinner.

"I don't know about that," Mumma said to us, where we were gathered around a table piled high with corn on the cob and, probably, fried chicken. "I don't have anything to hide."

"Maybe it's not *you* she wants to talk about," grumbled Amy.

Mumma knew better. "You girls think

you're the center of the world, but I can assure you that's not the case. I'm a pretty interesting person myself, aren't I, Spencer?"

"I've always thought so," Pops answered.

Satisfied, Mumma made eye contact with each of us, one after the other. We all ate in silence for a minute until, tired of waiting for somebody else to say it, I pointed out, "So's Pops an interesting person."

"I'm going to keep the appointment," Mumma announced. "I'm doing it for you, Amy, so don't say I never did anything for you. But only once."

Olympia, of course, wanted to tell Mumma to leave Amy her privacy, and Mumma, uncharacteristically, cooperated; although, of course, she never reported back to us about her appointment. We pestered her, to find out, and deduced from her subsequent conduct what had been said, but, "It's none of your beeswax," she insisted. "I'm not going back, but I've got a lot of respect for Olympia."

Amy, being practical, was the easiest sell on psychotherapy, and when the times came that Mumma wanted first Meg and then Jo to Talk to Someone, Amy's experience made that a non-threatening suggestion, even for teenagers. "She used Olympia instead of dealing with us herself," Amy says, and the others agree. "I guess I'm the only one who didn't have the crazies," I say. "Right," they agree. "You and Mumma." I throw my absolute proof down before them like a gauntlet: "I'm the one who never had to talk to Olympia."

They have had to concede the point. We all know how unusual it was for one of us *not* to do what the others had done. "Those mothers who play favorites don't do anybody any good," Mumma told us. "I don't want you girls having a mother like that." Mumma's standards required that all four of us be offered, and accept, the various activities that marked well-brought-up girls of our era — lessons in piano, ballet, sailing and tennis in the summer, riding in the fall and spring; we went to Sunday school three seasons a year and, when we were old enough, to the ballroom dance classes offered at the Club at Hyannis. Mumma drove us to our various appointments and commitments, fulfilling our separate schedules. Of course, in spite of the careful similarities in our upbringings, Mumma also wanted us to be individuals, separate and private, and this complicated the schedule. "I grew up with eight girls to a room," she said. "I want my girls each to have her own room, and decorated the way she chooses." She told us, "You'd like a cheerful yellow," or, "You're the feminine lacy type, with flounces," and we tended not to contradict her.

In fact, I liked my Spartan bedroom, with its wooden bookcases and desk, its dark blue curtains and rag rug. It was the kind of room a person could study in, Mumma said, and I was the kind of person who studied. "Like your father, you're just like your father," she told me, explaining me to myself.

Olympia advised Mumma that their adolescence was easiest on the families of girls who had activities, so Mumma made sure we each developed one of our own. I was easy: I studied. Meg played tennis well enough for that to count. She won at least two Club trophies a year, which Mumma displayed in a living room bookshelf so that anyone who noticed could ask. Jo was dramatic and creative, one summer taking drawing lessons, the next an acting class, then a ceramics course, until she was old enough to volunteer at the Hyannis summer theater, where she painted sets and rehearsed lines with professional actors, some of them famous. Amy was a problem, until Mumma decided that her third daughter had a gift for languages, specifically French, so she took French language and conversation courses at the high school and was even sent off to Maine one summer for two weeks of French camp, where she spoke only French and ate only French food.

Being nothing if not symmetrical, Mumma also assigned to each of us some activity we particularly disliked. Amy tried to avoid having to cook, which made sense to Mumma since "We're all such good cooks, both of her big sisters, which is sibling rivalry, and don't forget *me*. Whatever people might say, a girl *can* have sibling rivalry with her mother. Why should she want to compete with us and lose?" I myself hated tennis and Jo dreaded the sailing classes offered by the yacht club, so unimportant a place at that time that it didn't even have a pennant. Jo actually liked boats, and being out on the water, where the rhythms of wind and waves and the sun-warmed air enabled her to lose herself in her own thoughts. But sailing classes involved four or five teenagers packed into an eighteen-foot Lightning, one of them transformed into a skipper and desperate to win, and this as far as Jo was concerned sucked all the pleasure out of the sport. She hated those classes, although she has always owned a kayak, which is the only place in Jo's world where, once she discovered smoking, cigarettes were never in evidence. However, none of us could equal the intensity of Meg's dislike for dance classes. Then again, we didn't have her reason.

MUMMA AND MEG

The nadir of Meg's youth was the dance class into which, in the fall of 1959, Mumma enrolled her. The Boston Cotillion was a full school year of instruction in ballroom dance, which Grandmother assured Mumma was necessary for a Howland. Through the Boston Cotillion, Gemma Hustling and her husband had for decades offered well-born young Bostonians an opportunity not only to learn the dance steps but also to gain experience in social behaviors. The Cotillion's classes led up first to a Christmas Ball and then to the great May Cotillion, to which the three previous graduated classes were also invited, for the purpose of giving the girls a chance to look over the crop of possible escorts for their debutante year.

Predictably, Mumma objected, until Grandmother reminded her, "Even Spencer attended Cotillion, Rida. You don't want the child to be socially inept, do you?"

Unspoken: *Like you.* And Grandmother had read Mumma correctly; she planned for her daughters to have any advantage they could, and she determined that Meg should do it. "The rest of you will get your chances after," she promised us.

Nobody, especially Meg, agreed with Mumma that Meg needed to do this, but every Saturday that fall, Mumma and Meg drove off after lunch to the Louisburg Square house, and for three hours every Saturday evening Mumma joined other mothers on rows of folding chairs set up behind the line of slim pillars at the back of the ballroom of the Park Hotel to watch their sons and daughters learn the box step, the foxtrot and waltz, the three-step and the tango, all the basics for ballroom dancing. Sunday mornings, while back on the Cape Pops delivered the rest of us to Sunday school at Saint Stephen's in Wampanoag and Meg went to Trinity Church with Grandmother, Mumma made a tour of her properties and talked to her managers, picking up the bills and receipts for the week. On Sunday afternoons she brought Meg home, the car loaded with pastas and Parmesan and porcini mushrooms from the North End, greens, sauces, and sometimes even fortune cookies from Chinatown.

After ten such weekends, it was time for the Christmas Ball.

Meg didn't want to go.

"You never want to," Mumma pointed out.

"This time I really, really don't want to," Meg said. "All the other times you get your way, so why can't I get mine this one time? It's not fair."

"I never said I was in the business of fair. Did I, girls? Did any of you ever hear me say that? Spencer?"

"They hate me," Meg told her.

"You mean you hate them," argued Mumma the psychologist. "And you don't," added Mumma the humanist. "Hate's a big word."

"I'll have a terrible time," Meg predicted.

"No you won't. I'll be right there, and your father, too."

Maybe Meg believed what Mumma said, or maybe she just gave way to the inexorable. On the Saturday of the Christmas Ball, Pops, in his tuxedo, escorted Mumma, in a scoop-neck, floor-length, orange, white, and black plaid taffeta gown with some family diamonds around her neck, and Meg, who wore a green velvet dress with lace at the cuffs and collar, to the Park Hotel. Meg was delivered into the hands of the Hustlings, after which Mumma led Pops to the front row of the seats assigned to the parents. *("I don't know who they thought they were, these Hustlings, or these parents, either, the way we sat to watch like we were an audience, or maybe like those society people in ancient England. You'll know I'm right when you read her books, Jane Austen. And those dance cards with little gold pencils attached, and everybody wearing white gloves? As if Boston was England. And England in 1815, which even in 1815 Boston wasn't. Boston's America.")*

Except for Jonquil and Francis Cartenbury, with whom she didn't mix, Mumma didn't know the other parents, and while Pops had grown up with many of them, he had nothing to say to them. They, in their turn, had no interest in the Spencer Howlands. So Mumma and Pops talked to each other over the background noises of friends greeting one another, offering brandy from sterling silver flasks, offering flames from golden lighters to cigarettes concealed behind cupped hands.

The occasion began with a procession, the young people circling the dance floor arm in arm, an equal number of boys and girls, in their finery, on parade. This display completed, the girls went to one side of the room, where gilt chairs had been set in a line, and the boys to the opposite, chairless side. The Hustlings put on a Frank Sinatra record and boys drifted over to the girls' side of the room and girls wrote with tiny pencils on their dance cards. That done, Lester Lanin's arrangement of Glenn Miller's "In the Mood" was played and the couples went out onto the dance floor. Girls placed their gloved hands on boys' right shoulders, boys placed their gloved hands at the backs of girls' waists, they joined remaining gloved hands, and couples danced.

Nobody had asked Meg for the first dance. She remained seated.

Skirts swirled in a two-step, and dark-clad legs executed turns. When the music stopped, gloved hands clapped in muted thanks, as if the record player were a real band, while couples left the floor, speaking in murmurs, then separated to change partners for the second dance, the girls consulting their dance cards before looking around, waiting to be claimed.

Nobody had asked Meg for the second dance either. Records changed and partners changed and Meg, sometimes the only girl sitting alone, occupied a chair at the side of the long room, during the third dance, the fourth.

Mumma and Pops fell into a silence. Pops took Mumma's hand. This, he knew, had to be endured. He had been born in Boston, he had grown up going to cotillions. Admittedly, he was aware that it was up to the Hustlings to make sure that a girl danced at least a few times in the course of the two and a half hours, to see that the boys understood that no girl was to be embarrassed in this way. He remembered, further, that other boys would cut in on the unlucky fellow, that they all understood what was expected of a gentleman. Pops also knew the parental roles on such occasions. He knew, for example, that even though Mumma first asked him to, then told him in a furious whisper that he should, and even though he desperately wanted to, he could not cross the dance floor and ask his daughter to partner him, putting her into the protection of his arms.

Meg knew this too. That would be a humiliation worse than being a wallflower. She never once looked over to where Mumma and Pops were sitting. By unwritten rule — most rules in these situations being unwritten — the overseeing parents were like the audience at a theater, in the theatrical convention not present.

Mumma knew none of this, and when it

was told to her in apologetic whispers, she was unconvinced. After half an hour, perhaps a little more, she had stood as much as she intended to. She rose from her seat, a plaid avenging apparition, her red hair flashing more brightly than her diamonds. She marched around to the Hustlings, to whom she had a thing or two to say, and then down the length of the dance floor, cutting her swathe through the foxtrotting couples.

Meg's face burned red with embarrassment. Mumma's face burned red with anger. Meg tried to deter Mumma by shaking her head, and tried to refuse the hand that Mumma held out to her by putting both of hers behind her back.

(Years later, when she could talk about it, Meg said that she thought her mother was offering to be her dance partner. She had thought she had been doing a good job of sitting there with a smile fixed on her face, her eyes fixed on the hands clasped on her lap, joining in the pretense of her own invisibility. She knew that all she had to do was wait out the time. That was what you did. You endured. She could do it.)

Mumma had no intention of offering to partner Meg. She just wasn't willing to sit there and watch her daughter be treated like this, in this apparently acceptable way, or anybody else's daughter, either, but other people's children were their business. Meg was hers, so she seized Meg by the elbow and walked her along the dance floor, past the dancing couples and the record player, past the Hustlings and out the door.

Pops waited in the lobby, ready to take them home. He had his own chesterfield on and carried the other two coats over his arm. He held out Mumma's fur for her to slip her arms into before he took Meg's coat to hold it open for her. By that time Mumma had decided on her course of action. "Take us to the Rose Room," she told Pops. "You can dance with her there. She's a good dancer." But Meg was in tears, tears streaming down her cheeks, and Pops gave her his handkerchief and Mumma was thwarted in her attempt to make it all up to her child. "I couldn't take her anywhere, looking like that," Mumma said later. "I don't know what people would have thought."

Meg wept all that evening, and all the next day, weeping into her pillow at night and then oozing tears out of swollen eyes at Grandmother's Louisburg Square breakfast table, where Mumma announced, "She doesn't want to talk about it. Don't ask her." Meg wept all the way back to the

Cape, first in the back seat and then, in an unprecedented privilege, in the front seat, Pops having been relegated to the back. "Don't ask her," Mumma told us, when they arrived home.

The next day, Monday, Mumma promised Meg, "You're never going back there," to which Meg, being the firstborn, didn't respond that she hadn't wanted to go in the first place and had, moreover, specifically asked *not* to go to the Christmas Ball. "And neither is any other one of my daughters," Mumma decreed. She called Olympia then, and Meg got to have therapy all that winter and spring. "I don't want there to be any long-range repercussions from this," Mumma said, and when Meg became one of the popular girls in high school, with boys standing in lines to ask her to parties, dances, movies, sailing, ice skating, roller skating, drive-in eateries, drive-in movies, and riding around in cars, Mumma was satisfied with her handling of the situation. "Don't ever think I wouldn't do everything I can to make you happy," she told us. "You girls think life is like Christmas, nothing but presents all wrapped up in pretty packages. Or maybe — I know you; nobody knows you as well as your mother, never forget that — maybe you think life is like a birthday, only for you, your special day when every-thing goes the way you want it to and every-one gives you what you want."

"Not me," I said. "I don't think that."

"You always want to be different," Mumma observed.

"Unlike you." I was in the sarcastic stage that lasted, for me, from about third grade until Mumma decided I was old enough to be left at home alone, not dragged around behind her to her every commitment and activity, which might have been when I was about in tenth grade.

"You've got me wrong. I want to do things right, and if that makes me different then so be it," Mumma riposted. "Miss I'm-Smarter-than-the-Rest-of-You. You don't know as much as you think you do, Beth."

"I know that," I told her. "How dumb do you think I am?"

"Not as dumb as you sometimes act, I hope," Mumma said. "I hope I'm not wrong about you. I don't think I'm wrong about any of you."

MUMMA AND JO

Mumma had theories about her daughters. She had her ambitions for us, too: social ambitions, career ambitions, marital ambi-tions, character ambitions, and personal happiness ambitions; not to mention a list of the errors and misjudgments we were likely to make, all of which she set down before us at various times and from varying perspectives.

It was Jo's future that she focused on, because given Jo's emotional, impetuous nature, she might throw away future happiness to satisfy some impulse — get pregnant, get thrown out of school, get in trouble with the law. Or fall in love with a seriously wrong boy. Or become addicted to drugs, since she obviously had an addictive personality. Didn't she refuse to stop smoking even though Mumma *and* the Surgeon General warned against it? Jo was first sent to talk with Olympia when Mumma realized how often she lied for her friends, both boys and girls, to cover up for them, to protect them from some hostility, sometimes even to give them undeserved credit for an assignment, an opinion or deed, although never, Mumma reminded us with satisfaction, to get herself out of trouble.

Mumma intended Jo to be happy in life, whatever that might mean, and she knew that the line between delusion and idealism could be wavery, unless of course a girl was an artist of some sort, an actress or writer, which Jo did not have the talent to be, of which Mumma was confident. So Mumma aimed for Jo's happiness to be based on something solid. At the dinner table, appearing to talk to all of us, she offered advice to her second daughter: "You girls will never have to worry about money," she promised us, then added to Jo, "So worry about what work you're good at, so you can be happy in a job. Don't ever think work is only about money." She included the rest of us in the next observation: "Right now you think life is like watching some TV show, where you sit on the sofa and there's nothing you need to do except watch what you're going to be given, but life's not like that. Unless, really, it's like a TV show and you're the director, which means," she announced, "you *have* to make the choices. Think about it, especially you, Jo. You can't daydream a life, don't ever think you can. All you can daydream is a daydream."

Amy, with her inherent practicality and her knowledge of French, Mumma pointed toward an economics degree. "There's the World Bank, isn't there, Spencer? Or the United Nations, they have plenty of committees for economics. But don't ever think there's anything wrong with staying home, especially you, Meg. Home is where the heart is, they're right when they say that, and a heart needs to stay home." In high school, Amy signed herself up for bookkeeping and business math, leading Mumma to dreams of having a CPA in the family, and Meg's social and academic high school successes met with her approval. For Jo she needed a different kind of plan, more direct instruction. "You're a communicator, really. Don't forget that just because you think you're in love. Not that I'm against love, or marriage. You know better than to think that. You could study psychology, even if college is still school and you know how bad you are at school, but I'm your mother and I've read everything. I can help you."

Jo got to go back for a second round of Olympia's counseling when, for the third time, her heart had been cruelly broken and her good nature abused by the kind of young man who is in trouble at school and at home, misunderstood and in existential crisis, also heavily into pot. "Not the right kind of boy for you," Mumma told Jo. "You liked him," Jo wailed at Mumma, who didn't deny it. "But not for your boyfriend, I never said that."

"You said he was interesting! You said he was gifted!"

"He was, he maybe is, how would I know a thing like that? But just because someone's interesting, and maybe gifted, that doesn't mean he's a good person to fall in love with. I told you, Jo, I told you he wants someone who will spend her life making him feel important and I don't want you to be that. I know you think you want someone who needs you, to take care of, but that's just a big baby. You're going to be bad enough with a real baby, if you ever have any which, if you ask me you shouldn't."

"But I told you I loved him and you didn't say anything to stop me!" Jo argued but Mumma declined to accept that responsibility.

"If something's gone as far as loving him, what can I do? I don't know about you, Jo. I really don't. You girls think love is like some boat that comes up to the dock to pick you up, and you step aboard and off you sail. I don't know why I bother bringing you to live so close to the ocean if you can't look and see what it's really like. Or maybe, some ocean liner, the ocean liner of love, and you've got the movie star suite. But really, it's a rowboat and you have to propel it yourself, or if you're lucky you get to row in tandem. And you have to build it yourself, too. Unless it's more like a canoe, because of how tippy canoes are. Some boys — don't ever think this isn't worth knowing, girls, and you especially, Jo — Some boys are leaky boats, their love is a leaky boat, and you'll spend all your time patching it. Or working the pumps to keep from sinking, and I can promise you that's hard work, but you're afraid you might drown. So because you think you might drown you keep patching and pumping when really, you know how to swim, if you weren't so afraid of drowning. Are you listening to this, Jo? Of course," she continued, with a considering glance at her second daughter, "some people want to drown, with their death wish." That was the perception that brought Olympia in for a second round with Jo.

Mumma and All of Us, Again, until, Eventually, Me

Mumma didn't talk to me about love, or boyfriends, or marriage. To me she talked only about aiming high. That I was not ambitious was a constant irritation to her, just as her many and various ambitions were a constant irritation to me. If I told her I'd like to be a nurse she would say, "Why not a doctor?" and if I gave in, agreeing to want to be a doctor, she would say, "What is it with you? What is this doctor business? Why not a surgeon?" It was Mumma who caused me to undertake an academic career, because — witness Pops — higher education removed you from her range. So I determined on a doctorate and a university teaching career, and in mathematics, which, as Mumma told anyone who asked, was always her weak suit. But she had Amy, didn't she? To help her with the books and taxes, so she didn't need math, and she didn't see why I persisted in that field, either. Or why at least I wouldn't find some practical use for it, like banking. And what did I have against the World Bank anyway?

Mumma never went after Pops about his work, but there *were* limits to her admiration for him. "Your father's the smartest person I know, just — not about everything. But don't any of you ever think I don't respect your father's intelligence. I wouldn't think of telling him what to do. A man's job is up to him if his wife loves him," she told us.

"Right, and that's why you made him leave Harvard," I answered, having just learned that my father had given up a place at the most prestigious university I knew of, an institution to even the distaff side of which I had little hope of being admitted.

"You're spending too much time with your grandmother," Mumma decided. "It's not good for a young person to spend so much time with an old lady."

"I'll remember that when you're old. Besides, I like her."

"That's just the kind of thing I expect from you."

It was clear to me, from early childhood, that my mother didn't concern herself with me the way she did my sisters. It wasn't neglect, because Mumma did fuss, but she fussed *at* me rather than fussing *over* me. I was accustomed to her lack of interest in my grades and activities, in my friends. Pops, on the other hand, could talk to me about math, and all my school courses, too, which he did as if I were . . . not his equal, exactly, he was too honest-minded for that, but as if I were a gifted pupil. In return, I became a Latin scholar, doubling our areas of commonality. Mumma knew little about either of my two chosen fields, so I got to know my father without her interfering vision of him; I got to know his mind, how it worked, how he practiced his trade, what he valued, and how very deeply he loved his wife, aka my mother.

Besides friendship with Pops, there was another advantage to Mumma's uncharacteristic lack of concern, and that was that I didn't have her pushing her way into every corner of my life, as my sisters did and about which they frequently complained. Any boy any one of them got a crush on or dated or even simply had hopes of entered Mumma's sphere of interest and had to be brought around for Mumma to get to know. Our friends mostly liked our mother, which I for one could never understand except that they didn't have to have her for a mother. My sisters' boyfriends all thought she was terrific. Mumma in her turn maintained that they were all in love with her, "especially that Alan." Alan Penning, who dated first Jo and then Amy, and then hung around Meg although she was more than a year older than he, probably did do it to be around Mumma, not that he would ever have admitted anything like that, being a teenage male. "Your mom's cool," was all he said. "I can talk to your mom."

Our girlfriends said the same thing, but it was the boys that Mumma, being Mumma, preferred. She welcomed them and enjoyed having them in the house, in the kitchen, in front of the TV, at the dinner table. "Don't try to tell me you're the kind of boy who's afraid to taste eggplant," she challenged, and they rose to the challenge, those eaters of hamburgers, hot dogs, fried chicken and steak, when she set a moussaka down on the table in front of them. Or if they had come to pick up a date not yet dressed and ready, it was, "Sit with us, have a cappuccino, you'll like it, it's Italian," or "Sit, sit, have a cup of Earl Grey, it's one of the smoky teas," and they, who in most circumstances would drink only Coke, or beer, with the occasional bold foray into V-8, which was rumored to make a good bloody mary, sipped cooperatively. Mumma liked to think of herself as broadening their horizons. *"That boy needs his horizons broadened and you're the girl with the mother to do it."*

I am the only one of the four of us who had only Mumma and never Olympia to counsel me. I had only Mumma, and I learned from watching her with my sisters that she was an unreliable counselor — or, at least, a counselor so intrusive and authoritative that seeking her advice gave her permission to ooze all over all of your life, and enlisting her aid was tantamount to having sworn knightly fealty. Mumma, of course, denied that she was anything but supportive and helpful. "You can't boss me around like you can the rest of them," I told her, more than once.

"You'll see," she warned me.

"See what?"

"See where it gets you. Don't say I didn't warn you."

Mumma's style of parenting involved looking ahead to dismal possibilities and then warning us, individually or collectively, about them. "The wind will change and your face will stay that way," she predicted when we were little and pouting, or whining, or making faces at a dinner plate, or being too wildly happy or too obviously jealous. It was Jo whom she first warned that fast girls get pregnant and Meg to whom she pointed out the pitfalls and shortfalls of romantic love. "Nobody can be as perfect as you think he is. Don't ever try to make some other person perfect, Meg, even if you know how to do it. And you don't know how, don't ever think you know that."

For all of our girlhoods, she advised us what to look for in a man. Some of it was old chestnuts, "Handsome is as handsome does," or, "Why would a man get married if he can get what he wants for nothing?" She also made economic predictions ("That boy will never have two nickels to rub together") based on family histories ("They don't have a pot to piss in, excuse my French") or on character analysis ("A man with that kind of twinkle in his eye, don't think he'll be faithful"). "Marry the one that loves *you*

291

the most," she advised Amy, when the choice arose in Amy's senior year at Smith. (Amy married neither of them.) "I'm going to see to it you have a college degree," she told Jo, when our family doctor reported to Mumma that unmarried Jo wanted to go on the pill, "but the rest of your life is up to you and I hope you remember that I warned you."

"Don't be in such a hurry," she counseled Meg, when for the sixth time Meg arrived home from Tufts displaying an engagement ring or a fraternity pin. "You aren't in love with these boys, don't ever try to fool me about love. You're just husband hunting. If you're just hunting for a husband, a husband is all you'll get." But Meg went off and married Jack Cartenbury in the fall of her junior year, dropping out of school to follow him to Los Angeles and fame and fortune. Mumma couldn't decide which to dislike the most, the abandoned degree, the youthful marriage, or Jack Cartenbury; she settled for vacillating among the three. However, and to her credit, Mumma never said *I told you so* when things went wrong, nor when they went the way she had predicted, which two eventualities were often the same.

These conversations, like the many conversations with Mumma when we were girls, in which she talked and we nodded our heads, took place in one or another of our bedrooms. Mumma liked to climb up onto the twin bed — we each had a set of twin beds, for convenience when having friends for the night — and lean back against the headboard, her neck propped by a pillow, her bright red hair exploding around her face. "What's wrong between you and your sister? And don't pretend you don't know what I'm talking about," or, "We have to talk about your social studies grade," or, "Polly tells me you . . ." At about the age of eleven *("I was thirteen," Meg corrects, "and I'd had the curse for almost a year by then"),* we would come into our room and find the two thin hardbound sex education books propped up against the pillow.

"We managed, didn't we?" my adult sisters always remind me.

"She was *nosy.* She wanted to know everything we were doing, everything we were thinking," I say. They protest, "She wanted to be the best mother ever. Your memory is a little skewed, Beth, because, when I think about it, Mumma was way ahead of her time, just like she always said. She understood about adolescent girls. The kinds of stresses and pressures. Think about it, Beth. She just wanted us to find good husbands, like she had."

"She wanted *you* to. She was always talking about the kind of man you'd marry, all of you — all right, not you, Jo. But you she talked about the kind of man you should love. She never did any of that about me, not to my face and I bet not behind my back either." They don't argue, since I'm right, and also because we all know that whatever else Mumma did, she would never say something behind your back she wouldn't have already said to your face. "She didn't think I'd even *get* married. She didn't think anyone would fall in love with me."

"You didn't date," they remind me.

"Yes I did. I just never let my date pick me up at home. I'm not dumb," I say.

"We wouldn't dare even *think* that," they assure me.

"You know what I mean," I say.

"She knew what you were doing," is what they prefer to believe.

I know better. Mumma, having decided that I was the studious one, decided further that, like Pops, I was socially immature as well as being not the kind of girl boys wanted to date. To threaten, that is, with all of dating's concomitant dangers. I also wasn't the kind of girl a man would want to marry, not any man with any brains about him, given how quarrelsome and opinionated I was, how determined to get my own way even when my mother, who knew better, advised against it. When I announced that I wanted to attend Saint John's College in Annapolis — and not even apply to Radcliffe, Smith or Bryn Mawr, Wellesley or Wheaton, and not even Swarthmore, which was coeducational even at that time "and a really good school besides" — Mumma threw up her hands, literally and rhetorically. "I throw up my hands," she said, "I wash my hands of you. My hands are tied, if your father thinks Saint John's is a good school. I've never heard of it."

"She can learn Greek." To my father, this was a major advantage.

"Oh, well, that explains it. But Spencer, there are no majors. It's just like you, Beth, to go to a place where there are no majors and how are you going to earn a living?"

Even though I knew better, I tried to explain. "I can study Euclid from the *Elements*, and then work out the same problems Ptolemy solved, and everybody else will be doing the same thing, so there will be people to talk to about what I'm interested in."

"I'm throwing in my hand," Mumma said.

This was a much calmer conversation than the kind we were given to enjoy throughout my childhood, from the age of seven to about sixteen, when I at last got my driver's license and all of the lovely sense of freedom, if not actual freedom, that accompanies that achievement. Our earlier conversations tended to be heated and irrational. It seemed clear to me that whatever I did, my mother got angry at me about it. "You're always mad at me," I would tell her. "You're projecting," she'd tell me, and I hadn't at that point read Freud, which happened also to be part of the Saint John's curriculum, so I couldn't make any counterclaims about systems of denial.

Everyone agreed that Mumma was relieved when I at last went off to Saint John's. "I don't know what will come of you," she said to me in farewell.

Neither did I.

"Don't make it too hard on yourself," she advised. "You catch more flies with honey."

"That's good advice if you want to catch flies," I told her.

I thought that, having left home, I would no longer be the person I had been all of my life, the stubborn, uncooperative person my mother had had to deal with. In many respects I was correct in that assumption, and so, for the first time in my life, I invited a boy to come visit my home. This was George, who was a junior when I met him at the end of my freshman year and a senior when we started dating. Mumma took to George right away. On his part, from the first moment, he took her on, calling her by her real name, Elfrieda. "It's good to meet you, Elfrieda." Mumma glared at me — How else could he know this? — but George didn't notice; he was moving on to Pops, "And you, too, Spencer," holding his hand out for them to shake, first Mumma, then Pops. "Beth never says very much about you two, and I have to admit I'm curious," George said, and I glared at him.

Mumma took to George and he also took to her. They had lively conversations first about Freud and then about Hegel, whom Mumma had never heard of before but whose world views she approved of. At the dinner table on the second night of his two-night visit during the Christmas break, Mumma told him, "Beth's only nineteen," by way of letting him know I was not mature enough for a serious relationship.

"I'm thinking of law school," George answered, letting her know he was in no hurry.

"I'm thinking of a doctorate in mathematics," I said, forcing my way into their cozy conversation. Because if George, or Mumma, thought I was trying to get him to marry me, they could both think again. And they could think again together at the same time, since they seemed to like each other so much.

"I'm thinking of Cambridge," I added. "England."

"You'll like Cambridge," Pops said. "You're used to that kind of bad weather, and you could cross over to visit Brundy, which he would enjoy mightily. He'd show you Paris."

"Brundy?" George asked. "Who are they talking about, Elfrieda?"

George stayed only two nights, and on the morning he was leaving we wanted to walk on the beach (translation: neck in the dunes) before we parted for the rest of the holiday. When Mumma suggested that she might come with us to see the ocean, she would take us in her car, I don't think I shrieked "Mother!" but I might have.

George was readying himself for the law. "Elfrieda," he reminded her, "I want to say a proper goodbye to Beth."

"That means No Mothers," I said.

In the car beside him, I said, "I will never, never, never understand my mother. For a smart woman, she is *so* dumb."

"I know exactly what you mean," George said. "Amazing is the only word."

"Everybody always says that about her," I responded glumly.

"No, not her, you. I mean, I already knew you're strong-minded, but I think you must also have an unusual strength of character. I'm impressed, Beth. Elfrieda's not a mother, she's an experience."

I found myself defending her. "She's a good mother."

"I didn't say she was bad," George corrected me. "Is this where I turn? I said exactly what I mean. I'm not sure an experience is what a child wants from its mother. It must have been hard to be her daughter," George said, thinking about it. Then, being fair-minded by nature, he added, "Some of the time."

"More than some," I assured him.

After George had driven off to celebrate the holidays at his home in Delaware, Mumma found me in my room. She lay down on my spare bed and arranged the pillow behind her. Her hair was bright all around her face. I practiced thinking of her as an experience.

"You dye your hair," I realized.

"You don't love that boy," she told me.

I snorted at my desk, where I was reading Saint Thomas Aquinas in preparation for the seminar that would meet the night I returned to school.

"But if you aren't careful you will," she warned me.

"You're always telling me what you think and never asking me what I think," I pointed out.

Mumma lay silent for a minute, her legs crossed at the ankles and those high heels pointed straight at me, like miniature rifle barrels. "Don't ever think you don't love me," she told me.

At that, I burst into tears. Mumma rose from the bed and left the room, satisfied.

She was often right about me, about all of us, Mumma. You could trust her acumen. Because it turned out that I cared less about whether or not she loved me than whether or not I loved her. So perhaps Mumma was right not to have marital expectations for me, since it was only when George and I eventually decided that after all we did want children that we took that step. She could also have been right to be always wanting more, for me, for herself, for all of us. All except Pops, that is. "Your father is just fine, he always was," she told us. "I have no complaints about your father. Of course, he's not perfect. Don't any of you ever think any man is perfect."

And maybe she was even right never to offer me Olympia's counseling services. I bearded her once on that subject, when I was in high school and counted it a major proof of her disaffection. "Why did you send Amy? Or Meg, too, when it was only Jo who had a real problem, with her lying, and then all the boyfriends, the promiscuity problem. But what was so seriously wrong with Amy and Meg?"

Mumma always had her answers ready. "The kinds of things that happened, that Mr. Smithers and those boys at the dance . . . Girls can turn insecure and it makes them shy, when things like that happen to them when they're young. I don't want any of my daughters being like that. Life is hard enough without having a shy daughter."

6.
Mumma's Marriage

For years, I kept the secret. It wasn't until we had settled our Alzheimer-undermined mother into a nursing home that I told my sisters. We had made our farewells to Mumma, one at a time, one after the other so as not to distress her, and now we were having lunch together at The Captain's Wheel. We made our usual choices — chef's salad, the fried clam plate, a turkey club, and a medium-rare cheeseburger with fries. We had two pitchers on the table, one of iced tea and one of lemonade, to combine in whatever proportions each of us preferred. We had a table with an umbrella, out on the deck overlooking the harbor, where Jo could smoke and where, on a mild spring midday, pleasure boats far outnumbered the working boats that had filled the harbor when we were girls.

The round table meant nobody sat at its head and we would split the bill into four equal sections, no matter who did or did not order dessert, or coffee, or even, as Meg or Amy sometimes did, glasses of wine. Spring had come early and settled down gently over the Cape that May. Tulips bloomed in the planters that edged the deck. We had worn stockings and heels, even Jo, dresses and hats, to settle Mumma into her new home. In case she noticed, in case she cared, in case she needed the reassurance of things being as she understood they ought to be, we had dressed up for the occasion, purses and pearls. Despite the disparate nature of the paths our lives had taken, there were no real differences between us that day. We were four sisters, we were equals, we were Mumma's daughters, and I thought it was time they knew. So I told them.

"Pops had an affair."

"I don't believe it," they said. "Although I don't blame him. Do you?" they asked one another. "That's *if* he did. *If* it's true."

"It's true," I assured them. "He had a mistress, I don't know for how long, a woman he was seeing and I think they had to be sleeping together. Although, that doesn't sound like Pops."

"I don't know," Jo said. "He was a really attractive man, and he got even better-looking as he grew older."

"I was thinking of his moral integrity," I told her. "Although," I realized, "I guess it wouldn't show much moral courage or integrity to *not* sleep with her. I mean, if you're having an affair with someone, you *owe* it to them to sleep with them."

"Who was it?" Amy demanded. "When was it? I don't believe you."

"Why are you telling me this?" Meg demanded. "And why now?"

"Although," I realized, in the rush of thoughts that came to me, once I relaxed my hold on this secret, "I can see Mumma doing just that. Having an affair but no sex," I added, when they looked confused.

"Mumma would never have . . . she just liked . . . She liked toying with the possibility," Meg said. "She just . . . She liked *flirting,* she was a *flirt.* She would never have *done* anything. She just liked *thinking* men were in love with her."

It was an article of faith with us that Mumma was crazy nuts about Pops, and we could see why. What we couldn't always understand, even if we had no doubt the feeling was mutual, was what he saw in her. She wasn't his mother, after all; he didn't *have* to love her.

"Or maybe they weren't just flirtations,"

Jo suggested. "After all, she did have all those fiancés. She was pretty sexy."

Amy turned to me. "How *do* you know? About this woman, this mistress, if she was one."

"Did he confide in you about her?" Meg wondered, but Amy assured her, "He never would. He never really talked to any of us about his personal life, you know, feelings, fears, hopes. I figured he talked to Mumma about all that. Except work, he talked to Beth about his work. Was she someone from work?"

"Let her tell," Jo said. "Let's stop interrupting. Interfering," she pointed out.

I began. "Remember when George and I were living in Cambridge, and Emily was a baby?"

"The mid-'70s," Amy located it. "I was pregnant with Kelly and Jason was two and a half."

"The gas shortage of the '70s," Jo said. "Bennet and I weren't the only people riding bikes those days."

"I remember Bennet," I said. I hadn't thought about him for years, the first of the men Jo hadn't married, although she lived with them for extended periods before breaking it off and sending them away. "Bennet was a lot of fun."

"He had his moments," Jo agreed. "Pops was teaching a course at BU, wasn't he? Those years, what was it? Grad school Latin?"

"No, it was a community outreach course for adults. Continuing education, reading the Greeks, Homer, Aeschylus, you know, Sophocles, Sappho. All in translation," I told them. My sisters had never studied in Pops' field.

"A student?" Meg guessed.

"He wouldn't do that, not even with adult students. You have to know that about him," I scolded.

Meg fixed me with a level gaze. "Until today, until this lunch, I would have said that Pops wouldn't do that with anyone. So my mind is open."

She spoke precisely to the point, of course. I hesitated in my telling, taking stock. Here we were, the four of us, middle-aged now, hair fading and graying unless, like all of us except me, we highlighted or tinted it. I looked good standing beside him just as I was, George assured me, and I chose to believe him. We four, Mumma's daughters, sat around a table as we so often had, talking. Meg looked fit and tailored in a white-and-black linen dress, dark glasses perched on her thick short curls. Jo had grown her hair long and had perhaps twenty-five surplus pounds disguised, as she thought, by the high-waisted and loose-fitting flowered rayon dress; her eyes were heavily made up, which emphasized how much their blue had faded. Amy wore a tan blazer over a navy skirt, and low heels; she had a small signet ring bearing Wilfred's family crest on the little finger of her right hand, and Wilfred's great-grandmother's engagement diamond on her left, next to her wedding ring. I was the only one of us who had kept her hat on, one of my summer straw hats, because for college professors summer vacation begins early and I had already had enough sun. I wore a simple rust-brown cotton shift and dress sandals. We looked just like our childhood selves, only much older, and dressed up, and also a little mellowed by time and experiences, both good and bad times and experiences. Beyond us, cars had only begun their seasonal clogging of the street, searching for parking places. I met Meg's eyes and said to her, and to my other sisters, "I hope you'll agree that I was right to keep it to myself."

Not surprisingly, it was Jo who said, "What good would it have done to tell us?"

"Or Mumma," Amy guessed. "Although I'd have thought you'd have thought you

307

should."

"I didn't want to ruin her life. I outgrew that years ago."

Jo said, "Maybe it wouldn't have. Maybe, once she reacted — blew up, threw him out, sold the house, whatever — maybe her life would have been better."

"How better?" Meg wondered. "I always thought . . . I mean, she thought Pops was fascinating."

"I know," we agreed, smiling indulgently, "she really did." Pops was a lovely man, but *fascinating* wasn't a word anyone but Mumma would have applied to him. "She loved talking over his theories with him, and what he was reading, or his course outlines."

"If she'd thought he was unfaithful . . ." Amy didn't finish that sentence.

I agreed. "Talk about loose cannons. I don't know *what* she would have done."

"It would have been extravagant," Jo agreed, her voice not entirely free of longing. "It would have been uncompromising. I wonder what."

"Pops unfaithful? That would have undermined her sense of the natural order of the universe," Meg observed. "More than most women."

"Anyway," I said, "it turned out I didn't want to tell her."

"And maybe it wasn't true, anyway," Jo suggested.

I began again. "Remember when George and I were living in Cambridge, and I was getting my doctorate?"

"Not particularly," Amy said, "but it was the '70s, we've established that, and those years Pops came into Boston one night a week, to teach."

"He stayed at the Alumni House," Meg remembered. "I had dinner there with him once. It was sweet, he was worried about Liam and me. He was worried I'd get another divorce, I think. He was really concerned about me." She smiled at the fond memory, Pops as paterfamilias, and then she remembered, "And you're saying that at the same time he was having an affair?"

I'd had years to get used to the idea, and all that it implied, perhaps most significantly that our parents were just real people, ordinary people who could be unfaithful to their wives, like stories we read or heard or lived ourselves, like friends, not parents.

Jo said, "I don't know, Beth. How can you be so sure?"

"For one thing, I saw them together. And for another, I asked him."

"You didn't."

"How could you? No, I don't mean how could you do such a thing," Meg said. "I mean, how did you bring yourself to do it? I can't imagine."

"She was always closer to Pops than the rest of us," Amy reminded them and there they were again, the three of them, and there I was, alone and at odds, all of us once again reduced to our childhood configuration. Then I laughed out loud, at myself, at them, at the four of us, being sisters. Here we were with our father three years dead and our mother no longer a fully functioning human being, and we were still measuring the attentions we had been shortchanged of. I laughed out loud, and they stared at me with tolerant impatience. Here we were, four aging women, with the cellulite to prove it and lines around our eyes, chins starting to double, stretch marks and varicose veins, and buried in each one of us was the child she had been, who looked at her sisters as if they too were still children, a child glaring around her with the same resentments and jealousies.

By now, however, those were mixed with geographic distances from one another, as well as admiration and sympathy, too. Sisters. I would always be the youngest of the four Howland girls, and I was proud of my sisters. I liked us, our achievements, our hopes, our persistent attempts to live honest lives in whatever direction we were moving or in what position we had settled. *Mumma should be satisfied with the job she did,* I thought, and then I thought, *I wish she could remember us, so she could see the way we are now.*

That thought saddened me. I told my story quickly:

"It was a Wednesday night and we were both ready for a break, me and George. I'd finished the draft of an article, George had gone stale on a brief, so we hired a sitter and went to see *Coming Home*. With Jane Fonda, remember? And Jon Voight, it was at the Church Street Theater. As we were leaving I saw a couple ahead of us, and I recognized Pops. The woman he was with wasn't Mumma, but he was definitely *with* her."

"Is that all?" Meg demanded. "You thought it was Pops and you decided it was an affair?"

I remembered what I had seen, the tall man with the military bearing he'd never lost, and his dark chesterfield coat, his pale hair, the outer rims of his glasses; and the slender woman beside him, tall enough herself to come up to his chin, wearing a dark blue woolen coat, gloves, low, practical heels, her short hair a nondescript brown, and when she turned to glance at him, her eyes on his face and the little smile on her mouth, obviously a woman in love with her escort. I remembered the way he placed his hand on her back, to guide her through the crowd, as if she needed his help to successfully make her way, and the way she then took his arm, not his hand, as if she were accepting his support. He held the theater door for her and she moved through it. Once on the sidewalk, she turned to wait for him. She was an undisturbingly pretty woman, with regular features and a slim, delicate neck, curved eyebrows and large, deep-set brown eyes, which gave her face a doelike expression of helplessness, or weakness.

Before Pops let go of the door, he turned to whoever came after him to pass on the responsibility for holding it open. That was when he saw me watching. Without thinking, he smiled and raised a hand, waving, to greet me. I raised my hand back, but didn't wave and I think my face must have given my thoughts away, because Pops seemed to realize then that he wished I hadn't been there. Concern flashed across his face, then he turned to join the woman on the street, and she took his arm, and he leaned slightly toward her, protective, as they walked away together.

"It was Pops," I assured my sisters. "I saw his face. He saw me. He waved at me before he remembered."

"That is just exactly what he'd do, isn't it?" Jo asked us. "For a smart man, he was pretty slow to catch on. Even when it was a matter of self-protection, he was slow. So he saw you, and then what?"

"He just walked away. She was waiting for him outside. He'd been holding the door, the way he did."

"But why are you so sure it was a date?" asked Amy.

"They walked like people who were together." I clarified it: "People physically aware of each other, maybe lovers? People in love, sometimes — you must have noticed this — sometimes it shows? When they're walking together?" They nodded and I promised them, "It showed."

They digested this without speaking. I gave them time to do so. After a few minutes, Meg asked, "Who was she?"

"It took me a while to find that out," I admitted. "I had to sort of trail Pops, when he came to town on Wednesdays. I had to sort of follow him from his class —"

"How did you know where he'd be?"

"That was easy. I called BU about continuing education courses, and they sent me a catalog."

"A real little Nancy Drew," Amy commented. None of them added, "Just like Mumma," but we were all thinking it. The reason nobody said it was not to spare my feelings but because we had just left our mother, who at that point neither reliably recognized nor reliably remembered any of us, not even Meg, and who, in fact, had picked up the silver-framed commissioning photograph of our father and handed it to one of the attendants, saying, "Somebody left this." Then, with a secretive little smile that could have meant she was teasing us, or could have meant she was getting away with something, she took it back. "Maybe I'll keep it. He's a good-looking young fellow, isn't he?" Our mother, who all of our lives had been disquietingly sharp-witted and opinionated, even domineering, was now losing her brain, and with it her character. Our own loss of her remained too sharp for invidious comparisons. Our only consolations were: first, to know that we were suffering more than she was, that she wasn't suffering at all now, really; and second, to remark wryly to one another, swallowing back tears, that this was just like Mumma, wasn't it, arranging things to suit her own convenience.

Not that we forgot the first years of the disease, especially before Pops died, her denials about symptoms and her disguised compensatory tactics. We noticed. And of course we asked her. We were worried. "Your father has always needed me to keep his life in order. To pay attention too, because nobody appreciates him the way I do," she told us in response to hesitant, exploratory inquiries, asking, What would Freud say about this frequent losing of car keys?, or, Had she forgotten Emily's birthday, or, Was the check made out to Amy's oldest child, Jason, but sent to Jo, supposed to be for Emily so we should just give Emily the hundred dollars? "Wait until you get old," Mumma responded. "You'll know what it's like then. For now, bug off why don't you?"

Mumma was frightened, we knew that, and we were frightened too. Never one to be fiscally self-indulgent, however, she gradually handed over the management of her real estate business to Amy, with George continuing as the company lawyer. But while Pops was alive, that transfer was her only acknowledgment of encroaching limita-

315

tions. "Your father couldn't stand to lose me," she had told us, all of our lives. "I hope he dies first, because without me his days would be terribly empty."

We knew she was right about that, and this made the question of the mistress all the more puzzling.

"How long did it take you?" Jo wondered. "Finding out who Pops' woman was, I mean."

"It only took a day to find his class, but then I had to figure out how to discover who she was, and it wasn't as if I could go sit in on his classes."

"Unless you wore some kind of disguise," Amy said, and my three sisters smirked at one another. Then Amy realized, "You did, didn't you. You wore a disguise."

"Not really. Just a hat, dark glasses. And a wig. You could get fatigues at the Army Navy store on the Square. Don't look at me that way. It was just so I could follow him."

"You *followed* him?"

"It's not easy, it wasn't easy, and Pops was a creature of habit so he must have been easier than most. Although," I remembered, "she wasn't so hard, either. Maybe I missed my calling? Maybe I should have been a detective?"

This time they laughed out loud, which I

always prefer to sisterly smirking.

"So how *did* you do it?"

"Well, he stayed at the Alumni House the nights he was in town, and I followed him there, after the class."

"You got in a cab and said 'Follow that car'?" Meg asked.

"Actually, I had my own car." I continued my story. "I followed him and after that I just waited. What he did was, he went into the Alumni House alone, carrying his over-night case, he sat in the dining room, ate supper, and came out about an hour later with this woman. It was the same one I'd seen him with at the movie. So instead of watching his class, I started watching the Alumni House beginning at about the time class got out. But I didn't see her go in, although she came out with him again."

"She worked there?" Amy guessed, just as I had.

"In the dining room. A waitress. So what I did was, I wandered in, pretending . . . But not in fatigues, of course. That day I wore a skirt and sweater. My cover story was a father who had gone to Harvard but he'd been killed in Korea. You must remember how during Vietnam people felt bad for anyone who had lost someone in any war. Everybody felt so guilty, remember? I told

317

them I was working at Radcliffe, which was true, and I just wanted to see for myself the places where my father had been a young man. Before he was killed. Because I'd never known him and now I was having his grandchild . . . That was my story so they let me walk around, and I saw her. In the dining room. In her waitress dress."

For a minute, I remembered vividly how it had been. I stood in the doorway looking at the long room with its many-paned windows and bright white tablecloths and little glass vases of flowers, the leather upholstered chairs set around the tables and the woman moving among them, putting down silver, napkins, plates, glasses. She was one of those narrow-shouldered, slim, small-breasted women, although oddly enough not at all boyish-looking. Such women are unquestionably feminine, dainty, fragile, their gestures always a little hesitant, their glances often looking around for approval, their smiles hopeful. She saw me standing, watching, and straightened up to smile, and blush a pretty pink before she turned back to her work.

It never crossed her mind to come over and ask what I was doing there, or why I was staring at her. It crossed her mind only to hope that I would go away soon. Which I did.

"She was a waitress? How young was she?"

"Not so young. She looked to be in her thirties, mid-thirties, maybe. Actually, I learned she was thirty-four and divorced."

"You're amazing! How did you find *that* out?" Jo asked. "Did you find out who she was, too?"

"I tried to get George to get the information, because he went to Harvard Law School so he's an alumnus so he could ask, but he refused, he wouldn't even do it for Mumma. So I had to ask a friend who was married to an investment banker who had gone to the Business School, ask *her* to go there for dinner and find out. Because I couldn't go myself. I mean, what if she recognized me? But once I had her name, which was Na—"

Meg interrupted. "I don't think I want a name."

I didn't insist. "Once I had that, I looked her up in the phone book, and once I did *that,* I had her address, and once I had her address, I could go see where she lived. It was a house. In Somerville," I reported.

The house, in need of paint on its clapboards and its door and window frames, was a tall, three-story building with a bit

319

more yard than its neighbors. The two metal mailboxes told me that two families lived there, hers and one other. My guess was that she either rented or rented out the apartment to which the exterior wooden staircase led; the bicycles leaning up against a rear door led me to think she had children at least eight years old and lived on the ground floor. I already knew that the phone was in her name.

I ascended four broad steps up to the porch, where she'd hung a porch swing, even in Somerville; Mumma would approve of a porch swing on a city street, I thought, and took the two steps across to peer through a window into the house. Inside, a golden retriever came toward me, bounding down a dim hallway and barking ferociously, leaping up to the window. So I fled. But I returned, two days later.

That year we had snow in April, between April Fool's Day and tax day, six inches of a wet, heavy snow that fell all night long. In the morning, instead of clearing the patch of sidewalk in front of our rented house, as required by law, I walked over to Somerville. There, a man was shoveling the steps. He was old enough to be her brother, I thought, maybe she lived with her brother? The same golden retriever jumped about in the yard, taking big bites of snow.

"Hey," I greeted them both. "That was a weird storm, wasn't it?"

The dog barked and the man turned to say, "Quiet, Vi, it's all right," and at that news the dog bounded up to me, wagging its tail in excitement.

"Vi?" I asked, bending down to pet it with my mittened hands. "That's an odd name for a dog," I remarked, although I was unqualified to judge that question. Mumma hated pets, dogs or cats. ("What do I need with a pet? I've got four children," she said, and waited, before adding the clincher, "Daughters.")

"Viola," the man told me. His cheeks were red with cold and exercise, his eyes a trustworthy brown under straight eyebrows. He was a nice-looking man, not too tall, not too heavy, not too handsome — a nice, normal man. "After Twelfth Night. Because Vi pretends to be a fierce watchdog but she's really a sweetheart."

"Is she yours?" I asked, busily stroking the dog on the shoulders, pushing down against her willingness to stand with her forefeet on my shoulder to make it easier for me to reach her ears.

"She belongs to my landlady, but Vi and I are good friends. I walk her when the boys

321

are at school and my landlady's at work."

"You have boys? How many?" I asked.

"They aren't mine. Mine," he said with careful expressionlessness, "are in Wisconsin. Living with their mother."

"Oh," I said. He waited. "I'm sorry," I said. He shrugged. "You must miss them," I said.

"Yeah. I do."

"But you have the landlady's boys to keep your parenting skills honed," I observed.

He looked at me more sharply. "What makes you say that?"

"Well, you didn't say anything about a landlord, so I deduce that she's —"

"We're friends. Good friends, but that's all," he said. "I'm really fond of her boys."

"Boys need a father," I observed.

"Boys need a responsible father," he clarified. Then he seemed to think of something. "What can I do for you? Because I've got this shoveling to finish, and then . . . You ask a lot of questions. What do you want?"

I didn't have to fake embarrassment; that was real enough. I presented the story I had prepared. I was looking for a friend who was staying with another friend, I said; on this street, I thought, but I wasn't sure of the exact number. "A college friend," I specified, then realized I hadn't chosen a name, so I grabbed at the nearest to hand, "Rida is her friend's name. Not like Rita Hayworth," I said. "Rida with a *d,* Rida Smith, do you know her? Does someone with that name live on this street?"

He didn't believe me but pretended he might. I was female, I was pregnant, he would give me the benefit of the doubt. "No," he said. "Is there anything else?"

"No," I had to answer. But it wasn't what he thought, whatever he might be thinking. I only wanted to know what he meant by implying that her husband (ex-husband? late husband? criminal husband?) wasn't meeting his responsibilities. And if she had many boyfriends, I wanted to know that too, and were any of them *my* father, until just recently one of the world's most responsible husbands. At least, as far as any of us knew. But I was pretty confident that one of the boyfriends would be Pops, and probably he was the only one, especially if she was a working mother with two children in school and a very presentable tenant, who was moreover fond of *her* children, but whom she was keeping at friend's length. Mostly, I knew that anything else I was going to find out, I was going to have to find out from Pops.

I gave my sisters the synopsis: "She had a

house, and rented out the third floor, and she had two sons in school, no visible husband. She was working at a low-level, no-future job. I guess there's some éclat in that, but academics aren't good tippers."

"I always thought he really liked Mumma, really enjoyed her," Meg said. "An affair doesn't make any sense."

"This woman was the fragile feminine type. The kind Jonquil Cartenbury Heolms pretends to be. You know the type. I expect that's what attracted Pops," I told them. "Not that he said that, he didn't say exactly that. But she was one of those women, they just *look* helpless, and needy. She looked like that kind of woman and I think probably she really was."

"What *did* he say? When you asked him," Amy wanted to know.

"Did he deny it?" Jo asked. "I would have, but Pops had all that integrity."

"I know," I agreed. "That's what made it so weird. We met at Mrs. B's — the hamburger place? — for lunch."

"With George?"

"No. George kept out of it. He never even told me what he thought about it. I did all the talking with George, and I did most of the talking with Pops, now I think of it, especially when . . . He didn't deny it. I was dreading one of those conversations, you know? You have them with boyfriends, but you never think you'll have them with your father. You ask accusing questions: *How could you? What about . . . ?* Then he presents his defenses, his rationales, the reasons why he couldn't have done anything else."

"You mean denials," said Meg. "In my experience, mostly with Jack, but he was a classic, denial at all levels is the knee-jerk response. Even Liam thinks that way under pressure."

"So do I," I admitted. "But Pops didn't. In fact, he was sort of wonderful. 'Who is this woman?' I asked and he said, 'Someone who's had a hard time of it and is making the best of things.' That's verbatim. His exact words."

Saying that, Pops had looked straight at me, across the platter of onion rings at the center of the table. We both had grease on our chins, which we mopped at with paper napkins. We both sipped tall sodas from straws. We both weren't quite sure where this conversation was going to go, although neither of us wanted a battle. We both understood that, once I had seen him at the movies, and he had seen me, this conversation was inevitable.

I have to admit, I admired my father. I

continued my report to his other daughters. "I asked him, outright, if he was in love with her. He didn't answer me."

"You mean he didn't say anything? The silent nonresponse?" Meg asked.

"It wasn't that obvious, but he said Mumma was his wife."

"He called her Mumma?" Amy demanded.

"No, of course not, he called her Rida. He wouldn't ever call her Mumma, you know that," I said. "Pops never called her Elfrieda, either."

Three of us ordered the hot fudge sundaes that had been established during childhood as the best of all possible desserts, and Jo returned us to the subject. "So do we deduce that Pops *was* in love with her?"

"*I* did," I told them.

Amy greeted this statement with the irritated impatience that characterized so much of my childhood relationship with my siblings. "Do you really believe someone can love two people at the same time? Because you're not going to convince me he didn't love Mumma."

"Maybe he loved Mumma," Jo fine-tuned, "but maybe he wasn't still *in* love with her. Come on, you all know what I mean. Beth, for example, are you still *in* love with

George?"

I had to admit, "A lot of the time, yeah, I am. Most of the time, in fact, although I do know what you mean. So maybe that was it. He was *in* love with the other woman and he still *loved* Mumma. Although, I have a hard time with that. If it was George . . ."

"Never mind George," Meg said. "So you asked Pops if he loved this mistress person and he said Mumma was his wife . . . then what?"

"I asked him, What if Mumma found out? And he asked me, How would she?"

At the time, all I could do was stare at my father, his eyes serene behind round gold-rimmed glasses, his expression one of intelligence being applied to a problem. I had never realized before how compartmentalized my father's life was, or, more to the point, how separated in his own perceptions those compartments were. I stared at him in amazement across a table that suddenly seemed to me to resemble the uncompartmentalized lives of everybody else I knew, especially my mother. The table was littered with remnants of our lunch, the half-eaten platter of onion rings, straw wrappers accordioned up on the speckled Formica, mounds of crumpled, greasy paper napkins. But you could see, in the puzzlement on Pops' face, in the unselfdoubting, untroubled blue of his eyes, that as far as Pops was concerned, Boston, Cambridge, Wampanoag, and Brown were as distinct in his mind as they are on maps. They had nothing to do with one another. He had roles and duties, each appropriate to its own locale, none overlapping. You could see that he believed they were as separate in reality as they were in his perceptions. So he was entirely sincere when he asked me, "Why should your mother find out?"

"Did he think you were going to tell her?" Meg asked.

"He knew better than that," I said at the same time that she answered her own question, "I guess he knew better than that."

"*I* would have told her," Amy said.

"Anybody but Beth would have thought seriously about it. But you didn't, did you?"

They were right. I had asked my father to have lunch with me not to make a scene, or to threaten him, but so that I could put a stop to his affair so that my mother's . . . My mother's what?

They weren't *illusions,* that her husband loved and admired her, and was grateful to her, and enjoyed her company. I didn't know *why* he felt that way about her, but I knew that he did. So it wasn't her illusions I was protecting.

It was my mother's whole life I didn't want to see going up in flames, or down in flames, or crumbling into ashes, or whatever would happen if she were to find out that Pops had another woman. Mumma's vanity, and her own integrity, would require her to leave him. Or, I wondered, was she the kind of woman who would throw *him* out? The important aspects of his life comprised his teaching, his scholarship, his marriage, and his family. But he was the *only* core and center of her life. If the marriage ended, Mumma's life could be utterly changed.

I admit it, that insight left me breathless, poised at the edge of possibility. What would Mumma do? Without Pops, a single woman, what would she do? Would she liquidate her assets and leave Pops to live on his salary and a much diminished trust fund income, re-situating herself? Where would Mumma go? Where wouldn't she go? After their first visit to Brundy in Paris, Mumma's opinion of Europe had undergone a complete revision. She bought records to teach herself French and had Brundy ship her cases of fig jam. Also, she had always spoken longingly of California weather, and California soil, and the kind of people who wanted to live in California, as opposed to New England, and Boston, and even the Cape. As well, she was fascinated by politics and knowledgeable about issues; she was a dedicated member of the League of Women Voters, the ACLU, Common Cause, Planned Parenthood, generous with her donations and her time. What Mumma might get up to next — I would have loved to have seen it. I would have loved it to have happened for her.

What she wouldn't have done (there was no question about this in my mind) was mope and mourn. "Life's short," she always said, meaning, Life's too short for whatever useless mental or emotional occupation a person might waste her time on. That was, I always thought, good advice, and she followed it herself, never becoming disheartened by her various losses of the various elections for presidencies (PTA, garden club) or chairmanships (library board, hospital board), or even, twice, town council seats. She also always accepted the appointments her former rivals asked her to undertake after they had been elected to the higher position. "Life's too short not to be generous," she said when, for example, Jonquil Cartenbury needed a friend and no one else stepped forward. So if Pops had betrayed her, it seemed clear that Mumma would have moved on and arrived . . . My imagination soared. It would be an adventure, no question. I was almost sorry that I would never tell her.

Now, years later, I was finally letting my middle-aged sisters in on the secret that until then only George had known. "The only person I wanted to tell was Pops, and I wanted to talk to him because I wanted to make him stop."

"Stop seeing the woman, you mean."

"Yes. I thought that if he knew I knew, and knew I'd face him with it, he'd give her up. But that wasn't what he was saying to me. So I had to think of something else."

"Short of telling Mumma, what else *could* you do?" Meg asked.

It was Pops himself who had shown me how. He'd said, to comfort me, "You should understand, Beth, that this doesn't mean . . . This is about Nanette, not your mother. Whatever happens, your mother will be fine. You must know that."

"I do," I told him.

"She doesn't need me. She doesn't need anyone."

"But she likes having us. She *wants* us."

"I know that, of course, and I respect it. I'm just trying to reassure you."

"But what about Nanette?" I had asked him then, and that was my brainstorm. Because I understood then that this woman *did* need Pops, or someone. She was a needer, and needers attract people to take care of them, to fall in love with them, or to shovel their sidewalks for them. I could see, also, that to be needed, for Pops, might be utterly seductive. "If she's in love with you" — he nodded his head, smiled shyly, amazed at this unexpected gift — "and I can see that that's great, and I don't blame her, but . . . If you're not going to leave Mumma for her, what about her? That's not much of a life for her, is it? I mean, unless you don't love her."

"Your mother couldn't bear it if I loved somebody else," Pops said, shaking his head. "Nanette doesn't mind that I'm married," he confided, a proud secret.

"Well of course not, but I'd think *you'd* mind. Treating her that way. Using up her life, I mean. You know what I mean, Pops," I said, and I could see in his face that I didn't need to say any more.

"All right," he said, vague and inattentive now, rethinking everything. "Thank you," he said.

"Because," I said years later to my sisters, "he really hadn't thought about it from that point of view, and he really did thank me for helping him see it that way, because he really did love her. Because Pops wouldn't ever just mess around, in some midlife crisis. He had integrity."

"After that spring he never taught the BU course again," Meg remembered.

"That doesn't necessarily mean anything," Amy said.

"Yes it does, because then he would have had to lie about going into Boston," Jo said. "Or anywhere else that would give him enough time. For an affair, I mean, to meet someone. And you could never lie to Mumma. She had a real good ratcatcher. She always knew."

We smiled, a little conspiratorially, remembering the several times she had caught one of the others out, and I didn't think I could be the only one who had, at least once, gotten away with it with Mumma.

Amy brought us back to the subject at hand. "Did he forget about the mistress, do you think? Eventually he must have. I never got the sense that he was pining for someone. Did any of you?"

The waitress came to clear away dessert and I asked for the check and Jo asked, "Did she marry her tenant? I bet she did. Propinquity."

"Or at least take up with him," I said.

"Does that mean she did?" Jo asked.

"I don't know," I admitted.

"You mean after all that detective work you never went back to find out what happened to her?" Meg asked.

"Pops wanted me to leave her to him, so I did."

Without taking the check from our waitress, I handed her four credit cards. Whenever we went out together, nobody was anybody's guest. Because Mumma had insisted on being the person who paid whenever she was out with any of us, or all of us, we were all stiff-necked about paying our own way. If you never allow your children to take you out, to dinner, to the movies, for coffee, it's a way of denying their equality with you, like never letting them drive. Mumma never let any of us drive, either, once we were licensed; she only ever let Pops drive her, and then only for social purposes, so that everyone could see that he was the man of the family. When we were young, my sisters and I shared the driving equally, and as adults, in restaurants, we split the checks four ways — among the four of us, there will be equality.

"Probably Pops' girlfriend had married

before she finished her degree," Meg deduced.

"Unless she never started it," Amy said. "If she got married very young."

"I can't imagine Pops with someone who wasn't educated," Meg said.

"Imagine him with Mumma," Jo advised.

"Mumma *is* educated. She's self-educated," Meg argued. "But Mumma is unusual. No, don't make fun of me, I mean, she was determined to be an educated person."

"Then why didn't she go to college?" I asked, not for the first time. "When we were little, before Polly got married, she could have gone to school."

"Being Pops' wife was a serious job to her," Meg reminded us. "She was making their place in the community, which was what good wives did for their husbands."

"You want to hear what I think?" I asked, and gave them no time to decline the offer. "I always thought she was afraid to go to college."

"Would you blame her?" Jo asked. We all accepted our credit cards and our quarter bills from the waitress, did not consult one another about the tip, signed the slips, and replaced the cards in our wallets. Jo continued, "Anyway, this woman was probably smart enough. Although I don't see why she'd have to be, for Pops to fall in love with her."

"And then he gave her up," Amy said. "He *was* a good husband, wasn't he?"

"That was the summer he took Mumma to Paris, and rented an apartment for a month," I told them. "Remember? Pops stayed on, he changed all his plans, and they went to the Riviera to that nunnery, to see the Matisse stained glass because Mumma loved Matisse."

We smiled at one another, fond smiles, at the memory of our parents' marriage. "End of story," Meg said with satisfaction.

"Actually, no, it isn't," I told them, and savored — I admit it — the surprise on their faces. "It was the end for Pops, but there's more."

We left the restaurant and walked across the new grass, none of us having been so foolish as to wear more than the lowest heels even on that day. We were on the Cape, where we always wanted to drift off the roadway, or the path, onto the grass, or out onto the beach, up onto the dunes. In the harbor, sailboats rocked gently at their moorings and sunlight reflected off the water. It was a child's picture, the freshly painted hulls and the deep blue sky with impossibly puffy white clouds floating dreamily across it. I felt a swelling of contentment, to be where I was, in the company I was in, on such a day. Despite the sadness of Mumma, we had done what we all felt was the right thing for her. We were taking care of her together; we were sisters. "Remember Pops' funeral?" I asked them.

March is a good month for death. There are no holidays in March to be annually tainted by sorrow, and the weather is conducive to a sense of loss, and fear, and emptiness. At least in New England, that's how it is. Pops died in March. In fact, he died over most of March, having his stroke in the first sleety week and lingering on in a coma for eighteen days after that, with the wind constantly blowing and the skies constantly changing from gray to blue and back to gray again. For us — his family, his wife and daughters, their spouses and significant others, his grandchildren — for those of us who loved him, this was the kindest and most thoughtful of exits, entirely in character, as I think to myself every March while I watch winter make its slow retreat from the sky and sea, all that slow, sad month. A sudden exit leaves abrupt silences, too much unsaid, even unthought. A relatively slow exit, even if the dying person is unable to make the least gesture, gives you the chance to realize what it is you have wanted to say, whether you actually say it or not, whether you are responded to or not.

Not that that was the way I felt at the time. Not that all of us didn't hope fervently, at first, that he might make a good recovery. But then he didn't. He had his stroke, and after only three days he slipped quietly into a coma from which we eventually came to hope that he would never wake. Pops obliged.

During those weeks we gathered together at Mumma's house, taking turns visiting him in the hospital. The daughters taking turns, that is. Mumma was at his bedside almost constantly, and especially during the first long nights when his unconsciousness was incomplete. "He doesn't want to be left alone," she told us, and we believed her. Pops' eyes, when open, fixed on Mumma. He glanced at others of us, and at the nurses too, but he looked at Mumma.

Mumma dressed up to sit beside Pops and read aloud to him, in stockings and the high heels she always wore, something different every day, different styles, different colors. "He was always proud of the way I look," she told us. "He likes colors, so I don't want to see any of you wearing dark and gloomy. Not for your father, who was never gloomy. He deserves bright things."

I don't know what the nursing staffs made of us, either in the hospital or in the long-term care facility. We sat beside Pops' bed, Mumma and whoever, and sometimes we would talk to him, and sometimes we would talk among ourselves, but mostly we read aloud to him. Mumma chose the book, *War and Peace,* big surprise. "He loved that book and if you haven't read it already, you should, so now's your chance," she told us. "He likes to hear familiar voices," she told us, then clarified, "He likes to hear our voices."

Pops showed no awareness of our readings, but we carried on, page after page, making our way through most of the one thousand, five hundred and forty-nine pages of the Modern Library edition. *("Don't read the battle scenes," Mumma instructed us. "One war was enough for him.")* The machinery Pops lived on hummed and we sat beside his bed making equally monotonous sounds. Pops lay still, eyes closed, chest barely moving, and thus we each made our own slow farewell to our father.

Mumma, however, was not about to make

any farewells. She wasn't giving up. "After this, we'll read him *Moby Dick,* and after that . . ." She hesitated.

"Not *Little Women,*" Meg requested.

"No, he doesn't much care for women writers, except — you know the one, I can't dredge up her name just now."

"Jane Austen? George Eliot? P. D. James?" we suggested.

"That's her," Mumma said, her face brightening. "No, I was thinking of the Dickens novel next. About — You know the one, it's got that handsome boy who seduces the girl then dies in a shipwreck."

"Copperfield," we said. "Steerforth."

"I don't know the second one, but it's Copperfield, *David Copperfield,*" she seized on the title. "He'd like hearing that."

Mumma was tired and preoccupied, busy keeping Pops alive, and we were only too glad to supply her with names and titles, and whatever other help we could offer. The Howlands did what they could, or wanted to. Anne and Giancarlo visited the hospital regularly, she in the mornings before lunch, he in the evenings, after work. Pops' youngest sister Juliet came in one weekend from the western part of the state, where thirty years earlier she had established a Montessori school, now a going concern with more than two hundred students and its own board of directors, one of which was Pops. When she was in her mid-forties, long an established spinster who we all thought might be a closet lesbian, Juliet had married a man twelve years younger than she, one of her teachers, a plump, bearded, sweet-tempered man, so ill at ease anywhere away from the school that he never left it. At the hospital, Juliet sat beside Pops' bed and worked on papers she had taken out of her briefcase, while one of us read aloud. She raised her glance to him, every now and then, and sighed, saying softly, "He was such a nice boy, a good brother," and, "It's like a library in here. Conducive to good thinking."

From the West Coast, Uncle Ethan sent flowers that the hospital wouldn't allow in Pops' room. Ethan had moved west after Grandmother died and he inherited the Louisburg Square house, which he immediately sold. The rest of the family, as far out as second cousins, tried to dissuade him from doing this, but that only goaded him into quicker action. He sold the furnishings at auction, which those relatives, if they cared so much, could attend as buyers. It wasn't as if he hadn't given the family first refusal, but if nobody could meet his price, what did they expect him to do? Mumma explained it to us — and Pops agreed — "We don't want the house, that's the first thing, because if your father did, I'd find a way. And your uncle is the kind of man who when he knows he's in the wrong, he gets angry at you. You girls are lucky to have him for an uncle so you can learn what that kind of man is like. Women will use anger, too, although they don't do it in the same way, and you're lucky he's moving west because he's not the kind of uncle any mother wants to have around her daughters. Out there, he's just normal." So Uncle Ethan sent a huge bouquet of lilies that we left out on the porch, not wanting to take them into the house with us; they obliged us by being dead in the morning, after a single sharp Cape Cod March night. Brundy had died two years earlier, in Paris, and been buried there, but Tonio, his companion of twenty-two years, who had traveled with Brundy and Mumma and Pops, which he maintained made them all his relatives too, sent tulips every five days. Tonio's flowers we put on the kitchen table, changing the water every day and regularly cutting back the stems so that they would stay fresh as long as possible. Pops couldn't have flowers, but whoever was reading would bring a single tulip with her, from France, from Brundy. It sat in a bud vase beside his bed; she took it away when she left.

We daughters took turns coming to stay, for two or three days at a time. On weekends we tried to be there together for at least one of the nights. Meg drove down from Wayland, Amy from Wellesley, while Jo took a bus from South Station, unless I was driving down from our Avon Hill house and could give her a ride. We brought children when we had to. Sarah was often with me, and it cheered Mumma to have a baby in the house, someone to cuddle and complain about. My nieces and nephews, Meg's and Amy's broods, were all in their teens by then, old enough to make hospital visits. One of my sisters, usually Jo, would take care of my older girls when I sat with Pops, unless they came in with their older cousins for a visit. Those cousins met at Mumma's house before going on to the hospital or, after Pops was moved, to the nursing home. They were too young, too healthy, a blast of bright fresh air, and Mumma would abandon Pops to them. "I need a break. Those boys of yours, Meg, I don't know where they get the energy. If Spencer hadn't already done it, having them there with him in that shape would give him a second stroke. Don't get me wrong, I love them dearly, and it's refreshing for the staff to have them charging around the place. The nurses scatter, like ducks off a pond. They're not used to healthy people." While the grandchildren visited Pops, Mumma would go home, take a shower, "Put my feet up," and then get dressed. "He always liked me in yellow. Your girls have been with him long enough, Amy. I'm going to send them home. It's not good for young people to see too much sickness. It discourages them."

"They love Pops," we protested. "Of course they do," Mumma said. "That's why I'm giving them this chance to say goodbye to him. What do you think, that I'd be jealous of my own grandchildren? But he's happier when I'm with him. So go to bed, don't stay up too late talking about me the way you always like to."

Our disobedience of these instructions went uncharacteristically unremarked. We didn't go to bed. We weren't sleeping well anyway, so we made pots of tea, pots of cocoa, bowls of popcorn. We built fires in the big stone fireplace and sat in front of it, drinking, eating, with Jo — who couldn't seem to break the habit for all her attempts with hypnosis and clinics, elastic bands, special chewing gum — insisting that we go outside occasionally so she could have a cigarette or three. We wrapped ourselves up in sweaters and blankets, gathered up glasses of wine, bottles of beer, and an ashtray, and sat on the porch steps to look at the sky: Orion lounging along the horizon, the moon as it waxed from quarter to full, then waned to three-quarters, the clouds as they sailed across the darkness or spread themselves out like a veil between stars and earth.

We talked about our father. Our childhoods, and our adult lives too, had been dominated by Mumma, but Pops was always there. Quietly there, unimpressively there, profoundly there.

"He was the audience," Meg suggested. "For all of us, really."

"No, he was the backdrop, the scenery," Amy said.

"But not the stage manager, and not the sugar daddy, especially not once inflation hit the trust. It's lucky her real estate investments exploded," I reminded them, "or they'd have had to change their lifestyles."

"He made her really happy," we agreed. "And it's not easy to make Mumma happy," as we all knew.

Jo said, "Tell me . . . No, I mean, let's tell one another . . . I mean, let's exchange . . .

Pops *is* dying, we do all know that?"

We did, we understood that we were grieving, and we trusted Jo the therapist to know something we could do to help ourselves grieve well and begin to assimilate our loss. She said, "The best memories of him. I'll start. One of my best, and there are a lot of good ones, is the way Pops always gave me a book for Christmas. Remember? Even though I was the stupid one."

"We never thought that. Only you thought that."

"Me and Mumma," Jo reminded us. "He still does it, you know? This year it was *Pilgrim at Tinker Creek.* They're never new books, they've always stood some test of time. And I always read them. Some of them I've really liked. They all made me think, and I knew he'd read them himself and liked them, and that was why he gave them to me."

"He was great when I was divorcing Jack," Meg remembered. "He said I should do whatever I thought was best for me, for my character, and for my future. That was what he wanted. Then he told me that he trusted me to know what that was. I could count on him, he said. Unlike Mumma. She said that when you made your bed you should lie in it, at least for a year," Meg concluded, uncharacteristically outspoken.

"Mumma came around," Amy protested. "It was just because you're the first."

"First and only," Meg reminded us.

"Only because I've never gotten married to any of mine," Jo said.

"Is that a satellite?" I asked, taking my arm out from under the warmth of the blanket to point up into the sky. "It's too unblinking for a star, don't you think? Or could it be a planet, do you think?"

"How many years have we sat right here and looked at the stars," Jo asked, but it wasn't a question, it was a celebration. "Shall I pick up Mumma or do you want to?" she asked Meg, because I had brought Sarah, who would be awake early, and Amy was due at nine in the city to meet with George and the accountant about Mumma's taxes, so we two needed as much sleep as we could manage.

"I remember the way, when you were talking to Pops, he would look right at you, look you right in the eye," I said then. I was thinking of the time I had lunch with him to talk about Nanette, but they didn't know, then, what I was referring to. "Pops really listened to us," I said.

"He noticed," Amy added. "I mean, we heard a lot about how Mumma understood us, and we couldn't fool her, and that was true, but Pops noticed things. Remember when I won that Rotary Club prize in eighth grade? He wrote me a letter . . . I still have it, I have it in my safe deposit box, in fact. It was — it is — It's a wonderful letter for a father to write to a daughter. He said how mysterious I am to him and how proud of me he is. Whereas Mumma," Amy told us as we all looked up into the midnight sky, knowing that another hour would have to pass before somebody went to make Mumma leave her bedside vigil and get a few hours of sleep. "Mumma said that they gave me the award because I was *her* daughter."

"I remember," Meg said. "I thought it was sort of rotten for her to say that."

I remembered it, too, and remembered that I assumed Mumma was correct and that Amy's prize was thus not such a big deal, not nearly as big a deal as she wanted to make it. Sitting there, remembering, "I'm sorry," I said to Amy.

"I figured she was just jealous," Jo said, "the way mothers can be of daughters, although she'd deny that. Mumma's got a big streak of center stage, we all know, although she'd deny that too."

"She doesn't deny things," I told my

sisters. "She ignores them. Which — I know, Jo — you could argue is a deeper form of denial. But she wasn't ever jealous about Pops and us. How much we love him. I never thought she was, did you?"

"Pops wasn't an ordinary man," Amy assured me, "and she knew that. He was, he is, better than most people and she told me once, she told me she wanted to keep him that way."

At that, so exactly what Mumma would say, we all burst out laughing. Then we gathered up our glasses and blankets, Jo picked up her cigarettes and ashtray, and we went back into the house.

If it hadn't been for what I couldn't stop knowing was the contents of the coffin, Pops' funeral would have been a wonderful event. Saint Stephen's was crowded with family and friends, colleagues, students and former students, and the organist played Bach, the richly complex lines of melody intertwining like our own lives. The day was bright, the coffin plain polished pine, the flowers fresh and abundant, and the eulogies genuine, speaking of Pops as a man who in the course of his seventy-one years had done what was asked of him with a willing spirit, a loving heart, and a querying intelligence. My father. The immediate family followed the coffin out of the church, then in limos out to the cemetery, where final prayers were spoken before it was lowered into the ground, next to Aunt Phyllis. This was the only point at which tears trembled in Mumma's eyes, and her hand trembled in mine. Then we all returned to the big house, where Uncle Ethan, who had flown in from the West Coast to take up his position as head of the family, had arranged to receive the mourners. Guests filled the downstairs rooms and flowed out onto the sloping lawn, talking about Pops, sadly, but with that many-layered grief that comes at the end of a long, well-lived life, a grief that is in large part a celebration of how a life can be lived.

Most of us wore dark clothing. Mumma wore a bright pink dress, with a full skirt, its lack of printed flowers her only concession to the occasion. She assured us that pink was the Chinese color for funerals. Certainly, standing at the foot of the same curved staircase where decades earlier Grandmother had stood to greet guests at Anne's rehearsal dinner, Mumma seemed perfectly funereal, solemn and even dignified as she shook hands, kissed cheeks, accepted condolences, repeating over and over, "Yes, he will be missed," at home, in Wampanoag, at the college, whatever place was appropriate to the particular mourner. She accepted kisses on the cheek, even from Jonquil Cartenbury Heolms, and she stayed the length of Jonquil's sympathetic outpouring about widows over a certain age being in such a difficult position. Mumma didn't even round on her. She didn't show any sign of irritation at all. It was as if she hadn't grasped the meaning of the words.

Perhaps that was a sign we should have picked up on, but we didn't. Like the other people gathered at the Howland cottage to remember Pops, we assumed that Mumma was stunned by grief, and by the exhaustion of her long vigil. If she behaved, or responded, distractedly, we could certainly understand that. Two of her daughters were always beside her to welcome guests, to remind her of any names that might have slipped her mind; and in fact one or two of the older men who came had to introduce themselves anyway, saying, "I was in Spencer's OCS class, he was a good officer," or, "Spence crewed for me when we were at Choate, he was a fine crew."

I was standing on Mumma's left and Meg was on her right, when a tall, silver-haired woman approached, an elegantly turned out, tanned woman of about Mumma's age, with a long, straight nose and a strong, firm chin, her fingers festooned with diamonds and sapphires, all in old-fashioned settings. She wore full makeup, but of the best kind so that she looked glowingly younger than her years. It took all of us a minute to realize who she was: Abigail Smith. We had seen her photograph, we had seen her on TV accepting Oscars. Abigail Smith was so tall and slender and stylish that compared to her, Mumma looked like some TV sitcom grandmother, plump and plain and more than a little unkempt.

The elegant woman reached out a manicured hand, to take Mumma's, and followed it with another manicured hand, putting all of the rings on display. "How long has it been?" she asked, in a voice that had no interest in the answer to her question. "Rida, isn't it? Yes, Rida. I had meetings in the city, New York, that is, and I couldn't miss Spencer Howland's funeral. Not if I was on the same coast."

They stood looking at each other, Mumma looking up, waiting, Abigail Smith looking around. "I'm here for him," Abigail Smith announced, freeing Mumma's hands.

I was amazed. Pops the Don Juan, the lady-killer? Or was he just the one that got away and therefore the one that couldn't be forgotten?

"Because I loved him," Abigail Smith said.

"No you didn't," Mumma told her.

The tall woman glanced briefly at Mumma, then dismissed her and looked around, raising her hand. "Ethan, is that you?" Uncle Ethan was passing nearby with two drinks, probably both for himself. "Is it really you? Ethan Howland all grown up?" He stopped, puzzled. Abigail Smith smiled and reached a beringed hand out to him.

"If you had," Mumma continued, "you would never have left. Like Sonia in *War and Peace,* you'd have stayed near him, even if he was married to someone else. Have you read *War and Peace* yet?"

"It's Abigail Smith," she re-introduced herself to Ethan. "I know I've changed, but you remember me, don't you? *And* I hear you're on the West Coast now. Why have you never let me know?"

"Well, well," Uncle Ethan said, slithering an arm around her waist. "You haven't changed a bit since the time when you were the girl of my dreams. And those were quite some dreams, I can promise you," he said, pulling her toward him, carrying her away beside him. Over the years, Uncle Ethan had gone thick in the waist and ruddy in the nose. His wife of the time, his fourth by our reckoning, although we might have missed one, had stayed home, pleading a flu that none of us believed in. Probably she thought that at his older brother's funeral there wouldn't be anybody for Ethan to be tempted by, but she underestimated him.

At the end of the long afternoon, we all stood together, Pops' immediate family, to thank people for coming to his funeral. We placed ourselves just inside the front door through which all those years ago Mumma had first made her entry into this house, and this family, with Pops at her side and Meg in her arms.

The order of their going from funerals is well established. First to leave are the guests, and then the family has a quiet hour together, siblings, grandchildren, cousins. The hard liquor is brought out and people sit down to eat. They discuss the service, they discuss the previous generation of parents, and sometimes settle family business, such as the divided responsibility for and occupancy of a summer cottage. Every now and then, somebody looks up to remark, "This is a sad occasion, isn't it?" and the group will discuss, again, the way death took this particular family member and recall the deaths of others. Then, after another hour, either the larger, more distantly connected family will depart, leaving the immediate family to their sharper grief, or, as in this case, the immediate family being guests, they too take their departure, together this time, not in limousines but in the cars they came in.

George and I took Mumma home, and Meg rode with us; Liam took our older girls and their own boys, as well as Jo and Milton, in the Caravan. Amy and Wilfred had Sarah with them, because her Kelly was so good with Sarah.

In the car, Mumma sat in the front seat with George while Meg and I occupied the rear. Mumma never rode in the back seat. If she wasn't the driver, she was the primary passenger; that was as low as she could put herself in any hierarchy. "Well," Mumma said, without turning around. "That's over with."

I leaned forward to tell her, "I thought your dress was perfect. You looked" — I pictured it, Mumma greeting guests at Pops' funeral — "beautiful."

Mumma snorted. "*Now* you admit it. Life's too short to be stingy with compliments," she advised me.

I reached forward to put a hand on her shoulder. "But what do you mean, over with? What's over with?"

"That funeral, mostly, but — Oh, all of it, the going to the hospital, reading to him and we got barely three-quarters of the way through, you know. What was the name of that woman?" She looked impatiently at George. "You know who I mean. She's slipped my mind."

"Abigail," I suggested.

"No, in the book."

"Natasha?" George offered.

"No, the other woman."

"Sonia," I said, thinking that was the connection, but George, more in tune, said, "Hélène."

"Yes, that's her, with her white shoulders," Mumma said, contented.

I walked with my mother from the car to the front door. On the occasion of her widowhood, Mumma wanted to enter the house Pops had bought for her through the front door. She moved up the walk slowly, reluctant, I thought — and who could blame her? — to assume this new role. To become a widow. She and I fell back, letting the others get ahead, Jo and Milton following George in solemn procession, some sad variation on a bridal party. I put my arm around my mother's shoulders. Since having children of my own, I had grown bold about touching my mother, and comfortable too, even wrapping my arms around her to hug her in excitement, or sadness, or sometimes simple fondness. With my arm around her and her head close to my ear, Mumma said, "She was there."

"Abigail Smith? I know. Do you think Pops would have enjoyed that?"

"Your father would have been unhappy with all of it, all of this . . . this *ceremony*," Mumma answered impatiently. "It's what he'd have wanted, though. A Howland funeral. But I didn't mean the old girlfriend. I meant the new one. The Boston one."

I made my face expressionless.

Mumma ignored my silence. "I thought someone should know that I knew," she said.

"Did Pops tell — ?"

"No, of course not. He — There was no sex," my mother informed me. "If there had been, I'd have known. I wouldn't have stood for that."

"Oh," I said. I had to say something and *Oh* was all I could think of. Mumma was waiting for me to say something more, so I said it again. "Oh."

"I recognized her right away today, not that I ever saw her in person at the time, or any photograph either," Mumma told me.

"Your father wasn't the kind of man to make a Freudian slip like a photograph. But when she said, 'I knew Spencer years ago, in Cambridge. He was a wonderful man,' I could tell. She'd been really in love with him. Well, I'm not surprised. She's married now, she was wearing a ring, but I don't think she could have been, then. Your father wouldn't want to be a home wrecker."

"You knew and never said anything?" I wondered.

"Of course not. What do you think? He didn't want me to know, for one thing. And he was an honorable man. If he knew I knew, he would have thought he had to *do* something and I knew he didn't want to do that."

By that time, slowly as we were moving, we had entered the hallway and Amy was calling out from the kitchen that she had coffee brewing. Mumma let George take her coat, then settled herself at the head of the dining room table. Sarah came up and was allowed onto her lap, allowed to feed herself sugar by the spoonful and that day I didn't say anything about my authority being undermined. It was my father's funeral. Also, I was stupefied.

My first reaction was to berate myself: I knew *nothing* about my parents' marriage, I understood *nothing.* Then I realized: I was still learning about it and couldn't, in any case, expect to really understand it. Other people's relationships are always a conversation held in a foreign language, I know that. All you can do is grasp the occasional word or phrase, as much of it as you can if it's a language you're trying to learn. I thought: *Mumma knew all along. I should have guessed.*

"What's so funny?" George asked, passing me a mug of coffee with lots of milk and sugar, the way I like it in the afternoon.

"Tell you later," I promised.

Then Mumma started telling us what was what, moving on in her life. "I don't want you girls giving me a funeral like that one. I want a Quaker funeral."

"But you're not a Quaker," Jo protested. "You can't just *get* a Quaker funeral, like a rental car."

"I've read about them," Mumma insisted.

"We should talk about this later, Mrs. R," Wilfred said. Mumma's sons-in-law, and sons-in-law-equivalents, had always been told to call her Mrs. R, because she wasn't their mother and frankly — with a smile, and a glance from those eyes under their thick dark eyebrows — she didn't want to be. "You're young yet," Wilfred continued.

"We've got lots of time to worry about your funeral."

"Which reminds me of another thing," Mumma said. "One of you should be living near me now. Now I'm alone."

She looked around at her four daughters and we looked around at one another, alarmed and a little anxious.

"Someone who has a flexible career. Someone whose husband wants to go into private practice anyway. I mean Beth," she announced. "The schools are good enough out here, and it's a better place to raise children. I don't mean live *with* me," she clarified, looking right at me, as if she could read my mind, as if she was reading my mind right then. "And there is nothing to get all weepy about. It's not so great, living in the city," she told me. "I've done it. I know."

For once, she didn't understand. My tears were for sorrow, for the loss of my father, but for happiness, too, to be the one Mumma chose.

"When I was just a newlywed," Mumma reminded us, "and didn't know as much as I do now about how to be married."

7.
MUMMA HAS A FRIEND

It was at the April garden club meeting of
1981 that Mumma first heard the news.
They had asked her to be treasurer, again,
so she didn't have the option of missing the
monthly meetings. Jonquil Cartenbury, who
alternated between being the elected president and the elected vice president, was *not*
present, and this was entirely unexpected,
since, as Mumma often reported to us,
"That Jonquil Cartenbury just loves queen-
ing it over those women. They think she's
an intellectual. They think she's goodness
itself. They think they know her but they
don't have the slightest idea the kind of Ma-
chiavelli that woman is. They don't even
know how lucky they are to have me there
to keep an eye on her and keep her in
check."

The Cartenburys had moved out to Wampanoag as year-round residents not long
after Mumma and Pops did. "The woman

361

is my doppelgänger," Mumma complained, when she heard of the move. Pops was of a different opinion. "Francis Cartenbury wants to go into politics and Wampanoag will give him a good voter base. People around here — and I don't mean summer people, Rida, I mean everyone else — they know the Cartenbury name."

"Or nemesis," Mumma continued. "She wishes."

"He might make a good DA," Pops allowed. "He's smart, and pretty honest, and having been born to money gives him a better chance than most not to be corruptible. I'll vote for him."

"I'll vote for him to go back to Boston," Mumma offered, "if he takes her with him."

"Aren't you being a little narrow-minded?" Pops asked, and Mumma, who had a lot of respect for some of Pops' opinions, asked, "Do you think I am? Narrow-minded? Because I don't want to be that kind of woman, you know that, Spencer, or that kind of person either."

In Wampanoag, the Cartenburys winterized his family's summer cottage out on Beach Road, a low, gray-shingled house with a broad porch looking down to the water. Jonquil constructed elaborate gardens, in beds that spread back from the curved entryway to surround the house. During the summers we would sometimes be at the same events as the Cartenburys and their boys, but during the off-season we almost never saw them, since the boys went first to a private school in Hyannis, and then, as soon as it was possible, to boarding school. Only Mumma and Mrs. Cartenbury ran into one another. "We pretended to talk about the price of lettuce," Mumma might report, "and she asked after Grandmother's health, as if she knew something I didn't, some big piece of bad news that your grandmother asked her not to tell me." Even when Meg ran off to Mexico to marry Jack Cartenbury and soon after, when she ran off to Mexico again to divorce him, the relationship between the two mothers did not change.

They lived parallel lives, Mumma and Jonquil Cartenbury, running against each other for a garden club office, or a position on the hospital auxiliary, where Jonquil Cartenbury was regularly elected and Mumma never. "She's no more than a blip on my radar," Mumma reported, and she did vote for Francis Cartenbury, who was, as Pops had predicted, a good public servant. "Or maybe a mote in my eye. No, really, she's a gnat; most of the time I can barely see her."

But at that garden club meeting, when they were women in their fifties, Mumma noticed that Jonquil Cartenbury had absented herself, and she asked someone about that. "What is so important that she can't be here?" Mumma asked.

"You haven't heard," the woman answered.

Mumma didn't bother to affirm it. If she'd heard, she wouldn't have asked. She waited.

"Rida hasn't heard," the woman said to someone nearby.

"That's odd," the someone remarked. "Don't you think that's odd?"

Mumma continued to wait. They were talking in the kind of low voices used for serious gossip, for marital infidelity gone public, the birth of brain-damaged children, bankruptcy, drug addiction.

Looking carefully around as if to be sure they spoke privately, although everybody except Mumma apparently already knew, the first woman told Mumma, "She had a Bad Diagnosis."

Mumma said nothing.

"Her Breast," the woman said, confidentially. "The right one."

"When?" Mumma asked.

"A Biopsy," the woman continued.

364

Mumma repeated herself. "When?"

"And if it's Malignant . . . a *Mastectomy*," the woman said, with a significant nodding of her head. Then she relented and told Mumma, "The doctor just told her two days ago. She's barely had time to think, poor woman. To decide if she — to think about what she should do — if it's as bad as — if they tell her it's Bad News. Because sometimes they're wrong, you know. And then where would she be if she'd run off and had . . . a *Mastectomy*?"

"What does *she* say?" Mumma asked. She didn't much care for Jonquil Cartenbury, as everybody knew, but she wouldn't wish cancer on anybody. Life was hard enough without cancer.

"We wouldn't *ask* her!" They were shocked. "We don't want to intrude."

"We're not that insensitive!" they said. "We sent her notes."

"To assure her that Louise has agreed to take over the vice-presidency."

"Only temporarily, of course. Unless —"

"And we sent flowers. Not houseplants, they take too much attention and who can say how much time she'll have? For houseplants, you know, so we sent cut flowers."

The Garden Club of Wampanoag held its meetings at the Falmouth public library, in a paneled room with chairs set in rows facing a long table at the front. At the conclusion of the meetings, the women would leave their seats to gather around card tables at the rear, where whichever volunteers had come to the top of the roster set out their sliced cakes and crustless sandwiches, urns of tea and coffee, pastries from the one French pastry shop in business on the lower Cape at that time.

Mumma didn't stay for tea that day, or for her monthly efforts to improve the thinking and maybe even the voting habits of her fellow members. She went directly to her car and drove back into Wampanoag, where she turned on to Beach Road and drew the Cadillac up in front of Jonquil Cartenbury's low gray house. It was too early in April to expect to find the mistress at work in the garden, and she didn't. But it *was* midafternoon, so she didn't expect to find her in her peignoir, which she did.

It was a real peignoir Jonquil Cartenbury wore, a honeymoon peignoir of white lacy stuff that flowed all around the slender blonde woman. "Faded blonde, but still," Mumma admitted. "She always was a pretty woman, and she's kept herself up. She's kept her looks, Jonquil has, and it can't have been easy."

When Mumma was shown by the house-keeper into the conservatory, where Jonquil Cartenbury had stretched herself out on a wicker chaise with a pile of magazines on the table beside her, her hostess sat up straighter, arranging the filmy skirts of the peignoir around her legs, but seemed to address her own ankles, "How very good you shouldn't have —" Then she looked up. "Is that Rida?"

"Who did you expect?" Mumma asked. "Not one of those garden club friends of yours I don't think. They're all very well and good, but they're at a loss when it comes to real life."

"What a surprise!" Jonquil said, sitting up still straighter, setting her feet on the floor. "May I offer you some tea? I think I will have a cup after all, Teresa, and — some sandwiches? You just love my little cucumber sandwiches, Rida. Don't try to deny it. I've seen you gobble them up. Tell me everything that happened at the meeting," Jonquil Cartenbury said, rising to change seats and sit upright, hands folded in her lap and a bright smile on her face.

Mumma knew she was going to have to wait until the tea table had been wheeled in and she had been given a full teacup and passed a small plate of sandwiches, so she recapped the meeting even though it was clear that despite her bright-eyed expression, Jonquil was not paying attention. "Well, imagine," Jonquil said, whenever Mumma left space for a response. "Imagine that."

Finally they were alone and Jonquil Cartenbury was making no effort to drink her tea or even nibble at the one tiny triangle of sandwich she had taken, so Mumma could ask, "Who is your doctor and what did he say to you? What exactly, I mean."

"I don't think —"

Mumma brushed any protests aside. "I'm here to help."

"I don't think I want —"

"I didn't say you did. I don't think you do, but I'm here anyway. What are the facts, Jonquil? Spit it out."

Bullied, Jonquil Cartenbury admitted it. There was a lump. She had waited and waited, but it hadn't gone away and now the doctor . . . In her right breast. *There*, if Rida insisted on knowing the precise and exact location. She was going in for a biopsy. The day after tomorrow. To see what it was.

"Is it growing?" Mumma asked.

"Rida! How would I know *that*!"

"If it were me, I wouldn't be able to keep my hands off it," Mumma said, taking another sandwich. She didn't like to admit it, but Jonquil was right: She did love those little cucumber triangles, the cucumbers sliced paper-thin, the wheat bread crustless and brushed with sweet butter, just the lightest salting and even less white pepper. "You must be terrified," she observed.

"It's only a biopsy," Jonquil protested.

"I would be," Mumma said. "Cancer's a horrible disease, even if nobody wants to admit that it exists."

"Well, why anybody would want to talk about it . . . I can understand why nobody wants to talk about it," Jonquil said. "I am certainly hoping I *don't* have it, I promise you that."

"How is Francis taking this? I'm not sure how Spencer would react."

"Oh, I haven't told Francis. I don't want to worry him unnecessarily."

Mumma froze, the sandwich held suspended between her upper and lower teeth. She didn't move for a full five seconds, then she bit down thoughtfully and set the uneaten portion gently back on her plate.

Jonquil told her, "Francis is a man, and that means he's not one bit happy to hear about women's problems. I won't bother him unless . . ." And then, as if she were an inflated balloon let loose to rocket across the room, the air went out of Jonquil Cartenbury. She hunched over her knees, arms wrapped around her stomach. "What am I going to do?" she whispered. "If — if I really —"

"Probably you'll cry a lot," Mumma predicted. "But you have to do what the doctor tells you. You can't pretend it's not happening, not if you want to survive. You'll have to —" But she stopped talking because Jonquil was waving her hands in the air, either dismissing Mumma's words, or pleading with her not to utter them.

"I'm too young," Jonquil whispered. "I'm only fifty-five, that's too young. Isn't it?"

"I always thought you were older than me," Mumma objected.

"Really? How old are you?" Jonquil asked, perking up a little.

"Fifty-six," Mumma admitted. Then she said, "I'll go with you."

"Where?"

"To the hospital."

"It's in Hyannis," Jonquil protested. "It's overnight," but Mumma had made up her mind. "You won't want to be alone. I'll be there in the morning too, while they're operating."

Jonquil tried to decline the offer. "That's too much trouble for you, Rida, with your busy life and all."

"You'll feel better, knowing I'm there," Mumma assured her, contrary to any evidence.

So Mumma drove Jonquil Cartenbury over to Hyannis the next afternoon, and stayed with her while she filled out forms, and went with her up to her single room, and sat with her while she swallowed the pills that constituted all she was supposed to ingest before her early morning procedure. She did not visit Jonquil the next morning, but she sat in the waiting room — she had brought paperwork and a book to read, from six until ten, at which time the doctor emerged from behind a door, looking for Jonquil's family, to tell them the bad news.

"You're supposed to tell me," Mumma said. "I'm with her."

He recognized authority when he saw it, so he reported that it was in fact malignant and he himself would recommend a double radical mastectomy. If it were his wife, he assured Mumma, that is what he would advise her to do. The cancer, while not in evidence in the left breast, was of a type that spread rapidly and was in its later stages peculiarly resistant to both radiation and chemotherapy. He didn't trust it not to have already spread. Two lymph nodes on the right side were already impacted.

Mumma listened, with her arms folded protectively over her own breasts, as he made his diagnosis and recommendation. (*"Not that I didn't trust the man. He had a good reputation and he was sympathetic. He said that if he thought there were decent odds in its favor, he would be recommending a less drastic response, but . . . I knew what that but meant."*)

"Where is Mr. Cartenbury?" the doctor asked Mumma then.

"He's a district attorney so he's probably in court."

"The children?"

"Boys, both of them."

He nodded. "Family?"

"In Virginia, but I don't know if her parents are still living. I don't know if she has a sister, or cousins —"

"Because someone should be with her when she comes out of the anesthetic. To help her think about the decision."

"That's what I'm here for," Mumma said.

"Ordinarily a friend isn't . . . not being a relative, you see . . ."

"I'm not a friend," Mumma assured him.

"I'm just — I'm here with her. Does she know?"

"Not yet. I'll tell her when she's *compos mentis*."

Mumma didn't know *compos mentis*, never having taken Latin, but she could guess. At home, when she asked Pops what it meant and he told her, she announced to him that she'd gotten the gist of it, whether she knew Latin or not.

"I'd better go see her," Mumma decided. "What room?"

Who knows what Mumma thought about, sitting in Jonquil Cartenbury's hospital room waiting for her to wake up enough to recognize more than the little paper cup of water she occasionally sipped from. "I waited," was all she ever said about it. It was a couple of hours before Jonquil really surfaced, and the confusion in her eyes was swiftly replaced by memory, and fear. Then she saw Mumma.

Jonquil Cartenbury looked terrible, that midday; that was all Mumma said about it. She didn't look like herself, and it was more than lack of makeup. "I should call Francis," Mumma said, as soon as she saw that Jonquil knew who she was, who they both were. And where. And why. "You'll want him here when you see the doctor."

"No. No, please don't. I don't — He doesn't — Sit back down, Rida. *You* could stay. You said you'd be here," Jonquil reminded her. "Francis is a man, and you know how they are about hospitals."

"He should be here," Mumma insisted.

"It's fine," Jonquil Cartenbury responded, and motored the bed so she was sitting up. "I'm fine. You'll see, I'll talk with the doctor and be home by four. You'll let me stop off at the market, won't you? Everything's going to be just fine now," she announced. "Just hand me my purse, would you, Rida? I know that you think concern for appearances makes a person shallow, but I happen to believe a woman owes it to the world to always be at her best."

"Putting her best face forward," said Mumma, and Jonquil Cartenbury did something she had never in their whole long enmity done before: She laughed at one of Mumma's jokes.

Mumma knew then how perilous was the woman's mental state. So she didn't tell her the bad news she already knew, thinking that a last hour of hope was not to be begrudged, not to anybody. Mumma prided herself on not being so small-minded that she couldn't lie for a good cause.

"Won't Francis be wondering where you

are?" she asked. Jonquil shook her head and smiled brightly. Mumma grew suspicious. "Where did you say you were going to be last night, since you weren't at home?"

"Oh, that's not a problem. Francis keeps very odd hours. He works so hard, he can never keep up with the criminal classes, you know how they are. You read the papers, Rida, you *have* to know what people are turning into, what the forces of law and order are up against. Francis has his own rooms, of course. So he won't disturb me coming in late, working late, leaving early. He likes to eat breakfast at Maggie's, with people from the office; they have their own table and they start right in on the day's work, even if it's terribly early. I don't think people understand how hard public servants work. Tonight, however, we're engaged for dinner. So I have to be home by four, and I do need to do a little marketing because on weekends Francis likes to breakfast at home. Together," she added, lest the separate bedrooms give Mumma any ideas about the Cartenbury marriage, as if she had already heard Mumma's opinion, which began with the declaration that "Single beds are bad enough, even in the same room."

Mumma gave Jonquil Cartenbury her privacy with the doctor, to hear the bad

375

news. They left the hospital together and stopped by the grocery store, where Jonquil waited in the car while Mumma purchased her groceries. Then Mumma dropped Jonquil off at the low, gray-shingled house. Jonquil stepped tenuously out of the Cadillac, and Mumma took her overnight case out of the trunk, to carry it inside for her. Jonquil was carrying the bag of groceries.

"I surely do thank you," Jonquil said, bending her mouth into a smile shape. She still looked like someone walking away from a train wreck. Or a bombed building. Or someone who had crawled out of a collapsed mine shaft.

"When do you go in for the mastectomy?" Mumma asked.

"We don't have to talk about that now, Rida. We don't want to dwell on *that*."

"Yes you do," Mumma said.

"Oh, honestly! Really, Rida, sometimes you — The doctor said not until Monday."

"And Francis will be with you?"

"I don't know. He's — You know how busy he is, his work is *important*."

"Who would you like me to telephone?" Mumma asked. "To tell."

"Oh, no one," Jonquil said. "Really, there's no need."

"Someone, maybe from the garden club?"

Mumma insisted.

"Oh, Rida. You know how it is with women. Those women aren't *friends*. They don't like me any more than they like you," Jonquil told Mumma.

"They elect you."

"That doesn't make them friends. That makes them people who think that if I'm running things, things will be done right and nobody will be insulted. They can be sure that I'll *look* like they want their president to look. It's not about *me*. It's about them staying comfortable."

Mumma thought about that. "You think I make people uncomfortable."

"You make *me* uncomfortable. But I never hold it against you because I know you mean well."

Mumma was amazed to find herself talking with Jonquil Cartenbury like this, amazed to learn that the other woman had understood her. "I do mean well."

"Well of course you do, my goodness. You can't help what you're like."

"Will Francis drive you in on Monday?"

"It's Sunday, actually, that I have to go in. Sunday evening. But I imagine he will. He'll be back from his golf game by five, he always is. That's plenty of time to drive to Hyannis."

"I'll be there Monday, then," Mumma announced. She could see that Jonquil was about to tell her not to bother, so she preempted whatever the other woman was going to say. She thought that Jonquil had no more idea than she herself did about just how Jonquil might be feeling on Monday, so she added, "Monday, if you want me to, I'll leave you alone. You won't have to ask me twice, I promise. You don't have to spare my feelings."

"You're not giving me any choice," Jonquil complained, temporarily diverted from her distress by irritation at Mumma, who was acting entirely in character. Jonquil was clearly of the opinion that by their age Mumma should have outgrown this kind of behavior.

"What would be the point of giving you a choice?" Mumma asked. "Although, really I have. A choice between me or someone else. Or actually, a choice between me or someone else or Francis, because if Francis is there of course I'd leave. Anybody would know that."

Mumma didn't believe for one minute that Francis Cartenbury was the kind of man who would spend hours at the bedside of a postoperative wife, and as to what would happen after that, she had her doubts.

About how Francis Cartenbury would feel about being a man whose wife no longer had breasts, she had strong doubts.

That spring, Mumma made Jonquil Cartenbury her first priority. As she had predicted, Francis consistently came up short. It was Mumma who went to the hospital, carrying flowers, bringing books and puzzles, needlepoint projects, messages from Jonquil's friends — friends who, somehow, for a wide variety of urgent reasons, could almost never make the trip in. In the hospital, Mumma was unflaggingly cheerful, as she reported it to us, but sympathetic, too, although she never allowed fear or despair to get in and run the show. Mumma was running the show.

When Jonquil was sent home to complete her postoperative recovery, it was Mumma who went over every day to do the physical therapy exercises with her, and whom Jonquil taught to play bridge. "It was that or mah-jongg, and I at least already know what a deck of cards looks like," Mumma told us when we wondered at what she was getting up to. "But maybe I should give her a Scrabble board. For all that she has a college degree, she doesn't have much of a vocabulary. I don't know what they teach you all in college. Maybe it was different then, and in the South, too. Growing up in the South, even in a college town — I think it was different in ways I could never have imagined. Jonquil did a brave thing, marrying a Northerner. I never thought of that before, but she has qualities I never realized."

Mumma was the only person Jonquil could count on, for attention, for casseroles and card games, for company. "Those women, they think cancer's contagious and it's not. It's life. They think death is contagious, but if it is they've already got it. I don't know what's wrong with people," Mumma said.

"At least it's not wrong with you," I remember answering, by that time tired, I admit, of hearing about Jonquil Cartenbury.

"Well, I *know* better. There's lots I don't know, but I know better than to waste time being blind about things. Life is too short."

That Mumma persisted in being helpful to Jonquil Cartenbury didn't surprise us. For one thing, she no longer had children at home, so her bossiness needed an object. For the most important, it was in Mumma's nature to do thoroughly whatever she set herself to do.

What did surprise us was the pleasure she

took in Jonquil Cartenbury's company, her obvious interest in the close companionship of another woman, in a friendship. Mumma did the physical therapy exercises alongside Jonquil, and they talked. Mumma drove the woman to her radiation treatments, and they talked. They talked on the phone, often at length. Our mother was behaving like a teenager, not able to do anything without talking it over with her best friend. Mumma seemed half enamored of Jonquil Cartenbury, who was, Mumma said, a complicated lady, full of dignities and prides and insecurities, and she had not had an easy time of it, Mumma assured us. "Just that husband, to start with," Mumma said.

When, after six months of intensive treatments, Jonquil was given a necessarily temporary clean bill of health, Mumma took her into Boston to shop for prosthetics. Rowdy as teenagers, they came to see me afterward at my new Avon Hill house, for a cup of tea or coffee before they headed back out to the Cape. Their eyes were sparkling and their cheeks pink, and they would sometimes just look at one another and start to laugh. "Your mother," Jonquil Cartenbury said to me; then she started up laughing again and couldn't speak. I thought, watching her, that I might after all get to

381

like her, that perhaps this illness (Knock on wood, she really had it beaten; the doctors wouldn't be really hopeful until a year, or confident until five) might have changed her fundamental nature. It had certainly transformed her into someone who would be friends with my mother.

They had good times together, those months. Jonquil Cartenbury tried to tone down Mumma's habits of dress, and Mumma insisted that Jonquil wear higher heels. "You have nice slim legs," Mumma told her. "You should show them off, and you could wear shorter skirts, too." They talked over their pasts, and their husbands, and their different experiences of being outsiders married into Boston society, and their similar experiences ditto. They talked about their children, fears and worries, and occasionally they allowed each other to boast about conquests and victories. They had friendly exchanges about politics, and Mumma listened to Jonquil's advice never to run for office again. Mumma advised Jonquil about managing her money, since, as Mumma pointed out, it was likely that she would survive her husband, and inherit his wealth, and she would need to know how to do more than pay monthly bills and balance a checkbook. Although, "I just admire your mother so much," Jonquil told me, when Mumma was in the bathroom. "I would surely enjoy being a successful businesswoman, but I know it about myself, I don't have the heart. Your mother is a lion. I'm more of a peony."

On another day, while Jonquil was powdering her nose, or spending her penny, or any of the other euphemisms she had for peeing, one of which was even "visiting the little girls' room" — on the subject of which expressions Mumma maintained an uncharacteristic silence — Mumma admitted, "I never thought a woman could be so interesting. If she wasn't my daughter, I mean. Especially Jonquil Cartenbury. I never thought a woman would like me, either. Well, you must have noticed, women are competitive and for some reason they don't feel as if they ever win against me. But then, you're not supposed to want to win, if you're a woman. That's the trouble." Briefly, Mumma considered this statement. "I always want to win, so I guess it's simpler for me. Jonquil says she's fragile, but really she isn't. She's been tested," Mumma admonished me. "I don't mean just cancer, either, I mean life."

Even after cancer, life wasn't through with Jonquil Cartenbury. Or perhaps it wasn't life. Perhaps it was just Francis. It all blew up at a belated Thanksgiving dinner.

Because both Jonquil and Mumma had family commitments, they had to wait until the Sunday after the holiday, to have their own Thanksgiving celebration. This included husbands, of course, even if despite the women's friendship, the two couples had not become a foursome. Jonquil felt that Pops found her uninteresting and Mumma couldn't deny it. Francis Cartenbury found Pops recondite, while Mumma could barely bring herself to be polite to Jonquil's husband. Notwithstanding any of that, the women decided to make a dinner reservation for the four of them on the Sunday, at The Paddock, where the evening did not go as planned.

Or, rather, it went as Francis Cartenbury had planned it. On the drive to join Mumma and Pops at the restaurant, he told his wife of more than thirty years that he had wanted them to have this last good holiday together with their boys, wanted to give the boys one last good memory. He told her that it was their last holiday together because he was leaving her. He had met a woman at his work, another lawyer, in fact, someone who understood what he did and understood him, too, and would be an asset to him in his political life, because these days being divorced wasn't that much of a handicap, on the state level at least. The woman wanted Francis to marry her before she was too old to have children of her own. Francis knew Jonquil would understand. He had stuck by her in this illness, but now that she was better — although she was not the woman she had been and she did understand how that had to affect a man, didn't she? He was sorry. He didn't want to hurt her. But he had promised this woman, he'd made promises. Jonquil had never liked the house on the Cape all that much anyway, had she? She'd always wanted to move back to Cambridge, he knew that, she thought he hadn't been listening to all those complaints over the years, but he had. Because he wasn't a bad guy, and he hoped they'd always be friends, and there were the boys and the grandchildren now, so a peaceable divorce would be to everybody's advantage. She'd inherited money of her own, so she wouldn't need anything from him, or want it, he was sure of that. Unless, he suggested, ignoring the sounds coming from the far side of the front seat, she would want to move back to Virginia? To Charlottesville where she had family and friends and a familiar way of life. He wouldn't object if that was what she decided to do. It was going to be hard enough on him being divorced and remarried — think of Nelson Rockefeller and Happy — with his political career, and she could actually help him, now he thought of it, by moving south. Not always around to remind people, he admitted.

"He'd rather you'd died," Mumma interpreted. She and Pops had waited at the table for the Cartenburys to arrive, and when they were half an hour late Mumma had gone to ask if there had perhaps been a phone message. That was when she saw Jonquil, standing alone outside the glass door. Mumma immediately sent the headwaiter back to tell Pops to pay the bar bill, and leave a twenty on the table, please, to make up for the lost tip on the dinner they wouldn't order. "You'll have to watch and make sure he does it. The man has no idea about tipping," she told the headwaiter. "Tell him I need him to take me home. Emergency," she explained.

"I can't just abandon her," she told us later, explaining why she hadn't had time to stop by on her regular business days in Boston, or to invite grandchildren out to the Cape and give their parents a needed respite, or done anything more than write a generous check for Christmas. "Not when her life is falling down around her like a bombed city. Or like hail, maybe, because it's only natural for men to be unfaithful. Not your father, but some men. It's the urge to propagate, it's Darwin. But it's more like an earthquake in her life, really, and she can't think clearly yet. She was going to let him have her house!" Once Jonquil had stopped weeping and emerged from the subsequent rabid fury at Francis, Mumma could mention other men to her.

"I'm too old to get another man," Jonquil said.

"Don't be stupid," Mumma advised. "You're a pretty woman."

"I have no breasts," Jonquil reminded her. "I'm too old and I have no breasts."

"You know how to get along with people."

"And those supposed friends who didn't disappear with the cancer don't want a divorcée at their parties, making uneven numbers. They don't even invite *widows*, Rida. You don't know them like I do."

"And you'll have a nice sum of money when your lawyer finishes with that nogoodnik."

"He is the father of my children," Jonquil reminded her, which Mumma interpreted as Jonquil making sure she had the moral high ground, so that she would be well thought of in the community. "It's important for a woman to have the moral high ground in a divorce," Mumma told Jo.

Mumma stood beside Jonquil through all the long months of the required period of separation for an uncontested no-fault divorce and never once complained about the repetitive conversations, as Jonquil turned over and over the cancer, the abandonment, and the stinginesses with which Francis responded to her refusal to "do the right thing by him."

To celebrate the actual divorce, Mumma and Pops suggested that Jonquil join them for two weeks in Paris over his spring break, but Jonquil had already been invited by some South Carolina cousins to join them at the Mill Race Club in the Bahamas for Easter. "I didn't know how to tell you," she told Mumma. "They're family," she said apologetically. Mumma suggested that she might go, too, because the cousins asked if Jonquil had a friend she wanted to bring. But Jonquil told Mumma that two single women would be a social disaster for her cousins, and she wanted to be a good guest since they'd been nice enough to think of asking her. Mumma reminded her friend that *she* wasn't a single woman. Jonquil told

Mumma that wasn't what she meant and Mumma knew it, Mumma was just being her usual perverse self. They talked frankly, about everything, or at least that's what Mumma thought, but it turned out that there was a man at the Mill Race Club, a man her cousins wanted her to meet. They were fixing her up, but she didn't tell Mumma that. "Probably," Mumma decided, "she was worried that he'd fall in love with me."

After phone calls that were cut short and lunch dates it was impossible for Jonquil to make, Mumma found herself dropped by the only real friend she had ever had. There was one dinner when Jonquil brought her new husband to meet Mumma and Pops, again at The Paddock. Then, all the long summer holiday season, while Jonquil and Jake were living in her Wampanoag house to escape the South Carolina summer, they couldn't accept any of Mumma's invitations. Until, finally, Jonquil snapped. "I wish you'd stop telephoning, Rida. I don't know what's wrong with you. You never did have any subtlety. Or any tact."

"So you're avoiding me on purpose," Mumma said to Jonquil, and later, having repeated what Jonquil said to each of us, separately, she concluded, "She was avoiding me on purpose, so that's that."

Mumma refused to discuss it. "You never liked her," she reminded us, one after the other, and that was true enough. For Mumma, the door had shut on Jonquil Cartenbury Heolms. We were never given an opportunity to say we were sorry about the way things turned out, or to tell our mother we thought she'd been treated badly.

So I find myself agreeing, whenever Jo reminds us about that odd interlude in Mumma's life, that Jonquil Cartenbury Heolms might be the example where the essential Mumma could be seen. "Including being dumped, because whoever her parents were dumped her at the emergency room door at the very beginning of her story," she says.

"*We* were the only friends Mumma had," I realized.

"As if it wasn't bad enough being her daughters," said Amy.

"I don't know that I was much of a friend," Meg admitted.

"Neither was she. A friend to *us,* I mean."

"She was our *mother.*"

Jo had the last word, and it was a question: "Do you think that any mother and daughter *can* be friends?"

8.
MUMMA AT THE
END OF THE ROAD

We did become uneasy, when Mumma virtually retired from the business two months after Pops died. Mumma's financial successes gave her satisfactions that marriage and family life could not, that being a useful and publicly acclaimed citizen of Wampanoag didn't offer. She always remembered that it was Pops who started her out, but she knew it was her intelligence and her proven judgment that made its great success, that made her what she was. It was Mumma against the world and she knew she'd won when she had made her own fortune. Amy understood it best. "For Mumma, making profits was like getting a good grade in school. Making money, making A's, they're the same thing. They stand for approval. They stand for visible success."

We worried about Mumma's life without work. We couldn't imagine it, any more than we could imagine her without her various civic activities, the library and the hospital, the garden club, all of which she also retired from before the end of her first year of widowhood. We couldn't imagine her without anything to be fixing. She had said it so often, "I'm going to save the world and then I'm going to get it running right." She said it most often to the television set, or the newspaper: "You can't get away with that, not with *me*."

But it wasn't until Mumma bought herself a pair of sneakers, and wore them, that we became anxious.

Then she stopped cooking, and we knew. We couldn't any longer avoid knowing. Anyone who had ever shared a meal with Mumma knew what it was to enjoy food. Her pride in her cooking was equaled by her enjoyment of eating, and it was simply *fun* to watch her savor her proud twin pleasures. She cut a ravioli in half and held a chunk on her fork, anticipating. She brought it under her nose, inhaling slowly. Then she dipped it into whatever she'd sauced it with, put it into her mouth and, as soon as she closed her teeth into it, closed her eyes too, so as not to let anything distract her from experiencing that first taste. It didn't matter what she was eating — a slice of warm pecan pie à la mode, a glazed carrot, an unadorned steak, a bouillabaisse — each offered her its particular delights. Mumma maintained that she didn't care what she ate, but anyone who shared meals with her knew better.

So when there were foil trays from frozen dinners in her kitchen wastebasket, we had to recognize it for what it was. Stouffer's lasagna in her freezer, Captain Bob's fish sticks, Sara Lee cheesecakes, Swanson fried chicken pieces — they all gave it away: Mumma was no longer herself. We could no longer pretend. We had spent too many years, too many meals, wishing that we had her ability to enjoy eating, and cooking too, too much time envying her relationship to food, to be blind to the mute evidence in her freezer and her trash. Obviously, Mumma was failing. Most obviously, it was time for Mumma to stop driving.

But as long as any of us could remember, the world had featured Mumma behind the wheel of her fire-engine-red Coupe de Ville.

Mumma always drove a bright red car and it was always a Cadillac, the make Pops originally selected because of her long drives into Boston for business. It was the safest car he could find, and he was looking for the safest because he had taught her to drive, for one thing, and for another, this was Massachusetts. "The only thing worse than the standard Massachusetts driver," Pops told us, "is your mother. I wish I could buy her a Sherman tank."

On the winding roads of the Cape, Mumma habitually drove ten or fifteen miles per hour above the speed limit, and she exceeded it by more on highways. Also, she responded to traffic controls like the natural outlaw she was. Stoplights she was willing to respect, but a stop sign had to prove its worth. "I can see everything I need to," she would say, slowing down to perhaps ten miles per hour below the speed limit to enter or cross a roadway. "I saw him coming, I had lots of time, don't be such nervous Nellies." Or, if our fears were well grounded, "Where did he come from? He was going like a bat out of hell, he's lucky he didn't cause a wreck."

Mumma was proud of her driving, just the way it was, proud of her reflexes and her fearlessness, her ability to charm policemen and be unmoved by irate drivers. She was also proud of her car, proud of the care she always took of it, keeping it washed and waxed, lubricated, taking it in for the checkups, having the tires rotated, the wheels balanced. It follows as the night the day that Mumma refused to share the pleasure of driving, especially on short trips when it was such a bother repositioning the seat, and also especially on long trips, when an open road required long periods of good concentration. When she drove, Mumma put her foot down hard on the accelerator and kept it there, her ability to maintain a steady speed the mark, she assured us, of a good driver. She parked wherever convenience decreed, and in Wampanoag she could do that with impunity. Characteristically, however, when reserved places for handicapped drivers began to appear, despite any personal inconvenience she honored those restrictions. "Life is hard enough without being handicapped," she told us, and was vigilant about checking the license plate of anyone parked in the restricted spots. If she spotted an undeserving vehicle, she would park her car directly behind it. "He won't be making that mistake again," she reported with satisfaction. "Not in this town."

So to take Mumma's car away from her . . .

For me, for all of us, that was the worst moment of her Alzheimer's, worse than the time of ever-increasing anxiety, worse than the diagnosis itself, even worse than those last miserable months before Mumma had entirely detached herself from herself, when her waking hours were filled with a nervous and fearful fussiness. The time we understood that it was really, inevitably, happening was when we admitted to ourselves that we would have to get Mumma off the road. In the event, however, Mumma seemed to forget immediately that she had ever had a license, and a Cadillac. I say "seemed" not because she gave me any reason to doubt but because I couldn't believe it had been so easy. Without her car, Mumma took to walking around town, a little bright-haired lady in a bright flowered dress and sneakers, with either a shopkeeper or a daughter (me, usually) to help out if she had too many packages to carry home. "You should walk more," she told me. "You always were lazy, always with your nose in a book. A woman needs exercise, more than a man," she declared, forgetting that she had always maintained that being a mother and keeping a house kept her trim enough. Forgetting it or ignoring it, that is. With Mumma, you could never be sure what was Alzheimer's and what character. "I've been wanting to get rid of that gas guzzler for years," she eventually told us, "but you girls wouldn't let me. If I didn't know better, I'd think you didn't want me to get the benefits of walking. At my age, especially, it's important to keep fit."

We put off the crisis of Mumma's driving until the third time the police called me. "I'm sorry to bother you," the officer always began. "The old lady's fine," he always assured me. "We've got her safe here with us." Mumma had been a great supporter of any Police League activity and lobbied for increases in benefits too, for all public servants; she was an advocate and so they cut her slack, her credit good for years of indulgence. But she had become a menace. "Three strikes and she's out," we had decided after the first call. "Three strikes and we get rid of the car," we said after the second, hoping it wouldn't come to that.

My sisters were as reluctant as I was, but they knew as well as I did how dangerous she had become, to other drivers, to herself, and even, when we couldn't stop it from happening, to the grandchildren, who gleefully rebelled along with her, by not strapping themselves in when they rode with her, by riding in the front seat. "Gran's not afraid," they told their mothers. "She's not afraid of anything. Gran's fun."

"You'll have to get her car away from her, Beth," my sisters told me. We met regularly after Pops died, as well as talking frequently on the phone. That day we were in Wayland. We had had one of Meg's lunches, lasagne verdi, pear and walnut salad on a bed of mixed young greens, and with our coffee a selection of lovely little pastries, miniature tarts, cream puffs the size of gumballs, tiny perfect napoleons.

We remained at Meg's dining room table after lunch, the green lawn and the asphalt tennis court visible through the open windows, the vista framed by two stately horse chestnut trees and a clapboard corner of the four-car garage. We drank our coffee out of Limoges cups, with saucers, and made our selection from the silver platter of pastries, moving the tiny delicacies onto dessert plates of clear Finnish glass.

"Why me?" I asked.

"You're the one who sees her every day," they reminded me. "You're her primary caregiver."

"All the more reason it shouldn't be me," I said. "I'll hear about it forever."

"What forever?" asked Amy, but Jo had a less fatal view. "We all know that at this point, she's forgotten what she knew about driving."

I couldn't argue. After all, there had been the third call from the police, and the last few times I'd been on the road with Mumma I had seen Death with sickle raised over me, more than once.

"She absolutely should not have a car," Meg maintained.

I agreed. "I know, I'm the one they call, but why don't *you* take it away from her, Meg? It would take some of the heat off of me."

"I can't imagine Mumma without her Caddy," Meg mused sadly.

"Imagine her *with* her Caddy," Amy advised. "Imagine her going nose to nose with an eighteen-wheeler. Or nose to nose with a car full of children. Imagine that. That Caddy could take out a Chevy, easy. Imagine the publicity."

Meg continued, "Just thinking about Mumma without her —" and blew her nose.

"Imagine the lawsuits," Amy advised.

"Mumma trusts Beth," Jo announced, then turned to me. "She's used to you. The rest of us . . . She's not used to having us around. When I go home, it takes her about five minutes now to figure out who I am. She's fine then, well, mostly, I agree, but —"

"Imagine the guilt," Amy advised.

"What am I supposed to do?" I demanded, hoping for an idea. "Just get into her car and drive away with it?"

"You could bring it to my house," Amy said. "Wilfred would love a red Caddy."

I was pleased to be diverted. "And then how would I get back home? And who says *I* don't want it, anyway, or any of the rest of us, what gives Wilfred first refusal? Or one of my children, or one of any of yours?" Of course I knew it would have to be me and I dreaded doing that to my mother, taking her car away from her, taking away her driving privileges, her independence. But my sisters were right. I gave up the quarrel.

I made a date for lunch with Mumma, writing it on her calendar, calling her in the morning to be sure she had looked at the calendar. I agreed to let her drive me to the restaurant. I agreed to let her pay the bill. I agreed to "look nice." By then Mumma had grown suspicious. "You're up to something," she told me. When I didn't deny it, she said, "Save it for after the meal. Life is too short not to enjoy lunch."

So I did. I enjoyed my lunch with Mumma and it was over coffee and warm pecan pie topped with a scoop of fresh-churned vanilla ice cream that I told her, "You shouldn't be driving anymore. It's not safe. We don't want you to drive."

She fixed me with a mahogany gaze, and

chewed. She swallowed and stared at me. Ice cream melted in my mouth as I waited, unable to swallow.

At last she said, "All four of you? You all agree?"

I nodded.

"That's it, then."

I swallowed gratefully. Mumma reached into the purse she had hung off the back of her chair and rummaged around in it for the car keys, which she set beside my coffee mug in a gesture of surrender, Lee at Appomattox. We finished our desserts in silence. Then, "So who gets the Caddy?" Mumma asked me. "Not you."

"Not me," I agreed.

"That fine husband of yours," Mumma suggested, and I knew that she had temporarily lost George's name.

"I'll ask him," I assured her, although I was pretty sure what his answer would be. "I'll take care of it."

"Yes. Well. It may be a good thing for me not to drive anymore, because sometimes I'm not sure of the way home. With all of the building that's been going on around here, all the new streets springing up." She fixed me again with her gaze. "About getting old, I can tell you, the only good thing about it is that half the time I can't remember how old I am because I don't know what year it is. Getting old is like trying to see through a fog. Or maybe it's like walking through a spider web, in a thick woods, when you're trying to peel sticky stuff off of your face, pull it out of your hair . . ." She pulled fretfully at her bright, unnaturally auburn hair, miming this. "And at the same time as you pull you're walking into more of it. Or it's like wearing snowshoes, you can't just walk normally, you can't trust your balance or your instincts. But really, it's like trying to see through a thick fog. I think. Or did I already say that? I already said that, didn't I? I think I did."

"Don't worry, it's worth saying twice, to make sure I get it."

Mumma opened her purse. "I'm not worrying, I'm paying and that's all there is to it. *Now* what have I done with the car keys?"

By the time we got back into her car, and I'd reminded her that she would have to ride in the passenger seat, and she'd told me in no uncertain terms that she was not about to strap herself in, Mumma was in a fury. She didn't say anything to me, but she muttered to herself all the way back to her house. I didn't understand a word of what she was muttering, although I did get the gist, which was, "Can't do this to me." But by the time I walked into the kitchen with her, to retrieve the second set of car keys, the insurance information and the title to the car, her mood had changed. "When is my new car coming?" she asked, and then, without waiting for my response, said, "You didn't get black, did you? You wouldn't do that to me." She fixed me with another mahogany look and then a broad and happy smile that was, more than anything else, certain that she was about to get her own way. "You wouldn't dare."

9.
BURYING MUMMA

The nursing home called me, I telephoned my sisters, and by evening we had gathered at my house, which used to be Mumma's house, the house we had grown up in. None of them had wanted to come with me to view the body and make a final farewell. "The day she no longer knew my name is the day I said goodbye to her," Jo said.

Amy said, "I have to admit, I expected her to last much longer. I was actually sort of hoping she'd make it into the next millennium."

"She'd have liked that," Meg agreed, and pointed out, "She almost did."

Jo said, "It would have been just like her to keep living on, sticking to it no matter what. Like you, Beth, the way you went to see her every day even though she never had any idea she'd ever seen you before. Stubborn."

I thought I should apologize. "I live so

close, I couldn't not go. It didn't feel right not to."

"It didn't feel right to me when I went," Meg admitted. "That's why I stopped. I used to think, when she was so irritating and know-it-all and wouldn't let me grow up? I used to think I'd like the chance to boss *her* around and be the one who knew more, but I really . . . When push came to shove? I hated it."

"Having her be so anxious and unsure."

"Helpless," I added.

"Needy," Amy defined it.

Ceremoniously, Jo lit a cigarette. She moved over to the open window before I could protest, and from there gave voice to what we were all thinking: "We're a fine set of daughters, aren't we?"

"I don't know about the rest of you," Amy said, "but I did the best I could."

"She thought we *were* good daughters," Meg said. "Especially compared to other people's children."

"Just not much good compared to her," I pointed out.

"Well, Beth," Meg said, as if I didn't already know this, "Mumma didn't think anybody could compare to her."

We all thought about that until — "Maybe she was right," Jo said.

"Of course she was right," I answered. "That's what made her so annoying. And I don't know why you think that's so funny."

George had taken Sarah out to dinner and a movie, even if it was a school night, leaving the four of us to accomplish unhindered what had to be done. We had ordered out for pizza. Jo was drinking beer, Amy mineral water, Meg and I had glasses of wine. Amy had insisted on making a salad and Meg insisted that we eat on plates, and I had surrendered, setting the table with place mats, silver, and cloth napkins, just as Mumma would have, except I put candles on the table, and lit them. Mumma for some reason made a stand against candles on a dinner table.

"It was quick," Amy observed. "Not just in terms of how long we thought she'd hang on, but she had a quick death."

"I bet she'd claim she died of a broken heart," I said. "If she could come back and give us her personal diagnosis."

"Doctor Rida," Jo laughed.

Meg temporized. "But she did, didn't she? Isn't that what a heart attack is? A heart that's literally broken?"

Amy got to the point. "She can't come back and tell us." She helped herself to pizza and piled salad on her plate. "But —"

Jo interrupted to echo, "I guess she's really finished with us now."

I took two pieces of pizza and had no room on my plate for salad and decided that I might just treat myself to a meal without any green leafy vegetables in it.

"Not *quite*," Amy said.

"Good pizza," Meg said to me as if I'd made it myself, and I accepted the praise, "Thank you."

"What do you mean not quite?" Jo asked Amy. "In that I-know-something-you-don't voice, the way Mumma used to."

Amy merely looked gravely around at all of us, which gave Jo time to say, "Sorry. I didn't mean to be . . ." before she told us.

"There's a letter. Mumma left a letter. And before you all get bent entirely out of shape, it was George she gave it to. Years ago. This was just before Pops died, when Pops was in the nursing home in the coma. George asked me to keep it."

A letter was Mumma reaching back from the great beyond, defying death, or trying to, thinking she could, which was so like her that we were stunned into silence. Finally I asked Amy, "What does it say?"

"I haven't opened it. What do you think of me?" Amy protested, and before anyone thought of it she added, "Neither has

George. I asked him."

Before any of them could wonder about me, I told them, "He never said a word to me," which was the truth. "So where is it?"

Amy leaned over to her attaché case and extracted a long creamy envelope. She set it on the table in front of us. It was Mumma's handwriting all right, a little shaky with age and encroaching Alzheimer's, but those were her large black letters, ramrod straight although some the *o*'s and *g*'s were left unfinished, as if the writer's mind had moved much faster than her hand. She had addressed it: *To My Daughters.*

"*I* should open it," Meg announced. "I'm the oldest," she reminded us.

She took the envelope and turned it over to unseal it. When she did that, we saw written across the back: *Meg should open this, she's the oldest.* So we were smiling when Meg took out the sheets of Mumma's heavy business stationery and read. Typically, Mumma had wasted no time on a salutation.

I'll tell you girls about this after Spencer dies, so don't pretend that it comes as a big surprise. I want a Quaker funeral. And don't get yourselves into a swivet: it will be easier than you think. Surely, between the four of you, you can do this last thing for me.

Not exactly and precisely Quaker, I know that. I mean, Quaker-style. What I mean is my body should be disposed of before the service, and I don't want a service either. By which I mean: No prayers. No minister. Anyone who wants to get up and say something is free to do so but nobody is required to. It should last at least twenty minutes but no more than forty. Or maybe forty-five.

Also no flowers. Also no memorial donations, no memorial plantings, no memorial plaques. Life is too short for all these memorials. It's supposed to be short, and when it's over, it's supposed to be over.

Except for a tombstone. After the cremation —

"What cremation?" we interrupted, almost in unison. "Did she ever say anything to you about a cremation?" we asked one another, and we all denied it. "Do you think she meant it?" we asked, remembering how Mumma drifted in and out of full awareness even before Pops died. But those were also the same months during which she incorporated her business, making herself inessential to it *("But don't start thinking you don't need me. Nobody knows it like I do, all the ins and outs of the properties, all my connections"),* making Amy the CEO, George chairman of a board of directors, and naming the rest of us board members, making it possible for business to be carried on without her and therefore making possible our continuing incomes from it. Since she had designed and accomplished the transition during that same time, we couldn't tell ourselves that her mind had been failing her. "Maybe she really did mean it," we said. "But then, why didn't she cremate Pops?"

"I'm going to make us some coffee," I announced. "I need a few minutes to digest this."

"There's more," Meg said.

"Could I have tea instead?" Jo asked. "You have herbal, don't you? For Sarah?" Jo could smoke cigarettes and at the same time eschew caffeine without worrying over the contradiction. Only Sarah pointed it out to her. The rest of us went no further than refusing to let her smoke in our houses or cars.

"We won't read ahead," Meg promised me. "I don't know how I feel about cremation."

"I don't know how I feel about interments," I answered over my shoulder as I left the room. I cocked the swinging door open so as not to miss anything, and added, "About dressing my mother up in her good clothes and sealing her into a coffin so she can rot away more slowly than nature intended, for example."

"Please, Beth, don't start," they said. "Why do you have to do that?"

Satisfied, I set about putting on water for tea, filling the coffeemaker. I poured half-and-half into a little glass pitcher Mumma had brought back from Venice, took out the cut-glass sugar bowl she had taken from Grandmother's pantry after that death, and set them on a tray with cups and saucers. Then I exchanged the cups and saucers for mugs.

Meg came out to help me, so I must have been taking longer than they thought I should. But she still had to wait a few minutes; they would all have to wait. I assembled a selection of tea bags on a little plate. Meg studied my refrigerator door, photographs and silly magnets, cards reminding us of appointments and, occupying almost the entire top third of the door, the magnetized whiteboard on which Sarah kept current the family calendar. It was Sarah's schedule on that whiteboard that captured Meg's attention.

"How does she have the energy?" Meg asked — rhetorically, I assumed, since Sarah's energy level was as obvious to anyone as Mumma's had been.

"It's her organizational ability that impresses me."

"And she hasn't even included schoolwork."

"Exams, papers and reports, unit tests too. Those she does put on," I said.

"It's a little obsessive, you have to admit. For a sixth-grader."

"Kids can be obsessive about school. You were."

"But she actually checks things off." Meg pointed at the previous day, a Wednesday, which sported a column of red checks beside its list of activities.

I continued defending my unwieldy daughter. "Her self-discipline impresses me, too." I filled a teapot with boiling water.

"Maybe it's self-discipline," Meg said, "or maybe she's controlling."

I picked up the tray of mugs and sugar. "You bring in the teapot."

Meg followed me into the dining room. "I hope we can get this all sorted out before they get back."

"When does the movie get out?" Amy asked.

"Otherwise, Sarah will start finding faults in our ideas, and fixing them." Jo grinned.

"We've got plenty of time," I said, and passed out mugs. "So." I sat down again. "It's cremation, then. Agreed?"

"You've never been firm enough with Sarah," Meg told me.

"Unless somebody really objects?" I persisted.

Nobody did. We tasted our tea and coffee, refocusing our attention on the matter at hand, on Mumma.

"The nursing home will know how to arrange a cremation," Jo told us. "If Mumma hasn't already set it up. Finish reading the letter, Meg."

Also, I want my ashes buried next to your father, even if it is in the Howland plot. On the tombstone I want engraved "The rest is silence." Unless you think that's too intellectual, or too grandiose for me, so maybe I'd rather have "life's not a paragraph."

We looked around the table at one another in response to yet another of Mumma's allusions. "Life's not a paragraph? What does

413

that mean?"

Jo had the answer. " 'And death i think is no parenthesis.' " At the incomprehension on our faces, she added, "It's cummings. You know, e. e. cummings, he didn't use capital letters."

I knew that, but, "You read cummings?" I asked my sister.

"It's one of the books Pops gave me. I was . . . nineteen? Twenty? So I did read it, and you know what? I still do. But I didn't know Mumma had."

"Well," Amy said, "if it was a book Pops picked out for you, she wouldn't want not to know about it."

We agreed wordlessly, and Meg read on:

If you want to make me happy, you'll send everyone straight home right after the service. I never liked those parties the Howlands like to have after funerals, the way people come and eat and drink and talk about you behind your back. Your father would have wanted it, as part of being a Howland, so I gave him one, but do me a favor and don't.

Or maybe on my tombstone you should just put Beloved Wife, like on your father's.

We all remembered the matter of Pops'

tombstone. Mumma had decided that under his name and the dates of his lifespan, she wanted to engrave BELOVED HUSBAND. "Because he was," she explained, relaying her decision to us.

"What about us?" I demanded. "What about his daughters?"

"What *about* you?" she demanded right back. "You weren't married to him."

"What about 'Beloved Father'? That's what Beth means," Jo had said. Generously giving the benefit of the doubt to both of us, she added, "Beth means what about putting both on the stone, 'Beloved Husband' and 'Beloved Father.' Isn't that right, Beth?"

In fact, I hadn't thought about that. I'd only thought about being excluded, but of course Jo was right; that was it exactly. "We loved him, too," I reminded Mumma.

"Well I know that," she said. "Anyone who knew your father loved him. Just, not many people knew him. Not like how many people know me."

We got our way, got to declare our affection on Pops' grave, and now we were about to find ourselves in a similar position in reference to our mother. Sometimes things never changed, I thought, and I thought my sisters would agree with me. But I didn't expect that Mumma would too, so I was surprised when Meg read:

Whether or not you put down Beloved Mother, that's up to you. I have no say in that, especially now, although if you are wondering, I always thought you girls were fine daughters.

Or maybe I'd like you to put on it "She didn't waste a minute," because I didn't, did I? In plain letters, none of that fancydancy lettering like your aunt Phyllis has. Until this Alzheimer's, I mean, of course. I am writing this with a clear mind, so don't fool yourselves about that. But don't think I don't know, because I do. I mean, know what's wrong, I don't need any doctor to tell me about it when there is something wrong with me.

Or maybe there should be just my dates, none of this beloved business. You'll just have to decide for yourselves.

I hope you'll manage all this all right. It's work, as you'll find out, a funeral. Hard work and minimum satisfaction. But I was never afraid of hard work.

Maybe that should be my tombstone? "She wasn't afraid of hard work."

You'll miss me, and I apologize for that even though it's not my fault. You'll have already been missing me, but I hope for not too long.

She signed it:

With my love, and if you think it's not you ought to think again because you're not as smart as you think a lot of the time,

Mumma.

We were leaking tears, smiling ironically at one another, irritated and bereft. I brought out a box of tissues and we began planning our mother's non-funeral, her non-memorial, her burial.

"We're not in any hurry, are we?" asked Jo. "That's one of the advantages of cremation, you don't have a limited time. So the first question is the venue, not the date."

"I can write the obituary," I volunteered.

"No, we need your help arranging for the place," Amy said. "I'll do the obituary."

Meg objected. "Mumma wouldn't have wanted an obituary. It was Uncle Ethan who did Pops,' remember?"

Jo objected, "Yes she would, just not the *Globe,* not the *Times,* not a Howland obituary. She'd want the *Cape Codder.*"

I asked, "Why can't I do the obituary?"

Amy answered impatiently. "Because you're not only local, you're also the one who lived in Cambridge and you have friends who are Quakers, don't you? Somebody has to ask. If Mumma's going to have a Quaker funeral. You can *help* with the obituary, will that satisfy you?"

"The Cambridge Friends Meeting House?" I asked, astounded. "You don't understand."

"Not necessarily there," Amy said. "But at any meetinghouse. Ask if it would be possible for a non-Quaker to use the space. Otherwise, there's no point in trying to locate one, is there?"

So I telephoned one friend, then another, and for good measure a third, to discover that what Mumma wanted was not possible. I hadn't thought it would be, but I was still disappointed.

"We did tell her," Jo reminded us. "After Pops' funeral, we did."

I was trying to think of ways around the problem. A full family conversion? A donation to the American Friends Service so large that they couldn't refuse us the use — just for forty or forty-five minutes — of a meetinghouse?

"So we'd better ask at St. Stephen's," Amy said. "Although I can guess how they'll feel about a nonreligious ceremony."

"Who's the minister there now?" Meg asked me.

"It's a woman. Janice Lauter, a little younger than we are, never married."

"Why not?"

"Mumma told me —"

"Mumma actually asked?"

"Of course. She wanted to know. Everybody wondered, but Mumma asked. It turns out that when she was in seminary, Janice took a vow of celibacy. Janice is a real priest. Not Catholic, but, I mean, she's a real religious. She visited Mumma sometimes, here, and then at the home, too. I don't know if they were friends, but . . . I think Mumma respected her," I concluded.

"Will you ask her?" Jo asked me. "I'll go with you. Tomorrow morning? Do you think we need an appointment?"

"I'll call in the morning and find out. But you have to remember, I don't go to church."

"Neither did Mumma. That didn't mean she didn't think about God," Amy pointed out.

"She didn't think much of God," I pointed out.

"You're wrong," Jo told me. "It was organized religion she didn't care for. It was religious organizations. *They bring out the worst in people,* don't you remember her saying that?"

I remembered. *"As if they think heaven is a club that they can keep people out of. Or some election and they're running to win the seat."*

"She was always reading about religions," Amy reminded us.

"And she made us go to Sunday school," Jo added. "She wouldn't have done that if it hadn't meant something to her."

"I'll call Janice," I assured them.

That was everything. The staff at the home was packing up Mumma's few belongings, and I would pick them up in a day or two, so there was nothing for us to do right then. All we could do was sit together and watch the candles burn down.

The next morning, early, we met Janice in the church. She wore a plain priestly outfit, simple black skirt and black shirt with the white collar close around her neck, but her shoes were stylish. They weren't the high heels Mumma would have worn, but they looked like Joan & David to me, and they showed off slender ankles. We three stood together at the rear of Saint Stephen's. "I'm sorry for your loss," Janet greeted us, clasping first my hand, then Jo's, in both of hers, her expression sorrowful but her eyes serene and clear, accepting, hopeful. Her long graying hair curved up into a twist at the back of her head; she wore no makeup. *("The new minister at Saint Stephen's has style,"* *Mumma had reported, with satisfaction.)*

"Thank you," Jo said.

"Thank you," I said. I had always liked this church, with its tall stained-glass windows and white-painted traceries. I had always been comfortable in it, as a child in the Sunday School, as a bride, as a mother having my daughters baptized.

"What can I do for you today?" Janice asked in her unassertive voice. She wasn't the kind of person to catch Mumma's attention, I would have said, and not the kind of person to whom Mumma would have appealed, but once again I would have been wrong about my mother.

I told her that we'd come about Mumma's burial, and she frowned, slightly — at the seriousness of the occasion, I thought, not at the prospect of burying Mumma. She invited us back to her office, where she sat down behind a desk that simultaneously dwarfed her and made her more formidable. Jo and I sat facing her in high-backed wooden armchairs.

"Your mother wasn't a parishioner," Janet reminded us gently.

"My father was," I said.

"Yes."

"Doesn't that count? Like Social Security?"

"Then you would like me to conduct the service here for her? I want to say right off, I am honored that you ask."

I told her that Mumma had requested — "Well, instructed actually," I said, and Janice nodded, she knew Mumma — that there be no religious service. I told her that Mumma wanted a Quaker-style event and described the format she had set out.

Before I had finished speaking, Janice was shaking her head with pastoral regret. "That isn't possible, I'm afraid. If someone is to be buried from the church, it needs to be within the church rituals."

"Is there a definite restriction?" I asked. "I mean, would it have to be a traditional funeral? To be in the church, I mean. Like, are all of your weddings here, in the church, strictly traditional? Because mine wasn't," I told her, since she hadn't officiated at it.

"Your mother told me, you were all married out of Saint Stephen's," Janice said.

"I'm not married," Jo said.

"Yes," Janice smiled. "I remember. Excluding you, and also Meg's first marriage took place somewhere else, I think?"

"Mexico," I supplied, as if it mattered.

"The others," Janice said, and we had to agree. "But you see, Beth, I wasn't the priest at those times. At the time of your own somewhat nontraditional wedding, for example. Much of what happens here in the church falls within the discretion of the priest, yes, but this is first and foremost the house of God. I am God's priest in the Episcopal Church. So you see . . ." She spread her hands wide, in pastoral helplessness.

"Actually, no, I don't," I said.

"That I can't offer the church for what is essentially a pagan ritual."

"Quakers aren't pagans," I said.

"Your mother wasn't a Quaker," she reminded me.

"And it wouldn't be pagan anyway because there wouldn't be non-Christian gods," I said.

"I should have said secular," Janice answered serenely. "I really meant secular."

"Some of the people who speak — you can't be sure about this ahead of time — they might be religious and say prayers. Someone will probably say a traditional prayer," I offered. "Mumma knew a wide range of people, all colors, all creeds."

But Janice wasn't to be moved, so Jo and I exited with the problem unsolved.

"You have to respect her convictions," Jo told me as we got into my car.

"They're inconvenient," I answered.

"Convictions tend to be," Jo reminded me.

"What, are you trying to fill Mumma's shoes?" I demanded. We traveled on for several minutes of offended silence before I said, "I'm sorry, Jo, I didn't mean — But if Saint Stephen's won't bury her, who will?"

As it turned out, we did have other options. The day after Mumma's death, I had a visit from Yuri McGonigle, who had been Wampanoag's first selectman for at least twenty-two years, and maybe longer; I date his tenure from the time Mumma ran against him and lost. We were sitting dispiritedly around the dining room table, trying to decide if going out for lunch would lift or sink our spirits, and Sarah was in the kitchen making chocolate chip cookies on the theory that we all needed a sugar hit, when the doorbell rang and it was Yuri McGonigle.

We invited him to sit with us, offered him coffee and cookies, arranged ourselves to receive his sympathy.

"She was only six years older than I am,"

Yuri told us, stirring heavy cream into his coffee, taking two cookies, then a third, as if afraid the plate would be removed from his reach. His hands were pudgy, the fingers like little sausages, his earlobes unusually long, and altogether he was a fleshy presence. "But then, she had that Alzheimer's," and he looked sympathetically around the table, taking us in one at a time, with slightly bloodshot eyes. Mumma always said Yuri was a drinker. Not a bad drinker, just a heavy drinker, and always stone-cold sober for meetings, she assured us, she saw to that. He said, "Well, I can tell you, that was a sad thing. A woman like her."

We murmured agreement.

"It takes us three people to do everything she got done. Your mother . . . They broke the mold when they made her."

More likely Mumma broke the mold being made, I thought; but I didn't say it. Amy, from the expression on her face, might have been thinking the same.

"And she did a lot of good for this town," Yuri went on. He shifted in the chair, leaned forward to take another clutch of cookies. "The stoplight at Beach Road. The planting around Town Hall, and the fiberglass flagpole in front, too. Which is why I'm here, right now, in fact. We're agreed, all the selectmen, because we heard there was some little problem about where to hold the service."

"Not a service," Jo told him. "Mumma didn't want any kind of service."

"Well I know that, of course. That is to say, I didn't exactly know *that,* but it's what I would have expected. If I'd thought about what I expected, that is to say. Don't worry that I'm thinking religious service, Jo. Or any of you. That's why I'm here, because we thought you might like to use the Town Hall."

"Mumma would be pleased," I told Yuri, quite truthfully. I didn't say honored, because I didn't want to prevaricate. I knew that if Mumma had been alive, and if she had been herself, and if the offer had been made, "They knew a good thing when they got their hands on me," would have been her opinion.

"We need to talk this over. We'll call you if . . ." I said, not entirely candidly, "You see, Mumma left us a letter of instructions."

"We just want you to know, the space is available," Yuri said, rising, gathering up cookies.

"Pretty specific instructions," I said.

"Well, that's just what she'd do, isn't it?" he asked. "She was a fine woman," he told us, turning back, one hand crammed with cookies and his face sad as a bloodhound's. "There was no side to her, was there? She just got done what needed doing. If I hadn't been married already, I'd have gone after her," he told us, and left.

Sarah came in to scold us. "You shouldn't be laughing like that, with Gran just dead," but the empty plate deflected her and, "I guess he liked my cookies," eleven-year-old Sarah noted with satisfaction.

"Are there more?" I asked her. "Because people are going to be coming by."

"I *know* that," she told me. "I made lots, and iced tea too, and I'm running the dishwasher, but I have baseball practice this afternoon so you're going to have to take care of serving it yourselves and what's so funny now?"

"We'll be fine, thank you," I said. "We'll manage somehow."

"You're a good cook," said the more diplomatic Meg.

"It's in my blood," Sarah said. "Not from Mother, from Gran. These are Gran's recipe," she explained, and removed the platter from the table to take it out to the kitchen for refilling. We returned to our present difficulties.

"I'm right, aren't I?" asked Amy. "Thinking we can't do it there? Isn't the Town Hall about twenty by twenty? With one big plate glass window that faces the brick wall of the bank? I'm right that it's pretty scruffy, too. Aren't I? Bulletin boards on the walls."

"Not nearly big enough," Jo agreed.

"And those curtains," Meg added.

"What about the school?" I asked.

"An elementary school auditorium?" Meg asked, amazed.

"For our mother's funeral?" Amy echoed.

"What about separation of church and state?" Jo wondered.

"That makes it even better," I argued. "I mean, if it can't be at Saint Stephen's because that's a church, then there should be no problem for the school."

They didn't agree with me, not one of them, but then Uncle Ethan telephoned from San Francisco, a phone call that turned the tide at least in my general direction.

"It's 10 a.m. out here," Uncle Ethan told me. "It's Friday," he said, as if we might not know that fact, and then added, "I've got a game," and as if to hit us with the full weight of his thoughtfulness, he added, "Golf."

I turned on the speakerphone that any couple with children and joint business interests needs to have, to include my sisters in the conversation. They started out with the end of that word, "— *olf*."

Uncle Ethan continued, "The big house can't be made ready until Tuesday, soonest. I'll call young Grangery's nephew and get things moving. Or maybe you can call him? He's the caretaker now."

As long as Uncle Ethan, who lived on the other side of the country, and Aunt Juliet, whom we hadn't seen or heard from since Pops' funeral, were alive, the last survivors of their generation, they held ownership of the big house. "I'll be arriving Monday midday," Uncle Ethan's voice snaked out from the speakerphone.

"You're coming east?" I asked.

"For the service. For the interment." He took an impatient breath and I could almost hear him looking at his watch. "Your mother's funeral."

"How did you hear?" We had so far called only those few people who had kept in touch with us about Mumma while she'd been in the nursing home, and none of those were Howlands, or Spencers.

"McGonigle called me. Not the one your mother liked, that fat selectman she always wanted people to vote for. The McGonigle who used to be commodore of the Yacht

Club, the selectman's cousin. He called to tell me. Your mother was a Howland. By marriage, but still," Uncle Ethan reminded me. "You'll want the big house opened. I should be there." My sisters shook their heads at me, and for once we were all in agreement.

"Why?" I asked.

"For the reception following interment," he answered impatiently. "Are you alone there, Beth? Or is George with you?"

"We won't be needing the big house," I told him. "But thank you for offering," I added, my mother having insisted on good manners when dealing with one's elders.

"Don't be ridiculous," Uncle Ethan said.

"There's no need for you to come," I continued, adding another mannerly after-thought, "It's such a distance."

"Don't be a stubborn fool," Uncle Ethan advised me. "It's not as if I want to take the time, or travel the distance."

"She wouldn't want you to either," I told him. "So you better not. She wouldn't have gone to your funeral," I said, "not in California." (And not in Wampanoag, either, but I didn't see the need to tell him that.) "But thank you, Uncle Ethan. I have to go now. You know how much there is to do at a time like this."

"Put George on," he said.

"Goodbye, Uncle Ethan," I said, and hung up.

At about that time, people began to arrive with casseroles, hams and coffee cakes, bundt cakes and molded salads, and the phone began to ring, people offering sympathy, wondering when the service would be. Meg and Jo took care of the phone. I answered the door and talked with callers. Amy set food out on the dining room table, never neglecting to keep the plate of cookies filled. She was a well-trained aunt and Mumma's daughter, too; she knew better than to step on Sarah's toes, even inadvertently.

Consulting individually with each of my sisters, lest any one hesitation be taken up and turn into a groundswell of negation, I received the go-ahead to telephone the principal of the elementary school, at home, of course, and after school let out, the request being a personal favor and no school administrator in such a small town claiming the right to an unlisted phone number. But Andy was adamant. "It's not appropriate, it's just not appropriate, Beth." That was all he would say, no matter how I argued it. "I'm sorry for your loss. She was before my time, but I've heard how much she did for the school. Unfortunately, it's not an appropriate use of a school auditorium."

After consulting again, I called the library and got the same response, although couched in a different cliché: "Oh, Beth, I hadn't heard, I'm so sorry. But the meeting room for a funeral service? I can't say yes, I'm afraid. It would set a precedent, you see, and we're a public institution. We can't set a precedent like that."

In a lull among the callers, while we were washing the dishes and George had left to pick up first Sarah from the playing field, then Dot from Bourne where she had been spending the weekend with her cousins, and then Emily at the Buzzards Bay bus station, on her return from a shortened football weekend with her boyfriend at Andover, we four considered the problem.

"Here? Should we have it here?" I asked, dismayed at the prospect, but resolute.

"This house isn't nearly big enough," Amy told me. "Mumma knew a lot of people. And this doesn't even include Boston, or the business. You'd be surprised."

"No I wouldn't," I told her.

"We'll have to rent a hall somewhere," Jo decided. "Or the banquet room of a restaurant? It won't be so bad. Lots of people get married in restaurants, these days. Some of the larger places have event packages, they take care of everything. Anything would be better than the big house. We do agree about that? For Mumma, I mean. For Mumma's funeral."

"Not a funeral," I reminded them, adding, "and she liked *some* of the Howlands, Grandmother and Uncle Brundy, and Aunt Juliet. Okay, maybe she didn't *like* Juliet, but she respected what she did with her life. And don't forget Uncle Giancarlo. All right, he's not a Howland," I granted.

"I don't know why you keep wanting to quarrel about it," Amy complained. "It's annoying. You know the big house is impossible."

I didn't apologize. She was right, I did know that, but I wanted to keep Mumma's complications clear, to myself, to all of us.

Jonquil Cartenbury Heolms showed up in the early evening. She had brought her little husband with her, a pale man, his silvery-white hair thin across his scalp; she had dressed him out in white linen over a dark shirt, very stylish.

By then we were all fatigued, by the attempts to think of an appropriate and available venue as well as by the number of call-

433

ers, by all the sympathy extended and accepted, exchanged, by all the human intercourse of the day, the offering of food and drink, the washing of glasses and mugs and plates and silver, the grateful reception of plates and platters of food, by the *smiling;* and that after the big adjustment of the day before. People had come out of the woodwork, all day, to say they were sorry about Mumma, on the phone, at the door, in the mail. People I'd only heard the names of wanted to offer sympathy and praise and reminiscences.

Strangers telephoned. "Kathleen Ralster's great-niece? You know, the Ralster Children's Room at the Cambridge library? Well, Aunt Kitty always talked about your mother. She was so proud of that Children's Room, Aunt Kitty. It was a memorial for her two sons, did you know that? They both died in the war so I never met them, but . . . I think I would have liked your mother," she said.

I had been hoping to turn off the living room lights and withdraw with my sisters and a bottle of wine to the back porch, leaving George and the girls to arrange some kind of supper for themselves when they got home, so I was especially not pleased to see Jonquil Cartenbury Heolms at the door.

I was not in a mood to be responsive to Jonquil Cartenbury Heolms.

She had thrown Mumma over after Mumma had been such a good friend, and Mumma had (uncharacteristically, entirely uncharacteristically) not grumbled, or reviled, or talked analytically about it, not once, to any of us, and not to Pops either. I asked him. It had been Mumma in deep denial, full sail ahead. She had simply reverted to her previous position on the question of Jonquil Cartenbury Heolms, as if the two years of intimacy had never intervened. "Life's too short to waste time crying over milk somebody else has spilled," she told me, when I foolishly tried to offered a sympathetic ear, or shoulder, or embrace. "You're smart enough to forget about her," Mumma advised me.

Jonquil Cartenbury Heolms arrived at my house, that is to say at Mumma's old house, to offer us what she called "Aunt Ditsey's Southwestern chicken casserole," adding, "Your mother loved it so I didn't mind the trouble of making it. I'll just take it out to the kitchen, shall I? My goodness, it's been years since I've been in this house, you've done wonders, Beth."

Jonquil Cartenbury Heolms was wearing one of those Castleberry knitted suits, beige with dark blue trim, a beige silk blouse with a bow at the neck, low-heeled leather pumps with squared-off toes. She wore pearls and gold chains, bracelets and rings, pearl clip-on earrings in ears that had never been pierced; she wore full makeup and freshly coiffed hair. She had come to pay a sympathy call and she was doing it right, for everyone to see.

What I saw was what I had never been able to see when Mumma was sharing the stage with her, which was how very pretty Jonquil Cartenbury Heolms was, with her clean features and deep-set violet-blue eyes. I had to realize what a lovely young woman she must have been — dainty, delicate, almost beautiful. For the first time, I could see her appeal.

"You're going to miss her terribly, I know," Jonquil Cartenbury Heolms said to me, with a hand laid prettily on my forearm. "It's a great loss." She added, reminding me of her qualifications to say this, "Rida was a good friend to me when I needed one."

"Better than you were to her," I agreed.

Her eyes shone with unshed tears. "I know. I know. I always felt so bad. I always wanted to explain, about Jake, you know, he's . . . He looks so self-assured but he's really . . . He's very fragile, you know. Why — and Rida knew this, how serious it is — he sees his psychiatrist three times a week, poor man."

I said nothing. Out of the corner of my eye, I saw Jo, who is by far the kindest of us, move over to rescue me, or at least join us. Jonquil Cartenbury Heolms gave me a few seconds to say whatever it was I was supposed to say in response to that confidence, then, since I maintained my silence, went on.

"I tried to talk to her, you know. After . . . oh, about a year after, when she had had time to calm down. But she pretended she didn't know what I was talking about. 'You have a husband, you know how it is,' I told her, but she wouldn't listen. I don't like to speak ill of the dead, Beth, but your mother could be awfully stubborn."

Reaching out to clasp Jo's offered hand, I was pleased to remember that. "Yes, wasn't she? I always admired it in her, didn't you?"

"Yes, of course." Jonquil Cartenbury Heolms tried to smile. "But it could make her a little unforgiving."

"Mumma did have a strong sense of right and wrong," I agreed, and drew Jo in. "Wouldn't you say that about her, Jo?"

"We are speaking of your dear mother,"

Jonquil Cartenbury Heolms said, laying her hand on Jo's arm. "I was saying how much I missed her friendship, and Beth — if I may be frank? — I am getting the distinct impression that Beth thinks I did your poor dear mother some wrong."

"But you did, didn't you? Dropping her flat like that?" I said.

"You look so well, Jonquil," Jo said. "And that casserole smells delicious." She placed herself so that Jonquil Cartenbury Heolms would have to turn away from me to accept the compliments, and thus release me.

But I wasn't quite ready to be set free. "Not that she cared," I added.

"I was about to tell Beth," Jonquil said, "and it's in Latin too. *Nihil nisi bonum.* You both know Latin, don't you? Rida had such clever girls. She used to boast about her girls. Oh, and your father, too, of course. *Don't speak ill of the dead,*" she mistranslated. "But you're something of an academic yourself, Beth," and she turned to Jo, recognizing the safer sister, "isn't she?"

Then I did leave. I went through the dining room and out into the kitchen, where I found Jake Heolms standing in front of the dishwasher, facing a glass-fronted cupboard of baking supplies. He turned as I entered, wide-eyed like a deer in headlights, then as

I got closer (on my way to get myself a glass for a slug of scotch, or maybe just wine), he essayed a smile. It was the saddest, most hopeful smile I have ever seen. His eyes were a washed-out blue, his eyelashes and eyebrows colorless, and altogether he looked like someone unfit for this life. "Mr. Heolms, hello," I said. "Can I reach by you?"

"Oh. Sorry." He stepped aside, watching me take down a glass. "I wonder if I too might . . . ?" not quite daring to finish the sentence.

"Wine? White?" I asked, opening the refrigerator door. I had decided that scotch was not a good idea for me and a worse one for him.

"Just whatever you yourself . . ." he said. His voice was reedy, his shoulders narrow, and he kept his hands jammed into his jacket pockets as if to keep them safe from notice, or from misbehaving. "I don't want to be a bother."

"Why should it be a bother when I'm getting one for myself as well?"

"Well, two *is* twice one," he said with a nervous little laugh. "You do remind me of her. A little. Your sisters, too — taken all together, you really remind me. I only met her once, but your mother . . ." His sad voice faded away to silence.

I poured wine for both of us. He took his glass as if unsure what to do with it. I raised mine and offered a toast, "To Mumma."

A thin little line of tears leaked out of his eyes and dribbled down the sides of his nose. He didn't seem to notice them. "She took against me," he admitted, embarrassed. "Jonquil tried to spare me. I only met her once, but your mother was . . . She was like a transfusion, a blood transfusion. Have you ever had a blood transfusion?"

I shook my head, looking past him, through the window to where darkness approached from the east, spreading itself over the pine trees that edged the marshy field behind the house. I knew exactly what he meant about my mother.

"Your father, too, he was a nice man, wasn't he?"

"Yes. He was."

"And he knew what a treasure he had," Jake Heolms told me. "I've always wished she hadn't disliked me. She had lovely manners."

"Mumma?" I protested. "Mumma was a bull in a china shop."

"Not really. She noticed people, really noticed them, and cared about them, and she *listened*. She had her own way of doing things," this odd man told me. "At the time, she didn't *seem* to dislike me, although Jonquil knew her better and explained it to me, after."

I tried to remember what Mumma had said about this man, after Jonquil had brought him to dinner. Pops had said he was "a decent enough sort who had a bad time in the war," but Mumma? Then, as if I could hear her speaking in my ear, I did remember. "The man was wishing he'd met me, not her, at that fancy resort club. He was wishing I wasn't already married. He was half in love with me — Don't laugh, a woman knows. Wasn't he, Spencer?" She turned to Pops for corroboration and, "Anybody would be," Pops told her. "He's a sad specimen," Mumma said. "But I'll bring him around. You'll see. He might not get to have me love him, but he'll be glad he met me, you can bet your buttons."

I *would* have bet my buttons, and I felt even more sorry for Jake Heolms and, unexpectedly, for Jonquil Cartenbury Heolms, too. "She *did* like you," I told him. "She thought you had promise."

"I could have," he agreed. "She must have been a wonderful mother."

"I've spent my whole life working that out," I told him, and he giggled, then saw his wife enter the room.

"There you are, you elusive man. Have you spoken with Meg? She's dear, poor Rida's firstborn, you'll want to express your sympathy to her, I know. You'll excuse us, Beth? It's really Meg, by the way, Jake, not Margaret, don't make that mistake. I did once, but never again." She emitted a pretty little laugh. "You should have seen the dust fly. Your mother certainly knew how to get the dust flying, didn't she, Beth?"

I couldn't disagree. Neither did I point out that flying dust wasn't necessarily a bad thing. It could be said to clear the air, or at least to be an effort in that direction, the direction of a better world, that is. It wasn't that I wasn't just about to point out those things, but the phone rang and I answered it instead.

"Hello?" I said, and Jonquil waved at me, miming that she didn't want to take any more of my time, miming sympathy and farewell, leading her husband away by the arm.

"Beth," a woman's voice said. Not familiar, not immediately identifiable. "Janice Lauter."

"Oh. Hello," I said, surprised. "What can I — ?"

She cut me off. "I don't know what I was

thinking of. Or, rather, what I wasn't thinking of. Or how I could have not thought of it. Of course Rida can be buried out of Saint Stephen's. I'm sorry not to have realized sooner how wrong I was. *She* would have caught it right away, if it had been her making the mistake."

"She can? Really? I can't tell you, Janice, that's —"

"Your mother was always bringing herself up short," Janice told me. "She wasn't one to let herself get away with things."

Mumma? Self-aware? But Janice had gone on, before I had begun to digest that improbability.

"And whatever her faith — or, more accurately, lack of it, because she never lied to me about that," Janice said.

Not a liar. That I could entirely agree with.

"She was always generous with the church, which is the same as being generous with God, in my view of things. Generous to us in your father's name, the family name —"

For the Howlands? My mind reeled.

"— and it seems to me that the church, Saint Stephen's, can be equally generous with her. To her. For her."

Janice hesitated before concluding, "It seems to me that God will be, too."

And well He should be — I could hear

Mumma saying it.

"If, that is, you still want to have the memorial here?" Janice asked. "Beth?"

"Yes. Yes, we do. We would. That's exactly what she would have wanted. Thank you, Janice, I'll . . . It's pretty hectic around here right now. Can I call you Monday morning about details? After I've had a chance to talk with my sisters."

"Of course. I'm so pleased you haven't made other arrangements. Your mother was . . . Well, you girls were lucky to have her. I'm lucky to have known her."

Lucky? Well, maybe. "Thank you, Janice. Really."

"Thank *her.*" Janice laughed. "I don't know that I'd do it for anyone else, subverting my own principles."

"I'll call you Monday," I promised, and went to share the good news with my sisters.

We got through Mumma's non-funeral non-memorial non-service and its brief social aftermath by the cluster of oaks outside the church. After, George and my brothers-in-law, a category that includes one brother-in-law equivalent, took the grandchildren out to McDonald's and then dropped them at the movies, going on themselves to the Club for drinks and a stag dinner. This left

444

the four of us at home. Mumma's mother-less daughters.

We took glasses of wine outside, to sit on the back porch steps and watch the sky. The gold-rimmed gray faded to purple. Darkness approached, arrived. Only the brightest of the stars could make themselves seen through a thin layer of clouds, although the night was moonless.

"Well," said Meg, and Amy echoed her, "Well."

"Yes. Well," I said.

Beside me, in shadows, Jo exhaled smoke. "Well, that's it."

"Yes," Meg said. "That's really the end."

Jo asked, "Who has the tissues?"

We aren't big weepers, Mumma's daughters, but every now and then one of us needed a tissue. Not when we were on show, on parade, not when we had something to do, people to welcome, a non-service to manage, but at odd times, as then, when we were alone together, quiet.

"Gone but not forgotten, that's what I say," I announced.

"What's that supposed to mean?" Amy asked, while Meg protested, "Is that supposed to console me?"

Jo reminded us, "We lost her years ago. She didn't know who any of us even were for a long time. Isn't that right, Meg? It'd been months since she'd known even who *you* are."

Unexpectedly, Amy came around to my point of view. "But this does feel different."

"She was really — I mean, Mumma," Meg said. "Mumma really was — When she was herself, I mean . . ."

"Remarkable," Jo suggested.

"A handful," I said.

"She was really something, wasn't she?" Amy asked.

"Trouble," I said.

". . . one of a kind," Meg finished.

"Alive," I said.

"Frankly," Meg said, "I was always glad you were the one she lived next door to."

"Not exactly next door."

"You know what I mean. The one she chose. I couldn't have done it. None of the rest of us could have. She'd have eaten up my life."

"She'd have eaten up all of our lives, except Beth's," Amy agreed.

"Not mine," Jo maintained.

"You wish," Amy answered.

"I wish I was more like her," I admitted.

"So do we," they chorused. "But there's Sarah."

We laughed, little reluctant laughs and

mine, at least in part, ironic.

"Who has the tissues?" Amy asked. "I can't see. Jo?"

We sat silent then, for a long time. The filmy cloud cover faded and a few stars broke through its veil. From behind the garage, the insect light tolled steadily.

Meg broke the silence. "Nothing got in her way when she thought she was in the right."

"She always thought she was in the right," I pointed out.

Meg ignored me. "That time at Cotillion? I just remembered that, the way she looked, charging across the dance floor to snatch me up? Like Lancelot, riding to rescue Guinevere."

"Not exactly like that," I said. "Because he actually came to do battle for her."

"You know what I mean. I mean, heroic. I felt rescued."

"You said you were embarrassed," I protested. "That's what you always said. You said she'd ruined your life."

"I know, but really? She saved my life. If I'd had to sit there, doing nothing, which is the only choice I thought I had. I was doing exactly that, sitting there, doing nothing, like a good girl. But Mumma didn't do nothing. She didn't tolerate things. She walked right into the middle of it and got me out. Think of what an example that was for an adolescent girl," claimed my revisionist sister.

"What a role model for you as a mother, you mean?" Jo asked.

"I guess, but I was thinking more of a role model as a human being. That you don't have to stick it out, doing what people say you *should*. If it hadn't been for Mumma, I'd never have had the courage to give up on Jack Cartenbury. And then what would my life be?"

We couldn't argue with that.

"And Pops was so proud of her. Remember?" Jo said. "He'd tell the Cotillion story. She loved when he told that story."

"You always tried to get him to stop, you were so embarrassed," I reminded Meg.

"I know." She laughed, a low, self-effacing laugh. "But I got over it. Who lives may learn, like Mumma said."

Jo turned to look at us, her eyes dark hollows in the shadows. "That's one of the things I learned from Olympia. Didn't the rest of you? How to let Mumma give me advice. Not that Olympia ever said precisely that, not, 'Listen to your mother.' No therapist is going to say that. As we all know."

I reminded them, "Not me."

"Not that old song and dance," Amy said.

Jo continued, "Not that I'm anything like perfect, but I often think how if Mumma hadn't kept after me about the dangers of the way I treated people, letting them get away with anything? I don't know what I wouldn't have done."

"Wait a minute!" I protested. "Hold on!"

"It was sentimentality, really, which is just what she told me."

"You called her cold-hearted. You called her the Snow Queen," I reminded Jo. "And those were the polite names. Remember when she said that you were looking for pets, not boyfriends? And then offered you a goldfish?" and that made us all laugh, remembering Mumma.

Jo said, "I don't want to be like her and I never did, the way she bossed Pops around, and told us what we should be doing, and made such a big deal out of monogamy. But I've had some good relationships, and she showed me how. I'm having a good one now."

I gave up.

"I've never settled for less, and that's because of Mumma," Jo announced. "*And* I'd have made a truly lousy mother, we all know that. Of all of us, I'm the most like her. Don't look at me like that," she said, as if despite the darkness she could see our expressions. "You know it's true." I don't know about the others, but I had never thought about it. She lit another cigarette, and laughed, "I'm too old now, even to adopt. I'd be the mother of a teenager in my seventies."

"But you're a therapist," I pointed out, as if she might not have seen the connection.

"What else was there for me to do with all this empathy and insight?" Jo asked.

"How did Mumma show you how to listen to other people when it's something she never did herself?" I asked, then I was distracted. "You mean that because of the way she was, I'm the way I am. Like, the way I never brought a boyfriend home until George. Psychological cause and effect?"

"Too independent for your own good," they quoted Mumma.

"Because I knew he was for keeps or I wouldn't have brought him at all."

"Yes, but *how* did you know?" Jo asked.

"I've always relied on my own judgment," I answered. "You all know that. You've complained about it enough. If I hadn't, then Mumma would have filled my head with her opinions. Taken over my life, the way she did —" I cut myself short, to finish my thought privately.

They waited, not speaking.

"And that's why I never got to see Olympia," I concluded, surprised that I had never thought of it before. "It's not as if she thought I was so right or smart about things," I apologized to my sisters.

"No," they agreed. "But *you* did."

"Well of course," I said. "And I was." I thought. "Mostly I was, anyway, and for anything really important — *Now* what's so funny?" I demanded, but I could feel the sheepish smile spreading on my face.

"You're always complaining about Mumma," Amy observed. "Even still now."

"We've all had our complaints," I said.

Meg soothed us. "And they were all justified. She wasn't your normal everyday mother."

"No mother is your normal everyday mother," Jo announced with irritating authority. "So don't go thinking you've been deprived of something everybody else gets without even asking."

"Remember Mr. Smithers?" Amy said, almost dreamily. "I was thinking, when you were talking about Cotillion, it reminded me of Mr. Smithers, and I was thinking that Mumma really did a good job with him. Mumma was a fixer."

Meg doubted that. "She hounded the poor man out of his job. Out of his career."

"But you know, there really *was* something going on," Amy admitted, after years of refusing to speak about it. "We knew. Never me, but some of us, he'd stand too close, crowd up close to you, or call you to stand close when he was seated at his desk. Some girls said he'd touched them, nothing drastic, and Ellen Jablonski — Remember her, Beth? — Ellen claimed he'd kissed her. In the cloakroom. French-kissed her, she said, but nobody knew if it was true. You have to remember Ellen Jablonski, how she tried to be sexually ahead of us all so we never knew if she was making things up, but she didn't always lie, some of it was true. We were twelve years old, or eleven, it was the '50s, nobody knew anything. We had no way of dealing with him. We couldn't even talk frankly among ourselves. Girls didn't then. Anyway," she said, "he would have gotten worse, that's human nature. In my opinion, the man ruined his own career. But Mumma —"

"She even found him another job," Meg remembered.

"Those priests it's coming out about," Jo reminded us. "Think of what Mumma would have said about that."

"Where were those boys' mothers?" I suggested, then, *"What do you expect from an untaxed corporation?"*

"But with Mr. Smithers, I watched it happening. I saw how Mumma did it, and I've always tried to work that same way. Why do you think I've always had such good employees?" she asked us. "Besides being smart and hard-working."

"And ambitious," Jo added.

"That's not a crime," Amy pointed out. "Not in my book. And mine's the book I'm going by," she told us, as if we hadn't noticed. "Who has the tissues?"

"We're all going by our own books," Jo told us. "I mean, what do you expect? From people raised by our mother." Her lighter flamed in the darkness, again, so that I could see her face, and Meg's, and Amy's. Then there was just that round red glow and a pale wisping upward of smoke as Jo inhaled deeply, exhaled.

Somebody had to say it. We were all thinking it, even Jo, I was sure, so I asked the unwelcome question, risking the quarrel. "Isn't it time you stopped smoking? I mean, now that Mumma's dead," I said, as blunt as Mumma herself.

Sometimes, life is too short to worry about sounding just like your mother.

10.
AFTER MUMMA

A question I often ask myself is: How did Sarah come to be so like my mother? I do not ask my sisters this. Their answers would range from "It serves you right" to "You bring it out in her, just like you did with Mumma." Nor do I ask George, who would only avoid responding. "I'm not a geneticist, I'm a legalist. How would I know?"

I did, once, put the question to Sarah. She was in late elementary school at the time; I think that the occasion was her refusal to wear sneakers, or any shoe with laces, not ever, not for any occasion, not even — the immediate point of crisis — gym. "You didn't even know her and you're just like her," I complained, and Sarah explained it to me. "She's your hero, isn't she? So what's so bad about me being like her?"

"Nothing. Not a thing. Did I say it was?"

"What's *wrong* with you?"

"Wrong with me? I'm not the one refusing to wear sneakers, the world's most common footwear."

I don't remember losing that argument, but I don't remember winning it, either. Winning or losing isn't the point here. Sarah is the point, Sarah being herself. Two of the world's least low-key characters, my mother and my daughter.

I have put forward, and been mocked for, the theory that as Mumma's intelligence abandoned her, it systematically relocated its base of operations into the brain of my youngest daughter, who was transformed while still a toddler into my mother. When she says too often and with too judgmental a glance in my direction, "That's so *lame,*" I tell Sarah, "You're your grandmother all over again," and I add, so that she won't misunderstand me, "Twenty-twenty tunnel vision."

"Hunh," Sarah says, or, "You wish," or some similar mid-teen parent-dismissing phrase.

I point my youngest daughter in the direction of the nearest mirror. "Take a look. Gran reincarnated."

"Reincarnation is arithmetically illogical," says Sarah.

"Captain and high scorer of Team Denial," I say.

"You just think I'm homely," Sarah says.

"But Mumma was beautiful."

"I've got eyes," says Sarah.

"She just wasn't photogenic."

"Tell me about it."

I start to, but Sarah has walked away before I get two sentences into my speech about Mumma's vitality, comparing it to the thick, curly, improbably russet hair she took to the crematorium, and about how if beauty is something you just want to keep on looking at, even when your purpose is to land a fist smack on its snoot, Mumma was right: she *was* beautiful. Like my youngest daughter, to whom all eyes turn when she enters.

And before whom many hearts quail, that too.

Sarah, at three, banned the letter H from existence; she denied it. Reciting her ABCs, singing on-key, as we noted in fond admiration, she first tried simply omitting it, going directly from G to I, but that threw off both the rhythm and the rhyme of her song, so she merely pressed her lips firmly together and refused to utter the offending consonant. ". . . E-F-G-umm-I-J-K," she sang. "You forgot H," we coached her. "I don't want that letter," she explained.

"It's the terrible twos," my sisters promised me. When I argued that neither Emily nor Dot had been so terrible at two and Sarah was, moreover, no longer in her twos, they reminded me, "Children aren't all the same. Look at you and us."

"She'll outgrow it," I was promised by Sarah's nursery school teachers. Only George saw the same thing I was seeing. After careful observation, "Sarah's not going to change," he decided. "I'm going to relax and enjoy her," he said, and advised me, "You could do the same."

With Sarah, it has been one thing after another. It was books she didn't want to read — arguing that literate rats who wanted to create a utopian society exceeded credibility. It was foods she wouldn't eat — tomatoes for the first ten years of her life, raw or cooked into sauces, after which she adored them, not to mention, as their political seasons have come and gone, lettuce, green grapes, swordfish, beef, veal. All of her life Sarah has walked me out of movies, as being too scary, too stupid, too grim, too unbelievable, and also, more recently, too manipulative, too Hollywood. Everyone assures me, "It'll get better. Adolescence is a difficult time." Only George consoles me. "Your mother would have met her match with Sarah."

"*I've* met my match," I say.

"Do you think so? You don't act like you have."

I raise sarcastic eyebrows. "That's just because I never engage."

He raises eyebrows right back at me. "You make her take one bite of everything. You used to sneak tomatoes into dishes then tell her afterward that she'd eaten them and liked them."

"Tomatoes are a good source of vitamin C," I point out, and add, "That's about taking one bite of everything on your plate, about good manners and giving everything a try. That's what mothers do," I tell him. "They help their children learn how to get along in the world. I'm just —" but I can no longer not break into laughter. "I'd do better to help the world learn how to get along with my child, seeing that of the two the world is the easier to manage."

"Your mother would have approved of Sarah," George tells me.

"My mother liked trouble," I tell him. "I'm lucky they didn't overlap. Imagine — I can't even imagine it. What if I'd had to deal with both of them at the same time?"

"The two of them together would have made mincemeat of you," George agrees and doesn't sound all that unhappy at the prospect, although, "I'd have had to come to your rescue," he realizes.

My pride prickles, stung. "As if. I'm my mother's daughter. I don't get beaten down, not easily, not without a fight and not for long. Life is too short to waste it not living the way you want to," I say, then add, because it's an unavoidable truth, "If you can."

"Your mother would have said you always can."

"Mumma wasn't always right."

"She would have said that's not what matters."

A few weeks ago — long enough ago by now to have achieved the ease of a distant memory, like the remembrance of childbirth past ("Oh, yes, that was rather grim") — Sarah's oldest sister, Emily, married Elliot Brewster Adams, who is from one of those Boston families greater than the sum of the parts of its names. This was a textbook wedding, for which we consulted three separate texts lest we omit any significant step. The Adamses gave the original engagement party, and various wedding showers were given by various friends and relatives in various suburbs, but the main event was up to Emily's parents. That is to say, a full-dress, late August wedding with a guest list of over two hundred people for a sit-down dinner was up to me. Luckily for Emily, and for me, George is an actual *helpmeet.* Moreover, while he blinked at some of the bills, he paid up without questioning, and, frankly, I don't know which I value more, his generosity with money or his generosity with attention.

The expense of this large, formal wedding did, however, trouble my youngest daughter. "It's disgusting," she announced early on in the budgeting process, her mahogany eyes fixed on her father's hand as it totaled estimates on a yellow legal pad. Then she hurled a glance at me. "Don't you *dare* try to do anything like that to me if I get married."

"I wouldn't think of it," I promised.

It is, however, typical of Sarah that despite her strong and principled opposition to the manner of the wedding, she willingly masterminded the June bridal shower that Dot gave for her big sister, although whether Sarah did it from a desire to be in charge or in an effort to control some part of the expense, I couldn't say. I was myself at the end of an academic year and — quite happily, I admit it — unavailable. Because Dot attends a Midwestern college, she couldn't be on the spot, so Sarah took on the necessary tasks with her usual terrifying efficiency, selecting invitations, mailing them out to the three dozen invited guests and recording RSVPs in a notebook dedicated to the event, then choosing a menu (showcasing her individual key lime tarts, which Emily had particularly requested, but also organizing food preparation into a three-day period), planning the flowers, and rearranging the furniture. Everything was organized; we all knew what we were supposed to do, and when.

The occasion took place with only one crisis, and that not until the dessert course, when we were five tarts short. Fifteen of the invitees had RSVP'd acceptances and Sarah had made seventeen tarts, the correct number for guests, guest of honor, and hostess. Then twenty-two young women arrived at the party. To produce extra napkins, silver, plates, and glasses was simple. Following Mumma's model, I always prepared too much food. But seventeen tarts remained stubbornly seventeen tarts, not twenty-two. As the meal went happily and smoothly on in the dining room, Sarah and I, simultaneously chef, sous-chef, caterer, and waitstaff, addressed the difficulty in the kitchen. It was clear to me that the only thing to do was cut each tart into four wedges, as if it were a miniature pie.

"Mother!"

"I don't see any other choice."

"Everything's exactly the way it's supposed to be just the way it is, except for *them.* Whichever ones they are. Do you know who they are?"

"We have more dessert plates."

"Picture it — just picture it! And a knife will drag at the filling, you know it will, Mother."

(The other two call me Mom. But Sarah had gone directly from Mommy to Mother. I am not sure just how to take this and she is the last one I would ask. George, the first one I ask almost anything, advised me not to take it personally.)

I seldom try to govern Sarah, but on that occasion I did, and sternly. "Unless you are willing to simply ignore the fact that there are five more guests than you planned on, Sarah, you're going to *have* to compromise."

"Mother!" Immediately, the air in the room became sunny. "You're a genius!"

I assumed she was joking. "You know you can't do that."

"Why not? Is it my fault if there are five rude people out there? And that nobody does anything about it? They're not *my* friends." Once Sarah is convinced she has right on her side, she is entirely happy to let things make their own way along their own path to whatever disaster awaits them. "I'll ask which they are and tell them they can't have tarts. It's only fair."

"You can't *ask* them that, Sarah," I wailed and in that, at least, she let me have my way.

After all the guests had departed, my three daughters worked together to clean the kitchen and straighten the furniture, so it wasn't until late afternoon, the dishwasher ready to resume its final load, that I wandered into the kitchen with a coffee cup I'd picked up in the downstairs bathroom to hear Emily say, "I would have liked one of those tarts. They looked good, Sarah."

"That's because they were."

Emily laughed, asking her other sister, "Did you get one, Dot?"

"I had to be sure everybody else had dessert before I got one myself, didn't I?"

"Everybody liked them," Sarah announced with satisfaction.

"Why didn't you make enough?" Dot asked.

"I did," Sarah said.

"Palpably false," Dot said. "I didn't get

463

one, neither did Emily. Also, Sally Munro —"

"Although, in fact? Sally never eats dessert," Emily interrupted.

"And Elena and — who else, Em? We were five short."

Her sisters know enough to set their points relentlessly out in front of Sarah, giving her no time to interrupt. Sarah is at her best picking off one point after another.

"It was DeeDee, because she's a dessert freak but she eats so slowly that by the time she got back to the table," and at this point they both turned to face Sarah, "all the tarts were gone."

"Because *you* didn't make enough," Dot concluded.

I understand sisterly dynamics. I didn't interfere. Emily would not have made such a tactical error. Emily would have left Sarah to draw the appropriate conclusion. On the other hand, Dot had her little sister's measure and knew that when she feels wronged, Sarah and Appropriate head for opposite corners of the ring.

Sarah dried her hands and picked up her notebook. She opened it to a list of names and addresses and held it out for her sisters to look at.

"That's the invitation list, isn't it?" Emily

asked. "We all know who was invited," she reminded Sarah patiently.

"I know," Sarah said, also patiently. "And *I* know who accepted. *And* I know who regretted. And I *know* who never even bothered to respond at all."

Dot had the answer to this. "I told you, when you called me — I remember this conversation, Sarah, I told you not everybody RSVPs nowadays. I told you not to worry about them."

"I didn't," Sarah told her.

Emily understood. "You assumed they wouldn't be coming."

"So I want to know who the five people were," Sarah continued. "Because I don't remember that many of your friends," she explained. "It's not funny, Emily."

"Not a bit," Dot agreed. "I have to tell you, Sarah —"

"No, Dot, you don't." But Emily's attempt to warn her sister off was ineffective.

"— that I was a little embarrassed at running out of desserts," Dot said. "At my shower I was giving for Emily."

Sarah took a minute, letting all of us, especially Dot, consider the possible responses to this statement. Then, wordlessly, she exited the room, her victory complete.

As soon as the swinging door had swung

closed after her, it swung open again and Sarah reentered. We had expected this, Sarah being Sarah. Sarah likes the last word, and the epilogue, too. "I still want to know who they are," she told Emily.

"But why?" Emily insisted. "That's *if* I know. If I noticed. If I remember. I'm not even going to try to remember unless you tell me why."

"So I can write to them."

"Write what to them?"

"About their bad manners."

"You can't do that, Sarah," I said, even though I knew I should keep quiet.

"So you *do* know who they are."

"Yes, but I'm not telling. It would be rude to write to them."

"Ruder than to not RSVP? As long as they get away with it, they'll just go on doing it," Sarah warned. *She* would never have ceded the Sudetenland. "And what about the wedding? What if they do it at Emily's wedding at — What is Dad paying? A hundred and twenty-five a head?"

"Weddings are different," we assured her. "People feel differently about weddings. They know better."

"I bet I can figure it out," Sarah said. "Where do you keep your old yearbooks, Em?"

"What is *wrong* with you?" Dot demanded. "I feel sorry for you, Sarah."

Sarah's curiosity was aroused. "Why would you feel sorry for me?"

"Because you're never going to get it about yourself," Dot said. "Like Gran."

"Gran was more fun than anybody," Emily reminded them both.

"Yeah, but she was always making things worse. She made things blow up all the time. Explode." Dot's hands flew up in the air, gesturing explosions.

Why is it that whenever anybody else attacks her, I defend Mumma?

"Lots of the time, her exploding got good results," I told Dot. "You loved Gran," I reminded her. "And she loved all of you, she wouldn't hear a word against you. I'd have liked to have her for a grandmother, I can tell you that. Much more than the one I got. You girls were lucky."

We started in telling Mumma stories, then, even Sarah, who has none of her own but who has moved herself into many of ours, sometimes appropriating them entirely, and by the day's end, we had all forgotten about the tart shortfall and the manners shortfall. Or so we thought, Emily and Dot and I.

We always underestimate Sarah.

■ ■ ■ ■

In the weeks between the shower and the event, from June to August (it had to be August because until then weather on the Cape is so unreliable), it was Sarah who could keep us informed about the status of various segments. With her organizational gifts, she was a natural to be in charge of record keeping: expenses, guest lists, gifts received, musical choices, catering and flowers, driving directions from all nearby towns to both the service and the reception, available accommodations for out-of-town guests, travel options from airports in Boston and Providence, bus and train schedules from Boston, Providence, New York, and DC, a list of car rental agencies — each with comparative prices. In short, Sarah was irreplaceable, and she may well have been the primary reason for the equanimity, the serenity, the lambent happiness with which Emily remembers her bridal season.

I let myself slip into equanimity, too, and I should have known better. I'd lived most of my life within Mumma's sphere of influence so I don't know why I was surprised to be accosted on the phone one July morning by the groom's mother. "Do you know what your daughter has done?"

It had to be Sarah. People frequently approach a parent to ask, "Do you know what your daughter has done?" but when it was Emily they spoke of, the voice would be warm or delighted, and the message of some particular kindness Emily had performed. Dot elicited admiration for her team spirit and friendliness, but Sarah . . . When it concerned Sarah, the question always contained some level of outrage. "Do you?" Christina repeated before I had time to respond to her first inquiry. "Do you know what your daughter has done?"

Yes, I wanted to answer, *Yes, and I entirely approve.* That's what Mumma would have said. *No, and please don't tell me,* I wanted to say that, too. Instead, I responded with a mendacious innocence, "Which daughter?"

"She's written letters!" Christina spoke in tones of regal outrage.

"Oh?"

"To people we know! Friends of ours and even business connections!"

"Ah."

The phone at my ear, I wandered over to the sun porch window from which I could look out into a clear summer day and admire the day lilies, their orange and yel-

469

low petals highlighted with black streaks and spots, opened to the sky like hands in prayer, or at least in appreciation. Portable phones are to my mind one of the great technological achievements of the times. Bad enough that phones will interrupt whatever is going on, but worse when you can't move around, to empty the dishwasher, pick up scattered newspapers, look out the window, when the telephone imprisons your body as well as your attention.

"Did you know she was doing that?"

"No," I said mildly, and quite truthfully.

"I've never *been* so embarrassed!"

Lucky you, I didn't say. Neither did I apologize or offer sympathy. Mostly, I was curious about these letters of Sarah's. But I didn't want to fuel Christina's anger by asking, and besides, I guessed that the woman wanted to specify the offenses.

"People are calling me up," she hissed. "Friends of ours, and business connections, too. Asking who she is. If she's a psychopath."

"Sarah? I doubt it. If you ask me, the problem is that she's so relentlessly sane."

"I should have known better than to ask you." Christina took a long, audible, calming breath. "Nobody's called you?"

"No." *Our* friends knew Sarah.

470

Pale feathery clouds occasionally interrupted the perfect watery blue of the sky. I understood that the temperature outside was not as high as it looked, but I could believe it was tropically warm, as I stood looking out the window with the phone at my ear.

"They wouldn't, would they." Not a question, a bitterness. "They're probably used to being hounded about some arbitrary time limit." The RSVPs, then. "What has happened to the grace in life?" Christina wondered, sorrowfully.

"Well," I said. "I can't talk right now, Christina. It's a little frantic around here."

"You'll stop her, of course," Christina instructed me.

"Probably it's too late for that."

"You liberal parents . . . You ruin everything for the rest of us. Frankly, you're all very interesting and all that, you Middletons, you Howlands, but I just hope Elliot's not making a big mistake. I hope he knows what he's getting into."

"Oh, I'm sure Elliot and Emily will make a good life together. Emily's a lucky girl." Oil on troubled waters. Then I was temporarily possessed by the spirit of my mother and added, "Did you want to talk to Sarah?" A match to the oil on troubled waters.

"Don't be —" Christina stopped herself. We were, after all, going to be related, and it is, after all, politic to maintain appearances with the in-laws your child has brought down upon you. "What good would that do? I'll just fend these people off as best I can."

"Yes," I agreed, back in my passive persona. "Are we seeing you this weekend?"

Christina avoided the invitation. "Our plans aren't settled. Have a good day, Beth."

"I am," I assured her.

When I asked Sarah, "It's fourteen percent of the invitation list!" she exclaimed, and reminded me, "You said weddings would be different. And I wasn't the least bit rude." She explained it patiently to me: "You set the RSVP date two weeks before the caterers want to know, and that's another ten days before they absolutely *have* to know. You told me this, I remember, I thought it was interesting the way human weakness — See? I'm *not* calling it rudeness, Mother — is sort of factored into everybody's thinking. All I did was write a note to anybody who hadn't responded by the deadline. *Let us know if we can hope to see you,* that's all I said. It was entirely polite, I was charming. Really, don't laugh, I read Amy Vanderbilt and I cross-referenced Miss Manners and I included a stamped, addressed post-card for responses. You better hope they answer now, because fourteen percent of two hundred and seventeen people is a lot. At a hundred and twenty-five dollars a head. You're the doctor, you do the math."

She was becoming incoherent. I was about to become incoherent. George intervened.

This conversation took place over a Sunday lunch in Mumma's house on the Cape, which George had given me as a forty-first birthday present, buying out my siblings' shares when Mumma went into the nursing home. We ate Sunday lunches on the Cape together, simple meals like grilled cheese sandwiches or lobster rolls or, if Sarah or George felt like making it, there might be a pot of soup. That Sunday, with only the three of us at the kitchen table, I was about to tell Sarah in a blur of incoherent embarrassed fury that I wasn't that kind of a doctor, as she perfectly well knew, and that the cost of this wedding did not concern her, and that moreover I didn't believe even Miss Manners, whose righteousness almost equals Sarah's own, would condone sending reminders to people who haven't RSVP'd. Wasn't it time Sarah learned respect for social realities? Before she found herself out on her own in the real world. I was about to say something to that effect, when George stepped in.

"Elfrieda would have felt the same," he told me.

"I'm not saying I don't *feel* the same," I protested.

George turned to Sarah, and laughed. "Gran would have made house calls."

"One's in California, two are in Arizona, one lives in Idaho," Sarah explained. "Plus, a couple there's only a business address for. Wall Street, I'd have had to make an appointment."

"You're right, Mumma would have," and I had to smile, picturing it. "She'd have done it wearing a hat, and white gloves, high heels. A dress — something bright yellow, or orange, or yellow *and* orange. Flowered." I tried not to laugh. "Just like Sarah."

"I don't own any of those kinds of gloves."

"Or anything yellow because it's so unflattering," George added, and smiled benignly, not victoriously, at both of us, one after the other, and back again. George was wonderfully handsome when I fell wildly in love with him, and he has aged well, in terms of moderate paunch, moderate baldness, immoderate, although bespeaking much character, lining of the face; but I actually fell in love with him for his contentment, not his looks. And it might also be accurate to say I've stayed in love with him because of that contentment. Life, for George, is not a contest. It's a pleasure.

"Besides, if I'm correct, it's already too late," he said. "If I'm correct, the letters have already been mailed."

"Last Wednesday," Sarah said. "And I've already gotten four responses. They telephoned. They apologized," she announced.

"I can imagine," I said, letting her make of that what she would.

"I really *was* polite. I can show you my final draft."

"No." I stopped her before she actually left the table. According to her lights, she had probably been entirely decorous. It's just that Sarah's lights, like Mumma's, tend to be blinding, unless you keep them peripheral. "I believe you."

Sarah knows me as well as I know her. "No you don't," she said. "Don't ever think you can get away with pretending to agree with me when you don't, Mother. Life is too short to waste time trying to hide what you really think."

"Life is too short in general," George pointed out.

Sarah nodded her head energetically. "Exactly," she said, and her glance included me in the question she asked with, for Sarah, an unusual pensiveness, "What should we do about that? Since we can't change it."

As the receiving line at Emily's wedding reception was about to disband, George elegant beside me in a morning coat and I equally elegant in a dusty rose crepe mother-of-the-bride dress that flowed around my calves, Dot came up from behind to speak in my ear. "Mother," she said, giving the word an irritated elongated pronunciation, *Mo*-ther. "You better stop her."

I did not wait for an explanation. Christina Adams stood next to me, competing for the graciousness award, so I ceded it to her and slipped away. It had been a lovely wedding, traditional, tasteful, the bride and her attendants in simple long gowns of white and deep blue (so flattering to all skin tones), the Club with its wide verandas overlooking the Hyannis harbor an elegantly unostentatious setting for the reception, both Saint Stephen's and the clubhouse resplendent with flowers. We had done Emily proud and satisfied the Adamses: altogether, a promising start for the young couple. I didn't know exactly what offense Sarah was committing to upset Dot. Hectoring the kitchen crew was most likely, or arguing about how the cars were being parked by the teenage valet staff. Accepting compliments to my right and left, I followed Dot down a hallway where heavy gilt-framed mirrors alternated with engravings that covered a century's worth of racing yachts. We arrived at the entrance side together. "See?" Dot asked into my ear, and slipped away.

I saw. The heavy glass doors had been opened wide and I looked out into a golden summer evening saturated with the mingled scents of sea air and fresh-cut grass, infiltrated by the faint sound of an orchestra. On the topmost step of a broad staircase stood Sarah, like the angel with the flaming sword that guards the entrance to the Garden of Eden. The only weapon she actually had was her glance, but that was enough to keep at bay the eight people transfixed just beyond the lowest step.

All eight of them were dressed as if for a formal occasion — my daughter's wedding, perhaps. There were three couples of about my age, the men silver-haired unless bald, the women draped in pearls and gold chains, festooned about the fingers and ears with gemstones. With them stood two young single women, each carrying a wrapped gift.

The two younger women and the tallest and broadest of the older men were at the front of the group, all three simmering with anger. It was the man who gave voice to their feelings. "We are invited guests."

"You didn't RSVP," Sarah responded, for what was probably not the first time.

"We drove down especially," he insisted. "We were at the church."

"Anybody can go to the church," Sarah said. "The reception is different."

"We were invited to the reception as well," he said.

"You didn't RSVP," Sarah repeated.

George came up behind me and put his arm around my shoulders. He was there for solidarity and I stood within his embrace, trying to think of how to step in, how to make things better and smooth them over so that life might go flowing on.

"That was my secretary's error," the man maintained.

"You didn't answer the reminder I sent in July," Sarah said.

"That was an impertinence." One of the older women speaking up from the rear.

"We sent a gift," another wife said. "From Tiffany's."

"You didn't RSVP," Sarah said again, quite patiently. Like Mumma, when Sarah has right on her side she has the patience of Job.

"I *never* RSVP," one of the younger women said, and I recognized her, DeeDee Johnston.

"I know that," Sarah said, with so ominous a note of recognition that DeeDee took a step back.

"This is ridiculous," the man said.

"No, it's rudeness," Sarah said.

"And you consider what you're doing polite?" another wife questioned.

"Maybe rudeness begets rudeness," Sarah suggested. "Think about it. An eye for an eye. Fighting fire with fire. Tit for tat," she continued.

DeeDee caught sight of George and me, standing back. "Mr. Middleton?"

"None of you should be here," Sarah concluded to her assembled group of unwelcome guests. "I'm sorry to have to tell you that."

Following DeeDee's lead, the imposing man looked to George, a straight look between members of the same superior sex that wondered, *Are you allowing this?* and he asked, "You're the father of the bride here?" Subtext: *The host? Are you going to let this chit of a girl get away with treating me like this?*

Sarah gave us only the most careless of glances. We would agree with her: She was in the right.

George didn't hesitate. He pivoted me around and we went back inside, together, past mirrors and yachting prints, back along the carpeted hallway to the music and voices. We could trust Sarah to finish up fairly quickly and then join the party. George, I saw, was smiling.

I felt tears fill my eyes and then I felt my eyes overflow.

Not for long, not much, but still —

"Sometimes I just . . . miss Mumma," I told George as I wiped them away.

"I know," he said, and put his arm around me again. I put mine around his waist and we comforted one another. "I can just imagine what Elfrieda would have said, about all of this. And about Sarah too. Can't you?"

"Do you think Mumma would be back there with Sarah?"

"Maybe," George said. "But she'd be unnecessary."

"Maybe," I agreed. "But she wouldn't notice that. She had a wonderfully blind view of reality," I reminded him.

"She'd have driven Sarah crazy," he agreed.

"I haven't," I boasted, because that was one of the few things about my life I was certain of, that my unwieldy youngest child had emerged untrammeled from my hands.

We arrived back at the party to see that the reception line had disappeared and we hesitated just inside the doors to the long ballroom, surveying the scene. A small orchestra was seated up on a balcony. Half of the room held tables and the rest of the floor was free for dancing. When the orchestra began a waltz, we watched Elliot lead Emily out onto the dance floor. George and I moved toward the dancers, he contentedly, I with some dread: It had been years since I had attempted even ballroom dancing; dancing was not one of my proficiencies; I knew that soon, inevitably, Elliot would come to claim me, to lead me out onto the floor, where I was not sure I would do well. At that craven thought, I could almost hear Mumma's voice: *"Don't ever make the mistake of thinking I would have a daughter who can't dance."*

ABOUT THE AUTHOR

Cynthia Voigt won the Newbery Medal for *Dicey's Song* and the Newbery Honor Award for *A Solitary Blue,* both part of the beloved Tillerman Cycle. She is also the author of many other celebrated books for middle-grade and teen readers, including *Izzy, Willy-Nilly* and *Jackaroo.* She was awarded the Margaret A. Edwards Award in 1995 for her work in literature, and the Katahdin Award in 2004. She lives in Maine.

The employees of Thorndike Press hope you have enjoyed this Large Print book. All our Thorndike, Wheeler, and Kennebec Large Print titles are designed for easy reading, and all our books are made to last. Other Thorndike Press Large Print books are available at your library, through selected bookstores, or directly from us.

For information about titles, please call:
  (800) 223-1244

or visit our website at:
  gale.com/thorndike

To share your comments, please write:
Publisher
Thorndike Press
10 Water St., Suite 310
Waterville, ME 04901